I0562023

OLD SQUIRE

THE ROMANCE OF A BLACK VIRGINIAN

OLD SQUIRE

THE ROMANCE OF A BLACK VIRGINIAN

BY

B. K. BENSON

AUTHOR OF "WHO GOES THERE ?" "A FRIEND WITH THE
COUNTERSIGN," "BAYARD'S COURIER," ETC.

New York
THE MACMILLAN COMPANY
LONDON: MACMILLAN & CO., Ltd.
1903

All rights reserved

COPYRIGHT, 1903,

BY THE MACMILLAN COMPANY.

Set up and electrotyped April, 1903.

Norwood Press
J. S. Cushing & Co. — Berwick & Smith Co.
Norwood, Mass., U.S.A.

Not to defend slavery — but to do
justice to slaves

NOTE

WHEREIN this book departs from history, characters are affected rather than events.

Historically, the negro Barney — a fictitious name — must be considered only as the guide of the Union column in February–March, 1864; the actions ascribed to him before that time are purely inventional; in respect to these actions he is but a type differing from that which the main character shows; in other words, Barney is a foil to "Old Squire."

B. K. B.

CONTENTS

ix

CONTENTS

MAPS

OLD SQUIRE

THE ROMANCE OF A BLACK VIRGINIAN

OLD SQUIRE

CHAPTER I

FORWARD AND BACKWARD

"Of many worthy fellows that were out." — SHAKESPEARE.

A GROUP of horsemen had come out of the Ashby pike, and were making their way toward Hopewell Gap in the Bull Run Mountains. A dweller at a distance from the road counted four men, and said that they were Confederate cavalrymen trying to rejoin Stuart's column, which had passed on a road farther south many hours previously; and he was correct in regard to numbers and purpose, though only three parts right in his classification.

"Mahs Chahléy, how come you don't tek up yo' geahth? Dat saddle dess a-fixin' to th'ow you — dat it is. Ef you dess wait a minute I's a-gwine to git righ' down an' tighten dat geahth, feh de good book hit say tek heed least ye fall."

"All right, Squire . . . Boys, don't halt; I'll catch up with you in no time." And Charley Armstrong drew rein, and flung his left boot across his horse's neck.

"Not too tight now, Squire. Remember there's a hundred and eighty pounds on this saddle."

"Dat de troof, Mahs Chahley; dat w'at mek him ben' so in de middle, an' git jo' geahth so loose; you mek two o' ole Squiah, feh sho'. I'll dess tek it up a leetle bit," muttered the negro, who had dismounted and now had his white head almost under the horse's belly. "Hit's de Gawd's troof, Mahs Chahley; dis is a good hoss, but he so nahrow in de innahds of 'im dat it tek a mighty shawt geahth to retch roun' — dat it do; but I 'spec' he kin run feh who las' de longes'. Whah did Mahs Dan git dese hosses?"

"They're his carriage team; . . . going to ride the other himself; . . . bought cheaper ones to send away the folks."

"Yassah; I done heahd about dat, but whahbouts was de critteh raised, Mahs Chahley?"

"Down on Morgan's place in Augusta County, I suppose, where he's got plenty more. Good Lord, I do hope our folks will be safe there."

"Yassah; hit's de Gawd's blessin', too. W'en I tole Judy good-by aw'ile ago I's mighty proud 'at she gwine whah she be safe, an' not be 'bleege' to run f'om dem mise'ble Yankees no mo'e — dat I is. Who dat a-comin' yandeh th'ough de fiel'?"

Armstrong looked to his weapons, for at the north, riding rapidly, in a course evidently calculated for cutting off their march, was a single horseman.

"I 'spec' he's one o' ouah men," said Squire, doubtfully.

"I don't know. That don't look like a Confederate horse."

"Yassah, but some o' ouah men is got good hosses, Mahs

Chahley, an' den ag'in I dunno w'at dess one Yankee'd be
a-doin' out sheah by hese'f all alone ; he betteh be a-gittin'
fuddeh, feh all de res' of 'em is done gawn, an' I wisht 'at
dey'd stay gawn, too — dat I does.   I tell you who dat is ;
he Mahs Usheh Wes', — yah, yah, Mahs Chahley, you
dunno *him?* — I mighty s'prised at shu, Mahs Chahley,
feh not knowin',Mahs Usheh ! " and the old negro's mouth
twinkled still. " But I dess tell you, honey, dem Mosby
men izh sho' got good hosses — dat dey is."

The horseman shouted, and Armstrong replied to a
voice which he recognized.

" Hit's Mahs Usheh, dess lak I tole you he wus," said
Squire.

" Why, hello, Usher !   Thought you'd given it up ! "

" I've decided to go as far as Haymarket," said the
horseman, reining in ; " the major went last night though,
and I'm afraid I won't catch him."

Usher West was of some twenty-eight or thirty years
of age, of medium size, and fair complexion, with a short
sandy beard on lip, cheek, and chin ; his dress, unlike
Armstrong's dirty gray uniform, was that of the rural
civilian ; he looked the average son of the average farmer,
mounted upon a sleek bay which, however, showed no sign
of farm work. The man was without arms, so far as
could be seen, and none of his appointments in dress or
in trappings indicated military intention. He was a
typical " Mosby's man " — a member of the band of partisan rangers that gathered at the call of their leader to
swoop down upon the Federal outposts at night, — by day
to scatter and return to their homes.

"You'll never catch Mosby, Usher. Better try it with *us !*"

"Think too much of myself. What's become of Sency and Joe? I saw 'em back yonder."

"On ahead," returned Armstrong, waving his hand toward the east. "And Morgan is coming too. How are all at home this morning?"

"All well, thank you. But how do you expect Morgan to catch you?" and West's tone conveyed implication that Morgan had a difficult task before him.

"He's going to cut across and head us off before we reach the river."

"Pretty big risk. How is his brother?"

"Well, I don't know; there's a chance that he'll pull through, and we're hoping to get some Yankee surgeon to come for him."

"Good idea. They can do him more good than we can," responded West, in a matter-of-fact way.

"Yes, and not only that; our folks are leaving, and can't take him; he couldn't stand it."

"So I heard. . . . When do they leave?"

"Just as soon as they can get Dan's brother off; to-morrow, I hope."

"Charley, would you have believed that two people could look so much alike? When I first saw that Yankee, lying there almost dead, I pledge you my word I thought he was Dan himself."

"I reckon you did. I saw Andrew more than once and could have sworn he was Dan," cried Armstrong, bringing his hand down on his thigh with a great slap.

"Andrew? I heard the Yank's name was Dan, too; but I didn't believe it."

"Well, it was; but his right name is Andrew, I tell you."

"I don't know what in the name o' sense you mean," and West's voice contained as great wonder as was spoken by his words.

"Well, it was this way: there were twin boys; you couldn't tell 'em apart. And now that they are men, you can't tell 'em apart. Can *you*, Squire?"

"No, sah. Can't nobody tell 'em apaht w'en dey ain't togeatheh, 'scusin' hit be ole Juno."

"When they were about three years old, a man comes along; you see their parents were dead and their uncle had 'em; when they were three years old a man comes along, and to save your life you can't guess what his name was!"

"Morgan?" cried West.

"His name was *Daniel* Morgan."

"Well, that's nothing strange. I know three men by that name, myself."

"Yes, maybe you do; but this one was a rich old fellow who took a fancy to little Dan and adopted him. But after all, he got the wrong one."

"And got mad about it afterwards?"

"Knew nothin' about it. Never did know. He's dead."

"Well, but didn't his uncle know?"

"No—thought old man Morgan had taken Dan, and old man Morgan he carried Andy away, thinkin' he was Dan; of course it was all the same to *him*; he raised him

and he went by the name of Daniel; so now you have two
Daniel Morgans, twin brothers, just alike.　How does that
strike you?"

"Sounds like a book, doesn't it, Squire?"

"Yassah, hit do feh true, Mahs Usheh; hit soun' lak de
good book, w'at say de fust gwine to be de las' an' de las'
hit gwine to be de fust," the old man quoted with due
solemnity.

"Yes, but hold on.　How could there be *two* Dans?
Didn't you say his uncle thought *his* boy was *Andrew?*"

"Well, you see old man Morgan he lived in New York.
Now, Mr. Berry — that's Dan's uncle that raised him —
never could get a word from old man Morgan, and then he
thought he'd change *his* boy's name to Dan, because they
wanted the name to last, don't you see?"

"Oh, Lord, Armstrong, that's too deep for me.
Which is the right one now?"

"Well, Mrs. Berry, you know, she was the one that
knew all the time; she let Andy go instead of Dan, and
you can swear she kept mighty mum."

"And she told at last?"

"When she couldn't hold in, she did.　But you know
Andy never knew any better, and so he went into the
Yankee army."

"Yes; and he was shot in last Sunday's fight, and your
folks took him into the house, and I know all the rest of
it."

They had come to a halt where a narrow lane, running
south, left the main road.

"Good-by, Charley," said Usher; "this is my way to go

if ever I can reach Mosby; but I tell you now, I'm not
going farther than Haymarket. If I can learn nothing
there, I'm coming back home."

"You know all of Lee's infantry have crossed long ago,
and it'll be all we can do to catch Stuart before he goes
over. Come with *us*, Usher." Armstrong said the
words earnestly; there was but one man for whom he had
greater good-will — Usher's father himself.

"No; can't do that. Wish I could, though. Like to
be with you all again. Regards to Sency and Joe. Good-
by and good luck to you, old man," and Usher West rode
off upon the narrow lane, while Squire with his young
master continued to follow their advance, who had already
outstripped them so far as to reach the Aldie pike, having
taking a road running northeastward.

"Dat yotheth hoss w'at Mahs Dan kep' feh hese'f, he de
pie print o' dis un you's on, Mahs Chahley."

Armstrong was silent; his thought was elsewhere.
Last night he had seen Jennie West, and though his
urgent love-making had met with little success, her refusal
had not been such as to make him despair. There is a
time for all things : a time when hope refuses to go; a
time when an intonation will destroy it. Armstrong was
a man of immense vitality, yet one of those men whose
spirits are acted upon without apparent causes — a man
who at the bending of a straw would feel elation or mis-
ery, according to the degree or direction of the slant.
Jennie had indeed meant to refuse definitively, but the
girl had so disliked to grieve that the mere trembling of
her voice had given encouragement.

"How you gwine to tell dezhe yeah hosses apaht, Mahs Chahley?" asked Squire from the rear. "Dey mus' be twin brothehs, des lak Mahs Dan an' dat yotheh Mahs Dan w'at we thought wus Mahs Dan hese'f."

"Oh, no, Squire; the horses are very different — pretty good matches for a carriage team, though. What's become of Joe and George? They must have turned off."

"Yassah; dey done tuhned off up de yotheh road dat runs to de ribeh. I 'spec' dey sees Ginnle Stuaht's tracks is done tuhned off up dat a-way."

Joe Lewis and George Sency had not turned off; they had ridden on southeastward, Lewis merely dropping a green sprig in the fork. "They'll know that's the way for 'em to go," said he; "they know it anyhow, without tellin'."

"Half a mile will do," said Sency.

"Yes, an' maybe less'n that; from the top o' that hill yonder I'm a-thinkin' we can see fur enough. But what's the use for you to go at all, George? Might as well save your hoss an' wait till I git back."

"No," said Sency; "I'll go with you."

"Tell you what, George, I hate leavin' Morgan back yonder to come on by himself."

"Yes, so do I; but nothing else would satisfy him. I hope he'll overtake us before we cross the Potomac; he'll be in great danger unless he can fall in with some party or other."

"He's boun' to ketch us to-morrow if he gits his business in shape so he can make a start; but, George, I'm a-thinkin' that brother o' his'll never git well; he looks middlin' weak to *me*."

Sency replied with a nod. He was a slight fellow, thoughtful, earnest, almost intense. This was Sergeant Morgan's most valued friend, a discreet and upon necessity a daring man, one who could think for the best and would act regardless of danger. The other man, Lewis, was older, and far more formidable to look at, yet he had the air of relying on his comrade's judgment; both were veterans in service.

"An' then to think that he ain't able to talk. By George! It's the strangest case I ever heard tell of. There was this Dan Morgan in the Yankee army, an' our Dan Morgan in our army, an' nary one a-knowin' about the other. You believe they've got the thing straight now, George?"

"Oh, yes; Mrs. Berry knew all about the twins, and knew when they were separated. The other one's name is Andy, she says; but I don't suppose he knows it yet."

"It beats my times! . . . That old man Morgan that took Andy and called him Dan must ha' been a queer old case."

Sency looked grave, and more; a sudden cloud had overspread his features, an expression caused by tense concentration of his perceptive powers upon a single point. "What is it, George?" asked Lewis, who had not been unobservant of the change.

Sency seized Lewis's bridle, and led to the left, where thick bushes skirted the roadside. Hardly had they reached the sheltering thickets when hoof-beats became distinct . . . another moment and the noise had swelled and they knew that cavalry were advancing west. They dismounted ; each held his horse's mouth. Now, in the road, the sunlight fell on blue uniforms and bright metal, and the steady rolling mutter of many hoofs was pierced by higher irregular notes as the nearing column came — iron striking stone; scabbard clanking; and then, filling the road, there passed westward a company of Federal cavalry, with a large forage wagon and an ambulance, followed by a strong rear-guard.

Sency had waited until the last man was out of earshot; then he signalled, and the two rode through forest and field northwestwardly.

Meantime, Armstrong and Squire had reached the branch road.

"Dat's dess whah dey gawn to, Mahs Chahley ; dat bresh hit's a-pintin' to us to tek dat fawk."

" Yes, but I don't think *they've* taken it."

" No, no, sah. Dey's gawn down de road a piece to see ef de's any trouble down dat a-way. But shu'll see 'em a-comin' awn behime us toreckly. Dey done tole us wi' dat bresh which a-way dey's a-gwine to go."

" We'd better go slow, Squire, until they overtake us."

Suiting action to word they brought their horses to a slow walk, and at times halted and looked back. Armstrong was not without fear, however, that his comrades had passed on, and was about to quicken his pace when he heard hoofs in his rear.

"There they are at last, Squire," he said, without turning.

But the negro had turned, and had seen ; in an instant he turned again, and gave his horse the spur. " Run, Mahs Chahley ! " he cried, as he forged momentarily past the long bay; and as Armstrong caught the word, he, too, pressed on.

A shot whistled over their heads, but there was no pursuit. The Federals, while passing the mouth of the branch road, had seen horsemen whose flight advertised their colour and tendency, and without orders Private O'Donnell had let drive with his carbine, for which act he was not only sternly reprimanded by his captain, but ordered to do double vedette duty — the command was on special service and must not be diverted by small causes.

Old Squire and his young master had made but half a mile when they saw Sency and Lewis waiting for them.

" They took a crack at you, did they, Squire ? " asks Joe.

" Yassah, but ole Squiah still stickin' togeatheh, sah. Dey was a whole roadful of 'em, sah."

" Did you see them ? " asked Armstrong.

" Saw a whole company," Lewis replied.

" Armstrong," said Sency, "somebody ought to go back. Very likely those people are bound for Middleburg, and Morgan ought to be warned."

" Well, let's all go back then."

" No; I don't think that's the best way. One man can manage it better than four."

" Then I'm the man, George."

"No, Armstrong; we'd better —" and Sency paused, having barely glanced at Squire.

"Yassah," said the old man, interpreting; "you is dess right, Mahs Jawge; ole Squiah kin go back, an' nobody'll nuvveh know nothin' about it; dey won't nobody pay no 'tention to ole Squiah. You dess let ole Squiah alone feh dat."

"He's right," said Armstrong.

It was arranged that the negro should return at once to the Armstrong place, and secretly inform the Confederate soldier there of the advance of the Federal cavalry. Meantime, the three were to continue their march slowly, in the hope that Morgan and Squire would overtake them before the Potomac should be reached.

CHAPTER II

A LAST RESORT

"Abhorson. Do you call, sir ?
Provost. Here's a fellow will help you."
— SHAKESPEARE.

CAPTAIN ROBERTUS L. K. FREEMAN had been ordered to march his company from Fairfax Court-House, through Aldie, into Loudoun Valley. The orders given to Captain Freeman were specific.

First, he must learn whether on the Ashby's Gap turn-pike, west of Aldie as far as Goose Creek, there was any considerable force of the enemy. This order was consequent upon ignorance of the position and movements of the Confederate cavalry under Stuart. Ewell's corps was in Pennsylvania, while Hill's and Longstreet's were in Maryland, with Hooker moving at their right. Stuart had begun his ride between the Federal army and Baltimore, but had only begun it, so that no Federal authority knew the magnitude of the movement. On the preceding night Stuart had passed through Glasscock Gap eastwardly, and beyond the Occoquan would turn toward the Potomac to strike Hooker's communications.

According to the second order, Captain Freeman must proceed to the ground near Middleburg (avoiding Middle-

burg if possible and necessary), where the cavalry action
of June 21 had been fought, and endeavour to give
relief to any wounded Federals who might be found
there ; particularly was he to learn the fate of Lieutenant
Daniel Morgan, of General Pleasonton's staff, who had
been missing since the day of the battle, and to leave
nothing undone for his relief in case he was still alive —
otherwise to bring off his body if it could be found. Dr.
Lacy, a surgeon, of mature age, accomplished and peculiar,
accompanied the expedition.

The orders required celerity and alertness ; precautions
must be taken against the possibility of being surprised
by guerillas ; if any of the enemy's forces were in the
country, they were to be avoided.

Nothing worthy narration occurred on the outward
march : true, as already told, one or two horsemen —
rebel cavalrymen, or perhaps guerillas — were seen and
fired on as the column approached the mountain, but these
men had fled at once, and the command had moved on, a
strong rear-guard preserving the distance of four hundred
yards.

At noon the column halted, the horses were fed, and the
officers' mess assembled.

" Wonder where Lacy is now ? " growled the captain.

" Formulating a syllogism, and too deep in thought to
eat," suggested Lieutenant Brock, a sprightly, dark man
of thirty.

Captain Freeman laughed. " You know very well,
Brock," said he, " that Lacy and I are old friends, and it
wouldn't do for anybody to speak harshly of him in my

presence; but I must admit that for a man of good hard sense he is the damnedest fool I ever saw. Somebody call him up."

Before Lacy appeared the meal was half over. He was a long man, with an emphatic stoop that suggested a desk rather than a saddle — iron-gray side whiskers — spectacles—foot-gear No. 11, and hands to match—directly the opposite of Freeman — fair, fat, and fiery, who shouted, " Better hurry, Doc ; hardly anything left for you ! "

The officers were around a gum-blanket spread upon the grass. Lacy came up and squatted Turk fashion between the two lieutenants.

" What have you been driving at, old man ? " asked Freeman.

" O-o-oh, nothing of consequence," drawled the doctor. " Yet it is very unfortunate in this great crisis that there should be differences of opinion. Now, there's my driver ; he insists that Hooker ought to move into the Valley, and try to take Lee by the tail, as he expresses it."

" What do you trouble your head about that for? Was he arguing with *you* ? "

" No, with Tomlinson ; but I couldn't help hearing, and I feld id by dudy do zed de mad righd," mumbled Lacy, his mouth too full for distinct utterance.

" And you convinced him ; I'll bet my boots on that. "

" Yes ; he gave it up."

" I knew it," and Freeman winked furtively at Brock, who was biting his lip to preserve gravity.

" But, Doctor," said the second lieutenant, a very youthful soldier, unfamiliar with the surgeon's ways, and unheedful of Captain Freeman's warning signal; "but, Doctor, there are good critics who think Hooker's policy is just what your driver suggested."

The surgeon's reply was not immediate, adequate intonation being at the moment impracticable. "*Good* critics, you say, sir?"

"Yes, sir."

"Be good enough to name one."

"Oh, Doc, let up!" exclaimed Freeman, who detested argument; "let every man think as he will. And it's high time we were on the road again," he added, rising.

The march continued, more and more cautiously as the evening closed. When the company again halted it was already night, and preparations were made for the bivouac, strong pickets being posted in every avenue of approach.

*   *   *   *   *   *   *

Three officers were on their blankets under a great tree.

"We're not far from the battle-ground, Captain," said Lieutenant Brock.

"Yes; I think we're already on part of it, and I can't say that I greatly relish the duty we're on. Of course, it's all right to send us on a scout over here on this side of the mountain, and it's all right to give help to our wounded if we can find them, and I daresay it's all right to look for Lieutenant Morgan; but what I suspect is that the last order is really the first in importance, at least in the mind of General Stahel, and I'd prefer being told so directly. However, I'm not grumbling with the orders, and I'm going to obey to the letter, if possible."

"They say General Stahel is to be relieved," said Lieutenant Brock.

"Yes; the cavalry of the Washington Department is to form a division under Kilpatrick."

"Where are we to find them when we get through with this job, Captain?"

"North of the Potomac — about Frederick, I suppose; they are to cross at once — perhaps they've already crossed."

"And what's to be done for Stahel?"

"Oh, he'll land on his feet; there is a rumour that he's in demand to help organize the Pennsylvania Reserves; but I don't know how true it is. At any rate, when we get back we'll be under Kilpatrick."

"And are we all that are left here in Virginia?"

"I believe Lowell's scouts are somewhere about; but the division has gone, and we'd have gone too but for this bad business about General Pleasonton's aide."

"Morgan seems to be thought very important, sir."

"Yes; promoted for good conduct recently; don't suppose he knows it yet. I fancy he has powerful friends at headquarters, if not in Washington. They say he is very rich. Ever know him, Brock?"

"No, not at all," said the lieutenant; "I know, however, that the extensive preparation Lacy was required to make, indicates great interest in him. He's brought along the whole business — enough for a regiment. Isn't that so, Doctor?" he asked, the surgeon's long form having just shown itself.

"The preparation I have made is ample," said Lacy, with evident pride.

c

"Better than I was treated down at Kelley's Ford last March," said the captain; "yet I have no cause to complain; they did the best they could for me, I suppose; but they gave me no ambulance to ride in, nor any patent mattress to lie on."

"Your recovery was rapid, nevertheless," said the surgeon; "but are you thoroughly strong yet, Freeman?"

"Oh, yes; the day's ride hasn't hurt me at all. Do you really believe Morgan is still alive?"

"I know nothing more than I've already told you, Freeman. The colonel said he had received a note unsigned, stating that Morgan was over here; but I fear the whole thing is a trap; innovation is always to be suspected."

"Oh, no," said Freeman; "I don't believe they would be guilty of such a thing—not even Mosby. At any rate, I'm going to find out in the morning if any great force is near by, and if so I shall ask a truce to see after our men."

*   *   *   *   *   *   *

The night was cloudless, the concave moon was three-quarters down the sky, and the vedette doing double duty on the Ashby pike was thinking it was nearing the time for relief, when he heard a noise from his right—a sort of coughing sound, as though preliminary to salutation.

"And who is ut that's there now? Spake quick!" he called, abruptly jerking his horse to the left.

"Hit ain't nobody but me, Mahsta; hit ain't nobody but ole Squiah, sah; I done be'n sont to see de ginnle, o' leastways de cap'm."

With some fear of a stratagem, yet with full recognition of an unmitigable negro voice and speech, O'Donnell made ready his carbine, and said sternly, "Come out o' there at wanst!"

A small man approached; indeed, he looked smaller than he was, for he was bending very low, not in mock humility, but with the natural deference of the hereditarily weak.

"I ain't nobody but ole Squiah, Mahsta," he repeated, as, with hat off and coatless in the warm night, he stood before the horseman, who could now see that the little man's wool was very white.

"Whereabout d' ye belong, and what d' ye wantt, man?" Then the sentinel called aloud for the corporal.

"I b'longs to Mahs John Ahmstrong, sah, but he done gim me to Mahs Chahley, an' he done guv Judy, dat's my ole 'oman, sah, he done guv Judy to my Miss Lucy, an' I done be'n sont to tell you 'bout Mahs Dan Mawgin."

"Dan Margan, of all the world! And d' ye know where he is now?"

"Yassah; de good book hit say dat de man w'at fight is a-sho' gwine to be smit by de swoad, an' hit's mighty right dis time — leastways, ef it waun't a swoad hit mus' ha' be'n a cannon-ball, ef it waun't a bullet. But he's mighty bad off, sah — dat he is; he's pow'ful weak, Mahsta."

"And where is the poor craythur now?"

"At ouah house, sah."

The corporal came up, and O'Donnell explained.

" Well, I hope the darky is telling the truth. We've been afraid that Morgan was killed. Hasn't been seen since the fight on the twenty-first. Say you know where he is, old man ? "

" Yassah, we tuck good keeh of 'im. Blesh yo' soul, honey, we done tuck es good keeh of 'im es ef he wus a Confeddick. I done be'n sont to tell de cap'm how to come an git 'im."

" Yes, but you must tell *me*," said the corporal, with the desire of relieving his superior of any possible annoyance.

The negro scratched his head, and was silent for a moment ; then he said, " But, Mahsta, hit won't do no good, onless I tell de cap'm."

" Why not ? "

" Dess 'caze nobody can't git 'im, sah, onless dey comes right."

" Come right ? What do you mean by that ? "

" I dunno, Mahsta, 'scusin' hit ain't feh to come wi' de w'ite flag."

" Oho ! They mean to deliver him under truce, hey ? "

" Yassah, I 'spec' dat's hit ; I 'spec' dey wants de troof."

" Stand to your post, O'Donnell, and hold him here," said the corporal, turning rein. " I'll be back presently."

" And is Margan bad hit, now ? Where is the wound ? " asked the sentinel.

" In de top o' he shouldeh, Mahsta, an' hit's mighty bad. He ain't spoke but one time, sah, sence he got shot."

"Is he in yer own house, d' ye say, now?"

"In de big house, sah, an' in de baid; he done had two Confeddick doctohs, but dey ain't done him no good at all yit."

"Thrue for ye; more be token, they've nahthing to do good *with*. Can he ait, now?"

"No, sah; but Miss Lucy, she fo'ced some broth down his th'oat dis mawnin'. Dat's dess w'y I done be'n sont, Mahsta, so de Feddick doctohs, w'at's got all de tools, kin do 'im some good. De Confeddick doctohs dey done said dat was de onliest chance."

The negro's tones and manner of speech would have betrayed great deliberation had any familiar acquaintance heard him; old Squire was certainly doing his best to conceal, and at the same time to accomplish.

When the corporal returned, he ordered Squire to march before him, and soon halted the old man in front of four officers.

"This is the man, Captain."

Squire saluted to the ground, and stood there in the moonlight, looking unabashed in the presence of the powerful.

"I'm told you know where Lieutenant Morgan is," said the captain. This speech surprised Squire; he had not known that the wounded man was an officer.

"Yassah, he's at ouah house, sah, — leastway Mahs Dan Mawgin's dah, sah, — an' I done be'n sont to tell you dat shu kin come an' git 'im, sah . . . dess about a mile, sah, atteh you go by dem chimbleys."

"Where are the rebels?" . . . "What is the character of the wound?"

The question written as second in order, though the two were spoken simultaneously, came of course from Surgeon Lacy, and was more to Squire's taste than was the first.

"Mahs Dan, you talkin' 'bout, Mahsta?"

"Yes; tell me how he is hurt."

"Oh, hold on, Lacy; plenty of time for that. Old man, where are the rebels?" repeated the captain.

Now this, in Squire's opinion, was a very unparliamentary question — one of the questions against which he had been earnestly cautioned; and he thought the best policy was to split the difference — to tell half-truths and half-lies, and to exaggerate lavishly.

"Dey is all about, sah, 'scusin' dem w'at's done went away. Some of 'em is in Loudoun, an' some of 'em is in Culpepeh, an' some in Mellan' an' Penns'vania, an' some is in Richmon,' an' some is in ole Fihginny, an' den some mo'e of 'em is done went to Washin'ton."

"Washington!" exclaimed Captain Freeman, angrily; "you know very well that's a lie. Who put you up to say that?"

Dr. Lacy seemed as angry as the captain, though on a different account. "Freeman, let the man tell all he knows in his own way and get through. I want to hear about Morgan's wound."

"Now you just hold on till your turn comes, Doc. — Say, old man, what do you mean by telling me such lies?"

Squire was inwardly trembling because of his mistake, but thanks to the respite brought by the surgeon's intervention, had seen his way out.

"Yassah, mayby dey did tell me wrong, 'caze I didn't go wid 'em, an' cou'se I can't tell it feh true, an' some men is mighty deceivin', Mahsta, but I seed some of 'em tek de back track feh Washin'ton w'en de mos' of 'em ride down the road to'ads Leesbuhg."

"Back track! Do you know where Washington is?"

"Yassah; de big Washin'ton hit's down de road, an de Little Washin'ton hit's up de road. You b'lieve I talkin' 'bout de big Washin'ton, Mahsta?"

"Oh," grunted the captain, "you mean Little Washington in Rappahannock County?"

"Yassah."

"Now, Freeman, give me my turn," said the surgeon, chuckling.

"No; I'm not through with him yet. Are there no rebels left about Middleburg?"

"Oh, yassah," replied Squire, lying superbly; "dey is some dah yit; but dem. dat done sont me dey ain't a-gwine to fight shu all; dey say you dess sen' an' git Mahs Dan Mawgin; dey not a-gwine to fight shu all; dey says zhu dess put up de w'ite flag an' dess come along; dess put up de w'ite flag, Mahsta, awn yo' am'lance, an' come right along an' git 'im,—dat's w'at dey want shu to do,— you kin tek 'im an' keoh[1] 'im up, 'caze he mighty bad awff, an' he sho' is a-needin' de tools w'at shu got an' w'at dey ain't got; dat's w'at dey says, Mahsta, an' dat's w'at dey done sont ole Squiah to tell you, sah, dat dey ain't a-gwine to fight shu ef you dess puts up de w'ite flag."

[1] Cure.

" Now, Freeman, will you graciously permit me to do my duty ? " said the doctor.

" Go ahead, Doc," replied the captain, his tones indicating surrender without bitterness.

" Tell me, my friend, where the wounded man is hurt."

" In de neck an' shouldeh, Mahsta."

" By what sort of weapon ? "

" Sah ? "

" Was he shot, or cut ? " explained Freeman.

" Hit mus' ha' be'n a bullet, sah."

" Whereabouts on the neck ? "

Squire put his forefinger somewhere behind his right jaw, as it seemed to Freeman ; perhaps Lacy, even in the mild moonlight, knew what was meant.

" Can he eat ? "

" No, sah, an' he can't talk, nutheh ; he dess stays right still all de time, sah."

Lacy continued to question the negro, who, however, was really unable to give him other information than that the wound was very serious.

" Where are Mosby's men ? " asked the prudent captain.

" I dunno, Mahsta."

" Where are White's men ? "

" I dunno, Mahsta."

Yet, even guerillas would respect the white flag, thought the captain. There need be no hesitation in accepting the negro's news as valid, and there need be no fear in sending for the wounded officer, so Squire was dismissed with a verbal message to the effect that the ambulance would be sent to Armstrong's at eleven o'clock on the morrow.

Daniel Morgan had been warned by the Confederate surgeons that his brother's case required appliances impossible for them to procure ; he had seen, therefore, that the only hope was to deliver him into Federal hands, and for this purpose he had risked another day's delay, so when Squire before daybreak returned with the report of a successful mission, it needed but few hours to make everything ready, not for his own departure merely, but for that of his friends also.

* * * * * * *

The Armstrongs — father, mother, and daughter, with Mrs. Berry — took their seats in a great carriage, while the servants climbed into a heavy wagon loaded with what the refugees felt compelled to save. The adieus had hardly been said when old Squire trotted up.

"Lawdy! You gwine now, Mahs John?"

Mr. Armstrong found himself unable to reply. This home which he was deserting had been his home since his birth—the only home he had ever known ; the only place he would ever know as home.

The old negro sidled up to the carriage, and took one by one the white hands extended to him, and called down all the blessings of heaven, while unrestrained tears were visible on Lucy's cheeks, and Mrs. Armstrong sobbed convulsively. Then Squire went to the wagon where Aunt Judy, his wife, was sitting on a big trunk. He put one foot on a spoke, raised himself, took his wife's hand and placed it on his own white head.

"Gawd bless an' save you, Judy. I's got to follow Mahs Chahley th'ough thick an' thin, an' you's got to go

wi' Miss Lucy anywhah an' ev'ywhah. You an' me,
Judy — you an' me — dat's all. 'Membeh ole Squiah " —
and without another word he sprang from the wheel and
turned toward the house, leaving old Judy rocking from
side to side in her speechless agony. Hardly had the
horses started when Squire was at the doorway where
Daniel Morgan, bitter partings over, still stood, watching
the refugees begin their journey into hoped-for safety.

" Mahs Dan, you ain't a-gwine to hide ? "

" No, it's almost time for them to be here, Squire."

" Yassah, dey gwine to git sheah 'bout 'leben o'clock,
sah."

" We have only half an hour, Squire. They'll not
trouble you or me ; but you'd better take our horses and
hide them in the thicket down below the pasture —
we don't know what thieves they may have in the
gang."

Old Squire left him. He went to the room where his
twin brother lay. Soon he would deliver this brother
into the hands of friends — this brother with whom he
was even yet unacquainted. God, if he willed it so,
could save this life so nearly spent. Daniel Morgan
had in his own mind decided on this course — it was
the only hope. And, as he stood by Andrew's bed-
side, he felt that he had done for the best in sending
Squire for the Federals. But should he tell the Federals
his own great interest in their comrade ? They would
soon be here to take his brother away — would their kindness to the wounded man be greater if they should know
that he was of Southern birth ? No ; let Andrew, when

he should recover speech, tell whatever he might choose
to tell; to tell now would be to do so without his consent.
Daniel bent over and spoke.

"Brother, I know that you can understand what I say.
I have sent for your friends; they will soon be here, to
take you to some good hospital where you can get scientific treatment. I have done the best I could for you;
I cannot stay here, for my duty calls me away. When
you recover, I want you to send me word, if possible.
Until I know that you have recovered I can do my duty
without hesitation; when you have recovered, I shall
want to know it, and shall want to meet you, so that
we can arrange some way to prevent our ever meeting
in battle. Let us never run the risk of injuring each
other. If it be possible I shall send you some word, but
now I can do no more than tell you that my place is
usually with the First Virginia cavalry, though frequently
I am called on to serve General Stuart, and in many ways.
I shall not say to your friends that you are my brother;
it could do no good, so far as I can see. When you
recover, then decide for yourself whether you shall tell
anything. I know that enough has been said before you
to enable you to understand our real relations, and our
strange history. I pledge you, brother, that my hand
shall never be against you, and if we survive this war I
shall harbour no thought against you for serving against
us — you simply couldn't help it. And I know that you
give me credit for serving with equal honesty against
you. Good-by." The Confederate bent down and kissed
the wounded man.

An hour later the ambulance, under its escort, was moving slowly toward Aldie, while Daniel Morgan, with old Squire, was riding fast in a northeasterly direction, to overtake his friends and with them seek Stuart.

CHAPTER III

SANCTUARY

"Soften the wounded prisoner's lot." — SCOTT.

A CAREFUL examination had convinced the experienced
Dr. Lacy that Morgan's wound was not necessarily fatal,
and yet that the Confederate surgeons had been professionally correct in advising that the sufferer be handed
over to the Union army. The Federal surgeon could
only apply a medicated bandage and allow prompt removal; although he feared the effect, yet the journey
was clearly necessary, and for that he had already done
the best in providing for the easiest manner of trans-
portation possible. To stout elastic straps from the
ribbed roof of the vehicle swung a mattress, beneath
which were springs that it scarcely touched, permitting
only the minimum of oscillation, and furnishing the
basis of the doctor's pardonable vanity over his own
invention. To this mattress the wounded Morgan was
lifted directly from his bed; then mattress and all were
placed in the ambulance, screws and clamps were secured,
and orders given to drive eastward with extreme care,
two men walking ahead to remove every stone from
possible touch of the wheels.

29

The surgeon had mounted, and now rode in front at
the slowest walk, to guide the pace. A mile made,
Captain Freeman's company was found under arms by
the roadside. The surgeon reported, and was ordered to
proceed through Middleburg, the captain promising to
guard the rear, and to overtake the ambulance before
it should reach Aldie. Lacy learned that the parties
sent out over the battle-ground and into the houses near by
had failed to find any wounded soldier, so he was content
to know that his exclusive attention to Morgan was all
that could be required.

The slow progress under the midsummer sun was trying. Lacy tied his bridle to the rear of the ambulance
and got inside to avoid the heat, yet, although there had
been rain but few days before, and the fields were still
wet, the dust rose in great puffs from the hoofs in front
and balanced thick in the stagnant air, speedily powdering
the interior of the vehicle. This dust, Lacy reasoned,
might prove the preponderant grains in the scales of life
and death ; the doctor himself, well and sound, was suffering for want of pure air ; how was it with the patient,
whose air passages might already have become almost
choked by his wound ? At every firm spot in the road,
Lacy called a halt and allowed a breathing spell, yet
there before him he could always see the white line of
deep dust through which the horses and wheels must
churn ; and he began to cast about for some possible
manner of saving his patient from the noisome effects
of the way. He could see the road for a mile in his
rear: no cavalry were on it ; he had time to wait and to
think.

Only a furlong at the left of the road was an unpre-
tentious farm-house. Lacy sent one of his three men to
inquire whether it was possible, by taking some by-road,
to avoid the deep dust in front, and yet secure comfort —
a good level surface is the main requisite in any road.
The man soon returned, bringing with him Mr. West, the
resident, who calmly introduced himself. The surgeon
pressed his questions.

" Yes, sir," replied the Southerner, curtly, " there is a
way through my place."

" Then I'll ask you to show me the way. I have a
soldier here who is badly hurt."

" I suppose you are a surgeon, sir, and on the Union
side ? "

" Yes, and I trust you are a true patriot."

Mr. West smiled doubtfully. " I think I am, sir ; yet
there are two sides to that question. However, that shall
not prevent my helping a wounded man."

" I acknowledge no two sides," said the surgeon,
emphatically ; " but if you are not for the Union, I accept
your help as man to man. Will you lead the way ? "

Mr. West walked toward his home, Dr. Lacy, who had
remounted, riding near the farmer, and the ambulance
slowly following.

" I suppose the wounded man is the one that was at
Armstrong's ? "

" Yes, Lieutenant Morgan."

Mr. West had heard of the case of the two brothers,
but thought best to say nothing about it.

" Very badly hurt, sir ? "

"Yes, a quite serious wound; an interesting one, too, to a man of my calling. I'm hoping to pull him through, but I know that to do so I must make no mistake."

"Yes, sir; I can imagine your interest. I've often thought that a devoted surgeon gets as much out of real life as anybody : he saves others, and lives large himself. But for accident I should have followed your noble calling. Now, here we turn off through my lot. I'll take you by a road through my fields, where there is no dust, and not a stone. The way is longer, but you'll come out into the pike again near Aldie, and save quite a long pull through the dust, sir. I'll go with you until you can't miss the — But, hello ! Look yonder ! "

Mr. West had been in the act of opening his big gate, and in doing so had turned, and he was now looking toward the pike. From down the road a single horseman was riding westward with all speed, the dust flying, the horse's head, neck, and tail almost one straight line.

The surgeon had turned, but had shown no discomposure. Though the horseman's clothing was so completely covered with dust that the colour of his uniform was all guesswork, yet Lacy knew by his perception of many minute particulars merged into one general aspect that the man was a courier ; and, if a courier, he must be a Federal, riding with orders for Freeman. Bending low, the man was storming by, regardless of dust or hill or hollow ; yet, as he passed the outlet of the homestead lane, he turned his face, no doubt perceiving the ambulance, and shouted, but the words could not be distinguished.

"I believe that man is Stahel's courier," said Lacy,

almost mechanically; then, "Could you tell what he said?"

"No, I couldn't make it out."

"Perhaps Mosby's men have cut us off."

"Perhaps so, sir," said Mr. West, smiling, and thinking of Usher.

"Mr. West, I wish to hide this ambulance."

"I don't know that I ought to help you in that, sir. I'll do what I can for your wounded man, but I ought to do no more."

"Then I must do the best I can. Lead on, if you will. The courier will soon get to Captain Freeman, and they will learn the news. Until I know more than I do now, I shall be afraid to risk my patient farther east."

"As you wish, sir; I shall not object to your waiting till you know more. This way, sir."

The ambulance was driven behind a clump of plum trees near the horse lot. One of the surgeon's men was stationed at the gate, where he could watch the pike. Mr. West lingered near the vehicle and occasionally looked into it. Morgan was still stretched out, on his back, with eyes open—intelligent eyes which seemed to say that he knew all that was passing. And it was true that, with the exception of intervals when he had slept or had been giddy from pain, he had known all the while his own condition and somewhat of his immediate surroundings. At this moment he had begun to rise out of a semi-conscious state of suffering; he had felt his body oppressed, as with a weight preventing breath, and he had believed himself about to succumb; but now, in pure air, relief had

D

succeeded, and yet almost intolerable thirst. He could not remember that he had wanted water — it seemed a long time since he had thought of water — a long time since he had been brought into the Armstrong house — a long time since he had fallen. Snatches of recollection came to him, — women, men, one man above all, who had claimed to be his brother, yes, whom he knew to be his brother, for Daniel Morgan the Federal had learned of the relationship before the Confederate had known. He had slept much for the past two days, and his sleep had been marked by disturbing dreams ; so now, while wide awake, he was unable to know dream from fact, and as he lay there on the mattress the past became to him a past of confusion wherein things lost their right proportion and mixed irrelevantly. Yet his old actual service, before he had been hurt, loomed in his memory intact, and he knew that he had discovered his brother's existence while his own body and mind had been sound. And the present moment was clear : he had heard and understood the last words of Mr. West and Dr. Lacy ; he knew that the surgeon had suspended the march, and he hoped that the delay would be long, for movement was very painful.

Morgan's thoughts were forced into another channel. The voice of the surgeon sounded sharply in his ears.

"How long since ? "

"Only two hours, sir."

"Was it known who they were ? "

"Yes, sir ; Stuart — Stuart's whole force. They went through Glasscock Gap night before last, sir, and they are now passing through Prince William ; but nobody knows where they are making for."

" When will Captain Freeman be here ? "

" Coming now, sir ; he ought to be here in a few minutes."

Captain Freeman's company had been halted on the turnpike ; the commander rode alone to see the surgeon.

" Bad news, Doc ! "

" Yes, I'm told that Stuart has cut us off from the east."

" Fact, I guess ; at any rate, there's no doubt that rebels are between us and Fairfax."

" And what orders have you received, Captain ? "

" I've been ordered to march through Hopewell, or Thoroughfare, or Glasscock, and get back as quickly as possible. The rebels are reported moving northeast, and I am to strike south of them and get back. This road is completely blocked east of Aldie, and there's no telling how long it will be blocked. Stahel has marched into Maryland, and my instructions give me choice of moving after him by Leesburg ; but I'm afraid I'd run into a trap, for Pleasonton has no doubt crossed by this time. I prefer the southern gaps."

" And you go at once ? "

" Yes, orders are imperative. I expect a long ride, and a rapid one."

" Well, Freeman, this ambulance with my patient in it cannot go over those rough roads."

" Yes, I understand, Doc ; your case gives me the shakes, my friend ; I'm compelled to let you decide what you'll do."

"Decide? Decide be damned!" exclaimed Lacy, roused to rare emphasis. "The thing decides itself; I stay with my patient."

"Of course, I knew you'd do that. How about your men?"

Lacy seemed not to hear; he was thinking — trying to determine quickly what was best to be done. When he spoke again, his tones were full of energy.

"Can you give me an hour?"

"No."

"Half an hour, then? Order your men to feed, and give me half an hour."

"What do you mean to do?"

"I mean to use my men, and some of yours, for half an hour, and then let my men go back with you. There's no good in getting them caught here, and the more of us that are left the more danger there'll be. Mr. West here seems willing to help us, out of pure charity."

"Well, Doc, take your half-hour; but be lively now, man, and don't delay me longer."

"You'll see me ready in twenty minutes. Send me two or three of your best men up here."

Lacy had his patient, without removing him from the mattress, taken into the house, West giving up his best rooms. Then the chest of instruments and medicines was brought in, and finally Lacy's personal baggage.

"Now, Mr. West," said the doctor, "won't you let me hide this ambulance somewhere? I can have it taken to pieces and scattered here and there, ready to put together again when I can get away."

"No, Doctor, I can't help you do that; besides, what would you do with your horses? I don't mind telling you that I should be tempted to notify the first Confederates I see where you have hidden your horses. As for the wounded man, that's a different thing, though I don't know, after all, that I shouldn't tell our folks so that they can get his parole."

Lacy reflected; this man West was stubborn in his adherence to his cause. "Morgan's parole would be worth nothing," said he; "he is at the door of death, and even if he recovers it is very doubtful that he could ever serve again; but I shall not urge you to do violence to your conscience. Here, Hawley!"

"Yes, sir."

"Lead my horse. — Jamison, drive the ambulance down to the road. It can follow empty without any trouble."

Down at the pike the bugle sounded to saddle. Captain Freeman pressed the surgeon's hand. "Lacy," he said, "I always knew you were a tiptop fellow, and you're doing now only what I should have known you'd do in such a case. You may feel sure, old man, that Bob Freeman will tell things on you at headquarters. And we're coming back for you as soon as possible. Good-by," and Freeman turned and galloped after his company, which was filing southeast over rugged roads to avoid Stuart's column and work back to safety.

Though the wise submit to necessity, they feel the necessity. It is needless to say that the sudden invasion of his home was as disagreeable to Mr. West as it was to Dr. Lacy. Mr. West was known in all the country

round about as a discreet man, a long-headed man, a safe
man. His adherence in sentiment to the Southern cause
had been open, even while Loudoun was occupied by
Federals; yet he had given no offence, unless indeed to
mere sentiment contrary to his own. None had ever been
known to impugn his motives, or to point to any objec-
tionable act; for while to the Federals he admitted without
obtrusiveness his political views, at the same time he
condemned the voluntary activity of civilians here in this
fought for corner, and even had shut his doors upon his
own son until Usher proved to his father that Mosby was
regularly commissioned, and his men formally enlisted in
the service of the Confederate States. He had said that
he would be tempted to divulge the hiding-place of Lacy's
horses, but such temptation would have been overcome, as
always, by his sense of the impropriety of any civilian's
engaging in help of either side when not forced by law.
He was in the vigour of middle age, — sturdy, well pre-
served, frugal, hardy, thoughtful, — stern, his neighbours
thought. Except for Usher, who was almost always
away, his only daughter, named for his native State, was
all his family, Mrs. West having died before the war
began. Jennie, now nineteen, was everything her father
wished, save that by responsibility and care she was
forced into a life from which he would gladly have elevated her. Almost every negro had gone, and Virginia
was mistress, cook, housemaid, sempstress, all in one,
except for the help of two superannuated slaves; and at
times it was difficult for her to obtain their yet more
servile work, so that her hands were full and her brain as

well. True, her family was small, and her father's tastes
were not exacting, and her own simple nature demanded
not the unattainable ; but she was wise enough to feel that
their life, in the midst of contrary-minded men and
differing now so widely from her former life of ease, was
unwholesome, and that it could not endure. There were
times when she wished her father would abandon everything and take her with him out of the country, yet she
knew it almost impossible to live without this home
which could not have found a purchaser, and she
gave no utterance to her vain wishes, which she knew
were not his, he being very ardently attached to the
place.

"Well, Jennie, I'm to tell you serious news," Mr.
West had said, as the surgeon began to supervise the
removal of Morgan.

The girl had known that some important event was in
the air ; she laid her hand on her father's coatless arm,
and smiled. The faces were almost on a level ; her form
was erect and tall ; her face full of dignity unalloyed
with any shade of pretence. She did not speak — she
smiled assent and' comfort.

"We have a wounded soldier to help care for, for God
knows how long. I should not be distressed at all, but
that I know it will add to your cares and your work. He
is in a very bad way, and it would be brutal to refuse,
even if we had the power."

Miss West had many times seen troops of all arms, —
Confederate and Federal, — she had even seen them in
action, for her home was where the cavalry frequently

rode and not unfrequently fought. On this day she had seen cavalry ride past; she had seen her father guide the ambulance.

"Father, of course we must take care of him. Which side does he belong to?"

"He is a Federal. There are two to provide for, — the wounded man and a surgeon."

Jennie became very busy with her arrangements. The front room on the west — shaded by a great oak — had been chosen for Morgan, the adjoining room for the surgeon, who, however, insisted that all plans should take into account that his place was with his patient, and that for himself no apartment was necessary.

It was past the dinner hour, and Dr. Lacy had not dined. Jennie's slender meal had long been ready. The girl added what she could, and the three sat down.

"Miss West, this would be a very great pleasure were it not for the necessity that is upon us."

"You mean the condition of the wounded man, Doctor?"

"Yes, that and more. I mean of course, the necessity for disturbing your manner of life. I hate to do it. If you knew how I hate it, you would pardon me."

"You need no pardon, Doctor; you are doing no wrong. I can imagine how you feel."

"If I could only get *ice*."

"Ice?" said Mr. West; "you can have as much as you want. I've got ice older than you are — ice that the neighbours say has got worms in it."

"Is it possible? My dear sir, you don't know what a

weight you take from me.   I can almost say now that I
can warrant Morgan's recovery."

"Whose ? " asked Jennie, curiously.

"Morgan's — my patient's."

"Is he the soldier who was at Mr. Armstrong's ? "

"Yes.   Do you know anything of him ? "

"No, sir, I have never seen him ; but I heard they
were taking care of a wounded man named Morgan."

"They have all gone," said the surgeon.

"Yes, sir, they have long wanted to go, and have just
now found their opportunity.   You saw nothing of
them ? "

"We saw but one man — a Confederate soldier ; he
was wounded, too, to judge by the bandage over his
face.   He told us that the family had gone, and that he
had remained to the last, in order to see that Morgan was
safely delivered to us.   Strange thing about this business
is that we were required to come with a flag, and yet
found no authority entitled to receive us — nobody at all
except that one man.   I guess they outwitted us, but
for what purpose I cannot yet understand."

To all this speech Jennie said nothing.   Two years of
war had taught the girl prudence, and she felt that it was
her father's place to speak, if reply should be made.

CHAPTER IV

A SONG SIGNAL

"Ah, me! What act that roars so loud,
And thunders in the index?"
—SHAKESPEARE.

AT first Stuart's march had been southeastward, beginning the movement which, in its relation to the Confederate campaign, has caused the greatest condemnation by military men. Of course Stuart's purpose was not as yet understood by his enemies. Constantly overrated as the Confederates were, their cavalry division might be the curtain behind which heavy bodies of infantry were marching eastward upon the Capital. Prudence demanded that the outlying Federal troops still south of the Potomac be brought together to resist the possible assault, and they were quickly concentrated by order of General Heintzelman, in command of the Washington defences, and were deployed across the Little River pike, down which from the west the threatened attack seemed likely to come. But Captain Freeman's company found no enemy blocking the roads, for Stuart's column had passed beyond, and the captain, now deploring his inability under his orders to send back for the surgeon, pursued his way without hindrance, or even alarm, and reached Centreville, where he found orders requiring his immediate march to the Potomac to rejoin Stahel's cavalry division.

Meantime, pursuant to the plans laid by Sency, he and his two friends, after learning that all of Hooker's army had marched northward, turned toward Gum Spring, and continued to ride slowly in the hope of being overtaken by Morgan and Squire, who were to ride directly north-eastward and join Sency before he crossed the Potomac. Taking Salem as his starting-point, Stuart had marched almost on the arc of a circle, first southeastward through Glasscock Gap and until beyond the Occoquan, then northward through Fairfax Court-House to Rowser's Ford. Although Morgan's ride was to be on a chord of Stuart's arc, straight for Rowser's Ford, yet almost twenty hours had passed between the time of Sency's sending Squire back to Morgan and Morgan's start, and in these twenty hours Stuart had crossed the river and Sency was nearing it. Stuart's ride from Salem to the river was a ride of seventy miles; Morgan's was only thirty miles, but the last of Stuart's column had crossed before Morgan and Squire started.

Sency knew the danger of waiting. He knew that just so soon as the Federals should learn that the column had crossed, they would follow its rear, endeavouring to pick up stragglers, to cut the column off from the south, to harass its rear in every way possible. The case looked gloomy to Sency. It looked as though he must choose between deserting his friend and being almost certainly captured by the enemy. The three men had spent the night in the forest; they had this day moved cautiously, skirting the roads, riding through hollows, keeping sharp watch at all times, and on the hills pausing long and examining the ground in fear of seeing dust rising from the march of their enemies already cutting them off from Stuart.

Armstrong was too moody to talk; Lewis was never moody — just the opposite now — for he had abundant confidence in Sency's ability. Sency himself doubted not that Morgan would come, though he feared the coming would be so late that they would find all the river fords in the power of the enemy following Stuart; yet, as he neared the Potomac, his hopes rose, for here he was sure that he was following Stuart's column, known by the tracks of many unshod hoofs.

Three miles from the river a by-road running northeast enters the road to the Potomac; at the junction Sency halted.

"Here's the last chance, Joe."

"George, I'm a-thinkin' that Dan won't git here much before midnight. He'll want all this mornin' before he starts. If he started before noon, he might git here before night; but then, you know, he might have to ride in a roundabout way. I don't think he'll git here much before midnight." Fully fifty times had Joe Lewis made, on this day, a similar utterance.

"He'll ride like hell," said Armstrong.

"It won't do to stand here, boys," and Sency led the way into the bushes and dismounted.

"Suppose I go back on that road a mile or two," suggested Armstrong, to whom action was a necessity; "I might meet 'em coming."

"Your ride would be useless. They'll get here just as soon by your staying," replied Sency.

"Then suppose I ride on to the ford and see if it's all right?"

"Won't it be night by the time you get there? Can you see anything?" Sency asked.

"No, it won't be dark. I think I'd better do it, George. I can get up close and maybe see the other side. Then we'll know better what to count on."

"All right, Armstrong. But be careful, my friend — don't be too risky. Find out what you can; but be sure you look to your rear; and you'd better stay down there till we come."

Armstrong mounted and rode north.

"If he don't git into some kind of a row, it'll be a God's wonder," said Joe.

"Sh-h-h!" whispered his comrade.

Southward on the road over which they had lately ridden a thin dust was rising. In a second hoofs were heard. Expectation became painful. Was it possible that Morgan's route had merged into their own road far below this point? Neither man spoke, but they looked by instants into each other's eyes, and by instants up the road. Sency knelt down, to see better beneath the limbs of the trees. The sounds kept coming, louder and louder, and now Sency felt that more than two horses were making all that noise, and Joe could see by George's face that suspense had changed to disappointment.

Six Federal cavalrymen passed north on the road.

The two men again looked into each other's eyes ; the thought of one was the thought of both — how to warn Armstrong.

"I better go, George ; I can fetch a bend an' strike him, I'm a-thinkin'."

"No, Joe ; I'm afraid they'd hear you."

"Then I believe I'll ride out after them fellers an' fire off my carbine. Charley'll hear it an'll know some'h'm's up."

"Wait. Don't be in too big a hurry. Armstrong may find out without — Sh-h-h !" and Sency crouched low again.

On the road there was no dust rising, — the branch road to the southwest, — but there came again the sound of hoof beats, rapid ones, and fewer, and coming from far, and Joe knelt by George's side in an agony of hope. The sound of the gallop continued to come, and louder it grew, and the dust now rose in their sight, and with bated breath and joints all stiff the men saw first a curling mane, and a horse's head, and then Joe Lewis broke out loud : —

"Morgan ! Goddomighty, all hell couldn't hold him !"

"Heaven, you'd better say," laughed George.

Sency handed Lewis his bridle and rushed to the road.

"Morgan, Armstrong has gone to the ford, and six Yankees are following him. They passed here not five minutes ago."

Old Squire had come up, and had heard. Lewis had come up.

"We must follow the Yankees at once, and see what they're made out of," exclaimed Morgan. His tone was anxious but decided.

"No, no," said Sency, "that's not good policy; we want no trouble ; our business is to get across the river. What I fear is that Armstrong will cause an alarm, so that we shall be guarded against."

"How long since he left?" demanded Sergeant Morgan.

"Not a quarter of an hour."

"Got ten minutes' start ? "

"Hardly."

"Were they riding faster than he was ? "

"No, but before he gets in sight of the river he'll slow up, and I'm afraid the road runs between fences down there."

"Mahs Dan, I got to go awn," said Squire ; "I dess *got* to go awn."

"Go where, Squire ? "

"I got to go awn an' see 'bout my Mahs Chahley."

"The very thing ! " exclaimed Sency. "Squire, you ride on until you see the Yankees ; then — "

"Yassah, you dess leave 'em to me, sah; I'll fix 'em. I'll tell Mahs Chahley dey's a-comin' — an' dey won't know it notheh — dat dey won't."

"I see," said Morgan ; "and we'll ride as near you as we can, Squire. Go ahead, old fellow."

The negro started at a gallop.

"What is he up to, George ? " asked Joe, wonderingly.

"Don't exactly know his plans, Joe; but I'm confident he'll find some way to tell Armstrong to look out."

The three men rode northward, following the negro at such a distance as only to keep him in view. When the road turned and Squire disappeared, Morgan's men hastened until again they could see the old man, who even yet was at a gallop. And now another short stretch of the road was before them, and they saw Squire abruptly draw rein, and ride into a fence corner. When he appeared again he was afoot, running down the road.

When Morgan reached the bend, nothing could be seen in front. The sun had set, and the negro was far down the road. They moved on, Joe Lewis leading Squire's horse.

Squire had seen the backs of the Federals; he had known that mounted he could get no nearer undiscovered, and that the horse would excite suspicion. The old man was tough, but it was a hard run to overtake horses now at a trot; yet at last he saw one of the soldiers turn in the saddle, and at once halt, the others moving forward, but turning one by one and halting. Still old Squire ran on.

"Say, what the dickens is the row?"

"Mahsta! . . . Mahsta! . . . you's a-gwine to—Yassah! . . . you's a-gwine to," gasped the old man, truly lacking breath and pausing at every word. "Yassah, you's a-gwine to go de wrong way, sah!"

"What's that he says?" shouted the foremost man.

"Ha! ha! ha! Says we're going the wrong way, Corporal."

The men collected about Squire. "What do you mean, man? Speak out," said the leader.

The negro could see many expressions in the faces before him — expressions of ridicule, fear, doubt and hesitation, indifference, surprise.

"Mahsta, de Confeddick sojehs is gawn down dat a-way. Dey's done went down to de fohd."

"Oh, well, we know that; but they've all gone across. Much obliged to you all the same, Uncle," said the corporal, a fat young fellow smartly adorned and graceful, with evident pride in his own manners.

"But, Mahsta, I done seed 'em; I done seed mo'e of 'em, sah — seed 'em wi' my own eyes."

"When did you see them?" the corporal demanded.

"Dey was in de fawks o' de road, sah, an' dey rid down dis a-way; I seed 'em, sah; hit was dess fo'e sundown."

This startling bit of news clearly made a change in the corporal's estimate of the situation.

"Are there any of them in our rear — behind us?"

"I b'lieve dey is, sah, onless hit mought be dat dey tuhned roun' an' rid back, sah; an' dey done scouted down dis road, an' ef you don't mine you gwine to run up awn 'em — you gwine to heah de bullets a-comin' at shu ef you goes awn — tek my wohd, Mahsta, an' go mighty slow."

"How far is it to the river, Jim?"

"Not much over a mile, Corporal."

"There can be no harm in being cautious. Old man, how many did you see?"

Squire hated to lie, but he cared little for a lie that

E

stood between himself and Armstrong's advantage. Yet he compromised.

"Fo'e de Lawd, sah, I didn't see but one, 'caze I was a-peepin' th'ough de bresh, Mahsta; an' de good book hit say dat whah one man is geathehed togeatheh, dey is mo'e of 'em a-comin' dah, an' I heahed 'em a-comin' — dess a gallinup an' a gallinup. Dah now! I heahed 'em ag'in; don't shu heah? De good book hit say you got sheahs an' you don't sheah."

In truth the corporal had heard ; the sound of hoofs had been distinct, but had died away as Armstrong's horse trod soft ground not three hundred yards ahead.

"Which way was that ? " he asked, somewhat nervously.

"Right down the road," answered one of the men. "I guess they are our people."

"I don't know so much about that. Old man, you've got to obey my orders, or I'll string you up."

"Oh, Mahsta ! W'at shu gwine to do wid ole Squiah? W'en I done come to he'p you out, den you gwine to do me dat a-way? I's a-gwine right back — dat I is!" and the old man turned.

But one of the troopers blocked the way. "Halt, and don't you be so damned uppish. Nobody's goin' to hurt you, if you'll just behave yourself."

The corporal must have given further consideration to the necessity of serving a friend in a friendly way ; he said more mildly : "Old man, march straight down this road, and get as near the river as you can. Even if the rebels are there, they won't hurt you."

Perhaps it was well for Squire that darkness had almost

come, and that his face could not be clearly seen. The corporal's plan was of the negro's devising, though the soldier took all the credit for the campaign. Yet it would not do to accede too readily.

"Den w'at shu gwine to gim me?" asked the old man.

"Well, I guess we'll say a dollar; won't we, men?"

The men quickly assented; under the circumstances, the small contribution required of each would be well invested.

Old Squire's spirits rose; he laughed loud and long, loud enough to be heard by Morgan and his men, loud enough to have been heard by Armstrong, had he been alert toward the rear. The old man started down the road, laughing over the easy-to-earn dollar. The corporal tried to restrain the negro's merriment, but Squire replied that he would be in less danger by signalling his approach, to which statement the soldier mentally agreed so far as possible danger concerned the negro himself, but deemed it wise to follow this noisy scout at a sure distance.

Presently old Squire raised his voice in song. One of the old-time melodies, half sacrilegious and at this moment wholly hypocritical, rolled out on the night, the words undistinguishable to any but familiar ears.

> "Sisteh Mary, whah izh you?
>   Whah izh you?
> Sisteh Mary, whah izh you?
>   He's bawn de king o' de Jews!
>
> "Baptis', Baptis', is my name,
>   He's bawn de king o' de Jews!

Baptis', Baptis', is my name,
He's bawn de king o' de Jews!

"Mahs Chahley, whah izh you?
Whah izh you?
Mahs Chahley, whah izh you?
He's bawn de king o' de Jews!

"Yankee, Yankee, dat's dey name,
Dey's a-comin' right behime;
Yankee, Yankee, six o' seben,
Dey's a-ridin' right behime!

"Mahs Chahley, betteh pray!
He's bawn de king o' de Jews!
Mahs Dan he say go way!
He's bawn de king o' de Jews!"

Far down the road Armstrong had heard and recognized the tune, though not the words ; and through some uncomprehended influence he halted and hearkened. But he had not reached the slope that goes down to the river, and his halt was brief — he must go on ; he feared that he was too late to see the ford, yet if enemies were there he hoped to see their camp-fires on either side. He went slowly forward, the song continuing to reach his ears, — for the singer prolonged the chorus, repeating and repeating, — and once he fancied that the words had been distorted. He reached the brow of the hill, and dismounted ; he would tie his horse here, outside the road, and go forward afoot. He could see nothing in front except a sunken zone of darker gloom, where the river valley lay — no camp-fires, no light in any dwelling. The fence at his right was of stone, that at his left of rails; he went to the left . . . was not the singer approaching? Surely the voice was louder and clearer, the voice of some negro coming, and who would soon be here. This soldier feared no negro, but he knew the necessity for secrecy — negroes were friends to the Yankees, and if one should see him here, his plans would be upset. He began to take down the rails, still keeping bridle in hand. He would hide his horse in some thicket; he would let this negro pass.

And now the voice came loud, and Armstrong worked fast to let down the gap, and the words were clearer, and he knew Squire's voice and some of the words, and such wonder took hold of him that for a moment he well-nigh ceased to work, but already the gap was almost low enough, and he passed through just as a man marched by singing clearly, but now not so loudly : —

> "Mahs Chahley, git away!
> He's bawn de king o' de Jews!
> Git in de bresh an' stay!
> He's bawn de king o' de Jews!"

Armstrong led his horse rapidly from the road, and tied him; then he crept back, hearing, as he came, the sound of marching horses, too numerous for those of his friends, and hearing still the voice of old Squire singing in the distant front. The Confederate saw and counted his enemies as they rode by his hiding-place; he knew that Morgan had come and was near at hand; he understood the negro's stratagem, and saw how the distorted song had been employed for his own salvation

CHAPTER V

DELINQUENCY

"Pryde will have a fall ;
For pryde goeth before and shame cometh after."
— HEYWOOD.

IT was not so dark that Armstrong was unable to see
the three riders who soon appeared opposite his hiding-
place in the fence corner. As he lay flat, he knew Morgan's form outlined against the sky, and Sency's smaller
frame, and Joe Lewis's long legs — one of them at least —
and knew also Squire's horse led by Lewis in the rear.
They were moving slowly, not abreast, but strung out
along the road with spaces of many feet between. Armstrong gave a low whistle, and as they halted spoke out,
"Boys, ride through the gap." They obeyed ; he put up
the gap, and led to the thicket. The horses were grazed
— no telling how long they must wait for Squire.

Meantime the negro's song had died away. As he approached the river, his fears, relieved in regard to his
young master, took larger scope. Would the Federals
suspect ? When they should get to the river, and the
guards there should say that no Confederates had recently
been seen, would not this corporal and his men scour the
woods for the party whose nearness the negro had pro-

claimed? Yes, the guards would tell the corporal that
they had been at the ford for hours, and that no enemy
had shown himself, and then Squire would be suspected
of having made false report for a purpose. Ought he not
to slip away? If he should be seriously questioned, — and
surely he would be, — there would seem no way for his
vindication except by stoutly maintaining that the party
of rebels were still lurking near, or had ridden along the
river seeking to cross at some unguarded spot, and this
defence of himself was an alternative too near the truth,
too dangerous to his master. Oh, yes, all he had to do
was to step aside in the darkness, and let the soldiers go
on; but they *would* go on, and would soon learn of his
abandoning them, and would suspect the truth and would
search, and then it would be almost impossible for Morgan's men to cross the river. No, Squire would endure
much before bringing such a condition to pass . . . besides, he wanted that dollar.

Poor old Squire was in a close place. He felt the con-
traction; it had already closed his voice; it began to
affect his legs. Behind him he could hear the soldiers
coming — gaining on him; if he was ever to run, now
was the time.

But Squire did not run; he halted; so did the corporal,
and the men in his rear.

The corporal halted because he saw that the negro had
halted; the corporal wanted to know why the negro had
halted, but the case demanded silence; the soldier dared
not speak, for there stood the negro, stock still in the
road, evidently fearing something in his front.

The corporal rode back to his first man. " Jim," said
he, in a low tone, " dismount and go forward and find out
what the man means by not going ahead."

Jim obeyed at once. He halted ten paces in rear of the
negro, and asked : " What's the matter ? Why don't you
go on ? "

For all response Squire merely pointed straight down
the road.

Jim looked with all his eyes, but could see nothing to
get alarmed at. " What is it ? " he asked.

" I b'lieve hit's cows, but den ag'in hit mought be
hosses, sah. Won't shu please, sah, go awn down dah an'
see w'at dey is ? "

And now the soldier, more clearly directed to the spot
under suspicion, could see objects dimly prominent against
a background almost equally dark.

" They are bushes," he said.

"No, sah ; I done seed 'em move about — dah now !
you heah dem cows ? " and the darky, forced by a gentle
lowing to admit what he had already known well enough,
began to march forward again, having succeeded in gaining a little time, in spreading greater nervousness in his
guardians, and perhaps in causing them to feel stronger
confidence in their scout.

But Squire's confidence in his ability to dehorn the
dilemma had become no greater ; yet a feeble hope was
beginning to flutter in his breast, that, so near the river,
and still unable to see men or camps, they would find the
ford unguarded. Why were they not challenged ? The
river was at their left ; the ford was just down the bank,

and at neither right nor left did any fire show, nor did any noise reveal the presence of enemy or friend.

At every step Squire's hopes grew rapidly, and when he stood at the mouth of the ford, and knew there was no guard, he felt that his case was good.

"Come awn down, Mahsta," he cried cheerfully; "dey is all done went acrawst."

In his rear fifty yards the Federal horsemen had halted; the corporal ordered to dismount, and he alone rode forward to the negro's position on the verge of the stream. Squire was kneeling.

"Yassah, heah's de hufs; dey's all dess a-pintin' acrawst; an' heah's fresh uns, too; dey ain't full o' no wateh yit, but de ole uns is done fulled up. I 'spec' dem dat went acrawst fust is done got fifty mile by dis time. Ef you all is a-gwine acrawst, Mahsta, now's de time."

"Not yet; we are to guard the ford until — " and the corporal abruptly ended his speech, remembering that his orders were not to be divulged.

The negro's disappointment was so great that he came dangerously near self-betrayal; but the exclamation forced from his lips found excuse in a pretence of losing his foothold and almost measuring his length in the mud.

"Good Lawd! now I done done it. I sho' thought I's a-gwine into de ribeh."

"Where's the nearest house?" asked the corporal.

Squire did not know, but he knew that he *must* know, for he had been accepted as a near resident.

"Didn't shu see dem cows, Mahsta?"

"Yes."

"Dey b'longs to Mis' Jones's, sah; leastways I 'spec' so, sah, up awn de hill 'bout a mile back, but dey is some ole houses down in de bottom, sah; leastways dey was dah oncet, an' dey mus' be dah yit ef de freshet ain't done washed 'em away, sah."

The corporal rode back to his men, Squire following timidly.

"Give me a dime apiece, boys; I'll stand half of it."

The negro was profuse in thanks; hat off, he bowed and scraped and lingered and talked, lingered and talked, until he saw one man posted on the river bank, another stationed to guard the rear, and the others preparing to rest under the trees. Then he bade the corporal good-by, and started back on his road, chuckling agreeably, patting his pocket to hear his well-earned coins jingle, humming softly at times — humming "Rutheh be a niggeh dan a po' w'ite man."

But the leaf had not yet been turned on which Squire John's name had been written in that night's book of fate; before he could reach his friends he must be an actor in an adventure difficult for him, in his present state of mind, to foresee or to avoid. The corporal and his men were merely an extra force sent in advance of Captain Freeman's company, which, having reached Dranesville with horses greatly fatigued, had been ordered to proceed to Rowser's Ford, and march to Frederick on the morrow, leaving a picket at the river. Freeman's march must necessarily be slow, and fresher men and horses had been sent forward to picket the ford until he should arrive.

The negro had made half the distance back to the gap through which Armstrong had escaped, when he heard noises in his front; he stopped to listen; soon he knew that horsemen were approaching, — a small squad by the sound, — certainly not more than three or four. It would have been prudence for Squire to step aside and let the men pass on, but alas! pride in suddenly acquired wealth had destroyed his usual sense of relations. Ordinarily, he would have roughly and intuitively compared chances — those favouring the approach of his friends, and those against; but in his present state of elation his mind was sealed against adverse possibility; he never doubted that the coming horsemen were Mahs Chahley and his comrades, and walked boldly forward into the presence of Freeman's advance guard.

"Halt!" came abruptly from a voice new to the negro, almost above him, for he had but turned a bend to find himself confronted by four strange horsemen.

"Who are you? Give an account of yourself. No; take him back to the captain, O'Donnell; we must ride on."

"Oh, Mahsta, I ain't nobody, sah, but ole Squiah. I dess now be'n down to de fohd, sah, to show 'em de way; dat's all, sah."

"Bedad, and Oi know that v'ice," said O'Donnell. "Ye're the same ould man who tould us about Margan lahst noight. How the hell did ye get here so quick? Hwat're ye doing here, now?"

Although it was too dark in the woods to see faces, Squire knew at once that a denial would be but vanity.

"Yassah. Oh, Mahsta, I's so proud to come up wid ju ag'in — dat I is. You come an' tuck Mahs Dan — dess as I axed you to — dat shu did, an' I hopes he's a-gwine to git well now, feh de good book hit say de Lawd kin save f'om de pleg awn thing dat shu ketches in de night — "

"Oh, shut up that. — And you too, O'Donnell, take him back. But hold on, one second. — Old man, how many of our men are at the ford?"

"Six, sah; dey is good men, too, sah; dey gim me a dollah feh waitin' awn 'em, sah."

Between question and answer there had been but the hesitation of the smallest measure of time, Squire considering and resolving instantly that here the truth would serve him — yet the sergeant had noticed the hesitation — more perhaps by the trembling utterance of the negro's first words in reply than by the lapse itself.

"Damn him; — O'Donnell, take him back — Forward!" and three men marched on, leaving the negro guarded by the vedette whom he had approached on the preceding night, near the Aldie road, thirty miles away.

Since ten in the forenoon O'Donnell had ridden almost without a halt. He had come through Hopewell Gap to Centreville; thence to Dranesville by sunset; thence to this spot, almost fifty miles in all. He did not take Squire back, but stood where he was. He would wait for the company to come up.

"Ould man, I'm damned but ye're in a bad shape intirely. Better make a clane breast of ut now. Ye

may take yer Boible oath Captain Frayman's not a-going
to shtand anny nons'nse."

"Mahsta, I ain't done nothin' wrong. All I done was
to show de men de way to de fohd. Izh you all
Confeddicks?"

"The divil! You know well enough hwat we are.
And was thim ribels it was that ye wint with to the
ford?"

"No, Mahsta, I went wid de Feddicks to de fohd—de
good Lincum sojehs, sah. Dey'll tell you all about it,
sah. I seed dem dah Confeddicks a-ridin' down de road,
an' I tole yo' men, sah, an' dey gim me a dollah, sah, to
go wid 'em an' fine out ef de Confeddicks is done got
acrawst, sah—dat's all."

The tone of innocence was well-nigh convincing, but
O'Donnell's heart was hard against this man that seemed
almost independent of locality.

"Tell yer tale to Captain Frayman—here he comes
now," and the steady tramp of many hoofs warned the
negro that his time for action was brief. Terror had
gained on Squire. It needs not to be professed that he
was no consistent, invariable hero. Born subject to the
influence of detrimental heredity, the germ of his individual merit might never be developed, personal want and
personal fears clamouring so continually that time lacked
for enlargement of worthier considerations; then, too,
Squire was no Confederate—he was simply an Armstrong, a humble member of a family whose heads had
been gods and goddesses from their birth, his hierarchy
of palpable divinities to whom he and his fathers and his

children's children were bound by a fate whose justice
was unquestioned and unquestionable. At this moment
the negro's fears had blotted old Judy, and even the
Armstrongs, from his mind: he thought of nothing but
his own mortal peril, and of device for escape. The soldier confronted him with drawn revolver; the distance
was not six feet, and the captive had been made to stand
in the open road. The old man feared wounds and
death; possibly he could run into the bushes and get
away before the soldier could empty his pistol, but he
lacked the courage to try it. Yet the noise of the advancing cavalry was constantly loudening — he must run
now, or must risk the rope for having betrayed the Union
soldiers. He made a great resolve — he would run. . . .

"And who is ut ye belong to?" asked O'Donnell.

"Mahs Chahley," came the prompt reply; but earlier
still had come the negro's return to the actual relations
of his life, and to the recognition of the fact that he lived
not unto himself alone. No, he settled it there, in that
moment, that he could not run; to escape would be to
put Mahs Chahley in danger; he must submit and wait,
and endeavour yet to mislead his master's enemies.

The company halted. O'Donnell reported to the
captain; "The same ould naygur we had lahst noight,
sor," he said.

"Yassah, I's de same man, Mahsta; but I ain't a-
doin' no hahm,' sah."

"How did you get here?" asked Freeman.

"I dess come, sah, to git to see one o' my chillun,
sah."

" O'Donnell, does Sergeant Walker preserve his distance ? "

" He does, sor."

" Bring this man along with you in the rear, and report to me at the ford. Be sure he doesn't give you the slip," and the company marched on, leaving old Squire yet under guard of O'Donnell.

To the ford it was but half a mile. On arriving, the company replaced the former guards with greater numbers ; then the tired horses, unfed as yet because the forage wagon had not come, were picketed, and the men prepared to take hard-earned rest. O'Donnell marched Squire up to the captain.

"Now, old man, I want you to tell me the truth. Understand me ? " asked Freeman, loudly and sternly.

" Yassah, Mahsta," replied the negro, hat off, bending low, and speaking with all the insinuation of the deepest humility.

" What time was it when you started from home ? "

" Bout 'leben o' twelve o'clock, Mahsta ; but I dunno zackly, sah ; hit was in de middle o' de day, but I didn't had no dinneh yit, sah."

" How far do you call it ? "

" I dunno, sah ; but, Mahsta, I knows dat dis ole man is mighty tiahd, sah ; won't shu lemme seddown, Mahsta ? "

" Oh, yes, sit down. Who came with you ? "

" Wid *me?* Nobody 'tall, sah, didn't come but me. I come by myse'f, sah, an' I didn't hatto say a wohd to nobody, sah, tell I seed dem dah Confeddicks way back yandeh, sah ; an' den I didn't hatto say a wohd to de

Confeddicks notheh; but w'en I seed de Feddicks, den I hatto run to tell 'em, sah; I runned mos' fo'-five mile, sah, an' I is dess about broke down. I tole 'em, sah; dey'll tell you de troof."

Freeman sent for the corporal and his men, and questioned them closely, but of course failed to get any definite knowledge of the negro's character. They had paid him a dollar, they said, for guiding them. Yes, he had run after them, and had told them that the rebels were in their front, moving toward the ford. They had seen none, however; if there had been any, they had doubtless got across long since.

The captain dismissed the witnesses; but he was still suspicious, and his suspicions pointed nearly at the truth. He did not believe that this old negro had come afoot thirty miles to see one of his children; such a thing was possible, of course, but the fact that the same negro had been brought before him on the preceding night was a coincidence he thought remarkable. Freeman believed that a party of Confederates, to whom the slave was attached, had crossed the river on this day, and that his captive had been cut off from them — cut off, say, while foraging — cut off by the corporal and his little command. And Freeman wanted to know how strong a force it was. He knew that Stuart's main column had crossed on the preceding night—perhaps Stuart had been reënforced.

"Who do you belong to?" asked Freeman, suddenly.

"Mahs Chahley Armstrong, sah."

"Where is he?"

"He live down dah, sah, whah you come to git Mahs

Dan Mawgin, sah, but he ain't dah now. Don't shu 'membeh me, sah, w'at come to tell you 'bout Mahs Dan?"

" Yes, I know ; but how was it that you knew his name so well ? " and now Freeman wondered why he had not asked the question on the previous night.

" Yassah, he done had some lettehs in his pocket, sah, an' dem lettehs, dey tole Mis' Sarah an' Mahs John w'at his name wus, Mahsta."

It sounded plausible enough ; but the captain was not satisfied.

" Where is your master now ? "

" Mahs Chahley ? "

" Yes, if that's his name."

" He done gawn wi' de Confeddicks, Mahsta."

" Infantry ? "

If Squire's answer to this question had been truth, perhaps Freeman would have pressed him no further, except to try to learn of movements ; but the negro lapsed.

" Yassah."

" What regiment? "

The old man knew by the tone that he had made a mistake. Besides, the question was no doubt the first of a series bearing upon organizations inclusive ; some of these, indeed, a slave might well plead ignorance of ; but some he must know — for instance, the company in which his master was serving. Squire must recant without confessing.

" Ginnle Stuaht's, sah."

" But you said infantry," then in a moment, consider-

F

ing an untaught negro's ignorance of words; "are Stuart's men afoot?"

"Oh, no, Mahsta; dey all a-ridin' on dey hosses. My Mahs Chahley, he a-ridin', too, dess lak all de balance."

"When did you see them last?"

"'Fo'e Gawd, Mahsta, I ain't seed Mahs Chahley sence de day dat Mahs John an' Mis' Sarah an' Miss Lucy all done moved away."

"How long has that been?"

"Hit's be'n, sah . . . I couldn't dess tell you how long hit *hain't* be'n, Mahsta; hit's be'n a long time, sah; hit was w'en he come home f'om de battle w'at dey fit on de ribeh, sah."

"Fredericksburg, or what battle?"

"Dat battle whah Ginnle Lee got huht so bad, Mahsta."

"You mean Jackson? Stonewall Jackson?"

"No, sah; I means Ginnle Lee, Mahsta."

The fame of other Lees, in comparison with that of their illustrious kinsman, was much greater to Squire than to Freeman; and the captain, for some moments, was puzzled.

"I've never heard that General Lee had been wounded in any battle. Are you not mistaken?"

"No, no, sah; Ginnle Stuaht done hatto make Cunnle Chambliss tek Ginnle Lee's men."

"Oh, you mean Fitzhugh?"

"Yassah," replied the negro quickly, thinking that he detected in the question a desire for affirmative reply. Truth was, however, that Squire's invention had seized upon General W. H. F. Lee.

Nor had Freeman heard that the cavalry general had been wounded ; and perhaps it was well for Squire that he had not, for the battle in question might have been susceptible to the charge of having a date. Freeman was getting very drowsy. If this negro knew anything at all, he was successfully concealing his knowledge. The captain decided to adjourn the meeting. To-morrow he would test this man, and test him severely.

"Private O'Donnell ! "

The soldier, who all this time had been standing some yards away, stepped forward.

"Keep this man under strict guard until further orders. Repeat this order to Sergeant Dow."

*   *   *   *   *   *   *

The negro determined to get away.

CHAPTER VI

DEEP WATER

"Out of my lean and low ability,
I'll lend you something."
—SHAKESPEARE.

AT that day the southern egress from Rowser's Ford was through a narrow chasm dug with the spade, no doubt, but worn deeper in the bluff by years of travel. The passage itself was almost a mile in length, though not very difficult at low water, and required knowledge of its windings, a deviation being perilous because of the water's depth below the ford on the southern, above it on the northern side. From the great fall of rain up the river on the 23d the stream, although now falling, was still at least eighteen inches above its usual summer stage, and no one that was unfamiliar with the sinuosities of the passage, and at the same time aware of its bad reputation, would have dared to venture across at night. Stuart's column itself had been all night in crossing, the cavalry carrying the artillery ammunition in their hands.[1]

[1] ("As General Hampton approached the river, he fortunately met a citizen who had just forded the river, who informed us there were no pickets on the other side, and that the river was fordable, though two

68

East of the southern limit some sixty yards, and at equal distance south of the river bank, the guard reserve had been established, and to their post old Squire had been compelled to march. Farther south, on a swell of the ground, was a cluster of young trees, without under-growth; here the captain's bivouac had been prepared; still farther were the lines of picketed horses, vigilantly guarded by sentinels at either end of the rows.

The sergeant on guard duty to-night was an excellent soldier. He had chosen at once the correct positions for the sentinels and for his reserves, the captain approving, and he had now returned from his first relieving round and was lying on his blanket spread upon the grass already wet with dew — not lying in the posture of a man who would court sleep, but half reclining with his elbow for a prop, when O'Donnell, escorting old Squire, marched up.

"Got to kape him, Sergeant."

"Thought so; you're not on guard duty?"

"Oi'm not, sor; Oi'm going to get some slape. Who takes charge of this man?"

"Here, Laffney, wake up!"

A man sat up on his blanket, yawning. "What's up? I know it's not my time yet."

"No," said the sergeant, "time's not up; but we've got a man to guard. Take your piece, and keep watch over this negro here. You may go, O'Donnell."

feet higher than usual. . . . The residents were very positive that vehicles could not cross. A ford lower down was examined and found quite as impracticable from quicksand, rocks, and rugged banks." From General Stuart's Report.)

Laffney stood. Old Squire sat upon the wet grass, within a few feet of his guard. The sergeant leaned back upon his elbow and muttered, " Wonder if I hadn't better make a change . . . no, this is all right."

Stillness had come again — stillness complete except for the restlessness of horses yet unfed.

Between the guards and the bluff was no bush or other obstacle — a level space of sixty yards. The gash cut in the bluff by the road was sixty yards above. Here was a sentinel walking back and forth on a semicircular beat of perhaps a hundred and fifty yards, his beat at each end reaching the river bank, his position most distant from the reserve being nearly two hundred yards away. It was the duty of this sentinel to watch the river, and especially the far side of the ford, which, however, would be utterly invisible until daylight ; his rear was protected by the company's vedettes on the road, and his flanks by other guards, — on the east by the reserves themselves, on the west by another sentinel beyond whom a vedette had been posted perdu.

Squire was becoming desperate. Hours had passed ; he had confidence that his friends were still waiting for him — waiting, but almost hopeless. He knew that unless they could cross the Potomac this night, Stuart would so far outride them that they would hardly dare to venture. He fancied their suspense, comparing it with his own ; how long would it be before they should decide that he was lost to them, and cease to wait ? The thought caused a sudden fear that they had already gone. And the negro's small hope was not in Mahs Chahley, but in

Sergeant Morgan and Sency. He knew Armstrong was rash. If at this moment he had heard shout and shot, his surprise would not have been great; but he knew that force was not the means to use for success in his own case, or in theirs, and he knew that Sency and Morgan knew it. How much time did he have? Perhaps none — yet he must try.

Sitting there on the grass, his hand touched a hard and uneven substance, at first he knew not what. He had been almost at the point of springing to his feet and running hard for the river. Squire was an excellent swimmer, and, once in the water, might laugh at carbines fired into the night. Perhaps the sergeant's soliloquy concerning the advisability of changing his base had been concluded by the reflection that not one prisoner in a thousand would run for deep water under the fire of the guards, and that if this negro should do so, it would be for the purpose not merely to rid himself of present small embarrassment, but ultimately to escape slavery. But Squire had fully made up his mind: he would reach the river, plunge in, swim far down, and by a circuit reach his friends. The hard object, however, had induced a pause; he tried to lift it; it seemed a stump, immovable; in a moment he knew better; the thing was of metal, embedded in the earth. He pulled at it again, but failed. Then he began carefully to scrape the earth from its edges with his nails; he knew now what it was — a little broken pot, left here by some campers, no telling how many years before. He continued his work until he was able to shake the thing, and knew that at the opportune moment he should have no difficulty in pulling it out.

Laffney was looking toward the river; Squire was looking at Laffney. Laffney yawned, took a step aside, looked over his left shoulder . . . in that last moment the negro sprang to his feet, and, with the broken pot in his hands, was speeding toward the bluff.

The guard turned at the noise, saw the fleeing form, raised his carbine without a word — and fired.

At this instant the sentinel on Beat No. 1 had started on his tramp westward. He turned, and saw the negro just disappearing over the edge of the bluff; he fired.

The sentinel on Beat No. 1 heard a great splash in the water.

Laffney was running to the bluff. When he reached it, there was nothing.

Great commotion arose in the company's bivouac; a stampede threatened, many believing the rebels were upon them; men were running to their horses; men were shouting; horses were stamping and struggling.

Sergeant Dow, however, had seized upon the fact of the escape, and speedily reported to Captain Freeman, who at once restored quiet.

"That darky must want to follow his master very bad," said the captain. "I was right in believing that he had been cut off."

"Maybe he's running for freedom," said Brock.

"No, I don't believe it; he would have had no excuse for not saying so. He'd know very well that we'd send him along."

"Hawley believes he killed him, sir," said the sergeant; "says that when he fired, the negro was in the act of springing into the water, and that he never rose. I heard the splash myself."

"Hawley is a remarkable shot, and has remarkable vision," said Freeman, incredulously. —"Brock, give orders for doubling Dow's guards. We don't know a thing; those shots may bring some inquisitive people upon us. Let everything be alert. Wagon not come yet?"

"No, sir."

"More reason to be careful. Brock, have all the men to keep awake and ready for any emergency."

*   *   *   *   *   *   *

Squire had not felt the touch of lead or of water. On the brink of the bluff he had thrown the pot into the stream, and at once had leaped, not outward, but downward, risking the typical place — underneath him a narrow shelving shore from which the waters had receded. He had landed safely, his feet deep in the mud, and at once had crawled down the river, keeping under the bluff upon which the guards quickly stood. Soon there was no need of crawling; and he rose to his feet and climbed the bluff. He stopped, and looked up the river; he could see nothing, but could hear the noise of the alarm.

"Dem men not a-gwine to quit hunt'n' feh dis ole niggeh," he thought. "I betteh be a-gitt'n' fuddeh; hit ain't no sense in ole Squiah stayin' 'bout sheah no mo'e."

He turned to go on down; before him he could see deeper blackness, which he knew was a wooded hill; he would get to the wood, then fetch a bend and make his way back to his friends, and report the ford guarded; the little squad could not cross. Suddenly he stood still on the brink of a chasm; another step and he should have fallen. He got down on his knees, and could see the opposite wall of the ravine. He scrambled to the bottom, not more than ten feet, and bent his way to the river, chuckling.

An hour later, almost exhausted, he reached the spot where he had warned Armstrong. He climbed the fence and marched north, whistling a low note.

"George," said Morgan, interrupting Squire's report that the ford was guarded, "do you know any other ford near by?"

"None nearer than the one just below Edwards Ferry," said Sency.

"Too far up; eight or ten miles. We must risk it below."

"Mahs Dan, dey's anotheh fohd down dah — I mos' fell into de road, an' den I didn't do nothin' but go down de road to de wateh. Hit's a fohd feh true, 'caze I seed whah de people be'n a-gwine acrawst, an' I knows dat ef dey kin go acrawst, we kin too, leastways ef dat dah Cap'm Freeman an' his men don't sheah us a-comin'; dey is mighty clost."

"Captain Freeman? The same man we saw to-day?"

"Yassah, he de ve'y same man, an' he s'picion me pow'ful. He look at me lak he think me de debble."

"Got his whole company with him?"

"Yassah."

"How far above the place you saw?" asked Sency.

"Not mo'e'n a quauteh."

"We must risk it," Morgan exclaimed. "Think we can make it, Squire?"

"Yassah; de good book hit say de Lawd kin mek He chillun go th'ough de sea dess lak hit's dry groun'."

"Squire, you're a man all over. I wouldn't fail to cross to-night for — well, if we should fail to-night, we'd never catch up, and then what would the general say? Boys, we must try it."

"We can't afford not to try it," said Armstrong.

Squire mounted, and made ready to lead the way.

"Mahs Dan, dem Yankee sojehs is a-watchin' mighty clost. Dey ain't got a mou'ful feh dey hosses. Dey dess be'n a 'spectin' ev'y minute 'at dey waggin'd come up, but hit ain't come up yit."

"Lead on, Squire. Give 'em a wide berth."

They were in motion toward the road, riding in single file, when noises were heard. Squire halted, and his followers closed up.

"Mahs Dan, hit's dat waggin a-comin' now. Don't shu heah de wheels?"

"Yes," whispered the sergeant, "and that wagon ought to be ours; but we can't spare the time."

The noises came nearer. They could hear the tramp of a squad of cavalry, and voices, and the lumbering of the wagon in the rear. They still waited, for fear of a rear-guard; but soon all sounds ceased, and Squire started again, the soldiers riding silently one by one.

At length, past midnight, they halted on the river bank; at once Armstrong dismounted.

"Boys, it's my time now," he said, taking his picket rope from his saddle.

"Better strip, Charley," said Sency.

"That's just what I'm going to do."

Morgan walked up the river bank to reconnoitre; when he returned he found Armstrong ready to lead the way into the water. The ford was unknown; the stream was wide and deep; any misstep might be fatal.

"Charley," said the sergeant, "don't be in haste. Those men back there are as busy as bees. The wagon has come up, and they are feeding. Take your time, now."

Armstrong walked into the water. He had in his hand a slender pole, more than ten feet long; to his body was tied his picket rope, the other end fastened to Morgan's arm. Following Morgan came old Squire, while Lewis, leading Armstrong's horse, brought up the rear.

The moon had gone down, but the surface of the river could be seen. Armstrong slowly waded on with the water constantly deepening until it was up to his armpits; a moment more and he was swimming.

Morgan had halted. He felt the rope get taut; then he pulled steadily and brought the swimmer back to standing ground.

Now Armstrong waded to the right as far as his rope would allow, but found deeper water. He came back and waded to his left; here the water still took him almost to his shoulders; but he moved on some forty yards, Morgan following.

Again the leader struck straight forward, the water

lessening in depth. He was beginning to believe that he had found the right way; yet again the water deepened, and he paused. The rapid river was hard to withstand — not only was strength required to force his way forward, he must also resist the downward rush of the water; he would take breath.

As yet not a word had been spoken. The nearness of the Federal cavalry was such that over the surface of the river sounds might easily reach them. At length Armstrong, feeling rested, decided that he must make another advance. He would try the right again; he leaned his body in that direction; he struggled to move, but could not; he felt himself sinking fast, his feet embedded in quicksand; he struggled again, but could not move his feet; he shouted, and Morgan pulled, but seemed to pull against a rock. His horse was stiff in his tracks on a bottom fairly firm, but the body of his guide was immovable. Again Armstrong shouted, and at the instant a shot was heard on the river bank above them, and then loud voices, and the sound of running, and another shot.

"I's a-comin', Mahs Chahley," cried old Squire, making his horse plunge to Morgan's side.

"Hold on there, sir. What do you mean to do?" asked the sergeant.

"I's a-gwine to my Mahs Chahley."

"No; just take hold here, and help pull."

The strength of two arms speedily drew the exhausted man back to safety. Meantime, in their rear, the noises had increased, and they knew that men were running down the river bank.

"I'm a-thinkin' we'd better go ahead," said Joe, from the rear.

"Silence," said Morgan. He had no thought that they should be pursued into the water, and they were already too far to be seen; all he feared was some shot fired in the darkness at a noisy target.

Armstrong was too weak to continue; he stood in the water, leaning against Morgan's horse.

"Go back and tell Mr. Lewis to bring up your Mahs Charley's horse," the sergeant whispered to Squire.

"Yassah, an' den w'at shu gwine to do, Mahs Dan?"

"I'm going to lead, just as he was doing."

"No, sah, you dess lemme lead, Mahs Dan. De good book hit say de las' gwine to be de fust, an' I knows I ain't high, an' I can't do nothin' in de wateh; but I's dess a-gwine awn dry so widout gitt'n' awff o' dis hoss, Mahs Dan."

Now there was a great uproar,—men shouting on the bank directly in the rear. Morgan felt that Squire was right — something must be done at once, and the least risk was in doing what the negro wanted to do. Squire was a light-weight, and his horse could therefore lead with the minimum of peril to all.

Lewis ranged alongside and helped Armstrong, naked, to mount.

Then Squire forged ahead, giving his horse the bridle.

"Dish sheah critteh mought ha' be'n acrawst sheah befo'e now," muttered the old man to himself, "an' den ag'in he moughtn't; but I knows he got he haid down clost whah he kin smell de bottom, an' ef he ain't got 'nough

sense to keep he foot out o' de bog, he ain't fitten feh
dawg meat. De good book hit say de hoss got lots o'
sense; leastways hit don't say he ain't got none."

Whether it was that Squire's trust in instinct was more
accurate than his knowledge of Scripture, or that accident
favoured him, his beast turned to the right at a sharp
angle and was soon on better ground for depth, and though
the passage now was full of jagged rocks, they were making good headway in the middle of the stream. The
noise in the rear continued, and scattering shots warned
them to hasten. Morgan feared that the northern end
of Rowser's Ford was guarded and that the guards there,
hearing the shots, would come down the river and head
them off; so he rode almost by Squire's side, urging on.
The water again became very deep. Once Squire felt
that his horse was swimming, but in an instant bottom was
touched, and then the shore loomed close at hand.

Morgan ordered Squire to halt, and all the party ranged
alongside in the water. They listened intently, fearing
foes on the bank; but in their front, and now at the south
as well, there was no sound. Yet the sergeant would be
prudent. He could not know whether the exit was strongly
guarded, but he was going to take the venture. They could
not now return, and he gathered his men and prepared
to force the passage. He made Squire take the rear; he
waited until Armstrong had succeeded in partly clothing
himself; then, with weapons ready, he led the way into
Maryland.

CHAPTER VII

A LIVE PUZZLE

"I beseech you, what manner of man is he?"
—SHAKESPEARE.

A COMRADE farming near Haymarket informed Usher West that Mosby had already disappeared, having gone with a few picked men to the Potomac to find out for Stuart's benefit the condition of the fords, and had left orders for the remainder of the band to stay quietly at their homes until served with further notice.

"Jennie," said Mr. West, in low tones, "did you know that Usher has come?"

"Yes, Father; I let him in and kept him from going to his room."

Her fine, strong hands were white with flour; she stood at the kitchen window fronting the sunrise, her father on the outside.

"Your sleep was lighter than mine, then, for I didn't hear him; but I find his horse in the stable. What did you tell him?"

"Only that his room had guests in it. What are we to do?" she asked.

"I must tell him everything before he gets up; he may not want Dr. Lacy to see him."

" I'm afraid he won't like what we've done," said the girl.

" Why not ? "

"Because it may keep him from home, Father. When he can be at home he wants to stay ; and I know, too, though he never says so, that he's always afraid he'll bring trouble upon you and me if he's found out."

Mr. West looked very serious. Mosby's men were peculiarly obnoxious to the Federal authorities, who devised many plans for their capture, and sometimes refused to treat them as mere prisoners of war until they could show proof of regular enlistment in the Confederate army. The fact was that there were other bands —unjustly classed as Mosby's men, most frequently such as would join together for a single purpose and then dissolve forever—which did little else than plunder. Mosby was a partisan, yet in legitimate service, and his enterprises were directed mainly against the Federals' line of communications, in order that a feeling of insecurity might prevail throughout their army ; but his fame has suffered because of irregularity in the conduct of some of his men and more because of the deeds of bushwhackers with whom he had no connection.

" He may be compelled to hide out, Jennie."

" You haven't much time to lose, Father, if you are going to see him before he wakes ; breakfast will be ready in half an hour."

" How was Morgan last night ? "

"No change at all ; he just lay there with his eyes open."

G

At first, hardly roused from sleep, Usher gave speech to great dissatisfaction ; but when told all the circumstances, he said that his father could not have acted differently, and that it would be best to meet Dr. Lacy. Usher was not going to deprive himself of the comforts of home on account of a wounded Federal, and he knew very well how much to tell of himself to the surgeon and how much to withhold. ˙So at breakfast he was introduced as the son of the farmer, a Confederate soldier on leave of absence, and Lacy did not permit himself to ask possibly indiscreet questions, though he wondered how Lee in the present campaign could afford to grant furloughs to strapping fellows such as the one he saw on his right.

"And how is your patient, Doctor ? " asked Miss West.

"Our patient," he replied, with a stress on the pronoun. "You must not endeavour to shirk responsibility, Miss West ; he is just as he was, only he went to sleep very quickly after you left last night and is asleep yet. I shall probe for that ball just as soon as I think he has the strength to bear it. I regard the extraction all-important."

"Is he of the cavalry, Doctor ? " asked Usher, pretending ignorance.

"Yes — a courier — I think I've heard that was his position — and I reason he must have been in close action when he was shot ; it seems to be a pistol-ball."

"Last week ? "

"Yes, the twenty-first. Some persons admitted him to their home, where he remained until yesterday ; we

should have had him in the hospital at Washington but for
your friend Stuart. Mr. West, you were saying yesterday
that it might become your duty to notify the Confederate forces so that they could demand his parole ; now I
have thought that Morgan's delivery to us debars you ;
how does that thought impress you?"

"Possibly it does, not formally, perhaps, but actually.
What do you think of it, Usher?"

"Think you ought to let the man alone, sir. Doctor,
I'll make a bargain with you : you keep mum about me
to your folks, and I'll keep our fellows off while you're
here."

"Agreed!" exclaimed the doctor. "A very generous
offer on your part, young man, for of course the kindness
of this family would ever prevent me from bringing
trouble here. And even if the authorities should know
that my kind host has a son in the Confederate army,
what of that?"

"But I don't see the thing quite so plainly," said Mr.
West. "I am called on to aid a wounded man, and that's
all right as far as it goes ; but to wink at his escape when
he is practically a prisoner, looks like a different thing.
Of course the Confederates had no claim upon him after
they gave him up, but you find that you can't keep him
and actually throw him back on us. Have you not renounced your claim?"

"Really, Father, he has never been a prisoner, and is
not one now," said Jennie, her voice too low for Lacy to
catch all her words.

"Not strictly, I admit. But what I think of is the

duty of a citizen, not that of a soldier. I suppose that
my son here, in the absence of his commander, has perfect
right to make a bargain with the doctor — by the way,
Doctor, you say that a truce was made between your
forces and the Confederate forces which proved to be one
man. Can you tell me when that peculiar truce expired?"

The surgeon laughed. "That truce was indeed peculiar; it was demanded, so far as I have been able to learn,
by the family which was taking care of Morgan, — the
Armstrongs, — and the messenger they sent was an old
negro named Judge."

"No, Squire," said Jennie.

"Yes, Squire; a very ignorant old man —"

"The shrewdest old chap in the Confederate States!"
exclaimed Usher.

"Is it possible? I shouldn't have thought it. He was
very ignorant of everything except that he had been sent
to see us and arrange for turning over Lieutenant Morgan.
He said the Confederate forces were not going to fight us if
we'd put up the white flag! And of course we thought
that there was some scouting party with which we should
have to deal, — some squad or platoon that couldn't take
Morgan away, — but when we got there we found nobody
at all except one soldier with his head and face bandaged,
and the old negro himself. If this so-called truce is not
binding, sir, we are simply at your mercy, Mr. West."

"I have nothing but my conscience to guide me in this
matter, Doctor," interrupted Mr. West; "although
there was no truce in due form, yet it was accepted as
such by both parties, and I think one ought to be bound

by it just as if General Lee or General Stuart had been back of it."

" Then, sir, the truce still holds, if I understand truces; the purpose of this one has not been fulfilled. A Confederate soldier — rank and character unknown to me — asks to deliver us a wounded man whom he cannot provide for; he delivers him and goes away; then other Confederates intervene and prevent the accomplishment of the purpose for which he asked the truce — had they the right?"

" No, and yes; they had the military right to ignore an invalid truce, but have I the moral right? The question concerns *my* conduct, not Stuart's. You cannot suppose that General Stuart was bound in any sense to suspend his march because of that truce?"

" Certainly not, Mr. West; yet suppose that General Stuart had known the circumstances in all detail, do you think he would have stopped my ambulance on the road?"

" I know he wouldn't," exclaimed Usher.

Mr. West considered : better not express reluctance that he did not really feel; the doctor seemed honestly apprehensive ; it would be but common kindness to allay his fears.

" I am about to persuade myself that I have not the right to interfere," said the farmer — truth was that he had never intended to interfere.

" I'll stand by that truce," exclaimed Usher; " I was in the hands of your people once, Doctor, and shall never forget your kind treatment."

" What battle was it ? " asked Dr. Lacy, causing momentary dismay to two of his hearers ; but the one most interested calmly replied : " No battle, Doctor, no regular engagement—just one of the little skirmishes that we cavalry folks are always getting into. It was last winter, down on the Rappahannock."

From the first Lacy had observed that Usher was not wearing uniform, and had wondered ; yet tastes are different, he thought. He himself had laid aside his uniform here, and when on furlough always elected to go as a simple citizen.

" Yes," he said, " many of the skirmishes are unnamed."

" Not enough names to go round," said Usher.

" As you say ; even the names of some great battles are in duplicate, as Bull Run, for instance. A serious wound, may I ask ? "

" No, sir, an accident, really ; my horse ran under a limb and I was knocked off; disabled for a couple of weeks only."

" When were you exchanged ? " Lacy asked the question indifferently, moved by the necessity for showing a little interest that he did not feel. Mr. West glanced at Jennie, and saw that she was thoroughly composed. Usher at once replied : " Oh, never, sir ; I got away in a scramble that came up. I was recaptured while in one of your field hospitals. I'll tell you all about it," and then the young man went on to narrate one of his leader's daring raids, without giving names or disclosing the fact that his rescue had been achieved by his own comrades.

" That is very interesting," said the surgeon, dreamily ; doubtless he was imagining the possibility of such a deed in his own favour.

"And I'll tell *you*, Dr. Lacy, and I don't care who knows it, that it's part of my creed to give and take. You needn't fear my giving your hiding-place away, and you needn't fear my father, either, for all he is so particular."

Mr. West smiled feebly at this, but nodded his head, as much as to say that the question was settled.

Lacy rose. " I must be with Morgan. — Miss West, you and I are going to get him to take some food of some sort this morning, if you please."

"Yes, Doctor ; what shall it be ? "

" Can you get me a little chicken soup ? "

" Thickened ? We have no rice, but I can use flour."

" No, only the thinnest broth."

" At once, Doctor ? "

" Yes ; I should be glad to have it as soon as you can give it to me."

Usher went into the kitchen with his sister.

" Those men are outrageously in my way, Jennie. I thought I should have a good rest at home, and now I must be on my p's and q's all the time. I wonder how long they'll be here."

" There's no telling, Usher. It may be a month."

" Our army has all gone across the river ; so have the Yankees, but some of them are at Centreville and Fairfax, and could come after these men at any time. Why can't we send them word ? "

" And who would go for us ? " she asked.

" I'll find a way if you'll get that Yankee doctor to write a note."

"I'd never propose such a thing."

"Then I'll ask Father."

"But he won't do it.   You see that he almost wants to give them up to the Confederates.   Where are the nearest Confederates, Usher?"

"Blest if I know.   Culpeper, I reckon."

Jennie smiled at this.   Culpeper was far away.

"Then Winchester, or possibly the gap," said Usher, meaning Ashby's.

"I hope he'll get back to his own people," she said.

"Yes, I'm willing to that; all I ask is, not to be run out of house and home."

"They won't trouble you, Usher.   Dr. Lacy is in too great distress to think of giving you trouble."

"Yes, but when he goes back, won't he tell?"

"No; I have no idea that he knows anything."

"Yes, but the mischief of it is that to keep him from knowing anything I've got to be careful every time I open my mouth.   And then again, suppose Joe Dixon or Lem Roberts should happen to come over and blab.   I'm going to notify them all, so they'll keep out of the way."

"Oh, no!" she cried.

"Why not?"

"Because they would tell everybody, and somebody would be sure to cause trouble."

"Well, I'll try to keep 'em off some way."

He started to go, but turned again, and said, "Say, Jennie, I saw Charley Armstrong the other day."

"Well?" she said, looking curious.

"He was trying to catch up with Stuart.   Asked about

the folks here ; you know who he meant, you little hypo-
crite."

He laughed loudly, and started, saying that he was going to the mountain and should not be back before night.

Mr. West busied himself about the farm, and the surgeon was with his patient. Lacy felt himself peculiarly
fortunate in his host, whose character was so open, he
thought. If the farmer had professed to be a Union man,
there would be strong reason for doubting him, and for
always fearing betrayal. Your Virginia fellow-citizen became a Unionist only through compulsion, and disavowed
his conduct just as soon as the Confederates gained the
upper hand.

One thing, however, gave the surgeon a shade of anxiety: this young fellow Usher, who was so earnest in his
assurance of sympathy ; this soldier who gave no date or
name to the fight in which he had been wounded, and was
silent as to the organization to which he belonged, who
could get leave of absence at a most critical time to his
cause, and went without uniform — all these considerations
gave rise to uneasiness. Still, to take it on the whole, the
surgeon thought he might have gone farther and fared
worse : this young woman was charming and strong, if indeed somewhat unsophisticated ; she would be a great help
in pulling Morgan through. Women, you know, if they
have good sense, are the best of nurses, and this one
seemed highly endowed with that rare feminine quality.
He thought the daughter the stronger, when he compared
her with Usher, yet he admitted that the man might be
concealing his powers, with some purpose, though for

what purpose he could not imagine ; evidently there was
mystery, for ordinarily a soldier will let you know at once,
and with pride, the command to which he is attached, and·
if he has been distinguished by wounds he will tell you all
about the important matter ; then, too, Lacy had been
alert enough to perceive, and with some wonder, that
Usher, in his narration of the adventure which had for one
of its results his own release from captivity, had avoided
giving the names of the leaders in the daring exploit — a
thing hard to do when you come to think of it. All these
things tended to disturb Lacy, not that he felt great fear,
but simply because he had not yet reached a logical solution of what he regarded in the light of a small mystery;
and all through the morning, while with Miss West's help
he served his patient faithfully, he found his mind wandering from his important work and fastening on Usher
West. When dinner came the son of the household
assumed still greater prominence, for what rebel on
furlough was ever known to miss a meal? Lacy's bewilderment became almost extreme : a puzzle was here
challenging him ; he determined to lay hold of it;
puzzles were his natural prey.

CHAPTER VIII

DAHLGREN

"And what he greatly thought, he nobly dared."
— POPE.

GENERAL STUART, in his report of the operations of the Confederate cavalry in the Gettysburg campaign, tells us that early on the morning of the 28th of June he marched from the Maryland end of Rowser's Ford for Rockville. As a matter of fact it was fully midnight of the 27th when the rear of Stuart's column succeeded in crossing, and at once a rest was ordered until nearly nine o'clock; but for this delay Morgan's men would no doubt have found their purpose impracticable.

Rockville is northeast from Rowser's Ford some twelve miles, and it was past noon when Stuart's head of column entered the village. Here small parties of the Federals were seen, but they retired at once. Before the column passed through Rockville a long wagon train was reported in sight, coming from Washington, and W. H. F. Lee's brigade was ordered to seize it. This work took up the remainder of the afternoon, so that it was night when Stuart left Rockville for Brookeville, twelve miles north. At Brookeville he halted until morning, for the purpose of paroling prisoners. Hence when Morgan's men got across the river, the rear of the Confederate column was still at Brookeville, but twenty-four miles away.

No man in Morgan's party had ever ridden through the country beyond Rowser's ; yet Sency had learned much concerning the villages and roads, and especially in regard to the political feelings of the people.

"Dan, we must make for Quarles's," he said, giving the name of a Southern sympathizer.

"Know how far it is, or anything about it?" asked the sergeant.

"No; better send Squire on ahead to ask at the first house. All I know is that it's somewhere about hére."

"Squire, ride on hard and ask the first people you see where Mr. Quarles lives. Wake 'em up, if need be, and be on the lookout for us."

"Yassah ; Misteh Squalls's ?"

"Mr. Simpson Quarles," said Sency, and repeated.

Armstrong had recovered his strength; but Morgan thought best not to push the horses, and Squire hastened ahead, and did his work so well that before sunrise they saw him waiting at the mouth of a lane.

"Misteh Squalls, he say you mus' come up dah, Mahs Dan ; he say he not a-gwine to talk to no dam niggeh; he say ef w'at shu want to know is all right you kin come up, an' ef hit ain't all right shu betteh go 'long 'bout sho' bus'ness. Dat Misteh Squalls hese'f w'at tell me. W'en I axed him de road to Misteh Squalls's, he up an' he say he de man, an' dat he at he own house, an' dah he gwine to stay."

Sency rode toward the house, his comrades waiting.

For more than six months George had been held by
wounds at Mr. Radman's, ten miles above this spot — held
secretly for fear of captivity; he knew that Quarles was
friendly, but that was all he knew. There were evidences
of prosperity, — well-tilled fields on one side and well-kept
fences. The place was highly respectable, the outbuild-
ings having been newly painted, while the dwelling was
almost imposing — a much more pretentious residence
than the humble home of Mr. Radman. Sency began to
fear that he was making a mistake, and was almost ready
to renounce; but he had seen a man in his shirt sleeves
standing in the front porch, and he decided to go on. He
hitched his horse and approached afoot.

" Good morning, sir," said George.

" Good morning," was the reply, curt enough.

The man was about sixty, gray-bearded, short, but
strong-looking; rather fierce in his manner, thought
George.

" You are Mr. Quarles — Simpson Quarles ? "

" That is my name, sir."

An awkward silence followed; evidently each doubted
the other, and wanted him to open.

" I hear Stuart has crossed," said the Confederate, as a
compromise.

"Yes."

" Do you know it to be true ? "

"It is true."

Not much of an opening. Sency must develop.

" Can you tell me where he is now ? "

"I cannot. I suppose there are but few men who

know where he is now, and they are immediately about him."

Perhaps every man has a weakness. Quarles was no exception — he smiled at his victory over Sency. The soldier hastened to acknowledge defeat.

"You certainly got me that time. A friend of mine told me it wouldn't do for any common man to tackle you."

"And you are a common man?"

"Yes, sir."

"Common to what?"

"Only a private soldier — common to thousands," replied Sency.

"Who is that friend you talkin' about?"

"Oh, well, I won't call any names; but he's a friend of yours."

"What do you know about him?" continued Quarles.

"I know that he proved a friend in need. I owe him everything, sir — far more than I can ever repay."

"For what?"

"He took care of me when I was unable to go."

"What did he tell you about me?"

Quarles had become the questioner.

"Nothing whatever to your disadvantage, but much in your favour, according to my way of looking at things."

"What things?" The farmer was eying his visitor sharply. The man might be the opposite of what he seemed — might be a man sent to entrap him into treasonable confessions.

"The war," was George's reply.

" What about the war ? "

The question might bring truth to light ; there were two parties even at the North ; many there, although for the Union in sentiment, had tired of the long war, and wanted it to stop on almost any honourable conditions, and now with Lee in Pennsylvania and a decisive battle imminent — a battle on which would depend the safety of the Capital or of Baltimore — the peace party had become bold.

" I'd like to see it stop," said George, " and you know you would, too."

" Yes," says Quarles, indifferently, " I suppose everybody wants it to stop except the contractors and the officers who are hoping for promotion — but stop *how ?* "

" *Your* views are all right."

" But I don't know — " perhaps Mr. Quarles had been going to say "yours," and had thought better of it.

" You mean to say that you don't know mine ? I can speedily prove to you what I am, sir," exclaimed Sency, with great earnestness.

" How does that concern *me ?* But go ahead, and do your proving."

" I was born at Warrenton, Virginia, in 1843."

" That proves nothing, even if it be admitted."

" I studied at the Virginia Military Institute at Lexington."

Quarles nodded slightly, but said nothing ; indeed, his nod might mean a shake.

" I was under Professor Jackson — afterward Stonewall Jackson."

"You are proving nothing at all."

"I have in my pocket an old furlough that bears the signatures of Fitzhugh Lee, Stuart, and R. E. Lee."

"Let me look at that document, if you please," says Quarles.

Sency brought it from his breast pocket — a lengthwise folded sheet, on the back of which were the words, "Forwarded approved" — "Forwarded approved," with three signatures, followed by the great general's autograph, giving the final indorsement.

Quarles handed it back. "Yes, I suppose such things can be had."

"Do you know a man named Radman?" Sency asked.

"I know more than one Radman."

"And you know Tom Radman's middle name — so do I."

"What is it?"

"You know as well as I that he never tells it — Butler."

"Pretty good; anything else?"

"I know one more thing, and if that doesn't convince you, then good-by Mr. Quarles!"

"Let's have that one thing."

"Little Mac is a gentleman," whispered the Confederate.

"Come in," said Mr. Quarles, but at the same instant he stretched out his clenched fist — he had seen one of his labourers passing with face to the porch — and cried, "Get out of here, you damned rebel!" then whispered to the visitor turning in amazement, "Wait down at the road."

Mr. Quarles was not long in coming. He gave all needed information in regard to the roads and the country, but knew nothing of the movements of the Federal cavalry. He advised the Confederates to hide now, and make their way by night, for it was rumoured that Stuart's enemies were gathering in his front and rear.

"We must go on, sir," said Morgan. "Every hour's delay increases the danger."

"Your horses are none of the best," said Quarles; "and I don't see the U. S. brand on a one of 'em."

"No; branded nothing at all; they are private property."

"Well, I don't see how you men can make it by daylight. You might ride in your shirt sleeves, just like many of the Yankees do in this hot weather; but if you get any ways near 'em your horses would give you away, even if your breeches wouldn't." Mr. Quarles's voice was loud and his manner positive.

"Can't help it. We must risk it, sir. Stuart is pushing north, and we must overtake him this night, or we shall never do it."

"I think I could help you in the matter of the horses," said the old man with less emphasis, certainly, but more deliberation. "One of my neighbours has half a dozen good U. S. horses, and I think he'd like to swap. Good horses, too; he bought 'em when they were thin, and he's brought 'em out all right. He's afraid the Yankees may give him trouble about 'em some day, and he'll be glad to trade for cattle not branded."

H

"We must go on," said Morgan.

"Well, my friend, I'll tell you the straight truth. I'm interested in those horses myself, and I don't mind telling you that they never *were* broken down. They are good animals. I got 'em by a slant, and I'm in constant fear that they will be claimed by the government. They are a long way better than the ones you are on, and if you want a good trade now's your time."

"Where are they?" the sergeant asked, with some show of interest.

"Right on your road. You won't lose half an hour—you'll gain time, for they are fresh and will stand pushing. They are at the third place you'll pass on your left. If you say so, I'll get there before you do."

"All right, Mr. Quarles; come ahead; we'll look into it," and Morgan gave the word to mount.

"Dan," says Joe, "I'm a-thinkin' that old feller is in a clost place and wants us to help him out. I reckon he stole 'em. Anyhow, here goes for pullin' off my coat; I'll agree to that part of his doctrine."

The road was full of hoof prints, all pointing northward. In this thickly populated country farm-houses were all about, the smoke of preparing breakfast rising from many chimneys — hardly were they ever beyond sight of a chimney. Yet there were stretches of woodland on the streams, and many small groves and orchards. Their road now turned almost due northeast.

"What do you think about the swap, George?"

"Depends on what he offers," Sency replied. "I'm not going to be cheated in order to get a U. S. horse. I don't want one quite that bad; but I hope he is telling the truth, for ours are none the better for want of rest. He ought to be willing to do almost anything for the sake of safety. Don't you believe that he is interested in some of Mosby's people, or some other people like Mosby's?"

"Yes, I've little doubt of it," replied Morgan.

"You know I was with Mosby on one of his raids over here, and the men captured more horses than they knew what to do with. What do you suppose they did with 'em?"

"They ought to have killed 'em," said Armstrong.

"Yes, but they didn't — that is, all of 'em. Some of the men sold 'em for a song to the farmers, and some of 'em just gave 'em away, or turned 'em loose, which amounted to the same thing, for no doubt the farmers got 'em."

"But if they're branded, our men ahead would be likely to take 'em."

"Oh, Dan, he's got 'em well hid out; he's so afraid of the Yanks that I'm hopeful we'll get a good trade; it took my last word to convince him that I was not trying to get the best of him — he was afraid I was a detective or something."

"Mahs Dan, you betteh go mighty slow a-swappin' feh dem hosses you ain't nuvveh know noth'n' about. De good book hit say w'en you mek a trade you mus' jedge right; dat Misteh Squalls he in a mighty big swivet about swappin'."

"Yes, Squire, we'll not jump at the thing. When we

get there, I want you to keep both eyes open — look at all
of 'em — every point."

"Yassah, I 'spec' he done shut 'em up in de daytime,
an' tuhn 'em loose in his pastuh at night; an' den he ain't
fed 'em no cawn an' de las' one of 'em is got de scouahs
f'om eatin' noth'n' but green grass; an' hit'll be a
Gawd's blessin' ef dey ain't got de tendeh huf, too, feh de
good book hit say dat de hoss got to eat de hahd cawn ef
he gwine to stan' up to he bus'ness."

"You must look close, old man, and not let us be
cheated."

"If they swindle Squire, they'll have to get up before
day," says Armstrong.

"Yassah, dat de Gawd's troof; but dat Misteh Squalls
he done tuck an' got up befo'e day dis mawnin'; w'en I
come up to him, he dess a-smokin' his pipe dess lak it was
atteh breakfus', an' heah we is, ain't had not a mou'ful
yit."

The third place on the left was reached. A tall gate
was already open at the only entrance way through an
impenetrable hedge. Mr. Quarles had distanced them —
had known how to take a short cut, he said. He led the
way up to a dwelling of some former comfort, but now
greatly in need of repairs. Behind the house, on a
steep slope, stood a large barn, to which building the
whole party descended. In the stalls were nine horses,
all of them evidently ex-Federal. Squire went the
rounds.

"Dis un got th'ee w'ite hufs — dess es soon have a
cow," the old man muttered. He went out into the barn-

yard and returned with a heavy stone and struck repeat-
edly the hoofs of the animals he liked.

" Yassah, Mahs Dan, Mistah Squalls he say he done fed
'em awn dry feed all de time — an' some o' de cobs izh
heah yit, but you dunno how long dese crittehs can stan'
up undeh yo' weight an' Mahs Chahley's, noh Mahs Joe's
notheh; cou'se any of 'em kin git along undeh ole Squiah
—'caze I ain't noth'n' but a runt, nohow."

Quarles protested that the horses had had regular exercise; every night they had been turned into the pasture,
and occasionally one had been ridden. The trade was
struck, Mr. Quarles greatly rejoicing because he could
now sell unsuspected property.

Morgan's men, on fresh mounts, rode rapidly, Armstrong boisterously praising his new horse. Indeed, they
were all elated, except old Squire, who had felt his own
beast begin to stumble. Taking Quarles's advice they
pushed due north through Gaithersburg, cutting off the
great angle at Rockville, thus gaining miles on Stuart's
march, and at ten o'clock reached the road for Westminster. At the junction they paused: men were seen coming from the north, — five cavalrymen of yet unknown
colour. Morgan decided instantly that retreat was impossible — impudence alone was prudent; he gave the word
to his men — they must dash by the approaching squad.
Armstrong was with Sency in front, the sergeant was
with Joe at the rear; but where was Squire? Morgan
had just observed that the old man was missing; but there
was no time to lose — the meeting would be in a moment,
for the squad came at a gallop; the four rushed forward.

Between his teeth Morgan called, " Salute them ! "

In double velocity the two groups passed each other at
such a storm that the Confederates were uncertain as to
the character of those whom they had met, for they, also,
were in their shirt sleeves ; but Morgan looked back, and
saw the men coming to a halt and turning in their saddles
and gesticulating.

" Look out ahead! " roared Armstrong, and Morgan's
face came with a jerk to the right about, and he saw, coming, a troop of horse, which he knew to be the main body
for which the squad was but the advance guard ; the
speed had slackened.

" What are they, George ? " cried the sergeant.

" Yankees, undoubtedly — so were the others."

Morgan again turned ; the squad were pursuing their
way ; no doubt they had decided that the main body
would speedily settle the question.

The sergeant debated rapidly : would the commander
of this troop consider them orthodox simply because his
advance guard had allowed them to run into greater peril ?
Not much time did Morgan have ; the Federals were
within forty rods, coming at a trot.

" To the right, Charley ! " he exclaimed. He could not
expect this large body to give him half the road ; even if
unquestioned at the moment of meeting the head of the
column, his speed must be diminished for lack of ground,
and the colour of the trousers would be known easily.

A narrow lane was leading up to a farm-house some three
hundred yards from the highway. Sency and Armstrong
turned up the lane in a trot, Morgan and Joe following.

"Walk!" ordered the sergeant. He hoped that the
Federals would pass without attempting to examine them;
then he would wait for Squire.

At their left, by turning a little, they could see the head
of the cavalry column not more than a hundred and fifty
yards away and getting nearer, for the speed of the Federals was the greater.

Morgan ordered Armstrong and Sency to keep their
faces to the front and ride on; he ordered Joe to ride on;
he brought his own horse to a slow walk, and let his comrades distance him. He threw his right leg over his saddle
and bent over, seeming to seek timely comfort,

An instant more and "Halt! halt!" came from his
rear.

Morgan halted; the three others were riding on—some
sixty yards away.

Morgan turned his horse to face the challengers . . .
his party were riding on . . . three Federals were riding
up the lane . . . their speed lessened . . . the troop in
their rear was passing the mouth of the lane . . . the
foremost Federal turned and waved his hand . . . his
two followers went to the right about and followed after
the troop.

Morgan made sure that his right-hand pistol was easy
in its holster; he could see that the man approaching
was an officer; better to ride forward and meet him —
now he could see his shoulder-straps. "Good morning,
Captain," he shouted, almost guessing at his rank; then,
before any response had been made, "Can you tell me
where I can find the general?"

The Federal halted. Morgan saw that he was very
young — younger than himself; yet as he sat his horse
he looked all of a man — a stern soldier, and a hardy,
though handsome and of refined features. Not two rods
separated the horsemen — one trembling inwardly with
suspense, the other's face unmoved at first as he raised
his right hand and held it before him to shield his eyes
while he looked up the hill on Morgan, for the sun was
directly in his front; yet the palm of his hand was outward; even at the expense of awkwardness the owner's
dignity must not be permitted to suffer by discourtesy
to another. ·

All at once the Confederate saw that his antagonist's
countenance had changed : indifference had yielded to an
expression of bewilderment or other feeling which the
sergeant knew not accurately to construe; for up to this
point he had but attempted to play the part of *any*
Federal — not the part of one only Federal. Morgan,
also, had raised his hand, to return what he had momentarily conceived a salute, but his hand had dropped quickly
to his side, while the other's hand remained in the air.

Perhaps not three seconds had passed, the officer silent
and preserving his attitude, when, moved by some inex-
plicable cause such as affects one at peculiar times through
a sense of the ludicrous, Morgan smiled.

"Aha !" cried the Federal, instantly, and lowering his
hand, "is it you, really?"

"Really and truly, Captain," answered Morgan, with as
much coolness as his amazement would allow, his smile gone,
serious, alert, dreading this man of mysterious approach.

" Well, I'll swear," said the officer, coming nearer;
" who would have expected to find you here ? We heard
you had been killed, or at least so badly wounded that
you couldn't move. I believe I remember that you asked
me about the general, and in my perplexity I failed to
answer. Pleasonton is up above — near Frederick, somewhere. How in the name of sense do they spread such
reports ? "

" And where is Stuart with his gang ? " exclaimed
Morgan, his first wonder supplanted by a greater, yet
ready now to play the part forced upon him.

" Gone north toward Hanover. How did you get
here ? I'll swear I didn't know you till you smiled;
you've changed. Why, man, don't you know that your
conduct is disgraceful in the extreme ? You were given
up for gone — dead, wounded, missing, a triple casualty,
and yet here you are, just the same as ever, except that
you don't seem quite strong yet. For mercy's sake, give
me your recipe."

" Well, Captain, my horse *was* killed, but strange to
say *I* wasn't. But I was cut off and had to stay on the
south side. I picked up a darky who helped me ; he's
with me still, lingering behind somewhere. I'll be
obliged if you'll hurry him up when you meet him.
Can't you come up to the house yonder and help me get
breakfast, Captain ? "

" No, Morgan, I must ride on. I'm on urgent business;
the general has given me twenty men, and I'm after big
game. To tell you the truth," and now the officer's voice
was low, " we've learned that a messenger from Jeff

Davis is trying to make his way through to Lee, and I'm going to catch him if the thing can be done."

"But you don't expect to find him as low as this, surely?" exclaimed the Confederate.

"We are taking care of every ford. I'm now on my way up higher," said the officer, whose frank eye had not once left the rebel's face.

"And where is the army?" asked Morgan.

"I bet a pretty penny that you don't know a word of the big news," the captain exclaimed.

"No — tell me quick."

"You wouldn't guess in a week."

"Don't keep me in suspense, Captain."

"Well, then, here goes : one, two, and Meade is in command."

"Command of — you don't mean it ! "

"On honour. George Gordon Meade, Major-General commanding the Army of the Potomac ! That's been Lord George's style for the last twenty-four hours."

"By Jove ! "

"No . . . By George ! And once more . . . shut your eyes now ; the thing's personal to *you!* Ready ? "

Morgan nodded.

"It gives me heart-felt pleasure to tell you that you have been promoted to a first lieutenancy, Morgan ; and that, too, for a reason that all your friends will rejoice to hear and to speak of — gallantry on the field of battle."

Morgan gave no reply to this speech ; perhaps it was as well, for the look that dashed over his features as he thought proudly of the distinction to his family might

easily be attributed to proper confusion on his own
account.

"Truth, I tell you, and Pleasonton has had your name
read out in orders."

"Indeed that is news, Captain, and you make me very
proud. What does it all mean? and what do they all
say about Meade?"

"Well, they say everything. But I think that the
average opinion is good-natured at the bottom. Of
course everybody thinks it risky to 'change horses in the
middle of the stream,' as your Uncle Abe puts it; but the
thing's done, and Hooker's gone, and Dahlgren is out of
a job ... per*haps!* I'm on this messenger business, and
when I get back there's no telling what Meade will do
with me. Two to one he's already got four men spotted
for my place. Say, Morgan, do you know whether
Rowser's Ford is held by us yet? Really, that's just what
I halted you to inquire about."

"Was this morning about two o'clock. I crossed
there."

"Know who's there?"

"Captain Freeman is the officer's name, I think. You
going there?"

"No, I'm going higher. Was Freeman to come on?"

"Yes," was the reply at a venture.

"None of our men south of the river?"

"None nearer than Fairfax. I had trouble in getting
through, as you may well suppose."

"I see you have on gray trousers."

"Yes; put 'em on before I got to the river; and now

they're all I've got.   Will I have trouble above here,
Captain ? "

"Well, you may, but I think not. Stuart has gone
north, it's true, but all you have to do to avoid him is to
take the first road to your left; it's not more than half a
mile — but you'd better look out." The captain's voice
was growing louder at each word, for he had turned bridle,
and was moving away. "Give the general my regards,
and Cohen," and Captain Ulric Dahlgren, formerly
General Hooker's aide, galloped back down the lane,
leaving Morgan to follow after his comrades in peace, but
in a torment of curiosity to know more of this Captain
Dahlgren, who seemed so familiar with Andrew; and then
the sergeant chuckled at the thought of the scene when
Freeman and Dahlgren should compare notes.

CHAPTER IX

A CASE OF KNOWING

" And what's impossible can't be,
And never, never comes to pass."
— COLMAN.

WHEN, as already related, Morgan's men, at ten o'clock,
reached the road for Westminster, and saw the six cavalrymen who afterward proved to be the advance guard of
Dahlgren's troop, old Squire was not more than a furlong
behind. He heard the galloping horses, as his friends
rushed away, and, a few minutes later, the rapid approach
of the squad of Federals, but a swell of the ground hid
them as they passed southeast athwart the joining of the
two roads.

Squire's horse was in a bad way ; the rider knew that
he could ride but little farther, for he had exhausted the
influence of kicks and blows, and progress was becoming
slower at every yard. In momentary despair he ceased
to urge, and the beast began to nibble at the tall bushes
in a fence corner by the roadside, but soon ceased even
this exertion, and stood stock still. The negro dismounted and was examining the horse's hoofs when a
second and louder noise arrested his attention — the
sound of Dahlgren's main body, coming at a trot, scab-
bards rattling, a hundred horseshoes striking the flinty

earth, the noise of laugh and speech from many men;
and Squire, unable to know whether they were friends
or the enemies of his friends, cowered in the bushes
lest he be seen.

When the troop had passed at right angles to his
course, the negro again tried to help his horse, and soon
took a pebble from one of the hoofs, giving but the
smallest temporary relief, however, the case requiring
rest and food more than superficial treatment; yet he
was encouraged to remount, and by dint of loud speech
and violent bodily exercise succeeded in reaching the
junction of the two roads, where, looking north, he saw
a single horseman coming at a great gallop.

Captain Ulric Dahlgren, only twenty-one years of age,
was already distinguished for audacious ingenuity in war.
The son of Admiral Dahlgren, his social and military
prospects were great; and his own worth was unquestioned.   His first service had been to assist the ordnance
department in the important duty of disposing the batteries at Harper's Ferry; this engineering work accomplished, Dahlgren went to the field and served as aide to
General Sigel in the Valley campaign against Stonewall
Jackson.   On November 9, 1862, three days after General
Burnside had taken command of the army, Dahlgren rode
through the streets of Fredericksburg at the head of
Sigel's body-guard, seized prisoners, captured supplies,
and gained the knowledge that prompt action would
put the heights beyond Fredericksburg in the power of
the Union army, and that army on the right flank of
Lee's.   Dahlgren was at once appointed to a position

on the general staff; the army moved promptly, and it
was through no fault of Burnside that dilatoriness spoiled
his campaign. He reached the Falmouth hills before Lee's
advance had occupied the opposite range — the army had
marched well, but only to find that it was forced to a
protracted halt because the necessary bridge material had
not been provided by the authorities in Washington.

After Burnside, Dahlgren had served Hooker, and
now, although in Morgan's presence he had modestly
disclaimed the high esteem in which he was held by
the future conqueror of Gettysburg, was beginning service under Meade, who had already designated him as
a member of the general household.

When Dahlgren rode back out of the lane into which
he had followed Morgan, his men were no longer visible,
and he put spurs to his horse. At the top of the next hill
the captain saw a negro man, mounted, coming at a slow
walk, and, a little nearer, could see that the negro was
old and small, with none of the marks of a combatant.
Indeed, there were as yet no negro troops in the Army
of the Potomac, and but for the fact that this negro was
on a trooper's saddle, Dahlgren would have had no difficulty in attributing to him all the qualities that disfigure
and adorn peaceful rusticity and bondage.

The captain halted; so did Squire, with profound obei-
sance.

" Whose horse is that you're on, old man ? "

" Dis hoss, Mahsta ? Dis hoss he b'longs to de sojehs
w'at done went awn ahaid; he don't b'long to me, sah,
dat he don't. Ef he b'long to me I'd git shet of 'im, sah,

'caze de good book hit say dat de hoss rush into de battle ; but dis un he ain't wuff de salt dat he git ev'y Sunday. I done got so fuh behime dat I's afeahed I ain't *nuvveh* gwine to ketch up.　Did ju meet 'em, Mahsta ? "

"I met Lieutenant Morgan and two or three men.　Do you belong with them ? "

"Mahs Dan Mawgin ? "

"Yes."

"Yassah, but I ain't nuvveh knowed dat he was lieutenant, Mahsta."

"No, *he* didn't know until I told him.　Are you the man who helped him out over yonder ? "

"I dunno, Mahsta, dat I he'ped him out much wuff talkin' about, but I be'n stickin' to 'im long es I could, sah, feh de good book hit say be ye faithful to de eend, an' I 'spec' I mos' done got to de eend now, sah, 'caze de good book hit say de fust gwine to be de las', an' I knows I done be'n de fust a-leadin' de way in dat fohd, an' now I's de las' feh true.　How fuh is dey done got ahaid, Mahsta ? "

Dahlgren was moving on.　"Half a mile by this time. Morgan told me to hurry you up," he shouted, turning.

"Yassah," Squire replied, greatly rejoicing that the act seemed about to end so well ; but in a moment the Federal halted, as though a new thought had come.

"You crossed at Rowser's, didn't you ? "

"Yassah," Squire shouted in reply, then, feeling a necessity for providing a way to evade, "leastways hit wus down dah some'h's, Mahsta — dat's w'at dey called it."

"Deep?"

"Yassah, hit mos' swum de hosses."

The captain used his spurs and soon overtook his command. His thought was peculiarly tinged; ever since he had met Morgan he had suffered a sensation which he dimly felt was uncanny. He had been in some degree familiar with Junior (as Andrew was called), whom he had known as a daring courier serving Pleasonton immediately, and with whom he had been slightly associated in more than one small exploit. The news that Morgan had been mortally wounded had given Dahlgren pain, and the surprising discovery that the courier was well and strong had made him rejoice, yet there was mingled with the surprise and joy an indefinite feeling of discomfort which he could not analyze. "Wonder if I'm getting superstitious in my old age," he thought. "That fellow Junior Morgan makes me feel as though I'd met a ghost in broad daylight. I almost wish I hadn't seen him. Who was it that started that report about his being a dead man? He had heard of it, himself — at least he showed no surprise when I gave him credit for his resurrection. I'm going to make him tell me all about it when I get through with this messenger business. Ah! Yonder they are; wonder why they've halted."

Before him, at no great distance, was a larger body of troops than his own, all seemingly at a stand in the road; but in a moment there was a stir, and now Dahlgren saw faces as well as backs, and knew that his troop was meeting and passing some other command.

"Good morning, Dahlgren," cried an officer at the

I

head of the approaching column, and then halted while
his company rode on north.

"Freeman? The very man I wanted to see," and
Dahlgren reined up.

"Halt!" came Freeman's order to his company.

"Road clear to Rowser's, Captain?" asked Dahlgren.

"Suppose so; camped there last night and came through
this morning. Guess all of Stuart's are out of the way by
this time," replied Freeman, and then added with a loud
laugh, "but I don't know where Mosby is."

"You got there last night, did you, Freeman?"

"Yes; been over in Loudoun on a special job; the
general sent a runner to warn us. Thought we were going to have trouble, but found that Stuart had got out of
our way long before we knew he'd been in it," and Freeman's tones and movements of the head were not compli-
mentary to the Federal generalship.

"How far do you call it from Rowser's to Edwards
Ferry?"

"Just about ten miles; you mean by this side, of
course?"

"Yes; what I want to know is whether there is any
crossing place between Rowser's and Edwards."

"For troops, you mean?" asked Freeman, showing
great interest.

"No, for anybody; I'm to look out for a man with a
small escort."

"Ah! Well, people cross at many places; but there's
no good ford for public use between the two, so far as I
know. What's up, Dahlgren?"

"A messenger from Davis to Lee."

"Like hunting a needle in a haystack," exclaimed Freeman.

"Well, the hunt is good exercise. You know the news about Meade?"

"Yes, and between you and me I'm glad of it," replied Freeman. "Meade's a gentleman and a scholar, as well as a man and a general. Any news of Lee?"

"Not a word that means anything definite. Ewell has been at Carlisle and seems now to be making for Harrisburg, but what Hill and Longstreet are doing nobody knows. Meade is marching, but not rapidly — waiting for developments. I'm to report back wherever I find him — God knows where."

"You learned nothing of Stuart?"

"Oh, yes, he's somewhere up the road — about Hanover by this time. At what hour did you leave Rowser's, Freeman?"

"We staid there till eight this morning. It was thought that more of Stuart's people might be coming on — and in fact I guess a few of them did get through last night. We had quite a scurry for a little while. We're bound for Frederick; which road did you come?"

"Down by New Market."

"Wonder you didn't strike against the rebels that got by me at Rowser's last night," said Freeman, in a tone that indicated soliloquy rather than inquiry.

"How many were they?"

"Don't know — not more than twenty or thirty, I

guess. It was so dark you couldn't see — and then they
forded down below — not at Rowser's exactly."

"Possibly they were the very party I'm after, Freeman. What time was it when they got through?"

"Little before day."

"They must have been close on Morgan's heels."

"What Morgan?"

"Dan, or Junior, as they call him. Pleasonton's
courier, or aide, I suppose we should call him now. He's
promoted for gallantry at Aldie and elsewhere. The
same man that passed you at Rowser's this morning; a
downright good fellow all over."

"Dahlgren, to save me from sin, I can't understand
what you're talking about," exclaimed Freeman, with
great earnestness.

Dahlgren had dismounted; at this moment his left foot
was in his stirrup — he must ride on.

"Why, don't you know Morgan? He was reported
mortally wounded at Aldie last week and probably a
prisoner."

"Yes, I know Morgan; that is, I don't know him per-
sonally, but I do by reputation; and what I don't know
most is why you should say that the squad of rebels that
crossed at Rowser's Ford last night were close on *his*
heels, and that *he* crossed there also."

"Only this and nothing more: I met Morgan up
yonder about ten o'clock, and he told me that he crossed
there before you had left," and Dahlgren mounted.

"Hold on!" shouted Freeman. At the next instant
he saw difficulties; it would be a matter of delicacy to

tell Dahlgren — a man positive, peremptory — that he was duped by his own error ; yet something must be said, and Freeman recovered sufficiently to decide on adroitness.

"Well, what is it ? " asked Dahlgren.

"Are you sure that you know Morgan ? "

" Dead sure, and I thought you did too, for he told me that you were holding the ford," and General Meade's aide smiled to see the look of utter bewilderment that spread over Freeman's whole face, from which all shadow of adroitness had gone.

"Brock ! O Brock ! Come here at once ! " shouted Captain Freeman ; then, in a lower voice, he said : " I'm going to prove to you that Morgan is not north of the Potomac, Captain. *No*, sir ; nobody has passed Rowser's Ford except the squad of rebels — and they crossed below — and a man or two with passes who came over since daylight."

Dahlgren made no comment, except that which was indicated by the change that converted his smile of assurance into one of incredulity.

"Lieutenant," said Freeman, as Brock hastened up, " I want to present you to Captain Dahlgren, of the general staff " . . . the customary salutes, and words, and hand-shaking . . . "and to ask you whether you know Lieutenant Daniel Morgan of General Pleasonton's staff ? "

"Seriously, Captain ? " inquired Brock, with a dash of suspicion in his voice.

"Yes, seriously ; a question has come up," replied Freeman, his voice tremulous.

"Certainly, I know him ; at least in a sense ; I've seen him," said Brock.

"Do you know where he is now?" asked Freeman, assertively.

"Well," says Brock, "I can't swear it exactly, but I can come pretty near it. We left him yesterday at noon between Middleburg and Aldie, and I guess he's there yet."

"Of course, he *was* there — no doubt about that," Dahlgren broke in.

"But wait ! What was his condition?" asked Freeman.

"Well, I don't want to prophesy," said Brock, with an ominous shake of his head; "but if he was not at the very gate of death, then I never saw a living man in danger before."

"Yet I saw him hardly an hour ago, up yonder," exclaimed Dahlgren, somewhat huskily, pointing northward.

"Some other man, Captain," said Brock, who had not yet stopped his shaking of the head, and increasing that sign into one of vehement negation.

"Tell me what he looks like, Lieutenant."

Brock shook his head some more, saying: "Looked like a dead man, Captain. Face white as a sheet."

"Yesterday?"

"Yes."

"But don't I tell you that I talked with him for fifteen minutes? He told me himself that he had been given up for lost or dead."

"Impossible, Dahlgren, clearly impossible ; we were sent specially to get Morgan — my whole company — and Dr. Lacy — you know Lacy? — he was sent with us with all sorts of surgical things — an ambulance — a patent mattress, and God knows what else — and we *got* Morgan, I tell you, got him out of a house down there — why, man, he couldn't talk — he was perfectly speechless — partly paralyzed, Lacy said — and when we got orders to ride, we had to leave the man, and Lacy stuck by him — and is with him yet. You're dead wrong, " and Freeman's face had a desperate look upon it as though he would have chosen the proof of his own version rather than Morgan's safety and Dahlgren's triumph.

"You got the wrong man," said Dahlgren, coldly ; then, without waiting for any response, he said : "You see, *I know* Dan Morgan ; I've been with him more than once ; and I not only talked with *him* this morning, but I met the negro to whom he owes his safety. He told me about the negro, and then I met the old darky, following with a lame horse ; he asked me how far Morgan was ahead. You gentlemen have picked up the wrong man by mistake. Who told you that *your* man was Junior Morgan ? "

Brock and Freeman looked into each other's eyes. Could it be that Dahlgren was right, after all? That old darky again !

"We were notified that Morgan was lying desperately wounded at the house of a citizen named Armstrong. The people sent us a messenger — an old negro — to tell us that we might come and get Morgan — and, by the Lord ! I guess you're right, Dahlgren."

"What is it now?" asked Dahlgren.

"Why, that same negro turned up at Rowser's last night, and caused a rumpus that I've never been able to see into."

The superior smile on Dahlgren's face did not tend to assist Freeman's confession. Not every man bold enough to face battle without nervousness is sufficiently courageous to admit that some one has made a fool of him; but Freeman was both bold and brave. "I guess you're right, Dahlgren; we must have been worked, but for what purpose I'm at a loss to know. What sort of a negro was that you say you met?"

"Why, a most respectable old fellow; must have been about sixty; small, and tough-looking."

"Gray-headed?"

"Yes," says Dahlgren.

"Tell you his name?"

"No," says Dahlgren.

"Nothing peculiar about him?"

"I took him for a well-raised old darky — one of your privileged patriarchs that they call 'Uncle.' He said 'Mahsta' rather frequently, and showed a fondness for Scripture."

"God!" said Brock, and then roared with laughter, in which, spite of himself, Dahlgren soon joined more moderately.

Yet Freeman's consternation was but momentary. "I don't see what there is so funny in this mixture," he exclaimed; "here you go to show that the same old nigger that handed Morgan over to us tells you that he is attached to Morgan. And you saw Morgan. In one case the nigger delivers to us a dying man named Morgan, and in the other he follows a man whom you know to be Lieutenant Morgan uninjured. How do you account for the negro's conduct? Has he told two lies? If he told the truth once, which time was it? To you or to us? You are convinced that you talked to Morgan. If that negro lied to us, and palmed off on us another man for a purpose — he's too deep for *me!* What motive could he have? Even from your standpoint, what motive could he have? He helped Morgan to escape, according to your theory; how does handing over the wrong man to *us* help Morgan to escape? If he could hand any man over to us, why didn't he hand Morgan over to us? If he is really attached to Morgan, why should he wish to cheat Morgan's friends? And it looks as if Morgan himself had something to do with the thing. You say he passed me, and I say I know nothing about it. Damned if I can see daylight in the rotten mess anywhere."

"Well, gentlemen, I am compelled to bid you good morning," said Dahlgren. "I wish I could relieve this doubly dark mystery; but I must be riding. Tell you what I wish you'd do for me, Freeman," he added, smiling; "drop me a line if you are ever able to make heads and tails of this thing."

"I'll do it. And you do the same thing by me. There's something wrong about that old darky as sure as shooting."

"What's his name?" asked Dahlgren, still smiling.

"Squire," said Freeman and Brock.

CHAPTER X

SOLUTION

" Reckeners without their host must recken twice."

— HEYWOOD.

MISS WEST had consented with concealed reluctance to her installation as Dr. Lacy's assistant, and was devoting to her merciful work all time not exacted by pressing household affairs, which, indeed, suffered in her own fears as she thought of Usher's probable dissatisfaction when he should return to diminished comfort. Engrossed as he was, for the most part undoubtedly with his duty to his patient, but secondarily, it must be admitted, with his delicious perplexity concerning Usher, the worthy surgeon was utterly impervious to any effect from the girl's condition of enforced service, and accepted her aid without a qualm, and even without the consciousness that he was enjoying a lack of the irritableness that usually afflicted his temper when in the presence of a woman.

That the condition of his patient had become no worse was a source of great gratification, and Lacy felt no doubt of his own ability to bring the delicate case to a successful issue; for he furnished no exception to the rule respecting the union of genius and egotism — and he had sense

122

enough to know it ; indeed, his self-pride was so conscious
that he reasoned upon his own powers as justly as upon
another's, and felt additional pride at the accurate conclusion which, in such comparisons, he invariably reached,
that he had the right to be proud.

And Morgan, even in his condition of utterly passive
consciousness, felt the benefit of an atmosphere of safety
— the aura, so to speak, of a strong character with intellect
enough to throw eccentricity into invisible background :
men are to be judged as statesmen, as surgeons, as what
they profess to be, according to their purposes and achieve-
ments, and their foibles lessen not, but rather illustrate
their essential quality. The wounded soldier instinctively
knew that here was the man in whose hands his case was
safe, and saw as yet no flaw.

"Miss West," said the surgeon, "to-night I shall take
first watch."

Jennie would have preferred a different order of things,
as Usher was to be looked for before midnight, and she
could not readily sleep while expecting him ; but she had
had first watch on the preceding night, and she submitted
without protest. Turn about is fair play.

"Tap on my door, Doctor, when my time comes," she
said, not entirely void of hypocrisy perhaps, since she was
almost sure she would not need to be waked. Morgan
was already sleeping and Lacy was sitting near the west
window where he had drawn a small table on which he
had laid a paper ruled into parallel columns. He held a
pencil in his hand ; she was standing over him.

He nodded vaguely, whether for assent or concerning

some idea in regard to the marks which he was beginning
to make upon the paper, she could not tell, for he seemed
preoccupied. She went out.

Lacy wrote + over his first column, and the sign for
minus over the second, in his own mind the symbols
for argument pro and con. Then he set himself to thinking profoundly, so deeply that he had no knowledge of the
lapse of time, no perception that the light in the west was
dying, and that the lines on his paper could no longer
be seen.

At length he nodded emphatically, and made a movement to write; then he rose and went to a shelf and
brought his candle, and placed it on the table, and lighted
it, his body carefully intervening between the flame and
Morgan's face. He sat again, and took up his pencil, but
had lost his idea.

"What was it? Let me see now! . . . Oh, yes, I've
got it again," and he proceeded to write down the word
Deserter at the head of his paper. Then he began to
tabulate his reasons for and against a certain idea; that is
to say, in the first column and its opposite he wrote down
why and why not Usher West should be considered a
deserter from the Confederate army. Hours went by and
the sagacious doctor intently held to his self-appointed
task.

There was bright moonlight, and Jennie's one candle
shone upon the by-road beneath her window. She did not
sleep. Knowing that she could not, she worked at her
sewing, but frequently she went to her window, which
looked north over the rear of the farm, in the desire to

know the first coming of Usher, whom she would warn that the surgeon was not sleeping. On this night her thought was full : of Charley Armstrong, gone to the war, and of her father and Usher ; but more persistently than these came the thought of the Federal soldier lying almost dead in less than forty feet of her chair. It was very natural to think of him, and she gave no self-reflection in her thought. Thrown upon her care in a measure, he had become for the time one of her household ; yet not once did she wonder at the far greater prominence that the wounded soldier occupied in her mind over the doctor, he, too, in some sense almost equally dependent.

It was getting near twelve ; she did not wish Dr. Lacy to see light through her door and infer that she had kept awake, so she put out her candle and sat by the window, looking north over the farm, and then her thought took wider scope. Northward it went into Maryland and beyond, where she knew mighty armies were on the verge of bloody battle, each contending for a great principle. She was no logician, and her home ties were strong ; yet grave doubt was in her mind concerning the ultimate issue of the struggle, and even concerning the justice of this war in which all her manly young friends had taken part, and she heartily wished it to cease. She had seen mourning in families round about—dead brought home —and knew of more dead that could not be brought, but had been covered with a crust of earth in long rows wherein recognition of individuals was forever lost ; and here in her own house was now this soldier from the enemy's ranks ; perhaps he, too, would die, —this man with the pathetic eyes which seemed to look beseechingly upon her even here in the dark.

A sharp click noted five minutes till midnight; hardly had the sound ended; it seemed to merge into another click, but which she knew came from far — the ring of metal upon stone. She rose at once and went to the back door; there she listened intently, and heard again the sound, clearer and repeated. She went out that she might meet her brother before he came into the house. The clock struck twelve, but she did not hear it.

Dr. Lacy had pursued his lines of reasoning, and had reached the conclusion that Usher West's reluctance to speak openly could be accounted for upon the theory of his being a deserter, and upon no other; therefore, Usher West was a deserter; and the good doctor, while it must be confessed that the young man suffered loss of dignity by the involuntary transformation, chuckled over the result of his solution, feeling assured that his own wish to avoid armed Confederates was no stronger than that of the Wests.

Even the stroke of twelve had not roused the doctor from his revery consequent upon gratulation that his logic had found result at once accurate and wholesome. He still sat before his table, the light placed directly between his face and the small open window which looked west upon the walk leading round the house. At this moment Jennie had reached the position where she would wait for Usher, a hundred feet directly in rear of the back entrance to the dwelling.

The sound of a horse's hoofs continued to come, and

soon the young girl could see a dark spot in the moonlight, enlarging ; and then she was almost overcome with
terror as she thought that it must now be past the time
for her to relieve Dr. Lacy. She had forgotten to lock
her door, yet had pulled it almost shut, and suspense
became acute in wondering what the surgeon would do.
He would tap at her door ; there could be no response ;
then he would tap harder. For a moment she was divided
in mind ; ought she not to return at once ? But the
horseman was already near, and she felt that whatever
mistake had been made could not now be corrected. She
waited for Usher ; Lacy must not be allowed to hear her
brother and suspect the truth concerning the nature of his
service.

The horseman kept coming — coming, but only for a
few yards more. The girl was amazed to see him turn and
ride south on the walk that led by Lacy's window. What
could it mean ? Had Usher forgotten that enemies were
in the house ? No, that could not explain, — even if he
had forgotten, he would put his horse in the stable — no
need to ride round the house, — yet, after all, perhaps he
had thought best to look everywhere about him before
coming in.

The horseman had disappeared, the northwest corner
of the dwelling shutting him out of her vision, and the
sounds of the hoofs had ceased, making her believe that
Usher had halted on seeing the light of Lacy's candle.
And at the next moment she heard a voice that she knew
was neither the doctor's nor her brother's, and turned to
flee into the house ; but stood still yet, for she now heard

the rapid gallop of another horse, coming upon the north road.

Lacy had been suddenly confronted by a bearded face peering at him through the window.

"Say, old man," said a rude voice, but in friendly tones, "time's come for you to git. Been sent to warn you."

The candle was exactly between the two faces ; neither man could clearly see the other. The visitor was leaning on the window-sill, and Lacy could make out a bridle stretching from one hand.

The doctor doubted that he had heard aright; he had feared a flaw in his reasoning, and, distrusting his former conclusion, had been plunged deeply into new thought.

The man repeated : " Jig's up. Git ready. What's the matter, Ush, that you can't speak ? Wake up, and be dam quick about it."

Lacy heard distinctly ; he had recovered from both abstraction and surprise ; he knew that the man, accustomed to darkness, and now with his eyes suffering from the sudden glare of the candle so near them, thought he was speaking to Usher ; this room, devoted to mercy, was ordinarily occupied by Usher ; the man knew this, and had come to Usher's window to warn him that he was not safe — a conclusion almost correct, and one which rooted and grounded the doctor, more than all his previous depth of logic, in the certainty that West was a deserter.

Not ten seconds had passed between the visitor's two utterances. Lacy felt that he must say something, and knew not what best to say ; moreover, he feared that

his voice would at once disclose the fact that he was of
Northern speech; yet he must speak, and he opened his
lips at a venture, discreetly keeping his face directly
behind the candle.

At this moment the man turned his head toward the
north, and at the next withdrew, saying in a hoarse
whisper that betrayed discomposure : "Hurry up; I can't
stay here in this light — somebody's a-comin'. I'll wait
for you down the hill."

At once Lacy blew out the light. Then he rose and
stood still, not venturing to step in any direction. He
could hear the sounds of a horse led away, and from
farther the sound of galloping, and he feared lest the
house should be searched by Confederates coming to
seize Usher West . . . coming for that purpose, and
accomplishing more.

But not long was he left in this fear; the galloping
ceased, and voices reached him : one the voice of his
visitor, loud enough; the other, a low voice, some of its
words almost undistinguishable, yet by the responses of
the louder he knew it was Usher's.

" Who's that in your room ? "

" Hm — hm — loud ; hm — hm."

" Oh . . . Major . . . are you ready ? "

" Hm — hour — hm — wait ? "

" No — hm — hm."

" Hm — too loud."

For a short minute the doctor heard whispering; then
everything became silent again, and Lacy stood motionless
for a long time, while young West slipped into the house

K

and got his weapons and slipped out again, to ride with Tom Baxter to the rendezvous of Mosby's men, and then northward upon a raid into the Federal lines.

At length the doctor heard a light tap on his door.

"What is it?" he asked.

"Isn't it time, Doctor?"

"Yes, it must be past time." He lighted the candle, and looked at his watch. "Past one o'clock. Is it possible?"

"I've been expecting to hear you come for the last half-hour," said Jennie.

CHAPTER XI

"Endurance is the crowning quality,
And patience all the passion of great hearts."
— LOWELL.

SQUIRE's horse could do but little more. The old man
was alone in the land of the stranger, and knew not how
to overtake his friends, yet he must try ; though the case
would have been hopeless for a soldier, for a slave it was
only difficult.

"I dunno w'ich a-way dey's a-gwine to go," he mumbled ; "ef I knowed w'ich a-way dey wus a-gwine to go,
an' w'ich a-way dey's a-gwine to come back ag'in, den I
mought cut acrawst an' git ahaid of 'em . . . but I dunno
w'ich a-way dey's a-gwine to go. W'en we come oveh
heah oncet befo'e, we crawssed away up high an' den we
crawssed back ag'in into ole Fihginny away down low,
an' I 'spec' we's a-gwine to do de same way dis time . . .
but den we didn't crawssed away up high dis time. Dis
dam hoss is done ruint me, feh sho."

The beast had sunk down on the road and now
refused to budge. Squire took off the trappings, thrust
his head through the bridle, slung the saddle upon his
shoulders, and pushed on. He must outmarch Stuart's
cavalry, already many miles ahead. But his load was heavy,

and the heat was great.   Before he had made half a mile,
seeing that he was only breaking himself down, he went
a little distance into the wood and held a consultation.

"De ain't noth'n' but one thing dat ole Squiah kin do
now.   He ain't got to keep awn up dis road, an' he ain't
got to try to ketch up wid 'em no mo'e; but he dess got to
cut acrawst an' haid 'em awff, leastways ef he can't fine
anotheh hoss . . . but w'ich a-way to go, dat I dunno,
dam 'f I do.   De good book hit say look not, sinneh, to
de right han' road, noh to de lef' han' road, but keep
awn a-movin' awn de straight an' nahrow paf; but I
ain't seed no nahrow paf; an' I dess obleeged to do
some'h'm.   I's not a-gwine to go back ag'in; now I
let shu know dat."

Totally ignorant in regard to his immediate surroundings, as well as to the larger geography of this and every
other region, the negro was at an utter loss for a clew to
help his decision, and he remained long as he was, unwilling to take any step that might be for the worse.   But at
length he sprang to his feet.

"I knows dess w'at *I's* a-gwine to do.   I's dess a-gwine
to do lak I use to do w'en I was sont to hunt de cows :
dat's w'at *I's* a-gwine to do.   Now, you heah *me ?* "

He held his left palm, bowl-like, before him, and spat
in it; then the broad right forefinger descended violently
upon the artificial lakelet, he intently watching for the
direction in which the smitten waters would fly.

At once he stooped, picked up the bridle only, and
began to walk rapidly toward the northwest.

* * * * * * *

A mile north of the spot where he had encountered
the Federal captain, Morgan led his friends again into the
highroad. Sency was directed to ride a furlong in the
advance, for a repetition of past good luck could not be
hoped for ; no more squads of Yankees must be met.
The speed was not pressed, for all the horses were showing signs of weakness ; they must be saved for the possibility of a race ; besides, they still had a little hope that
Squire would overtake them.

Sency saw that many wheels had churned the crumpled
dust left by the cavalry ; many tracks, but not the broad
tracks of cannon. Stuart had begun his march without
encumbrance of wagons — whence these parallel lines that
had obliterated so many hoof prints? Sency rode on,
looking sharply ahead, but thinking of the tracks. " I'm
afraid of those wagons," thought George ; "if Stuart has
captured them, he ought to burn them. However, if he
doesn't he will play into our hands, for we'll soon overtake those same wagons; but he will play into the
Yankees' hands, too. I believe Stuart has captured a
wagon train, and he'll hang to it like grim death to a
dead nigger."

Sency met civilians, whom he passed without conversation. Some of them looked at him curiously.

Back at the rear Morgan had observed the tracks.

" See these wagon tracks, Charley ? "

" Yes ; what do you reckon made 'em ? "

" I'm going to get down and see if I can tell which way
they went."

But with all his experience Morgan was unable to deter-

mine, and he remounted and rode on. There were many
small hoof prints, — those of mules, no doubt, pointing
north, and a few pointing south; but in the road, between
the ruts and outside, the dust had been torn here and
compacted there, and so trodden everywhere — one hoof
print on top of another — that for long he could not
decide ; but at length a small brook was crossed, and he
cried: " There, Joe ! See that ? "

" Yes ; I'm a-thinkin' them waggins is gone on ahead."

" Beyond a doubt we're following them; the wheels
have slung the wet mud all about over here."

Civilians were met ; farmers were seen at work, some
of them pausing to look. One man shouted from his
yard gate : " Better be keerful ! Whole gang o' rebs
went by here last night ! They're not fur ahead of
you ! "

" How do you know they're not far ? " shouted the
sergeant in return.

" 'Cause they're goin' slow."

" None of our men up the road ? "

" Mighty few.   One company rid by an hour ago."

" Riding fast ? "

" In a trot."

" What made all these wagon tracks ? "

" Rebs got a whole raft of our wagons way down below.
They took 'em by here before day."

And now Morgan, as well as Sency, knew that Stuart's
column could be overtaken, because its speed must not be
greater than that of the wagons ; all that was needed was
to shun the company of Federal cavalry hanging on

Stuart's rear. The sergeant rode forward rapidly and joined Sency.

"There's a company of Yankee cavalry ahead, George."

"How did you learn that?"

"A man told me they passed his house an hour ago."

"A mighty little company, then," says George. "Look how few tracks have broken into the ruts — about one in every ten yards. That man has no idea how to count cavalry; he would think a company was a regiment."

"See these wagon tracks?"

"Been lookin' at 'em."

"Stuart has taken a wagon train, and has it in tow. All we have to do is to take care of ourselves; we have plenty of time."

"Yes, I see. Wonder what on earth the general means by holding on to those wagons; better burn 'em, and 'git furder' as the boys say."

"Not in him as long as he sees a chance to bring 'em in."

The two were riding on slowly. "There now, see that!" said George.

"Yes, but what are they?"

They had halted, and Sency was dismounting. He had pointed to the ground, where Morgan could see that the wheel tracks were now imprinted with a greater number of hoofs, the ruts broken into at every foot.

Sency walked, bending over, leading his horse.

"Our men!" he exclaimed, and began to mount. "Yes," he continued, "fully a fourth of 'em are barefoot. The general has put a rear-guard behind the wagons. Wonder what regiment it is."

"We ought to run against that squad of Yankees soon," said Morgan; "they're not strong enough to follow our folks very closely. Let's halt and wait for Charley and Joe."

The four held a council. Armstrong was for going dead ahead and rapidly, in order to end the thing; he had no fear that Squire wouldn't make his way. Joe left everything to Morgan. Sency advised prudence; it was evident, he maintained, that haste was not the thing needed now; the only thing to fear was the cavalry following Stuart's rear — following only to observe. All that Morgan had to do was to approach the squad of observation carefully, then flank 'em, and reach Stuart; better go slow and see 'em without being seen; then the rest would be easy.

Morgan decided in favour of Sency's policy, and the party moved on, George again in the lead.

"Dan," says Joe, "I'm a-thinkin' that old Squire must ha' fell in with that Yankee cap'm you been a-talkin' about."

"Let Squire alone for that," replied Armstrong; "I'll pit him single against any of 'em, big or little. The man that gets the best of Squire, has got to get up mighty soon in the mornin'."

"They'll not be likely to trouble him much," said Morgan. "I don't think they'd be hard on him, even if he should tell where he belongs. But he may be delayed in getting through."

"I'll bet he gets to Lee's army before Stuart does," says Armstrong. "Hello! hear that? Stand by Sency

now, boys," as two or three shots were heard a quarter
of a mile at the front, and then a scattering volley.

The three broke into a gallop forward, and, at the next
turn of the road, found Sency halted by its side in the
bushes, intently watching and listening; and now every
man could hear a far clatter of approaching hoofs from the
north.

"Hide and let 'em pass," ordered the sergeant, and
the group rode away into the wood.

Morgan dismounted and went back to watch the road.
The sound of hoofs was distinct, and increasing — coming, and soon he saw a mournful group on the road before
him. Three Federals were riding in the front at a slow
walk. A centre group was composed of two living men
and two dead, the bodies lying across the horses which
had doubtless been ridden by the men recently slain. A
group of four brought up the rear — all moving slowly, all
with heads bent down as though repenting the crime of
rashness.

No danger was to be feared from these men. Without
waiting until they had disappeared, the sergeant returned
to his comrades; they mounted and rode at an angle into
the highway, and then north, and when they had reached
the top of the next hill Stuart's rear was in sight, with no
enemy between.

The column was strung along the road for miles. At
five o'clock Stuart, at its head, was nearing Westminster,
Dan Morgan having reached its rear just north of the
railroad at two. The wagon train separated advance and
rear by almost three miles, while the troops themselves

took up as great a stretch of the road. The little squad was under protection, but had far yet to go, and with tired horses, before they could join their own regiment. Yet the horses of all the troops were in no better condition than Morgan's, for Stuart had not brought forage, and ever since the 25th, the day of his start from Salem, his animals had been given but little nourishment — the column halting early of afternoons to graze and to collect what little forage could be found on the devastated farms of Prince William and Fairfax. But on the wrong side of Morgan's account was the fact that he had on this day already ridden fifteen miles more than the column had marched, and his own beasts were no more vigorous than theirs whose speed he desired to outstrip.

Sency dismounted. "What you goin' to do?" asked Joe.

"I'm going to foot it. My horse'll give out if I don't."

George had not originated; many of the worst mounted of the troopers were already afoot and leading their horses, for the march was a slow walk, easy for a footman to equal. Sency's companions followed his example and the four went forward, slowly gaining distance on the moving column which was compelled to preserve its marching ranks. Rests were frequent; the Confederate cavalry now barely averaged two miles to the hour. At one of these rests, seeing that a great gain had been made, Sency proposed to take time — to hunt food — to give the animals one good rest, and then push on. He had some greenbacks, he said, and the Maryland farmers would sell them hay, oats, corn, anything . . . if that whole regi-

ment which they had passed were to halt and demand it,
they could find feed enough within a mile. Morgan consented, and Sency and Joe went off and returned loaded
with oats and dry forage, just what the grass-fed horses
had needed.

At dark, Morgan's men reached Fitz Lee's brigade at
Westminster, where but few hours previously the Fourth
Virginia had encountered the First Delaware under Major
Knight, who lost sixty-seven out of ninety-five men in
a contest brave but unwise. At Westminster the tired
Confederates found ample supplies for horses and men,
and rested until the column was well closed. Then in
the darkness the march was continued six miles farther
to Union Mills, where a halt was called for the remainder
of the night.

Stuart learned that a strong Federal force of cavalry
was at Littlestown, blocking the road to Gettysburg.
On the morning of the 30th the Confederates marched on
Hanover, ten miles north, making for York, where Stuart
hoped to find a division of Lee's army; but Kilpatrick, at
Littlestown, had been only seven miles from Hanover,
and when the Confederates came in sight of Hanover they
saw that it was held by their enemies.

The Confederate artillery opened on Hanover; the
Second North Carolina cavalry charged down Frederick
Street, momentarily causing confusion, but Farnsworth
rallied his brigade and the tide turned; the Confederates
were swept back, and Stuart was in great personal danger, saving himself by an extraordinary leap of his horse.
The Confederates withdrew to the hills southeast of the

town, and seemed to make preparations for vigorous
battle.

Fitz Lee's brigade, near the head of which rode Morgan
and his friends, was ordered to file to the right and make
for Jefferson — eight miles east, the wagon train following.
Stuart held the remainder of his command in open view
of Kilpatrick until nightfall; then he followed Lee. All
through the night the march continued : first to Jefferson ;
thence north to Dover, fifteen miles, where in the early morning hours a halt was called to allow the column to close up.

It was now July 1, the opening day of the great battle.
A. P. Hill was marching from Cashtown eastward upon
Gettysburg; Ewell was marching from Carlisle southward ; Longstreet was at Chambersburg, twenty-four
miles west of Gettysburg. At Hanover, Stuart had been
only eighteen miles east from Gettysburg, but ignorance
of the situation had led him to march a whole day and
night — east, north, and northwest — to find himself at
Carlisle, twenty-five miles north of the battle.

And when Carlisle was approached, instead of finding
it occupied by his friends, Stuart learned that it was held
by Federal infantry. Surrender of the town was demanded and refused, and Stuart prepared for action,
His artillery had begun to throw shells when mounted
officers from Lee rode up, bringing orders for the cavalry
to march at once to Gettysburg.

    *   *   *   *   *   *   *

Armstrong had predicted that Squire would make his
way to Lee's army before Stuart had reached that protection. Certainly Armstrong's words had been dictated

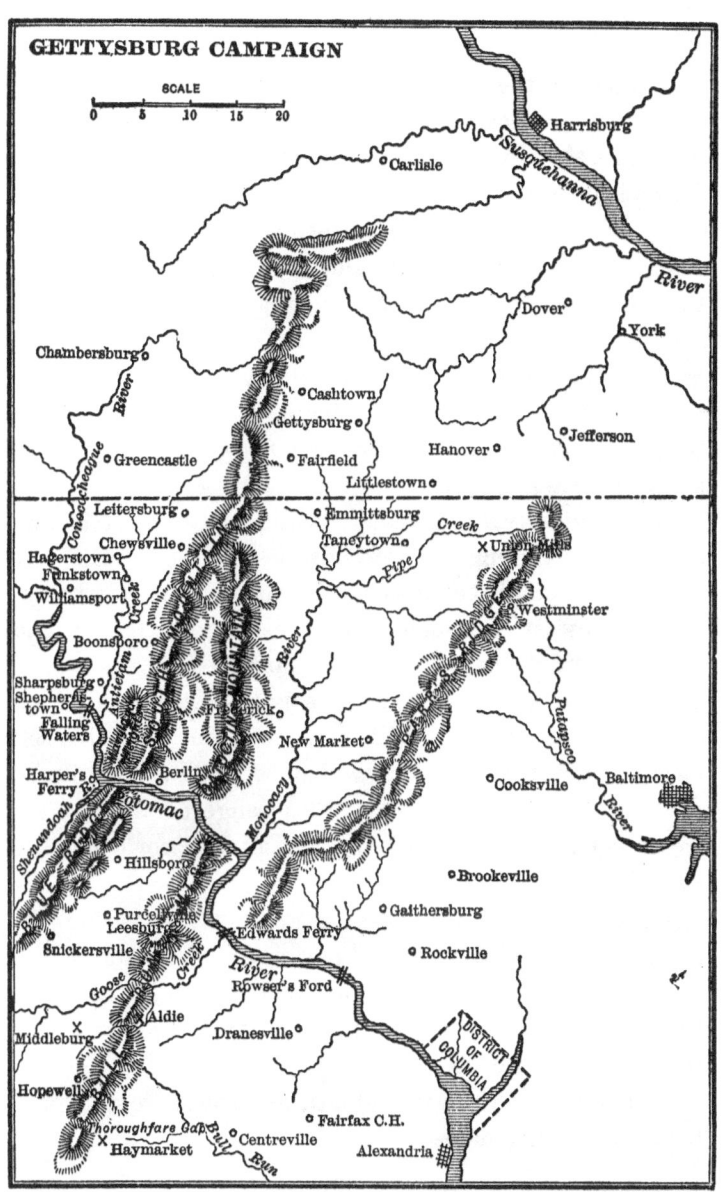

GETTYSBURG CAMPAIGN

SCALE
0   5   10   15   20

Harrisburg

Carlisle

Susquehanna River

Dover

York

Chambersburg

Cashtown

Gettysburg

Jefferson

Hanover

Greencastle

Fairfield

Littlestown

Leitersburg

Emmittsburg

Creek

Chewsville

Taneytown

Union

Hagerstown

Pipe

Funkstown

Westminster

Williamsport

Boonsboro

River

Sharpsburg

Shepherd town

Frederick

Falling Waters

New Market

Harper's Ferry

Berlin

Cooksville

Baltimore

Potomac

Shenandoah

Hillsboro

Brookeville

Monocacy

Purcellville

Gaithersburg

Leesburg

Edwards Ferry

Snickersville

Rockville

Goose Creek

River

Rowser's Ford

Aldie

Middleburg

Dranesville

DISTRICT OF COLUMBIA

Hopewell

Fairfax C.H.

Thoroughfare Gap

Centreville

Haymarket

Bull Run

Alexandria

by the wish rather than the assurance, for no Confederate knew the respective difficulties. At the moment of Squire's deflection to the northwest all the Federal army, divided into many detachments, lay between him and Gettysburg, the focal point afterward determined for the concentration of Federals and Confederates. Yet the Federal detachments were moving northwardly, and Squire's course, decided by augury, could not possibly have been better chosen: northwest was not a direct course to Lee's army when it should have reached Gettysburg; but it was the best course for avoiding the Federals marching northward.

Old Squire trudged along, bridle in hand. His way at first was through open woods, descending a hill. He sought no public road — his token was the northwest, and northwest he would go. He climbed fences, and went around fields, and avoided farm-houses; he waded streams, and plunged through small swamps, and kept on, tired and hungry, until, at sunset, he found himself near a shallow river beyond which he could see a railroad running across his course, with a range of hills at the westward stretching northeast, for all the world like his own Bull Run Mountains.

He waited until darkness came; then he waded the river and crossed the railroad; behind him an almost full moon broke through the clouds, and gave him light; he kept on across the hills until in his front he saw a wide road; then he sat down.

At this time Squire was almost due south from Gettysburg twenty-five miles.

The negro was resting in the woods, afraid to cross the highroad, for it was wide and straight for a long distance, and the moon gave a great light.   He was very hungry.

What with hunger and weariness, having had no rest for thirty-six hours, old Squire went to sleep.

And while the slave lay there in the woods, Hancock's corps began to march by within a stone's throw of his hiding-place.

CHAPTER XII

AWAITING THE VERDICT

"Of all the paths that lead to love
Pity's the straightest."
— BEAUMONT AND FLETCHER.

SURGEON LACY believed that the rest of a day and two nights, and especially the conservative effect of the bags of pounded ice which with judicious intermissions had been kept about his patient's wound, justified him in searching for the ball which he doubted not was somewhere near the spine. Possibly the doctor felt that he was taking a perilous chance, but by neither word nor look did he betray nervousness or fear.

Though Miss West had known almost from the first that the wounded man was Andrew Morgan, brother of Daniel, yet at sight of the pale face she had been shocked greatly by the wonderful resemblance, which for all time thereafter made her feel that something more than mere resemblance was here — something that approached identity in form, in feature, and in mind. While not allowing herself to remain in the sufferer's room, she nevertheless gave much help to the surgeon, who demanded without hesitation anything he conceived to be helpful. Jennie prepared strips for bandages, hunted for lost pins every-

144

where, — pins were rare in the Confederacy, — brought
fresh water, pounded the ice, and relieved the surgeon
of so much drudgery that he was allowed to give almost
undivided attention to his critical case.

When came the supreme moment of probing for the
ball, Jennie waited in the passage, ready to lend any aid
possible if she should be called on ; but so well had she
obeyed the doctor's injunctions that nothing, which under
the conditions could be supplied, was lacking ; she kept
her place in the hall, almost breathless, suffering a suspense which her own conscious acknowledgment of its
cruelty made none the less intolerable. In the chamber
she could hear footsteps — her father's and the surgeon's,
as first one and then the other moved about in preparation for the great trial, and then, after some minutes
which seemed innumerable, the room became very silent,
and she knew that his life on whom all her hopes of joy
now hung was being put into the scales of time against
eternity. She sat there, thinking no thought of herself,
but all of him whom she had so suddenly loved. Suddenly ? Yes, but if she had been at that moment egoistic
enough to analyze her feeling and its causes, she would
have known that this love of hers had its origin in the
very helplessness of the being thrown upon her care, for
her love was more maternal than passionate. He was her
possession, she not his, and there could be no claimant
against her claims — no rival but death. Death ! Yes,
death was even now fighting for its prize, and Jennie's
face was very pale and sad, and her heart had almost
ceased to beat. Yet she sat patiently, still as marble,

L

feeling incapable of attempting such devices as are usually employed for the illusive abatement of suspense ;
her suffering was precious to her, in that it was for him :
let all the woe, all the pain, all the death fall upon her,
and all the joy go with him ; then could she be happier
than he. In a maiden's first passion there is the great
piety of sacrifice ; in all following substitutes there is a
greater personal demand for more than reciprocation.
With Virginia West there was no wish but for the life
and weal of him she now first loyed.

The silence in the room was broken, and she stood. At
each successive minim of time, she thought to see the
door opened and her fate shown in the surgeon's eye and
face. But the door remained closed, though moving feet
could still be heard. Surely something must be wrong.
Had a first attempt failed, and must a second be tried ?
Oh, what torture to her love ! She continued to stand,
breathless, expectant, hopeful, despairing, her eyes fixed
on the door-knob that she might catch the first motion
of its turning. Again there was silence within.

There come periods in every gentle life — periods, halts
of time — when time ceases to move. The dial may show
shadows changing, the sand may run down in the glass,
the blood may continue to pump forth and back, but the
objects are unreal and the pumping blood is no longer
an experience — all of the subjective has concentrated
against one single point that fixes itself immovable and
becomes the world. So now to Virginia the door-knob
was the only visible thing, diminishing to naught all
other things ; it *must* turn, and in her supreme anxiety

and fear an almost uncontrollable impulse seized her to step forward and do the turning, for each second stood in the way of the next and prevented its coming.

But the door-knob turned. How long was it in turning? From the first movement, which the intent eye had detected by the varying light on its irregular surface, until she could see beyond the opening door, there had been but a fraction of a second; yet long enough for the girl to repeat a thousand alternations of life and death — death and life, let us say, for now her eyes lifted to the height of the surgeon's face all aglow with the superb light of professional achievement, and instantly leaped to the left a foot, and fastened upon a small round object which Lacy held in triumph between his forefinger and thumb.

The girl fled to her room and locked it, every nerve a-tremble, every muscle quivering; then she sank to her knees and bathed her coverlet with tears of love and thanksgiving.

CHAPTER XIII

BARNEY

" When I was at home I was in a better place."
— SHAKESPEARE.

OLD SQUIRE'S sleep was untroubled except from the pinchings of an empty stomach that brought on tantalizing dreams of huge corn-pones and big flat rashers. When his hunger woke him, he failed for a little while to know himself and his condition ; but cruel reality quickly came and prompted exertion difficult to determine and to effect. His Mahs Chahley was far, perhaps in a more deplorable case than his own, and the negro's heart sank in thinking vaguely of the unknown difficulties that must be overcome before they might meet ; then his mind went to ole Mahsta and Mistis, and to Miss Lucy, and to Judy, very far away in the Virginia mountains, safe from the touch of actual war, and he wished that he was with them.

Night had taken away fear of detection, but had added to the terror always inspired by the unknown. Squire muttered a prayer and started to cross the highroad. He would get on its western side and keep by its edge in the shadows ; for though by the stars he knew that the road here was running northerly, if not toward the east a little,

148

yet he would bend to suit it until it deflected too far from
his purposed course.   The moon was almost overhead ;
in the open road there would be no shadow to hide him.
He listened . . . was there not a sound at his left ? He lay
flat, with ear to the ground, and could hear many noises
mingling into a confused murmur which he at once recognized as the composite sound made by a marching infantry column, getting nearer and nearer.   And then he
was torn by hope and fear : were the advancing troops
Federal, or were they Southern ? He must not fly and
renounce the chance for protection, nor must he allow
himself to be stopped by a column of the enemy intervening to the west ; he ran straight across the road and
crouched in the bushes.

But after a little the noises ceased.   Perhaps a halt had
been ordered for rest ; perhaps the troops had turned off
on another road ; perhaps they had halted for the night.
Squire had sufficient knowledge of relation to know at
once that there were two chances out of three — three out
of four if he had thought of the possibility of a counter-
march — that the troops would not on this night pass his
present place of hiding, and he decided, whether wisely or
not, that his next step must be to learn whether they were
preparing to bivouac ; so he rose and stole along the roadside southwestward, but in less than a hundred yards he
reached the edge of the wood and saw a broad open field
before him.

He hesitated, considering that the field was large
enough to reach the point from which the sounds had
come, and even while he considered he saw a little point

of light far away, which was extinguished immediately; but another, and another, and then many, and he knew that a great body of soldiers were near him, in the act of kindling numerous fires, preparing, before they should sleep, to satisfy their own hunger, and increasing his own to agony.

Though bivouac fires are not peculiar to friend or enemy, yet Squire was almost convinced that the troops before him were Federal. In the South, matches were few and valuable; he knew that Southern soldiers were slow in making bivouac fires, — waiting to get a coal or flame from their fortunate comrades, — while in his sight a multitude of flames had started almost simultaneously. Yet this indication was not conclusive, and Squire waited; for there was another line of reasoning which would bring him to an entirely contrary opinion : he knew that Federal soldiers were not forced to do so much cooking as their Southern brethren were compelled to do, the Federal ration of bread usually being hardtack, and the Confederate, raw flour. In the light of a moon almost round there would be little need of other light for choosing places and spreading blankets, and the weather was warm; but then, thought the slave, many would want to boil coffee; he would wait and would be prudent — it takes no great fire to boil a cup of water.

A little at his right he saw that the ground sloped downward to a thin strip of bushes ; a stream was there, he thought, and at once he walked down the slope, for he was thirsty, and the bushes would screen him in his advance nearer to the fires. He found a brook, running

to his rear, and drank ; then he followed the line of straggling bushes, which stretched not directly toward his
object, but approached gradually.   The hollow deepened
and Squire felt secure.   Near enough, he crawled up the
slope at his left, and lying there could see many men
gathered around small fires, and others moving this way
and that ; but most of them had taken off their coats,
and he could not tell the colour of their uniforms.   Long
stacks of arms reflected the moonlight, and these arms
showed the bayonet — another indication that the troops
were Federal ; for many of the Confederate infantry,
through lack or through purpose, did not burden themselves with this comparatively useless weapon, and Squire
knew that, in the Southern ranks, stacks were frequently
formed by using the heads of the rammers.   And then the
negro heard the steady tramp of a few men near by and a
moment later saw a squad pass, — a sergeant no doubt,
engaged in the duty of posting a camp-guard, — and he
could see the diagonal shoulder belts for their cartridge-
boxes — a distinctly Federal token, for the Southerners,
almost to a man, placed cap-box, scabbard, and cartridge-
box on one single waist belt.

Squire crept back to the hollow, and went to the woods
again, and pursued his way northward, avoiding the road,
upon which he could now see moving wagons.   He was
greatly disheartened ; his hope for relief, for food, for
protection, had gone, and in its place were fear and
sharper hunger ; yet he trudged along, though painfully,
looking well ahead and about him for any evidence of a
habitation where he might beg a little food — he must

take risks or starve. He passed the spot where he had slept; it was at his right rear some forty rods, when he was brought to a stand by fires in his front.

Yes, there they were, stretching far on both sides of his road, and he knew at once that troops had marched past him while he slept, and had halted for the night beyond him — he was between two divisions of the enemy.

But for the negro's physical weakness, the situation would not have been perilous; strong and unweary, he would but have given himself the task of walking far around this encampment; but to the exhausted a mile more is an enormity. He sat down and then lay flat on his face, this time without alertness, almost in despair.

Then, in a moment, he stood again — the sound of marching came from his rear, and its meaning was plain: a great body of troops, perhaps a full army corps, was by divisions coming from rear to front, and successively taking up their places for the night, and the division or brigade which he now heard would soon bivouac in the interval where he was standing, ready for its position in the column on the morrow. Old Squire had interpreted correctly: General Meade was concentrating toward Gettysburg; the troops on the road were the Second Corps, under General Hancock; they had marched from Monocacy Junction, and were halting according to the order of the next march.

But Squire's fright soon diminished; he decided to be still and let the troops camp around him. They would not suspect him; he was not getting into their lines; they were getting into his.

A regiment filed to the left of the road, stacked arms, and broke ranks; another passed farther and filed to the left, parallel with the first, not a hundred yards separating the two, stacked arms and broke ranks, the negro between the lines. Other regiments filed on and formed.

The negro was standing still. All round him men were making lights, men were searching for fuel in the woods, the interval between the stacked arms thickly swarming with men. Under his feet lay dead sticks and leaves. Squire gathered an armful and walked to the nearest regiment, passing men who gave no attention to him. Before him were clusters of men, gathered about feeble flames on the ground.

"Mahsta, I's got some kindlin' fuh you," says the old man, showing his fuel.

"All right, sonny, hand her here. Where'd you come from? Live about here?"

"No, sah, I b'longs wi' de calvry; but dey's done went awn an' I couldn't keep up wid 'em no mo'e."

Old Squire's kindling flamed up, and lighted his face and the faces of six infantrymen, their eyes on the fire, each eager to finish and get to rest.

"What cavalry's that you belong to?"

"You know Mahs Dan Mawgin, Mahsta? He's de man w'at I 'tends to."

"Know where any water is?" asked another, but little interested in Morgans.

"Yassah, dey's a good branch a little ways out yan-deh. Ef you wants me, I kin show it to you, an' all I

axes is some'h'm to eat, an' to stay long wid ju all, tell I
kin ketch up wi' de calvry."

"All right, old man; come on, and show me the
way."

It would have been less irregular, perhaps, for these
men to report at once to their officers the presence of a
stranger, but the help offered was not to be renounced;
besides, there was the lieutenant, at the next fire but one,
and he could see for himself — why report a fact that is
already evident?

Squire found the water, picked up more fuel in returning, helped in the quick boiling of the coffee, made himself so useful to the men that each contributed from his
rations for the negro's wants, and on the next morning,
June 30, he found himself brevetted without ceremony
as the temporary camp-servant of the mess which he had
taken in, and followed, on July 1, along with other
servants, in the rear of the regiment in its march on
Gettysburg.

Many and wonderful were the questions which had
been asked him; but by simulating ignorance of organization and locality, he had evaded serious inquiry.

The old man had learned from the soldiers' talk that
a great battle was expected; he would march to the field,
knowing that thus he should reach his friends by the most
sure and direct road. Before the battle, or after, as the
case might be determined for him, he would slip away in
the night and rejoin Mahs Chahley. He had abandoned
his bridle, and had picked up an old blouse thrown away
by some burdened infantryman.

On the morning of the 1st the corps was near Taneytown, twelve miles southeast from Gettysburg. The
march was continued, and soon it became rapid, and rumours were thick concerning battle that had begun far
at the front. Officers rode back and forth along the
column, pressing the march, and all camp followers were
ordered out of the roadway. At length Squire found
himself in a crowd of non-combatants, white and black, at
the rear of the division; there were ambulances, baggage
wagons, teamsters too many, a few civilians, sutlers,
stragglers, the half sick, everything that swells the crowd
that hangs to the rear of an army about to engage in
battle. The old man easily succeeded in attaching himself to one of the sutlers.

The advance of the camp followers had been arrested.
The column had gone on; the roar of artillery could be
heard, though as yet miles to the northwest. The middle
of the afternoon had come. Squire was lying under the
sutler's wagon, drawn aside from the road which must
not be blocked; he had fed the horses, and had fed himself heavily, and was half dozing; yet with his head on
the bare earth he could not fail to feel the throbbing of
Hall's and Cooper's guns vainly resisting the advance
of Hill and Ewell into Gettysburg, and the sounds kept
him from actual sleep. Squads of mounted men were
galloping, some north, some south; from time to time a
courier would dash along, throwing the thick dust far and
wide — some runner sent by the anxious Meade to hurry
the march of a belated division. Not yet were the ambulances seen so far in the rear with their loads of wounded

and dying — the field hospitals were nearer the battle-ground.

"Say there, old man," shouted the sutler from the inside of the wagon; "get up and water the horses."

"Yassah; whah I gwine to git de wateh, Mahsta, — up yandeh at dat house, whah dem yotheh men's a-gwine?"

"Yes; a bucketful apiece will do."

Squire had to cross the road; he followed another negro who, with buckets in hand, had also started — a young man, tall, brown, sprightly; he had come from the direction of the baggage wagons. Just as they were in the middle of the road a horseman spurring hard from the south swerved to avoid the old man, and in another second reined up violently and turned.

"Well," he said, "how is it by this time?"

The young negro had stopped by the roadside; he lifted his cap, but the horseman failed to observe.

"Mahsta, dat no 'count hoss, he done guv clean out, an' lef' me awn de groun'; you seed Mahs Dan any mo'e, Mahsta?"

"No; say, do you know Captain Freeman?" laughed the rider.

"Cap'm Freeman? No, Mahsta; I mought ha' seed him, sah, but I dunno his name — leastways I done mos' fohgot. Is Mahs Dan wid *him*, sah?"

"Didn't you come to Captain Freeman over in Loudoun and tell him to come and get Lieutenant Morgan, who was wounded, you said? Now, old man, own up. Tell me what you meant by playing that trick. Who was it that Freeman got?"

Old Squire put down his buckets and scratched his
ead. "Mahsta, is Mahs Dan huht bad? I ain't nuvveh
otch up wid 'im, sah, sence dat yotheh day dess befo'e
met up wid ju, Mahsta. Is Mahs Dan huht bad?"

"Old man, you're a sharp one; but I tell you, Free-
1an's got a crow to pick with you. He says you fooled
im. Let me see — what's your name?" The horseman
7as laughing, notwithstanding his words. The presence,
ere in the Federal army, of the negro who had befooled
'reeman, could not possibly cause Dahlgren to suspect
hat he himself had been the deceived.

"John," said Squire, promptly.

"Do you know a man named Squire?"

"Oh, yassah, I knows de man dey calls ole Squiah.
quiah he live down in ole Fihginny; he ain't no 'count.
'ou know Squiah, Mahsta?"

"Where is he?"

"Squiah? I 'spec' he some'h's about, Mahsta. He say
e gwine wi' Mahs Dan hese'f, an' I 'spec' he tryin' to
ne him now, sah."

"Well, you and Squire between you have got the
aptain well worked up. Better settle it, old man,"
nd the horseman, still laughing, shook his whip at
quire and rode north, having already knocked up one
orse on his great ride this day, pushing on to carry to
is general the captured letter of Davis to Lee.

"Lawd Gawd fohgive ole Squiah feh tellin' lies awn
ese'f," muttered the old man, picking up his buckets;
but den de good book hit say dat dou shalt not mek no
lse witness ag'in yo' neighbouh — an' I ain't no Squiah's

neighbouh ; I is ole Squiah hese'f, — dat I is, an' ef I tell a lie ag'in ole Squiah de good book hit don't say nothin' ag'in dat. But I's a-gwine to fight shy o' dat man — now I is, feh sho'."

This soliloquy was hardly ended before the young negro, who had waited, accosted the old one.

"Unc John, do you know dat man you was a-talkin' to ?"

"Yas, chile — leastways I's seed him befo'e. Doezh zhu know him ? "

"Dat's Cap'm Dalgreen. I use to know him, but he's done fohgot. Whah you be'n all dis time dat I ain't seed you befo'e now ? " And the young negro looked curiously at the old man.

"Me ? Blesh yo' life, chile, I's be'n mos' eve'ywhah ; I's be'n in ole Fihginny, an' I's be'n oveh in Mellan' an' Penns'vania, an' in Loudoun, an' mos' down to Richmon', an mos' eve'ywhah. Who izh you wid ? "

"I'm with one o' dem baggage waggins. You done runned feh freedom, Unc John ? "

"Me ? W'at I want feh to run ? I's a-gitt'n' mighty ole an' stiff to be a-runnin', an' de good book hit say hit ain't no use to put yo' pennence in runnin', noh in fight'n' notheh. You don't go wi' de fight'n' men — doezh zhu, chile ? "

"Dey come an' tuck me away," said the younger man in a low voice.

"Whah you raised, chile ? W'at sho' name ? "

"My name Bahney, Unc John ; I be'n tuck away f'om my folks way down in Goochlan', an' I ain't had no chance to git back no mo'e. Lemme draw de wateh fuh you, Unc John."

"Dat's right. De good book hit say be ye kine to de ole man, 'cazhe you dunno w'en you got to lay in de same bed. How long you done be'n away f'om home?"

"Dey tuck me when dey come down dah las' yeah; I disremembeh how long hit's been exackly."

Old Squire did not approve of Barney's lack of enterprise; he had no doubt that many opportunities for escape had been neglected; this young fellow seemed deferential and obliging, but not yet did the old man decide to trust him, for Squire knew that the slaves were greatly divided in opinion as to their proper course. Given the incentive of freedom on the one hand and the centripetal influence of home on the other, those who held to home and kindred would be the old; while the young would covet liberty and the excitement of novel scenes even though dangerous; many would be incapable of a firm decision, and would act rashly and repent afterward.

"You ain't tole me who you is wid," said Squire.

"I've got a job wi' dem waggins. You see dem waggins right oveh yondeh whah dem gray mules is? Dat's my place now."

"You ain't be'n wid 'em all de time?" asked the old man, shrewdly observing the conditional ending of Barney's speech.

"No, sah; fust I was with Cap'm Freeman."

"W'at Cap'm Freeman dat shu talkin' about, chile?"

"Cap'm Bob Freeman; same man dat Cap'm Dalgreen was a-talkin' about; but he done got mos' kilt down to

Kelly's Fohd, an' I jest had to do the bes' I could. Who you with, Unc John?"

"Wid Misteh Woods — dat sutleh's waggin. Much obleeged, Bahney," and Squire picked up one of his buckets. "Ef I don't see you no mo'e, Bahney, I's a-gwine to tell you good-by," and they shook hands; but Barney whispered, "I'm a-gwine to come and see you ag'in, Unc John."

"Well, Bahney, you kin come, an' ef you sticks to me den you need'n' to call me Unc John no mo'e. I be'n call my right name John feh dat man w'at rid by wid he whup, but Squiah'll do feh *you*, Bahney, leastways ef you sticks to me."

As he went back, Squire was vaguely disturbed by fears and disconnected thoughts for his race. This Barney, like many others, had been enticed from home by alluring prospects that could never be made valid. Squire knew the type; his own fellows, whom he had seen grow up around him, had gone from home, most of them to a life of suffering of which from time to time he had indistinctly heard wretched rumours. He pitied them, and pitied Barney, whom he rated as wanting in decision; for he could not believe that for a whole year the young fellow had never found opportunity to abandon the life he was now leading. To Squire's mind there was no possibility of doubt concerning his own interest; his friends were all of one side; his home, which to him was not the uncertain possession of a few years to be abandoned for another when change should come, was the home of his fathers and his children — one lasting, earthly home that could not be disputed. The

sojourn in the Virginia mountains was but a visit; his
people would return, and home would be home again.
And as for Barney, the old man believed that he, too, loved
his home, and wanted to return to it, and he felt something
akin to contempt for the strong young man who allowed
slight difficulties to prevent his realizing the dearest of
joys.

Toward night the roar of the guns had died away, and
the highway was filled with infantry in double columns
hastening forward for the renewal of the battle. The
crowds in the rear held their places, the provost-marshal
having placed a guard in their way — a guard sufficiently
strong to keep them from moving toward the perilous front.

Slavery encouraged respect for the old. There were
other negroes around, in the disconnected camps of the
loose crowd in the rear, but somehow Barney was attracted
to Squire; he came to the old man.

"Unc Squiah, did ju come away f'om home willin'?"

"Chile, de good book hit say don't shu git in too big a
hurry to move de ole lan'mahk an' to fohsake de people
w'at shu raised up wid. I comed f'om home, Bahney, but
I's a-gwine to git back ag'in — leastways ef de good
Lawd'll be awn my side dess one mo'e time. W'at fuh
you ax me dat queshton?"

"'Caze I jest wants to see de Jim Riveh so bad dat I
can't rest. My ole mammy is down dah, an' my daddy is
lone dead, an' I don't know nothin' about what's become
of 'em all, an' I don't see nothin' no mo'e but trouble."

"W'at mek you done lef' 'em?"

"'Caze I ain't had no betteh sense. Dey done tole me

M

dat de white folks is mean to me, an' now dey is jest as mean — an' wuss. When de cap'm was heah he treated me right, but now I sho' wants to git back. Dis heah country ain't like what I wants. How you gwine to git back, Unc Squiah?"

"W'at shu ax dat fuh? You gwine to go wid me w'en I go?"

"Unc Squiah, ef you jest let me go too, I'll wohk my fingehs off to help you awn de way."

"But how we gwine to mek any staht now? Don't shu know dey's a-fight'n' up de road?"

"Yes, sah, but we can go *back*. We can staht back down to Vihginny."

This proposition had no charm for Squire; he must seek and find Mahs Chahley.

"But, Bahney, chile, de way to git back, hit ain't to go dat a-way — hit's to go dis a-way," pointing northeast, in which direction the old man had seen his friends of the Confederate cavalry ride.

"How come dat, Unc Squiah?"

"'Caze dat's de way to fine ouah folks, an' w'en dey gits done fight'n' dey'll go back to ole Fihginny, an' den we kin go back wid 'em. Ef dey gains de day, den dey *kin* go back, an' ef dey don't gain de day, den dey's *got* to go back."

Which reasoning convinced Barney, and a plot was laid for an attempt on the following night.

CHAPTER XIV

THE MEETING

"Where mingles war's rattle
With groans of the dying."
— Scott.

THE night of July 1 brought rest to Squire, but
little rest to the Union army. The First corps, — defeated, — the Eleventh, badly disorganized, were gathering their scattered men in rear of the Third and Twelfth,
who were intrenching, while the Second, near at hand, and
the Fifth and Sixth, a day's march behind, were hastening
to the relief of the discomfited on whom the brunt of to-
morrow's battle must not be allowed to fall.

The morning of the 2d came and went. Stuart had
marched south from Carlisle, and was now on Lee's left
flank. Squire, at Meade's far rear on the Taneytown
road, heard the pounding of artillery west, northwest,
almost north, and knew that a great battle was waging,
but knew not in whose favour. Among the crowds of
camp followers there had spread many startling rumours :
how that Gettysburg was occupied by the rebels, General
Reynolds killed, a great defeat inevitable ; and it was
said that a council of war had decided on retreat, yet
there were no strong indications of a withdrawal. Many

ambulances had gone by to the rear, and many slightly wounded afoot, and at times the road was almost filled with straggling men making their way from the battle in spite of the weak provost-guard; but ambulances and wounds and rumours of great losses may not mean a defeated army; no battle, in which the opponents number scores of thousands, is won or lost without many fluctuations of the bloody wave: here it rises high and submerges the foe, but it ebbs, and rolls back on those who think their feet have touched the solid earth; while at some adjacent curve the tide sweeps forward upon treacherous ground that lures to destruction. The long front lines of men sway forth and back, this way and that way, repulsed here, victorious there, and the average of the battle for or against, no man in the line may know. He must fight the enemy in his front; the brigade at the right may succeed; but if that at his left be repulsed, his own brigade gives way, so great is the dread of being flanked and captured.

In the afternoon the west roared for hours, too far away for Squire to hear the musketry of Longstreet and Sickles, except in its greatest volumes, but constant and loud with cannon.

The negro's instinct persisted in placing his friends at his right, and he had determined to seek the Confederate left, not knowing that he was separated from Lee's right by but half the distance to Stuart. When darkness should come, which would not be darkness, for a full moon would rise at twilight, the two negroes would meet at the well, where time and again they had gone for water.

Squire was taciturn, deliberate, resolved ; Barney, capricious, talkative, intermittently uncertain. Squire endeavoured to strengthen him but failed, and wished to be alone.

The moon was rising above the trees. In the yard around them were many men, some camping here for the sheltering grove, others waiting their turn for water. The old negro led the way, Barney closely following. In the northwest the noise of battle had died ; but it had broken out in the north, a little to the left of their course, where at this moment Johnson's division of Ewell's corps had carried the Federal intrenchments on the slope of Culp's Hill.

There was no need at first for stealth ; as yet there were wagons all round them, bivouacs of this and that, reserve artillery, officers' baggage wagons, medical people's tents deserted except by a servant or two, skulking stragglers, moving men, single and in groups — moving in every direction. Yet Squire avoided unnecessary publicity ; he kept away from the groups, away from the fires, and gave the wagons distance. No one accosted them ; their course along the rear fringe of the army was safe until the flank should be reached ; then they must beware.

An hour's march through field and grove brought them to the edge of a wide road, the road from Gettysburg through Littlestown and Westminster to Baltimore. In the front, or nearly so, the sound of fighting had become clearer, but its volume was not so great. Johnson had pushed on toward the Baltimore road where Meade's ammunition wagons were parked, but resistance to his advance had ceased until better preparation could be made, and his further advance itself had been at first timid, and at length was given over through fear of the unknown. At the road Squire halted, for it was blocked by a body of troops hurrying to the left. In neither direction could Squire see the end of the column ; he turned to the right : he would go down the road and cross it sooner by making his own progress in a contrary course bring him to the rear of the troops ; but almost at once the troops halted ; then loud voices commanded a counter-march, and the column faced about and marched down the road at the double quick. Squire had again come to a halt.

But the movement soon ceased ; the troops fronted north, and were allowed to be at ease — in line, however, and with musket in hand.

The night was going ; the moon had almost reached the zenith ; within the next four hours Squire must succeed or fail ; here was an impassable wall, its length unknown, perhaps impossible to flank. The negro was puzzled ; by waiting he might at any time see the road become free of troops ; to the contrary he might wait indefinitely — by going to the left he would be going into the battle lines at the extreme front ; by trying the right he would be getting farther from his object ; he knew not what to do. In his dilemma, Squire refused to consult ; he had found Barney lacking in fixed purpose and weak in suggestion ; he must decide himself, and he decided upon movement.

They crossed roads and small streams, and a creek

where they had great difficulty ; when on its eastern bank
they rested and slept. Before sunrise they set out again,
now northward, avoiding the fields ; when the openings
were large, they sought the hollows or crept along fence
rows. About nine o'clock they stopped on the edge of a
cultivated valley into which a wooded ridge projected at
its farther side, with a great barn over there near the woods
almost half a mile away. At the east the fields stretched
too far, but looking northwest for a way of approach
Squire saw a crooked line of small growth starting near
the buildings, curving about in its sunken course, and
growing wider and taller as it crossed the open.

Squire pointed. " Dat's de way. Dat dah's de spring
branch dat comes f'om de spring ; dat's dess de way de
spring branches does away back in ole Fihginny. I
b'lieve I kin mos' see de spring up yandeh. Come awn,
Bahney. Le's git down in de branch ; den we kin go ahaid
an' git acrawst. An' we's a-gwine to have some fallin'
weatheh, too ; don't shu heah dat raincrow ? An' hit's
Friday, too." Meanwhile, he had turned ; Barney followed, and still in the edge of the woods the two went
down the hill to the left, and then up the stream, creeping
through the fringe of bushes that grew on the west border
of Rummel's spring branch, and had made half the distance across the open when a shell shrieked above their
heads, and then another, and another.

* * * * * * *

The morning of the 3d was hot and dry. At a far distance in the southwest Armstrong could see Round Top,
opposite Longstreet's right, and all along Meade's line,

curving like a fish-hook, and all along Lee's lines enfold-
ing, he could hear the boom of cannon, mingled, near by,
with the ring of the sharp-shooter's rifle.   Yet there came
no volleying musketry from the dense lines of infantry
on either ridge.   Lee was holding and massing, in preparation for attack on Meade's centre.

General Stuart had connected with Lee's left on the
2d ; on the morning of the 3d he moved farther to the
left, making eastward toward Hanover, that, in case Lee's
assaults should prove successful, the cavalry could seize
the roads by which the Federals would be forced to withdraw, and turn the retreat into rout.

Stuart marched on the York road ; two miles east of
Gettysburg his column filed right, and moved toward the
rear of Meade's army, keeping in the forest in order to
avoid observation by the enemy.   At ten o'clock there
was a halt.   The head of Jenkins's brigade had reached
a sort of wooded promontory that overlooked a wide,
open stretch to the south and east.   Behind Jenkins was
Chambliss, commanding W. H. F. Lee's brigade; then,
with an interval, came Hampton, and, after Hampton,
Fitz Lee — a formidable body in all, if the organizations
had been full, but most of the regiments were little larger
than original companies.   One of the batteries had by
some mischance supplied itself with defective shells, and
some of the battalions were short of cartridges.   The
ridge on which the column had halted faces another and
parallel range of wooded hills at the south, where nothing
could be seen ; a gentle valley between, crossed by fences
here and there, and checkered with yellow wheat and

green corn, while the prominent feature of the interval
was Rummel's great barn, distant some two or three hundred yards from the edge of the wood in which Stuart
formed his line, the right of which held the promontory
— the termination of the wooded hills. Here Stuart
himself halted, and with his glass searched the surround-
ing fields and groves for indications of the enemy's presence; then he ordered Jackson's battery to fire three
shots, possibly a signal to Lee that the cavalry was in
position.

At the moment of the first discharge the two negroes
had fallen flat.

"Lawdy, Unc Squiah, how is we gwine to git out o'
heah?" asked Barney, for the moment showing great
fear.

"I dunno who dey is, chile. Ef I knowed dey wus
ouah folks, I'd dess go awn up to 'em; but we dunno who
dey is, an' we got to stay right down heah tell we know
who dey is."

Barney's terror soon gave place to reasonable apprehension; the low spot to which they clung was defended on
all sides but one by higher ground, the only view being
almost directly north toward Rummel's barn. He raised
himself to look.

"I see 'em," he said. "Dey's a-comin'," and when
old Squire got to his feet, and parted the bushes, he too
saw a line of skirmishers advancing from the woods.

The troops which the negroes saw marching toward
Rummel's barn were the Thirty-fourth Virginia battalion
under Colonel Witcher; they passed the barn, and, in

orderly alignment, took position behind a rail fence, their right flank some three hundred yards from Squire's position, too far to tell whether they were friends.

"Dey may be ouah folks, Unc Squiah," Barney said, "an' den ag'in dey may be de Yankees. Anyhow, dey's not cavalry. I b'lieve dey's got long guns ; dem ain't no cahbines. Dah, now ! I see some of 'em a-loadin'; dey's got long guns."

"Dat don't alluz count, Bahney. Some o' ouah calvry totes long guns." And, in fact, the troops they saw were armed with Enfields.

The negroes hugged the hollow of the spring branch ; to ascend either hill at left or right would expose them ; to go forward would be going into wrong lines perhaps; to go back was still less to be thought of, for they had already heard at their right rear many sounds which they knew were made by troops taking position.

Opposite Stuart was McIntosh's brigade, which the Confederate signals had warned to prepare for action. No sooner had the Virginians aligned along the fence than a shell screamed over and into the woods behind them. Jackson, unlimbered near the extreme right, replied, and drew the fire of the Federal batteries — a most destructive fire that speedily silenced the Confederate guns. As yet, the Confederates had seen no enemy, except far away and indistinctly; but now there came from the opposite woods and on down the slope a line of dismounted men, the First New Jersey advancing, and skirmishing began. Even yet old Squire knew not which side of the field to seek, He saw the Federal skirmishers advance, but skirmishers usually carry no flag, and he was unable to tell that they were Federals. The contest continued, the two lines facing each other, the negroes' position being three hundred yards to the west of the interval.

Three miles to the southwest a tempest was roaring ; the great cannonade of Gettysburg preliminary to the charge of Pickett and Pettigrew had begun, and the hostile cavalry here on the flank nerved themselves for the strife — the Federals to prevent Stuart from turning them, their enemies to seize the road in Meade's rear. Part of the Third Pennsylvania reënforced the skirmishers, extending their left, which almost reached the branch, yet was hidden from Squire by irregular ground. The firing was rapid on the hill at the negroes' right.

The Federal skirmishers had almost spent their cartridges ; the Fifth Michigan was ordered to advance and relieve them. The change was not made, for the old line was tempted to retire too early, and the Confederates, seizing the opportunity, pushed on with loud shouts, driving the Union skirmishers.

And then old Squire knew that the force at the north was Confederate, and that at the south Federal ; he knew by the sound of the yelling.

" Bahney, come right awn now ; dem's ouah folks right up dah in de woods beyant dem houses."

The negroes had made but a few paces forward through the bushes, when there came a great change in the nature of the fight. General Gregg having arrived upon the field, with Custer's Michigan brigade, had at once determined to take the offensive ; but even while he was giving orders to Custer, a regiment of gray horsemen moved out from the east of Rummel's and came sweeping down the open. This was the First Virginia, and could be seen by the negroes before it reached the level.   At once the Seventh Michigan charged, almost from Squire's rear, its left storming by within pistol shot, its whole length rolling toward the Confederate skirmishers, who had withdrawn to their first position behind the rail fence.

Footmen well posted are not afraid of cavalry. The Southerners, moreover, counted on two delays in the advance of their enemy, for two fences were in the front, and they held their ground, expecting to see the Federal cavalry broken by cannon ; but at neither fence was the halt prolonged or the integrity of the ranks seriously impaired. Men dismounted, threw off the top rails, and remounted in the rear as their comrades passed the obstructions. The skirmishers must run or be taken.

But the flank of the blue horsemen's line began to waver.   Off at the east the Virginians were coming, ready to strike and roll up the Federal right when it should have advanced sufficiently far.

And to the south of the barn the Federals were stirring— a long line of horse moving forward from Gregg's left.

The charge upon the skirmishers fell promptly, but not on all the line, the right of the Federals hesitating, and at length refusing to expose its flank to the Confederate cavalry. Horsemen were riding through the skirmish line, striking with sabre, firing close shots with pistol, making prisoners of men afoot, yet losing constantly from the fire of cannon, from the fire of the rear line in the woods, and from that of the survivors among the Virginians, who retreated firing. Disorganization in the Federal cavalry was certain ; it had come, and then the gray line at the east came thundering athwart the field.

From their sheltered hiding-place, Squire and Barney had watched intermittently all of the fight that could be seen. They had at length been able to tell the Confederate lines which surged forth and back, and to know the artillery at the north from that at the southeast.

But rolling ground intervened here and there, and even when an entire regiment might else have been in their sight, the dust and smoke made clear vision impossible. They had become so wrought up by excitement, that they had failed to watch toward their rear, where Custer had posted the Sixth Michigan, and the first that Squire learned of this regiment's advance was to find himself almost surrounded by blue skirmishers afoot who were moving up and across the branch. He dropped to the ground and pulled at Barney's leg, but he was too late.

" Hello ! What are you niggers doing here ? " shouted the nearest soldier.

The line was passing, moving toward the northwest, the men parting the bushes and speaking loudly to each other, that they might preserve rank as nearly as possible in the midst of the thicket.

" 'Tain't nobody but me, Mahsta ; I dess be'n a-layin' down heah to keep f'om gittin' kilt."

The line passed beyond the branch some forty yards, and halted in position facing northwest just at the edge

of the thicket, ready for the enemy if they should move
upon them from that direction.

And then Squire heard other noises ; clanking squad-
rons rode up from the south and halted in line at the east
of the branch, no doubt the main body from which the
dismounted skirmishers had just advanced ; and other,
louder, and more confused noises Squire hears, farther
away, where the great contest rages. Gregg hurls a reserve squadron of the Third Pennsylvania against the
Virginians, who at this moment are sweeping the field ;
but another gray line comes out from the northeast, a line
led by Hampton and himself waving the colour. There
is clash of sabres, with pistol-shot replying to blow of
steel, while the cannon throw their shells, striking friend
and foe. The fields are alive with moving men : here a
group scampering in flight, there, a mass commingled,
horses rearing, swords uplifted, smoke and dust ; here
the Confederates giving ground, there the blue cavalry
outnumbered and fleeing ; at the barn windows a few
skirmishers still hold, firing rapidly. Either side takes
prisoners, either side as it recedes leaves blotches on the
ground — dark spots only, but that writhe awhile and
then cease to writhe. Everywhere there are horses riderless, some of them mad with pain, stumbling on three
legs, or on two, others with tails horizontal and manes
floating, go storming into wrong lines, or race in front
with stirrups whipping their sides. Shock succeeds
shock ; right and left the battle swells, up in the open
field, between the reserve lines north and south, while
Stuart's batteries work upon the cavalry moving on his

right, the Michigan regiments under Custer, whose squad-
rons are touching the fringe of bushes where the two
negroes lie.

* * * * * * *

Even after the main battle had ended by the withdrawal of the Confederates to the position which they had
occupied before advancing, Squire and Barney held to the
thicket ; movement toward the northeast over the field
would have placed them in double peril from the opposing
sharp-shooters still seeking targets, while any attempt to
make progress northward would have been detected and
stopped by the skirmishers who lined the west margin of
the bushy flat. Indeed, these skirmishers, who through
intense expectation of becoming engaged, had troubled
them little, might at any moment destroy their hopes, and
Squire looked about for a spot in which he could be hidden from view until nightfall. Worming their way along
the ground, the two succeeded in crossing to the east of
the branch, and thus placed the whole width of the strip
of bushes between themselves and those whose observation they avoided ; then they lay close to earth, fearing
not only to rise but even to speak. The sky was cloudless ; the moon would rise a little after nine ; brief obscurity would be given them for protection in their
advance toward the Confederate lines. Squire communi-
cated with his companion by signs, and Barney, now fully
receptive, understood. The skirmishers, at their left
some sixty yards, were motionless in their places ; far at
the front and far at the rear there was the hubbub of
movement — groups and detachments disorganized by the

fight, shouting and riding hither and yon, seeking to re-
store their scattered lines — but at length all noises ceased,
save that from the field so recently given to the clamour
of battle the old man imagined the groans of the wounded
breaking the silence of twilight.

The time had come. Squire whispered to Barney and
crawled to his right oblique, parting the bushes with care; at
their limit he looked long up the hill. The skirmishers'
backs were toward him, and he knew that once on the rise the
growing wheat would serve as a screen; he crept on, encouraged. At length, just as he was at the top, a great shout
arose at his left rear, the shout of some skirmisher of the
hitherto silent line, caused by no telling what, but sounding
to the old man like the crack of doom . . . he rose and fled.

But only for a moment did he thus expose himself.
Twenty yards passed over, the brow of the hill hid him
from the left, and he dropped flat in the wheat to evade
detection from his rear. Barney had followed closely.

When the short darkness came, which was not complete,
for the coming moon already faintly silvered the east, they
rose, and made more rapid progress straight toward the
great barn; but after a little, hearing voices at the front,
Squire dropped again and crawled toward the east through
the wheat.

The old man was making his way slowly, pausing now
and then to raise his head and look.

"Unc Squiah."

"W'at de matteh, chile?" He had stopped, and
turned his head.

"Didn't shu heah some'h'm?"

"No," and the old man turned again to go on; but he did not go on; his hand had come down on something soft — something that felt unlike wheat, or grass, or earth, but smooth, nevertheless, and cold. Though his hand had been snatched away on the instant, he still felt the cold thing whose momentary contact had checked the beating of his heart. He knew at once that he had placed his hand on the face of a dead soldier.

"Why you don't go awn, Unc Squiah?" whispered the younger man, seeing no cause for the delay.

Perhaps there is none, who, such an incident coming into his experience, would have regarded it as trivial; to Squire the event was enormous. All men are superstitious; the negro is superstition. When Squire touched the dead man's face, strength left him. In his crude belief an omen of utter misfortune had been shown — his very life was forfeit, and dismay had so unnerved him that for an instant he was not able to reply to Barney, who again spoke, urging him to go on.

"Fah you well, Judy," the old man at length muttered; "fahwell, Mahs Chahley; fahwell, ole Mahsta and eve'ybody; ole Squiah done got his call; Lawd, do please fohgive dis mis'ble ole sinneh feh all w'at he done wrong."

"What de matteh with you, Unc Squiah? Why you don't go awn?"

"Bahney, chile, you go awn ahaid now. I done be'n whah I can't see de light no mo'e; you go ahaid."

Barney ranged alongside. "What dat dah thing awn de groun'?"

.   .   .

N

"Somebody."

.   .   .

The dead man's face was toward them, his length
stretched in the wheat.

"Which side he was awn?"

"I dunno, Bahney."

"What de matteh with you, Unc Squiah?   What make
you so change?   You feahed o' dead man?"

"Dat man he so cole."

"You done totch him, den?   Oh, my Godamighty, Unc
Squiah!"

For a full minute neither spoke, each absorbed.

*   *   *   *   *   *   *

"I'm a-gwine th'ough him," said Barney at length.
"He's a Yankee, an' he's got some'h'm."

The old negro made no protest, and the younger man,
horrified the previous moment to learn that his companion
had incurred disaster by touching the body, proceeded to
rifle it; but then every one knows the difference between
desecrating a corpse through inadvertence and doing it
for a purpose.   What Barney found he put into his own
pockets, telling the old man nothing; but his booty must
have been encouraging, for at once he rose cautiously and
looked about him, and then began to move away, saying,
"Don't go 'way, Unc Squiah; I gwine to be back in a
minute; dah's anotheh."

Now Squire followed Barney; the old man could not
bear to be alone with the ghastly object which had brought
him calamity; he found his companion bending over
another of the fallen.

"Dis ain't no Yankee," said Barney; "he ain't got nothin'; I ain't a-gwine to tetch him." He straightened to his full height and looked about. Objects, small and large, spotted the trodden wheat; the large ones were horses.

Barney moved on; he wanted more prey.

"Stop," said Squire; "who dem a-comin' yandeh?"

Some fifty yards in the front, two men were moving about; with their eyes just above the level of the wheat the negroes watched; the two men became invisible; they had stooped in the wheat.

"I 'xpec' dey's a-gwine to git it all," Barney grumbled.

A minute passed and the two soldiers rose to their feet. They seemed to struggle with some object between them; they moved away slowly, going toward the Confederate lines.

"Come awn," said Squire; "dem's ouah men; dey's a-gittin' up de wounded men; we's all right now," a true joy bringing the first little relief from his fear of portended death; but as he put his foot forward he heard a groan and stopped.

"Unc Squiah, jest wait a little bit; I be with you in one minute."

"I gwine to see who dat is," said Squire, willing to grant delay.

While the old man, directed by repeated groans, went straight forward, cautiously, however, lest he tread upon some hidden horror, Barney made to the right and bent over the body of a Federal officer. He turned the pockets and rose.

"Bahney! Bahney!"

The tones were loud and startling, making the young man shake with fear.

"Bahney! Bahney!" again the loud words rang, filling him with terror; front and rear specks of light flashed out, as the skirmishers fired across the wheat at the noises.   He dropped to his knees and crawled toward Squire, who continued to shout : —

"Come quick, Bahney! Hit's my young mahsta!"

CHAPTER XV

" Why, then, lead on. O, that a man might know
The end of this day's business ere it come ! "
— SHAKESPEARE.

SEVENTEEN miles, General Imboden tells us, was the
length of the trains and escort which the Confederate
chieftain on the 4th ordered back to Williamsport. In
one of the many wagons filled with wounded, Charles
Armstrong lay, uttering groans that went to the heart of
old Squire, who trudged along in the rainy night, refusing
to leave his master whom he had saved from captivity if
not from death. The old negro was alone, for Barney
had found it convenient to make some temporary business
arrangement which demanded that he follow Jenkins's
brigade, and Squire felt distress that was not unmixed
with relief. Mahs Chahley was more than enough on his
hands without having to take charge of another incapable.

The road was rough, the night was black, rain fell in
sheets, but the wagons were urged on desperately — all
through the black night old Squire walked behind the
wagon; where they were going he knew not; that the
Eighteenth Virginia led the advance, that the train was

181

as long as a county, that Mahs Dan and his friends were
in the rear with Fitz Lee's brigade, the old man knew
not — he only knew that Mahs Chahley was in the wagon.

Before getting well started Squire went to a barnyard
near by and boldly seized a great armful of hay, with
which he made Armstrong's condition a little less intolerable; and at halts on the encumbered road he brought
water, and worked in every way to lessen his master's distress; yet the considerable halts were few; the wagon
would go a long distance bumping over stones and washes,
rolling the wounded about and against one another; then
after an instant's halt it would jerk forward, causing cries
and moans, curses and prayers; and at sudden slopes
would lurch heavily, and wring a wail in which no voice
could be distinguished. Seventeen miles of human
agony.

Barney had attached himself to an officer of the Thirty-
fourth battalion, who had met the negroes as they were
bearing Charles Armstrong from the field of battle, and
had followed the part of Stuart's command which marched
by Emmitsburg across the mountains. He foraged and
found himself cut off by the Federals who were vigorously
attacking Ewell's wagon trains; but the negro gave them
great margin, fearing to be questioned closely. He went
westward, toward Hagerstown, hearing the sounds of
artillery in many directions.

July 6 Stuart moved upon Hagerstown. The great
trains had reached Williamsport, the point selected for
crossing the Potomac; but there was no bridge, and the
ford was impracticable from high water. Imboden looked

after the defences, for the position might suddenly become perilous. The rear-guard was not yet up.

The Federal cavalry division under Buford marched from Frederick upon Williamsport, that under Kilpatrick from Boonsboro upon Hagerstown. There were bright skies and highest hopes; no great numbers of the enemy could well be at Hagerstown; it was reported that Lee's army was making for the ford at Williamsport by the way of Greencastle, for General French had already destroyed the Confederate pontoon bridge at Falling Waters. The men were buoyant, full of pride in the great victory over Lee's army, and responded quickly to every demand upon strength and courage.

* * * * * * *

Barney was resting; his mind was not fully made up; whether to go on westward, to strike south at once for Virginia, to engage again with some Federal officer, were disturbing questions. He was not satisfied with his present way of living; alone, his courage failed him; with another to lead, he could follow. Squire had correctly read the young negro, who, even at this moment, was thinking of the old man's urgent advice to remain faithful to his Southern home.

Barney fell asleep, and his awakening was rude; he heard loud voices almost above him.

"Now, will ye belave me, Misther Hawley? And will ye give me the credit for the taking of 'm?"

"Oh, yes," says Hawley; "but how do you know what he is?"

"He's a ribel's naygur, he is; anny wan can tell it by

his skin; it nades graise, and the insoides of 'm no less."

Barney's eyes were still almost closed, and the men were standing outside of his line of imperfect vision, but the voices were perfectly familiar.

"Wake up!" cried Hawley, punching the negro with his foot.

With a jerk, Barney sat up, and looked about, pretending confusion. On either side stood a blue soldier, Hawley afoot, holding his bridle, O'Donnell mounted.

"Ho, bedad! And if it's not Barney, then it's his brother!"

"Yes, sah. Howdy, Mist' O'Donnell. Howdy, Misteh Hawley."

"And tell the blissed truth and shame the divil now, dam ye! D'ye belong to the ribels?"

"Who, me? Now, Mist' O'Donnell, you ain't done pokin' yo' fun yet? How come you think I done go back on you all? Don't shu know dat I stuck to you all jest as long as de cap'm staid?"

"Say, O'Donnell, we've got no time to be fooling here. The best thing to do is for one of us to take him back to the captain."

"Roight ye are, me b'y. Come, Barney, gettup, and marrch before me, and ye'll soon see that same captain that ye loike so well."

"And you get back here dam quick, O'Donnell," said Hawley. "This place is not as safe as an ironclad; the Johnnies are not half a mile off."

If Barney felt any distress at being thus haled before

his old protector, he was careful not to show it, and marched in O'Donnell's front without objecting; indeed, the negro hoped to end suspense by finding favour with Captain Freeman, who had treated him kindly, and whose service he was not disinclined to undertake again.

A quarter of a mile at the rear of the vedette post, near which Barney had been sleeping, Freeman's company was found drawn up as mounted skirmishers, and O'Donnell at once conducted his prisoner to the captain.

"Wan more for O'Donnell, sor, if ye plaise; the siventainth for the waik."

"You want to count this man a grayback?" said Freeman, laughing, and not yet having recognized his former servant; then, looking more closely, he cried: —

"Why, my Lord, man, what are you doing here?"

"Cap'm, I jest ain't quit a-wonderin' ef dat *izh* you, sho' nuff. I'm so glad to see you, sah. You done got well?"

"Yes. Where have you been, Barney?"

"Cap'm, I've jest be'n a-runnin' 'roun' loose mos' eveh sence you done lef' me. I've had a hahd time, sho'."

"But how did you get *here?*" Freeman was somewhat suspicious, simply because he knew that the ground had very recently been occupied by the rebels.

"I got los' in de woods way back yondeh las' night, sah, an' I jest kep' awn a-gwine, 'caze I was afeahed all de time dat I run up awn de wrong folks, sah — an' I did run up awn 'em, sah."

"Who do you serve now?"

The question was a poser. Barney knew names enough,

but he dreaded consequences ; any officer whose name he should give might afterward be consulted by Freeman, whom, though willing to serve, he feared greatly.

"De las' man I tuck up with was with de baggage waggins, sah, Misteh Dodson,"— giving the truth, so far as it went,— "but I done got cut off f'om de waggins, an' I jest didn't know whah to go, sah ; an' las' night I got in a crowd o' de wrong folks, Cap'm, but I got away dis mawnin'."

A bugle was heard somewhere in the rear. Freeman ordered an advance.

"Well, Barney," said he, "I'd take care of you if you could keep up with us, but I can't wait for you. What are you going to do ? "

"If I jest knowed whah yo' waggin's a-gwine to be at, I'd go to it, sah."

"Well, make your way to Hagerstown," said Freeman, pointing, and then marched on.

Stuart's two brigades under Chambliss and Robertson, the two not greater than a full regiment, marched from Leitersburg and occupied Hagerstown. Kilpatrick's first brigade, under Colonel Richmond, reached Hagerstown from Boonsboro, and drove the Confederates to the protection of Iverson's infantry brigade, which held the northern side of the town. Stuart himself was coming westward from Chewsville, and Kilpatrick's main body was coming into the town from Boonsboro.

Kilpatrick's advance had thus intervened between Stuart and Williamsport ; and beyond Kilpatrick the rebel commander could hear Buford's guns thundering upon Imboden, who, in awful suspense, Fitz Lee's brigade miles in the rear, called into momentary service his teamsters, the convalescents among the wounded, all men who could make a show, and as pretence of strength marched them up and down in sight of his enemy.

Stuart attacked and broke through Kilpatrick's advance, and passed on ; but the Federal main body now had its say ; there was bloody encounter in the streets, charge and countercharge, both sides fighting with almost unexampled stubbornness. Squadron after squadron charged, and dead and wounded littered the carriage ways and sidewalks. Captain Snyder was picked up dead, Captain Chauncey was fearfully wounded, and Dahlgren was found fainting from a smashed foot — the three officers falling in the last daring charge.

Meanwhile, Kilpatrick was swinging his flank across the Williamsport road. Behind the hills at Williamsport, old Squire could hear fighting east, northeast, and north, while the head of Fitzhugh Lee's brigade, forcing the march on Williamsport, could hear the same sounds southeast and east. Imboden was sorely pressed ; he longed for Fitz Lee as Napoleon for Grouchy — and, unlike Grouchy, Fitz Lee came.

Half a mile to the left of Lee's column, eight picked men, Morgan the foremost, rode at long intervals, covering the east of the whole brigade. The march of these men was very rapid, for the leader had only his judgment to rely upon, and his orders required him to keep at least three-quarters of a mile to the left oblique of the head of the column, which he was told would move at the rate of five miles an hour. Woods intervened here and there, and hills, so that the sergeant could not positively know at all times that he was preserving good distance ; as for the men in his rear, all each had to do was to keep his leader in sight and watch toward the east, toward Hagerstown, where the fight between Stuart and Kilpatrick threatened again to become battle. Dusk was gathering, and still they rode with great intervals, each seeing the form of his leader more indistinctly, Morgan guessing his way, almost unconsciously increasing his speed, and sheering gradually toward his left, for at the west in open ground he saw a dark moving body which could be no other than the head of Fitz Lee's column, and he feared that his own march had been slower than his duty required. But soon his fear was changed, for the moving objects were nearer, and he began to think that the brigade had left the main road and was marching southeastward. He deflected yet more ; for a few hundred yards he rode almost at the top of his poor horse's speed, a hill shutting from view the marching column; and when again he reached level ground he was astounded to see the column almost within a stone's throw at his right and to know that it was moving squarely eastward . . . and a column no longer, but a body of mounted troops marching in line.

Morgan halted ; any further advance on his part would have put him in easy speaking distance of these troops which now he feared were not Lee's. He turned in his saddle to see if possible how far northward the line extended, and as he turned he struck his spurs deep, and pulled bridle eastward, for he saw himself almost sur-

rounded by enemies, many of them already cutting in
between him and Sency, his nearest follower. It was a
vicious chase. "Halt!" — "Halt!" — "Halt!" came
from three sides, as his horse made the first bound; and,
at the second, shots were fired, and then loud shouts and
many thundering hoofs sounded in his rear.

Morgan was not a light-weight, but what he didn't
know about riding is not worth knowing, and all that he
feared beyond a stray bullet was the condition of his
already overworked horse. As luck would have it, the
ground was good, a narrow road, but firm, and, knowing
that if by a sudden spurt he could outreach the vision
of his pursuers he would change long doubt into quick
success, he bent forward and urged his tired beast to do
his uttermost at once, — and for a hundred yards the response was generous, — the mud flew from under the
horse's hoofs, and the sergeant believed he should escape;
but he could still hear the pursuers coming, many of
them it seemed by the noises, and he soon felt the speed
of his horse begin to slacken. Every moment was invaluable: rapidly increasing darkness in his favour,
rapidly decreasing strength against him, he knew that in
the time it takes one to count a hundred his fate must
be decided. Oh, for a descending slope, a long descent,
where the opposing hills would shut his form below the
sky line! But even as he thought the wish, the ground
in front began to rise and place him above his enemies.
He looked to the right — there the same condition; then
to the left, and he turned, for there he saw better chance,
though he knew that the very divergence had almost

destroyed his hopes, for he was compelled to bear away
from the Potomac, whereas, before, he had been fleeing
from the enemy's extreme right flank retiring (for it
was Buford's men that had cut him off), and he felt necessity so urgent that he dropped his carbine to lighten
weight, and even started to throw away sabre and pistols ;
but saw that he had not time, as his horse was even now
sinking. Yet, although in this dire strait, Morgan
was not utterly resourceless. He pulled rein, sprang to
the ground, drew his sabre, gave the almost exhausted
animal a blow which goaded it to fresh if momentary exertion, and as the horse galloped forward again, the man
slunk to the left through weeds and briers, and then lay
flat, while many horsemen passed.

Still he was very far from safety : would not the enemy
soon return upon their tracks ? He thought not ; no
doubt his horse, left to the influence of weariness alone,
would be overtaken almost instantly ; yet the enemy
had too serious business on hand to allow such scattering
as would be necessary for search in all directions ; he
would wait until reasonably sure that no laggard was
still to come, and then he would try to make his way
westward. The night was as dark as it would ever get
to be ; the moon would not rise until after ten ; he had
two good hours of obscurity. How far he had ridden
out of his course he knew not ; indeed, at the beginning
he had been ignorant of his position, and now he knew
nothing beyond the fact that the west was in the hands
of the Confederate cavalry, and the east in those of the
Federals. He had crossed fields and roads in his head-

ong flight, — not more than a mile he thought, or two
niles at the most, — yet he was in grave fear that his
narch to the rear of the enemy's right flank had been
:aused more by his own error of direction than by their
winging northward; and if this fear was based on
ruth, then there was no telling what distance separated
iim from his friends. Yet he must act, and after a few
noments, hearing nothing in the rear, he rose and walked
apidly away.

Kilpatrick, reaching the Williamsport pike, marched
he brigades of Custer and Huey down that road to con-
iect with Buford's right and overwhelm Imboden, while
Richmond's brigade should hold Stuart in check at
Iagerstown. Stuart cared nothing for Hagerstown; he
:new that Lee's infantry in a few hours would be there
n position; what he wanted was to break through Kil-
)atrick and relieve Imboden. At sunset he charged and
lrove Richmond's brigade toward Williamsport. Now
Kilpatrick was in danger, and, receiving word that
3uford was withdrawing, concerned himself mostly about
he safety of his rear under Richmond, which would soon
)e driven hard upon him.

Captain Freeman's company was retiring southward,
n tolerable order, after severe fighting in which many
nen had been lost, the survivors preserving distance as
vell as they could for the darkness, when Private O'Don-
iell raised a cry. Sergeant Dow, his file closer, moved
ip. "What's the matter, O'Donnell?" he called, seeing
he man bending over in his saddle and struggling, to
ill appearance, with something on the ground.

"Hould onn there, now! Don't ye be a-giving me anny of yer tongue; Oi know what ye are. Ye're a dam'd ribel, ye are; so come along. Oi've got ye."

"Is he armed?" asked Dow.

"Beloike he is armed, indade; but little do Oi care for that; his legs are hwat's giving me the throuble. Sergeant, be plaised to give'm a lift, will ye, and Oi'll put'm behoint me, so Oi will."

Morgan saw it useless to struggle, and after the first unavailing attempts to evade the clutches of a single opponent, submitted with all the grace he could to combined forces. He gave O'Donnell no trouble in mounting, and sat behind the Irishman in a way to embarrass him as little as possible.

"Now that's hwat Oi call acting loike a sinsible man. Be aisy, now, and kape the pace; ye'll do yerself no harrm by ut."

"All right," said Morgan, willing to conciliate; "I've got nothing against *you*, my friend."

"And Oi wantt to tell ye that it's me number eightain that ye are."

"Be kind enough to explain," said Morgan.

"Oi will; but ut's no koindness at all, at all; I mane that the eightainth wan that Oi've put me hand on the waik is named yerself."

"Oh, git out, O'Donnell," said Sergeant Dow; "the man knows you're drunk."

"And did Oi not? Oi tell ye, and it's Dennis O'Donnell that can back up his worrd, that this gintleman behoint me, and he's a-roiding so aisy and noice, he's

ne number eightain, and be dam'd to iverry wan that
gives me the loie."

The retreat had almost ended; the sound of battle
vas no longer heard; the men were silent, most of them,
s soldiers usually are after a hard day in which honours
all to the enemy, yet here and there along the ranks,
low formed into column, could be heard a shout of inquiry or reply.

"Nobody wants to give you the lie, O'Donnell, but
everybody can't quite agree to all eighteen points. You
till want to count Barney?"

"Oi do. Eightain of 'm and Oi'm not to be chaited
ut of wan by the loikes of anny wan of ye."

"Ha! ha! ha!" roared Hawley. "Black and white,
ll's alike to Irish. Just so he counts, he don't give
a dam what colour."

"And, Misther Hawley, will ye be so koind as to say
vhere me number siventain would be at this toime if
Oi hadn't laid me hands onn'm?"

"Be with the rebels, maybe; dam 'f I know where,
nd dam 'f I care; maybe they'd have got him and
maybe they wouldn't. What's that got to do with it?
Think they'd have made a soldier out of him?"

"Begod, and he counts wan, Oi'm telling of ye.
Whin he worrks for the ribels, doesn't he kape a ribel
n the ranks by worrking forr'm, Oi'm telling of ye!"

Morgan had begun to feel interest in the quarrel.
Hearing the word *Barney* had not at first kindled any
uriosity; he had not applied the name to any person
vhom he knew; but when it became evident that Bar-

o

ney number seventeen was a negro, he began to see a
possibility, and when, in addition, he heard that this
Barney was of doubtful standing as to his adherence,
the prisoner suspected strongly that number seventeen
was none other than old Squire's mate who had helped
to bring Armstrong in from the battle-field at Gettysburg,
and concerning whom Squire had given some little history. And if Morgan had become alert, Hawley's next
sally increased his interest unto excitement.

"Yes," says Hawley, "a nigger's as good as a white
man any day to Irish. That old fellow Squire that we
had down at Rowser's a week ago, ha! ha! damned if
O'Donnell didn't say he was the biggest take the company had made since we was at Kelly's Ford, by
God!"

"Oi did, sor, and Captain Frayman belaves it no less
than Oi do, sor; but Misther Hawley, bad luck to 'm,
he puts in his worrd that he kills the ould naygur at
that same Rowser's, and he takes all the proide out of
poor O'Donnell."

The laugh that followed this retort had the effect of
silencing Hawley, and the Irishman, restored to good
humour, never completely lost, said to Morgan in an
undertone : —

"Don't ye be failing downhearted now be rayson of me
number siventan ; sure, and it's no disgrace to be wan
behoint wan whin that wan that ye're behoint can cause
so sarious a quaurr'l."

"I don't know so much about that," says Morgan.
"Don't seem to me you are totin' fair with me. You

ought to count me ahead of that nigger, unless he's a mighty good one."

"Sure and he's a good wan. Oi'm to show 'm to ye, and ye'll be sinsible yerself that he's all roight for siventain."

The company halted, and the men were at ease, though in ranks, Captain Freeman having sent for orders. The first sergeant reported one prisoner.

"Let him be sent to the provost-marshal," said Freeman; "I'll let you know when and where as soon as I learn, Sergeant. Meantime, see that he is well guarded. We bivouac shortly; I've already ordered the wagon up."

Again the march was ordered; troops ahead of Freeman kept straight on for Boonsboro; his own company filed left, and after half an hour's tramp bivouacked in rear of Funkstown.

CHAPTER XVI

UNSTABLE AS WATER

" But it sufficeth that the day will end,
And then the end is known. Come, ho ! away ! "
— SHAKESPEARE.

THE Irishman and his number eighteen were on the ground by one of Freeman's extinct bivouac fires, Private Hawley erect above them, other guards near by on their blankets. O'Donnell, though not on duty, had persisted, nevertheless, in holding himself near to Morgan, whom he claimed as his own peculiar and labelled property ; and the sergeant of the guard, hoping that complete intoxication would speedily bring relief to all parties interested, had avoided a useless altercation which he knew would have resulted in the necessity of reporting a comrade for insubordination, by tacitly acknowledging the ownership and permitting the Irishman to lie near his prisoner. But O'Donnell, still feeling a certain consciousness of interest in what might happen, had refrained from the finishing cup ; occasionally he would throw out an arm and caress Morgan's head and give grunts of gratification induced by the combined influence of contrary powers — that over himself, and his own over another ; meanwhile, that other lay motionless, but with every sense alert.

Barney had succeeded in reaching Freeman's wagon, and, thanks to his skill as a caterer in both foraging and cooking, had prepared a supper which helped to reinstate him in the captain's good graces, as well as in the old position of chief serving-man for the officers' mess.

"Brock," said Freeman, lighting his pipe, "I wonder if that rebel that O'Donnell caught has anything to eat."

"If he has, Captain, he's in better luck in that respect than the rest of Lee's army, if what they say is true."

"Well, they don't tell me where to send him, and I suppose we've got to feed him ourselves. Barney, take him something. Sergeant Dow will show you where he is, if you don't know."

Barney already knew; he had seen Morgan under guard and had recognized him, and was in terror of revelation; yet he trusted that the only time he had been seen could not have sufficed for the Confederate to impress feature and name upon his mind; so, pulling his hat down to hide his face as much as he dared, he approached Hawley and without a word handed him the food, making a gesture with his hand as much as to say that the food was for the prisoner; then he started to go away.

"For the rebel, you mean?" asked Hawley.

Barney turned and nodded.

O'Donnell had heard; he scrambled to a sitting posture and saw Barney, who had again begun to retreat silently.

"Halt! ye dam black naygur," said O'Donnell; "and can ye not show yer manners better'n that? Oi wantt me number eightain to see ye. Halt there, now, and come back wid je."

Barney reluctantly obeyed; the man O'Donnell was important; he might become the negro's enemy, and make life a torture.

"Number eightain, yer rations is brought ye by number siventain, and sure ye mustn't have any more harrd failings."

No doubt the prisoner had already been prepared for quick recognition of Barney, whose embarrassment would have been betrayed, in any case, by his reluctance to approach; yet Morgan failed to interpret the negro correctly, believing his conduct but natural through shame at being found a turncoat from the Confederates, as it were.

"So, you are here," said the prisoner.

Barney was mute; he stood without movement, his head hanging; he must take what should come; at the worst, nothing more could be said against him than that he had helped a wounded Confederate, and his poor thought was concerned only in providing excuses before Captain Freeman.

"What made you leave?" asked Morgan; he had almost said "leave Squire," but had stopped, prudence telling him not to show knowledge of the old negro; yet the intonation of his interrupted closing was not unobserved by Hawley, who exclaimed: "Finish your speech, man. Tell what you know about this nigger."

The tone was rude; Morgan did not like it; moreover, he considered that everything he could say positively would be from his own point of view favourable to

Barney, and to give such testimony with the purpose of doing harm would be base.

"Why did you leave your master?" asked Morgan.

Barney had determined to preserve obstinate silence, but he felt relieved by Morgan's modified question, which was entirely unimportant and might have been addressed to any former slave. Fear diminishing, he reasoned that it would be better, if possible, to appease Morgan, who if angered might do more than retaliate.

"He's dead, sah," was the false reply. Then the negro said, "I ain't neveh done you no hahm, sah, an' I ain't a-gwine to do none, an' you oughtn't to be mad with me jest 'caze I don't know you, and when I'm a-tryin' to do de best I can." The last words bore an appeal that Hawley suspected and Morgan felt, and both became to all seeming indifferent, the one in order to betray no eager interest that would put the speakers on notice that their peculiar conduct was observed, the other because he had decided to end the trivial thing and give the poor darky a chance to get along in his new circumstances. But if the silence that followed proved embarrassing to Barney, it was felt as an insult by O'Donnell, who quickly broke in, addressing Morgan : —

"And have ye no more to say, now? And the naygur fading of ye?"

"No, let him go back where he belongs," was Morgan's reply, given rudely with two purposes, — one to allay Hawley's suspicions that Barney was an old friend to the prisoner, the other to put an end to a scene that might damage the negro.

Barney went back to the officers' bivouac, where his fears yielded to a feeling of safety, and doubtless he would never have dared to approach Morgan again but for an incident that he had not foreseen.

Hawley's suspicions had not been entirely laid by the prisoner's tone, and as soon as he was relieved he went to his commander, who, as luck would have it, was found alone.

"Captain," said he, touching his cap, "I'd like to say a few words to you."

"Very well, Hawley, what is it?"

"I've been seeing some strange things between that nigger Barney and our prisoner, sir."

"Well?"

"I believe they know one another, sir."

"And suppose they do. What of that? Barney is from Virginia, and perhaps the rebel is also."

"I shouldn't have thought very strange of it, sir, but I don't see why they couldn't say so at once."

"Say what, Hawley?"

"Say that they know one another, sir. The man spoke to Barney as if he knew all about him, and then Barney goes out of his way to say that he didn't know him."

"That so? What did the prisoner say to Barney?" asked Freeman, now showing interest.

"He asked him when he left."

"When he left what?"

"Well, sir, the thing hangs right there. When he got that far, he stopped, as if he might be going to say too much; and then I spoke up, and told him to finish; but the rebel is a sharp one, sir, — anybody can see that, — and he asked the darky when he left his master."

"And what do you think he was going to ask at first, Hawley?"

"I believe he was going to ask when he left the rebels — possibly the regiment that this man belongs to."

"I'll go see that man. Come with me. No, Hawley, you stay here till I come back. We'd better not go together," and Captain Freeman, his suspicions of Barney revived, walked rapidly toward the guards, muttering to himself conditional threats against the negro, and entirely unobservant of a dark form gliding through the bushes at his right and taking post behind a tree in earshot of the conversation that followed.

"What is your name?" he asked Morgan.

The prisoner was prepared and replied promptly, "John Berry, sir."

"I see you are a sergeant."

"Yes, sir."

"Your regiment, if you please."

"The First Virginia, sir," was the reply — the action was long over, and Morgan felt that he was compromising no interest.

Thus far well and good, thought Freeman; but how from inquiry of a military nature to make a transition to private questioning began to trouble him. He felt that he must use great tact, else the sharp rebel would suspect. Even now, perhaps, he was on his guard.

"Brigade?"

"Fitzhugh Lee's."

The captain had gained no information by his last question, for he had already known, if he had but thought of it, that the said regiment was a part of the said brigade, yet the reply brought helpful suggestion in regard to his real purpose.

"Is General Fitzhugh Lee with his brigade?"

"Yes, sir; he was this morning, at least."

"But I was told recently that he had been wounded," retorted Freeman, his mind now on Squire so firmly that he continued without a pause, "Say, do you know a negro named Squire?"

"Squire? No, I don't know anybody by that name, and I know every nigger that follows Fitzhugh Lee's brigade." Morgan gave the answer very readily. He felt pretty sure that Squire's actual name could not easily have reached Freeman's ears.

"And Barney? Do you know Barney?" asked Freeman, quickly seeing his chance, as he thought, to get at the kernel of his purpose without logical violence.

But Morgan was not to be caught thus; the leap from Squire to Barney was apparent in its suddenness.

The prisoner shook his head peculiarly, as though in doubt. "What Barney?" he asked.

In the rebel's manner, Freeman saw hesitation, but read nothing more; he paused a moment that he might add time to the weight of his words.

"Do you know *any* Barney?"

"Yes, sir," said Morgan, promptly; "I know more than one Barney. Down in Virginia, I know a whole family of 'em."

" You are talking about white people ? "

" Yes, sir."

" The man I'm speaking of is a negro named Barney, and nothing else, so far as I know."

" Who does he belong to ? " asked the prisoner.

" He is the man who brought your supper awhile ago. What do you know about him ? "

Morgan was now aware that suspicion of the negro had induced Freeman's visit. Simply by refusing to conceal he would bring disaster upon Barney, and for a moment he experienced a moral embarrassment more intense than he would previously have supposed possible in connection with an object ordinarily considered of paltry importance. But it would not do to hesitate. To gain time for deciding the ethical dilemma, he could only evade.

" I know that he was not very polite in his manner at -first," he said ; " but I don't care any more for that than for a dog's barking at me. You people take our negroes and set 'em free, and make fools of 'em —"

" I'm not talking about that," interrupted the captain. " I want to know if you ever saw Barney before to-night."

" I think I have, sir. Was he not raised in Fauquier County ? "

" No, in Goochland."

" Well, sir, I'm not from that county ; and if he is from Goochland — you know it's not easy to swear to every nigger you meet. I'd not like to say positively that I ever saw him. Anything wrong about him ? "

The captain tried to read the prisoner's face, but there

was so little light that he gave it up, and, without replying to Morgan, went back to his place.

"I get nothing out of him, Hawley," he said; "the fellow knows nothing, or else smells a rat and is on his
guard. I'm half persuaded you're right; but what I can
do more I don't see."

"Captain, let me talk to Barney in your presence, if you
please."

"All right, call him up."

It is needless to say that Barney was ready for any
ordinary examination; but armed though he was with
knowledge that he was suspected, he was unprepared for
the first words that Hawley hurled at him.

"Make a clean breast of it now, Barney."

The negro was silent, wondering, and might have betrayed himself through manifest hesitation had Hawley
here ended his speech instead of merely pausing.

"Own up, man. We know all about you. The rebel
has given you away."

"I dunno what he's got ag'in me, Misteh Hawley. I
ain't neveh seed him, an' I don't know him, notheh."

"Well, *he* knows *you;* and you can't deny that you've
been with the rebels."

Hawley's weakening would have been evident, even
though the negro had been duller and unprepared; the
descent from the high plane upon which he had cast his
first utterance was absurd in its abruptness, in its tone,
and in useless multiplicity of words: why wish the negro
to confess if he was already known to be guilty? Perhaps Barney failed to reason thus; he felt the substance,
nevertheless.

"Yes, sah, I done told de cap'm dat dey cut me off an' I had to git th'ough 'em de best I could; but dey didn't try to keep me, sah. Dat man, what he got to say ag'in me? Tell me what he say," and Barney looked full on Captain Freeman, though the words were directed at Hawley.

"Nothing against you except that he knew you, or thought so," was the reply, feeble and uncertain.

To Hawley, Freeman's disgust was not less apparent than was the negro's triumph; yet the captain said merely, "Go back to your place, Hawley," adding to Barney, "And you to your work, sir."

Barney's victory caused him no elation. He knew that henceforth Hawley would be hostile, and that Freeman's suspicions, though seemingly quieted, would be renewed upon the slightest provocation, and he longed for the time when he could turn his back upon the Federals and upon his dangerous employment. But, whatever else may be said in derogation of the negro's character, ingratitude cannot be urged against it, and this negro was no exception to the rule. He had overheard Morgan's replies to Freeman, and he wished for a way to help the captive, or at least to show thankfulness. A way was given him.

Hawley went past sleeping men and approached the guard post. It was now after ten o'clock. The moon had barely risen, but the sentinel's form was distinct as he stood on guard over the prisoner. At this instant a clatter of hoofs was heard toward the east, and near by, and then voices, one of which was clearly Captain Freeman's, and Hawley paused to listen, and he was not the only one that overheard.

"To Boonsboro?"

"Yes, sir, by midnight . . . how many . . . ?"

"I have only one."

"All right, sir; we can take charge of him without troubling you to send a detail. We have two other prisoners."

"Very well, I'll turn him over to you . . . Hawley!"

Hawley turned and answered the call, and began to retrace his steps. In another moment a different voice called "Hawley!" and from a different direction. He knew the voice to be that of the sentinel over the prisoner; he must not stop to talk while the captain was calling. But the sentinel persisted, "Hawley, haven't they come to get him?" violating military rule in his eagerness to know whether he should now be rid of this encumbrance, the only reason for his enforced watchfulness, and in his eagerness leaning toward the man whom he wished to reach with his voice.

A few moments passed and Hawley came back, leading the way for three horsemen.

"You are devilish impatient, Jackson; what do you mean by hollerin' so at me? Couldn't you wait decently a minute? Where's the sergeant?"

The sergeant rose in his place some yards away and came forward. Morgan could see him rub his eyes, and saw two horsemen with another rider behind each of them, and he knew that he himself was the chosen double to the third.

"Sergeant," continued Hawley, "these men are to take charge of the prisoner according to the captain's orders."

"All right — glad to hear it. Take him right now?"

"Yes," replied one of the mounted men. "Here, Frame, take him up behind you."

"Get up," said the sergeant, and touched the prisoner with his foot. "Give me a receipt," he added, and the horseman began to write.

Morgan moved uneasily about, as though he was hardly awake. O'Donnell was snoring heavily by his side.

"Get up, I say," said the sergeant in louder tones.

Morgan rose and looked about him in the stupid manner of one that has been rudely and but partly awakened.

"Johnny, you're to go with these men. . . . Jackson, you're relieved."

A horseman leaned over to grasp Morgan by the arm . . . Jackson was walking cheerfully away — and now Hawley started also . . . the sergeant had discreetly given room to the horses.

"Give him a lift, Sergeant," begged the horseman, in the act of bending over ; "here's your receipt."

The prisoner suddenly fell to the ground, and as suddenly rose again with the horse between himself and the sergeant, having dashed under the animal's belly. In an instant he was gone.

"Hell and damnation!" cried the horseman. "Why'n't you hold him? You are responsible for this."

"Not at all," replied the sergeant, coolly and quietly ;

"I delivered him to *you;* you are the responsible party
— not I."

"Pursue him!" cried the horseman, almost in frenzy,
more perhaps because of the laugh raised by his two companions than because of the loss itself.

"Pursue him yourself if you want anybody to pursue.
I'm done with it, except to report it," and the sergeant
walked toward Captain Freeman's place.

Morgan had not run far; he knew too little of directions, for the sky was hidden by the trees above him, and
he must not risk running wrong; he sank to the ground
and listened.

Behind him there was noise, but no great noise; he
thought it came from Freeman's company; the sounds
indicated preparation to march, yet there had been no
bugle. Soon there was another noise — a low hissing
sound near him — which at first he knew not how to
construe, but it grew in clearness and intensity until he
recognized the warning "Sh-h-h!" prolonged and repeated.
But toward whom was the signal directed? Doubtless
footmen were searching for the fugitive, and one had
stopped another with the command to hearken ... yet
would the sound be repeated? Why noisily bid a companion be silent when he is already silent? for Morgan
heard no noise near him except this one persistent growing "Sh-h-h!"

The fugitive wondered why the guards — he was as yet
not more than a hundred and fifty yards from the post —
were making no noise of pursuit or search. He could not
know that Freeman had received orders to march. Could

it be that he was surrounded, and that they felt so confident of his falling into Federal hands that they were refusing to make needless effort? No; such could not be the
case, for if he were environed by foes, his guards would
shout and warn the troops around lest he slip through them
in the darkness. Yet, could he believe that no effort to
retake him was being made? that his escape had been
taken for granted by his enemies? Surely not, unless —
unless there was for him some peculiar advantage of the
ground, something to make the Federals despair of success
— and with this thought Morgan raised his head as noise-
lessly as possible and tried to look about him, hoping rather
than believing that he should see near him a ravine or other
help that would give conclusion to his doubts. He saw a
man squatted less than five paces distant.

Morgan did not lower his head. He reasoned that the
man knew of his presence, or did not; in either case
additional attempt at secrecy was without profit, in the
first ineffectual, in the second needless, for he knew that
he was well concealed already; he looked at the man
squatted near a bushy tree. Again came the signal for
silence — and then he heard a rattling sound in the leaves
at his right knee, and knew that a missile had been thrown.

It was now impossible for Morgan to believe that his
presence was unknown, and almost equally difficult for
him to believe that the man before him was hostile;
yet the absurdity of admitting the hope of aid at this
place and time was so manifest that for the moment confidence in his own sight and hearing was shaken. Had he
seen aright? Had he heard aright? Was that object

P

before him really a man? Was it not, rather, some bush
or stump distorted by his fears? Had he heard a pebble
or stick thrown toward him? Had he not, rather, heard
the noise of some decayed acorn, some rotten twig, as it
fell to the ground? Had he heard a voice uttering a caution, or had he heard the swish of a bough, the rubbing of
branches against each other? Yet it was but for a moment
that he thus doubted — the next moment he knew that the
man near him was the negro Barney, the recognition being
due to a whispered declaration coming from Barney himself.

"Jest be quiet, sah; dis is me."

Instantly renewed fears and doubts swept through Morgan's mind. This negro was, to certain knowledge, a
deceiver; he had been with Squire and with the Confederates, but had gone to the Yankees and had denied his
former relation. The sergeant, ignorant of the fact that
Barney had overheard Freeman's questions and the replies
thereunto, had not the smallest thought of any claim upon
the negro's gratitude; and so confirmed was his belief in
the falseness of the man, confirmed by his knowledge that
Freeman himself was full of suspicion, that he refused to
respond, and thought rather of sudden flight than of awaiting the issue. But Barney was by instinct no mean logician; he knew and felt that Morgan could not be expected
to trust him, and appreciated the necessity for acting
quickly.

"Don't be afeahed, sah," he whispered. "I'm yo'
frien'; I heahed what shu said to de cap'm, sah."

"Are you going to help me?" whispered the soldier.

"Yes, sah, if I can ; but I ain't got much time. De company is awdehed to mahch, an' I got to git back mighty quick. You mus' go dis a-way, sah," thrusting his arm out almost in contact with the white man's face.

"How far do these woods stretch ? "

"Not mo'n a quauta', sah ; an' when you git to de aige of 'em you can see de big road."

"What big road ? "

"I dunno, sah, whah it goes to."

"Troops over there ? "

"Yes, sah, awn de yotheh side ; but shu nee'n' to git awn de yotheh side. Jest stay awn dis side, an' keep awn down de aige o' de fiel'."

"I'm greatly obliged to you, Barney."

"I done all I can do fuh you, sah ; you helped me out, an' I ain't a-gwine to go back awn sich as dat."

"Why didn't you stick to Squire ? "

"Unc Squiah, he jest went his way, sah, an' I jest went my way. I dunno what I'd ha' done if I hadn't met up wi' Cap'm Freeman ag'in. I've be'n with him befo'e, sah. Now, sah, I've got to git back, 'caze dey'll be a-gwine f'om heah. Good-by, sah."

Morgan did not wait; he started in the direction given him, fearing longer delay — not that he doubted the negro's faith in regard to himself, but because time was valuable. He succeeded in reaching the edge of the woods, and then crept south on the east side of the big road. But Barney's knowledge of the country and the troops that occupied it referred to a very small area, and Morgan soon found his way blocked by a great cavalry bivouac extending far

across his path. He endeavoured to flank it by going to
his left, and might have succeeded in achieving his escape
had not the bugles rang out "To horse" in every direction around him. He soon saw himself surrounded by
moving men and horses, and he tried to hide and wait till
the coast was clear, attempting the impossible. Men passed
near him without speaking, but the thing could not last—
a few minutes went by, and again he was in the hands of
his enemies.

CHAPTER XVII

WAYS CONVERGING

" Is the coast clear ?   None but friends ? "
— GOLDSMITH.

MORE than half the night was gone; the moon, changing to its last quarter, was fully two hours high.

Morgan's new captors were of Buford's division, which had retired from the fight near Williamsport, and was now beginning its movement toward Kilpatrick's left.   In the recent combat Buford's people had been sorely tried ; the company into whose clutches Morgan had stumbled had suffered greatly, the men being held too long to their work even after their cartridges were exhausted.   Its commander was not in the best of humour.

" How did you get here, sir ? " he asked sharply, when Morgan was halted before him.

The question brought with it the apprehension of a possible danger not hitherto thought of ; this Confederate, unarmed, in the midst of moving enemies, was peculiar. Yet a moment's reflection assured the captive that, in full gray uniform, he had no reason to fear being accused as a spy.

" I was captured, sir," was the simple reply, given in tones respectful and low.

"Can't I see that? But how the hell did you manage to get *here* in order to be captured?"

"Straggling and hiding out, sir."

"Where are your arms?"

"I had to throw them away, sir, and to abandon my horse; he was taken before I was."

"You were not in the fight this afternoon?"

"No, sir; I heard cannon in two directions, but I saw no fighting." The declaration, literally taken, was true.

"Your command?"

Morgan answered freely and fully, telling the whole inclusive organization.

The officer ended the matter by giving the prisoner in charge of two men whom he ordered to ride hard toward Boonsboro, that they might overtake a batch of prisoners sent back under guard earlier; they were to deliver the prisoner and return forthwith to their company.

"But if we don't catch up with 'em, Lieutenant?" asked one of the men.

"Then turn him over to the first officer you find in authority. You may be compelled to go as far as Boonsboro."

Morgan was made to mount behind one of the men, and the second trooper followed, his horse's head at the other's tail. The leader struck a trot and soon found his road, moving eastward. In the road, however, the trot was necessarily abandoned, for the mud was above the fetlocks and the foundation was slippery.

The great rains that began on the night of the 4th had proved Lee's advantage and later would prove to be his

peril. The Maryland mud, coupled with uncertainty, prevented the swift pursuit which the President, in agony of
suspense, urged upon his general. Lincoln's belief that
the rebels could not move more rapidly than the Federals
was borne out neither by facts nor by valid theory. In
retreating, Lee had one purpose ; in advancing, Meade
must have many ; besides, the retreat was conducted with
infantry leading, cavalry marching in rear ; the advance
necessarily was in reverse order, so that the Confederate
infantry had the advantage of roads wet enough in all
conscience, but not cut and churned into the loblolly
through which Neill's division was forced to splatter behind their own and their enemy's cavalry. So the bulk
of Meade's infantry was diverted from a direct pursuit of
the Confederates, and made a flank march to Middletown
through mud and slush, a slow march and painful because
of greater destitution than the Union troops often experienced. Though Buford and Kilpatrick had marched with
sufficient rapidity to bring Stuart to action, they had not
succeeded in defeating him. Stuart and the mud gained
Lee the great position of Hagerstown where the swollen
Potomac held him for a week.

"Say, Locke," said the rear-guard, "you lead out o'
this. Git out there on the right. Dam'd if ever I saw
such a mess."

"How the hell you expect me to climb that fence ? "

They were in a closed lane, on the left a fence of stone,
on the right, one of rails. The progress was the slowest
walk.

"Well, we might jest as well go on back," said the

rear. "Them fellers is five mile ahead before now, an' a-gainin' ground. If they got any sense at all, it's more'n we got, an' they tuck to the hard ground, you can bet your bottom dollar on that. Say, Locke, you halt."

"What for?"

"You halt, an' I'll show you. Look out for that Johnny now, an' I'm a-goin' to let down a gap."

"All right, Sam ; that's talkin'."

Sam rode to the rail fence and speedily lowered it so that the horses could step over.

The march was now better, yet the hoofs sank into the soil of a ploughed field. The leader guided right and left, seeking avoidance of the bog, and soon cried out, "Struck a good un, Sam," as the hoofs rang upon a stony, unploughed path stretching directly downhill before them.

The hill in front, wooded, obscured the moon. Locke's path as yet had diverged but little from the fence, and it was true policy to keep this path until its course should change. The horses trotted.

The prisoner had not spoken, neither had his guards addressed him a word. These were three veterans; curiosity as to unknown individuals was not a strong point with any of the three.

The woods on the hill were now distant but little more than a stone's throw. Locke cried back, "Guess you'll have to let down another gap, Sam."

But a moment more and he brought up at a stone fence.

"I'll be dam'd ! Let's go to the left an' git in the big road again."

But his horse floundered.   Sam tried it ; his horse
sank above the knees and was made to scramble out.

The weary horses stood still, and for the time neither man
spoke ; both were debating one and the same question.

" Be *damned* if I go back," said Locke at last.

" Then we got to go on down this rock fence till we git
some place."

" No, *sir !* Cock your pistol, Sam, an' I'll manage this
business."

The leader dismounted, and Morgan could hear behind
him the ominous click that had been commanded ; yet he
had hope . . . but it was gone in the next instant as he
saw Locke carefully thrust his left hand through his
twisted bridle reins.

Locke was now standing at the fence ; he gave a strong
push against a topmost stone ; its outward fall was followed by a loud splash.   He leaned against the fence,
peering over.   The shadows of the wood on the hill
were receding toward the east.   Locke's head was in
the moonlight.

" Sam, I'll swear the's a bluff here ten foot."

The rear gave no response.

Locke remounted.   The rear-guard returned his pistol
to its holster.

The leader urged his horse to the right, finding better
ground.   Now and then he rode to the fence and looked.
Men and horses were in the moonlight.   It must have
been almost two o'clock, Morgan thought, little more
than an hour until daybreak.

The fence at their left stretched southward.   Morgan

could not believe that this course would be kept long;
his guards would soon make other decision unless an
opening should be seen. The prisoner, weary, almost
hopeless, found himself debating what he should have
done and should yet do in Locke's place.

There came a halt. Locke was again peering over the
fence.

"What you see now?" asked Sam.

"I believe we might risk it."

Morgan himself could see, beyond the fence, the flat
sandy margin of a narrow stream.

Locke dismounted, bidding his comrade guard the prisoner. Now the stones fell rapidly and made no splashing
sound. In two minutes the passage had been effected.
Locke went forward afoot, leading his horse down the
stream to the right, searching for a safe place to ford.
The stream wound this way and that.

Again Locke halted. "Guess we can make it," he said.
"Won't do to go on this way all night; already lost half
a mile."

He mounted and headed his horse into the water, which
proved of little depth.

On the eastern side the party turned left, in order to
regain the road. After a few yards they struck into a
bridle-path, which Locke began at once to follow, for it
seemed to stretch due eastward over the hills, and he knew
not what marsh might stop him if he should continue to
ascend the flat. They were making good speed; and
soon the path joined a wider one, and Locke urged forward yet faster, believing his course correct — merely

believing, for zigzagging here in the wooded hills allowed
no real knowledge of this road.

On top of the hill the leader paused, for the moon was
now at their left oblique, while the road turned sharply to
the right.

"By God!" he exclaimed.

"What's the matter with you now?"

"Goin' straight southwest," he sighed. "And I'll bet
you that ever since we left that dam fence we've been
a-goin' round and round."

The horses stood motionless, with drooped heads ; they
had had but little rest in the past two days. Their
shadows were almost in the road at their front.

Sam spoke: "Locke, seems to me this road's just
a-turnin' up to some house on the hill. S'posin' we ride
on a piece an' see?"

For lack of better Locke started, and to his great joy
soon proved the soundness of his comrade's conjecture.
They rode up to the gate of a large dwelling.

"Hello! hello! hello!" shouted the leader, at each
successive syllable ascending the scale and exerting more
his lungs.

"Dam it, Locke, if the's a gang o' rebs in two mile,
you'll bring 'em down on us!"

"Hello! hello! hello!" Locke repeated, as though
Sam's comment was utterly unworthy of serious thought.

Footsteps were heard, and then the noise of an opening
door.

"Hello! What chu want?"

"Come out here."

"Who are you?"

"Buford's cavalry."

A man came forward into the moonlight—came hastily.

"Boys, I tell you right now, you better be keerful."

"What about? Anything rotten round here?"

"Well, I tell you right now, you're not as safe as you might be. The' was some men passed by here not half an hour ago, an' I don't know their names."

"How many?"

"Two — two's all I see."

"Oh, well, I guess they're all right; anyway, two men don't count. Which way'd they go?"

"East. One of 'em he comes on to the porch an' wakes me up; an' he was so quiet like about it 'at I knowed he was skeered, an' I says to myself, 'You must be a long ways f'om home,' says I; an' then when he asks me questions, I see at once 'at he wants to know too much."

"Make out his clothes?"

"No, only I see 'at he had a jacket on 'stead of a sack like your'n; an' then they started fust one way, an' then they don't go not more'n ten rod before here they comes a-ridin' back an' goes on east; an' then I says to myself, 'You two fellers is rebs, an' I can see it by your pore hosses,' says I."

"Well," says Locke, "let 'em go. I guess they'd be willin' to let us pass providin' we were willin'. I want to know how to get to Boonsboro."

"Go this way," pointing toward the back track; "a mile from here you'll strike the big road. No way to put you out; all you got to do is just stay on top o' the range an' just foller the plain road, don't matter how it turns. How'd the fight go, up higher ? "

" Went wrong. Johnnies had all the luck. Say, where does this end o' this dam road go to, anyhow ? "

" Winds about over the range and strikes for Harper's Ferry, but not all at oncet."

" Harper's Ferry ? Our folks there, or the rebs ? "

" Our'n, I hear ; but I hear a heap o' things that I don't count for Gospel."

They turned back. Locke had no desire to see Harper's Ferry, even though he were sure to find it in the hands of his own people, who were indeed at this time about to seize it. General Kenly would march at sunrise for Maryland Heights, which commanded the town. The Federals had already sent scouting parties in that direction, who had reported the coast clear ; but they failed to see and intercept some of Mosby's men, who, sent into Maryland below Leesburg, had been cut off by the swollen Potomac and had been forced to steal their way at night, by twos and threes, up the river, making for Lee's army on its retreat. On this night Usher West and Tom Baxter had reached the range.

" Hush ! " says Tom, bringing his horse to a stand.

Far in front there were sounds, but so indistinct that the two could only know that a man was speaking. Again the sound was heard ; then there was deep silence that continued long.

" How far, you think ? " asked West.

" A quarter, I reckon."

" Better wait awhile, hadn't we ? "

But at once another sound was heard — that of a horse's footfall.

"Coming?" whispered Baxter.

"Yes."

They dismounted and hid in the thicket; there Baxter remained, and West returned toward the roadside. Before him was an irregular open space strewn with great rocks and low straggling bushes. West lay behind a bush and watched the open. Sounds of hoofs were clear and sharp, more than one horse coming.

A minute later two horsemen came into the moonlight. They were riding abreast, in a slow walk, perhaps wary, possibly weary. They came on until they were against Usher's hiding-place — thirty feet from the road.

"Hello! hello! hello!"

The voice was clear, yet it came from a distance, perhaps the fourth of a mile, for the night was very still. The two horsemen halted and turned their heads, as though to listen.

"Hello! hello! hello!"

"Yanks," said one of the horsemen.

"I'm a-thinkin' so too, George," said the other.

West rose to his feet. At once two pistols were levelled upon him.

"I'm yours truly, boys," he said, laughing; "Usher West."

"What!" exclaimed two voices.

"Yes; come on down here in the woods; I've got Baxter with me."

In the thicket reciprocal explanations followed, showing

on the one part that Sency and Lewis had been sent out
by their colonel to examine the ground between Buford's
left and the Potomac.

"It's all clear below here for two or three miles,
George," says Baxter; "we've just come up that way."

"And what you fellers goin' to do now?" says Joe.

"Got to go up the river till we can get across. They
say Lee's making for Williamsport; and if that's true,
we've got to go there too."

Sency decided to turn back. He must make as early
report as possible; besides, it seemed useless to go on
— he had already found that the Federal cavalry were
leaning north rather than south.

The shouts that the men had heard were no more repeated. The four men rode westward, Sency and West
leading.

"Know the road?" says Usher.

"Yes, just come over it. Big house up here a piece.
We stopped there, but the man gave us nothing. Reckon
we'd better be sly; I think that's just about where we
heard that hello business a little while ago."

"How's all the boys?" asked Usher. "How's Armstrong and Morgan?"

"Both in bad luck, but might be worse. Charley's got
a sword cut on his head, and Morgan's missing since late
yesterday; afraid they've got him."

"Armstrong get it bad?"

"Don't know. Doctor said he wasn't sure any bones
had been cracked, and if they hadn't he'd be all right in
no time, if he could just keep his head cool in this hot

weather; but then he didn't know. They put him in a wagon, and I reckon he's at Williamsport by this time. Old Squire's with him," and Sency gave a great yawn of sleepiness.

"Say, Sency, did you know that Morgan's brother is at our house?"

"At your house? Why, no; how did that happen? I thought they were taking him to Washington." Another yawn.

"Yanks couldn't get through with the ambulance; you know they'd just found out about Stuart's march, and didn't know what to do. They could ha' got through, but didn't know it, so Morgan was left with Father; he's got a Yankee surgeon staying with him."

"And how is he?"

"Better, so the doctor says, but he hadn't said a word up to the night I left."

"When was that? Ah!" and Sency's yawn was stifled in an exclamation.

"Sh —" whispers West, and halts.

"I hear it," says Sency.

"How far, you think?"

"Close by, and coming; between here and that house we passed. Don't you think so, Joe?"

"Boun' to be."

"How many do you make 'em?"

Sency sprang from his horse and put his ear to the ground. An instant more and he had remounted.

"Two," he said.

"Suppose we gobble 'em up," suggested Mosby's man, professionally.

" I'm willing.   I don't want the men, but my horse is in need of repairs, and I'm willing to swap sight unseen."

Sency took command.   He posted Usher West on the south of the road, Baxter and Lewis on the right, all in the bushes, while he remained, sitting his horse, in the open road.

CHAPTER XVIII

BACK TOWARD LOUDOUN

"If they come off safe, call their deliverance a miracle."

— ADDISON.

THE two Federals, with their prisoner, were making good headway on the best road they had yet found, and were nearing the end of their outgoing journey — a mile more, they had been told, would put them in the main road. In a little while they would turn over their charge and then start on the return. As yet there was no sign of day.

The prisoner, actually asleep, his head resting against Locke's neck, was roused by the abrupt jerk with which the guard brought his horse to a stand.

"What's up?" says Sam.

Morgan, dimly conscious, at first awakening, of sudden perplexity in the manner of his guards, quickly became alert. He peered over Locke's shoulder. In front, some fifty yards away, stood a motionless horseman square in the road.

"Don't you see?" asked Locke.

Sam changed position a foot or two, and, as his horse moved, he thought he heard a noise in the brush at the left ; but his attention was distracted at once from this noise by seeing the single horseman begin to turn as though he intended flight.

Locke's first thought had been that the man in his front was a sentinel, posted by whatever Federal command had camped at Boonsboro ; he had expected a challenge, which would have been highly welcome to his ears ; now, seeing the man begin to retire, suspicions assailed him. Of course, in these parts, chances were great that the man was of the right colour — perhaps he was a Federal scout willing to compromise, choosing to slip away rather than run the risk of capture by two men whose degree of unfriendliness could not be accurately estimated at fifty yards under a half-moon. At any rate, the man had begun to retreat, and Locke had no objection to such movement on the part of the unknown. Locke had drawn his pistol, and he still held it as he again rode on.

But the singular horseman had made less than a hundred feet before he halted ; he turned his horse and faced the Federals once more.

" Who comes there ? " cried the stranger.

Locke had now heard the wished-for challenge, yet he felt a cold shiver run from the centre of his spine in contrary directions and back — not at the words, or at the tones, but merely at the low pitch of the man's voice. For an infinitesimal moment he considered. The reply to a challenge should be immediate ; but Locke was not thoroughly prompt. Never in his previous experience had he been challenged in a voice so little above a whisper ; yet he must speak, and he opened his lips ; but before he had made a sound there came to him a repetition, nay more, three repetitions of the challenge.

"Who comes there?"

Right, left, and rear, the low voices had sounded.

Sam turned, and saw a horseman blocking his way. From both sides came the noise of hoofs, sounds hardly heard in the greater noise of rustling leaves and boughs.

Morgan threw his arms around Locke. "Better take it quietly," he said; "you've treated me well enough, and I'll speak a good word for you." Then he called out, "Come on, George!" for he had recognized Sency's voice.

There was no clamorous rejoicing by the rebels; neither, on the other part, was there any weak display of sorrow. A veteran cavalryman looks to be made a prisoner no less than he expects to take prisoners; the only surprising sensation was the wonder common to Morgan and his friends at the unexpected meeting. The Federals were stripped of their arms and turned loose afoot without even the pretence of exacting a verbal parole, and the party, now five men with one led horse, made their way toward the cavalry lines.

"Boys," says Morgan, "what are these horses worth? I want both of 'em."

"Not worth much," says Sency. "I thought I was going to get a good swap, but I reckon I'll hold on to my own."

"How much are they worth?" repeated the sergeant.

"But whose are they?" asked West.

"You and Baxter could claim 'em."

"We never would ha' bothered with 'em if we had

been alone. I reckon they belong to the Confederacy. Joe and George were on regular duty."

"What do you say, George, you and Joe?"

"I think at least half the business is Baxter's and West's."

So said Joe Lewis, also.

"Well," says Usher, "neither one of 'em is much punkins of a horse. I reckon Morgan himself has a right to one of 'em, seeing that he's just lost his own in this same night's scrape. Maybe the other belongs to Tom and me. What do you want him for?"

"Want him for Charley Armstrong."

"But what are you going to do with him till Armstrong gets well?"

"He'll be well in a couple of weeks; at least I hope so, and if I don't save this mount for him, I can't see where he'll get one. Tell you what I'll do, boys, and I won't do anything else. We'll call that one a token of affection from all you fellows to Armstrong if you'll let me divide a thousand among you for this one I'm on."

The offer was taken. Morgan was rich and obdurate; the other men were poor and receptive.

Inside the Confederate lines, Morgan, Sency, and Lewis reported to their commander. Baxter and West continued toward Williamsport, leading the extra horse that had been voted Armstrong's property. They would see Charley, hand over the horse to old Squire, and as soon as they could would return to Loudoun that they might be ready for Mosby's orders; it was evident that the war would quickly roll back upon Virginia. But at Williamsport they found no speedy way to cross. Boats were crossing, but for a time not even prisoners or wounded were to be allowed a passage to the south side, the need of hurrying supplies, and mainly ammunition, to Lee's hungry men and empty ordnance train demanding the rapid, and therefore exclusive, use of the boats for wagons from south to north. West found Armstrong cheerful, who laughingly professed to have been more scared than hurt. In a mell of charging groups his horse had been killed just as his own head had been almost smashed by a descending sabre, and he had fallen unconscious and entangled. Drawn out by Squire and Barney, and taken to a surgeon who was up to his elbows in blood, his case had been declared serious yet hopeful, and the intense pain which had been prolonged and even increased in the rough journey by wagon, had but augmented his natural fear concerning his condition, which fear was not ended until the 6th, when his head was again and more thoroughly examined and pronounced whole and hard ; so he was almost overjoyed when he learned that his friends had provided him with a new mount.

On the 12th, after many skirmishes, Stuart uncovered Lee's infantry now in position. Armstrong, taken to the south side, was still under the surgeon, but as a rapid convalescent, the more severely wounded having been sent south. West and Baxter also had crossed the Potomac ; they greatly desired to return to Loudoun, but the Shenandoah was very high and they decided to wait.

Old Squire had his hands full and his pockets as well ; the work of foraging for three men and three horses kept

him busy while West and Baxter kept him supplied with
money. Somehow — by hook or crook — Squire had got
eight sections of tent cloth, and the men had rigged up a
shelter more comfortable in this hot weather than a house
would have been, for their fly was under a great oak, and
its sides were all open. But it came on to rain.

Morgan had reported to Stuart concerning the whereabouts and condition of West and Baxter, and the general had expressed gratification. " I'll need those men
shortly," he had said, and had sent them a message, bidding them remain where they were.

A day later Stuart sent for the sergeant.

" Dan, how'd you like to go into Loudoun next week ? "

" At your orders, General. Alone, sir ? "

" Oh, no, a few picked men. Those two men of Major
Mosby's battalion are over yonder yet ? "

" I think so, sir ; I heard yesterday that they were still
staying with Armstrong on the south side."

" Yes, I ordered 'em to stay there ; hold yourself in
readiness, Dan."

This was all that was said at the time, but Morgan
conceived that Mosby's two men were being held back
in order to lend strength to his own expedition into
Loudoun, of which the general had hinted.

Meade's infantry faced Lee's two full days at Hagerstown, but made no general advance. On the night of
the 13th, Stuart covering the retreat, the Southern army
drew back into Virginia. There was the customary skirmishing by the rear-guard, and on the 16th Morgan's regiment lost its commander, the gallant Drake. Repeated

rains had made the roads quagmires and had overflowed the smaller streams, even the Shenandoah being level with its banks.

The Federals crossed the Potomac at Harper's Ferry and below. The relative positions of the two armies were identical with those of McClellan and Lee in the preceding autumn just subsequent to the battle of Antietam. McClellan, in 1862, after long delay, had made the movement which Meade would push with greater promptness and vigour. The contrast in the activity of these two generals, prosecuting the same measures, but with seeming lukewarmness on the part of one and greater energy on that of the other, could not have failed to call forth many criticisms derogatory to McClellan, though it should be remembered in his favour that he had no precedent of experience to guide him as had Meade, who a year later repeated McClellan's movement, and that in 1862 the Shenandoah was easily to be passed by Lee's army. Yet, on the other hand, McClellan's enemy, relatively, was not nearly so formidable as Meade's. It is the common belief that Gettysburg was a field of glorious victory, and that Antietam was in reality a drawn battle, without the honour of success to the Union cause until it became known that Lee had declined a further contest on that field. Yet it would not be difficult to show that the converse was more nearly true: the battle of Antietam gave McClellan over Lee twice the preponderance that Meade obtained by reason of Gettysburg. And in so far as either battle should be regarded as a mere battle, that is to say, for the

moment leaving out of consideration all the moral effect
of the respective campaigns in their termination, it is
hardly too much to believe that Antietam was as great
a day for the Union rank and file as even the Friday at
Gettysburg, and certainly a very much greater day than
Wednesday or Thursday, either or both; for McClellan's
battle reduced his antagonist to a point almost beyond
hopeful defence, while Meade's had scarcely changed its
relative capacity to resist.   The future historian, doubtless, will mark the beginning and place of the Confederacy's military decay not the 3d of July in Pennsylvania,
but the 4th in Mississippi.

Be this and these as they may, the facts remain that
General Lee on the 17th of July found the Shenandoah
impassable except by bridging, and learned that Meade
showed signs of repeating McClellan's movement.   A
rapid march through Loudoun and Rappahannock counties to Culpeper might place the Federal army between
Lee and Richmond, for Lee must perforce march up the
Valley almost southwest in order to effect a crossing at
Front Royal.   True, a pontoon bridge might have been
laid at almost any point on the Shenandoah; but at
what point?   Certainly not at any of the roads that
passed through the northern gaps in the mountains, for
the exits of these gaps could be blocked by Meade's infantry before Lee's could cross the river; and if it should
be determined to cross into Loudoun, Lee must first get
trustworthy information, to be had only by sending men
across the brimming river and beyond the eastern mountains.

On the night of the 17th General Stuart sent for Morgan.

"Dan," he said, "I want you to get into Loudoun County and stay there till you find out something."

The sergeant bowed.

"Major, be good enough to give Sergeant Morgan all the information you can, and all the help you can, too. I am ordered off, Dan — got to go; but Major McClellan will fix you up all right. Take as many of the boys as you think you will need, or, I mean to say, as few as you can get along with. The major'll see you through."

Stuart rode off for a conference with his commander; his adjutant explained fully the intent of the expedition, and gave orders for the detail to be chosen by the sergeant — a detail of but three cavalrymen and four men of the signal corps. And so, on the morning of the 18th, our four friends, accompanied by Baxter and West, with the signal men, and attended by old Squire on a mule that Major McClellan had somehow managed to spare for the enterprise, made their way toward a crossing on the Shenandoah near Meyerstown. Armstrong's head was not well as yet, but he had refused to consider himself unfit for the duty required. Fears were felt that the hot summer sun would do him damage, and the journey was pressed with due regard to his condition, the shadiest ways being chosen, with rests called when he seemed to suffer, so that it was noon when they came in sight of the river. Here West's experience came into service: he rode to the nearest farm-house and demanded the use of a skiff, which after some little temporizing was pointed out in its hiding-place. Three stages landed the party on the eastern bank, the horses swimming, bridles held by the men in the boat.

Two of the signal men had been left upon the west side; the others were to attain some high point on the Ridge whence by smoke they could convey to their comrades the most important tidings. In case of necessity, one must return nearer the river in order to give more detailed information by means of the customary flag signals.

"Now, boys," says West, "you follow me. String out fifty yards apart or such a matter. Better let Baxter come next to me; then Morgan, to look after Charley; then you signal folks, and George and Lewis can bring up the rear."

"Den I's a-gwine to stay by my Mahs Chahley," said Squire.

"No, I want you to stick right by my side," said Usher. "I may want you to go ahead. I reckon I'll show you the devil to-night, Squire."

"I done seed him too many times," said the old man, but he obeyed orders and took his place.

"Now," said West, "everybody must halt whenever he sees his leader halt, and whenever the rear is obliged to make any report you must whistle and every man must repeat and halt, and then close up, and every man must take his cue from his leader; each man must follow on and do what you see the front man do."

Then there followed a display of woodcraft that had

been learned in perilous experience. West mounted and
rode up the river bank under the drooping trees, his horse
sometimes up to the belly in water. East was a great
field, with a road fenced on both sides running toward
the mountain through the open. No distant eye must see
this procession. The leader went on, frequently making
progress with great difficulty, until he reached a point
opposite the northern boundary of the field; here he
halted. He looked back and saw that Baxter had halted,
Squire's horse almost at the side of his own. He dismounted, gave the negro his bridle, and went forward
afoot, commanding Squire to be still. He was gone long,
possibly half an hour, but when he returned he seemed
satisfied. Remounting, he led on again, eastward now,
flanking the field, slowly ascending the wooded foot-hills.
At one place where the trees were sparse he dismounted
and walked forward, so handling his bridle that the body
of his horse intervened between himself and open ground.
Squire imitated the movement. Ever winding about —
south, east, north, sometimes even west — the leader went
on, his speed varying in accordance with the nature of
the ground and according to his estimate of the degree
of security from observation — a compound of conditions
evasive of mathematics and void of resolution to everything but experience coupled with delicate instinct. At
length he halted and ordered Squire to ride back and
tell all the men to close up.

Then he spoke to the signal men. "You see that bald
spot over yonder across the gulch? From that place your
flags can be seen by your men over the river."

" But how the devil can we ever find that spot again ? "

" By this tree," said West ; " I've come out of the way
to bring you to this big pine; it's the biggest one about
here. I noticed that spot and the pine when we left your
men back yonder. I suppose you'll have no trouble if
you can get here ? "

" Oh, no ; if we can get here, we can get over yonder;
but we must look out now for more guide-posts."

" Yes, all we've got to do is to find other points from
which you can see this tree ; but, mind you, don't go to
blazing any path."

And the winding way was resumed, Armstrong, here
in the woods, keeping bravely up.

Now they were at such a height that when vision was
open to the southwest the smoke of Lee's great camps
was visible above the Limestone Range, and once, when
the prospect was north, Morgan was almost sure that he
saw smoke rising from Meade's, near Harper's Ferry, an
opinion he was ready to revise on the next day. The sun
was setting, but the crooked march continued, with now
and then a pause in which West showed some natural
waymark to the signal men. Sharp ascents were made,
the riders dismounting. Though the peaks were still in
the sunlight, West knew that darkness would fall quickly.
He was yet far from the point he had wanted to reach ;
but as the gloom came on he stopped in a heavily wooded
gulch, where a clear streamlet was trickling over the
stones, and ordered all to close up.

" Got to camp, Morgan. Can't go any farther to-night,
unless we all take it afoot."

Morgan readily assented; he was more than willing because of Armstrong. They had brought forage and rations, and West allowed a fire, for the ravine was so environed with wood and peak that little fear was felt. Squire made a great bed of leaves for Armstrong, who, now that the stress of the day's journey was over, had scarcely strength to move. The halt had not come too soon.

After a hurried meal, West took Morgan aside.

"I ought to see to-night what's on the Hillsborough and Harper's Ferry road, and I'd better take old Squire with me."

"Hard work, Usher; better rest and go on to-morrow."

"No; you see I know where to find a man. The major keeps a man on the lookout in these parts. I don't know who's there at this time, but there ought to be somebody. And if anything has happened, you know we can't get word back too soon."

"Can you find your way back?" asked Morgan.

"Not to-night. See that moon? She'll be down long before I can start back. But it won't matter; I'll get back before sun-up."

"All right. Do what you think best," said the sergeant.

Armstrong was asleep. Usher West bade Squire to follow, and started across the mountain afoot. He was apparently unarmed, and Mosby's men wore no uniform — except upon occasion. For half an hour West went on as rapidly as possible, making the most of the moonlight, now and then pausing to look at the stars. The way was extremely rough, but at length he struck into a travelled road, and here their further progress would be a descent. They had reached the greatest elevation of this obscure gap.

"Squire," said West, halting, "you must lead now."

The speech had hardly ended when from far away came to their ears a familiar sound — directly from the east it floated — the sound of a bugle.

Squire muttered a prayer.

"Yes," said Usher, "they're there; but we must try it. Go ahead, Squire, and go mighty slow; as soon as you see anything skeery slip back and let me know."

The old man's teeth chattered, but he went forward down the road, Usher following at twenty paces.

* * * * * * *

On this day four of Meade's infantry corps had crossed to the south side of the Potomac, and his cavalry had advanced far into Loudoun. Captain Freeman's company was on the Hillsborough road.

CHAPTER XIX

IN THE MOUNTAINS

"What, a play toward! I'll be an auditor;
An actor too, perhaps, if I see cause."
—SHAKESPEARE.

"WHAT the hell do they mean?"

Captain Freeman had risen to his feet; he looked angry, or rather acted anger, his change of expression being unseen in the dim light of the fire which Barney, supper long over, had allowed to die.

"I guess they've got no notion that we are in any danger. Fellow was practising a little, I suppose." Lieutenant Brock was the speaker.

"Send a man back to Colonel Smith and beg him to see that that bugler is stopped. Beg him to allow no noise at all. He ought to have known better, dam it!"

Brock called a sergeant and gave orders. Smith's command, half a mile in rear, must not imperil the safety of Freeman's company, the advance guard.

Freeman sat down. "I don't like it, Brock. If there's a rebel scout in two miles he'll know how to bring his gang down on us. I have half a mind to patrol the road to the west. Yes, I'll do it," he said, again rising. "Sergeant Walker!" he called.

The orderly-sergeant came.

" Send a corporal and six men west. Have them go as far as they can, not to exceed three miles, and order them to be quiet, and to send reports back if they learn anything. And if they suspect any man — farmer, or parson, or pedler, or what not — take him at once and send him in. But you can send me the corporal first. Who is it to-night ? "

" Corporal Cliff, sir."

" Send Cliff to me, Sergeant."

A tall, handsome young man stood before Freeman. Corporal Cliff had but three days previously rejoined his company, wounds received at Kelly's Ford having disabled him for months.

"Corporal, with six men you will patrol the road over the mountain — the road to the west. Mind you now that you don't turn north at the fork — go west on the narrow road. You will find a picket there. You are to remain out until relieved, unless you are forced back. Be prudent. Keep one man out in front as you go, and better make him go afoot. Report everything suspicious — seize any suspicious man you may see — watch the houses — if you find any man returning home, why, take him and send him in."

Cliff saluted and started to withdraw.

"Furthermore," said Freeman, "caution your men against noise. Twenty yards apart. If any man runs from you, let him run ; don't fire. You can't hit anything in the dark, mind you now, and I want no noise. Catch 'em if you can, but make no noise. And be sure

R

you go no farther than three miles — and see always that
your rear is all right."

The corporal and his men were soon at the junction
of the roads. The picket stationed here could tell them
nothing more than they knew ; there had been no cause
for alarm.

Cliff told off his men by number : " Wilson, one ;
O'Donnell, two ; Jones, three ; Hamilton, four; Smithers,
five ; Ledbetter, six. Now, men, go forward by number,
twenty yards apart. Wilson, dismount and let Smithers
lead your horse ; at the first sign of trouble you will fall
back on O'Donnell ; I ride with Jones."

The choice of Wilson was the best possible ; the succession of the other men was without regard to the occasion. Wilson dismounted and went forward slowly, his
carbine resting in the hollow of his left arm. His sabre
made a rattling noise ; he shifted his carbine to his right
hand, and held his sabre steady with the left. Had the
ground been open, the starlight would have been sufficient
to enable him to see every step ; but here on the edge of
the mountain, with great trees overhanging the crooked
road, Wilson felt that he must depend more on ear than on
eye. His foot came down softly, that he might listen even in
the intervals of his strides ; but at each interval he could
hear only the clatter of O'Donnell in his rear, whose horse's
hoofs struck the flinty road without diffidence or respect.
For a mile Wilson bore this annoyance ; then he halted,
and waited for O'Donnell to close up. And now, waiting,
and looking intently ahead, all his mind centred on what
was to be seen, and none of his power wasted in listening,

he was sure that he saw two forms of men in the road before him . . . a second more and they had vanished.

"Come in here ! " he cried, but in a low tone.

O'Donnell was almost upon him, making a noise that rendered oral silence unnecessary.

"O'Donnell, you follow too close," said Wilson. "I'd swear that I saw two men ; but they've gone off. Halt here till Cliff comes up and ask him to spread you fellows out more. I can hear nothing for the noise you make, and anybody in half a mile can hear you coming."

"Begobs, and it's all wan to me, Wilson. And if the carpral says the worrd, Oi'll kape a moile behoint ye, so Oi will."

"Hush ! " said Wilson, peering into the wood. But if anything was there, it gave no further indication of existence. Wilson went on and halted some fifty yards in front of O'Donnell, on whom Jones and Cliff now closed up, while all the rear was closing.

"What's the halt for ? " asked Cliff.

"He wantts me to roide more in resarve. He says twinty paces dhrowns him with me horse so that he hears nahthing but me horse."

"Well, O'Donnell, I guess he's right about it. Keep fifty paces hereafter. You other men, however, may hold to your twenty. That's Captain Freeman's order ; but I guess fifty won't hurt for the first man."

The march proceeded, O'Donnell preserving the new interval.

When the last horseman had passed this spot a hundred yards, two men rose to their feet.

"Close shave, Squire," whispered West.

"Yassah," the negro whispered in return, "an' I knows dat man; I knows him feh true. Didn't shu heah dat Hirish?"

"Yes."

"W'at dat yotheh man call him, Mahs Usheh?" asked Squire in trembling tones.

"O'Connell, I thought," Usher whispered.

"Yassah, hit's mos' lak dat, but dat ain't hit ezackly."

"O'Donnell?"

"Yassah, dat's de ve'y man; an' he b'longs to Cap'm Freeman w'at had me oncet o' twicet befo'e, an' I ain't got no bus'ness wi' dat man no mo'e."

"What Freeman you talkin' about?"

"Mahs Usheh, ain't shu know 'bout dat same cap'm w'at come to ouah house an' tuck away Mahs Dan's brotheh?"

"Yes, but how do you know that he is the same Freeman?"

"I knows it dess 'caze dat same Hirish was wid 'im, an' he knows me too — you ax Mahs Dan an' Mahs Chahley. I went up to 'em in dey camp, an' I tole 'em to come an' git Mahs Dan's brotheh, an' den de nex' day dey got *me*, an' dey ain't got no bus'ness wid ole Squiah no mo'e."

"Lord, Squire, if that's the case, then that fellow that you and Morgan have been talking about so much — that nigger Barney — he's with Captain Freeman, and maybe you'll get to see him again," and West giggled. "He did you a good turn once, and he did Morgan a good turn, and I'd think you'd like to meet up with him."

" *Me?* Now, Mahs Usheh, I dess as soon meet up wi' de debble w'at shu done say I gwine to see to-night. Mahs Usheh, hit won't do to go awn down dis a-way no mo'e."

West saw that the negro was unstrung. " Come on, Squire," he said ; " you have done your part like a man, and now it's my time to lead."

West, with Squire following, crept along the edge of the road ; for an instant he had considered the policy of getting back to Morgan and devising the capture of the few men that he had seen ; but the thought had been abandoned as soon as suggested, for Stuart's purpose must not be hindered. He had learned already that Federal cavalry held the Hillsborough road — cavalry from the army under Meade, no doubt ; it was quite likely that infantry was following, and he wanted to make sure, and quickly, so that information could be sent west of the mountains. A day's delay meant peril to Lee's army.

Soon West turned northward, and, after stumbling through brush, and over rocks, and into ravines, in half a mile he stood on a narrow ledge of rock that overlooked a great scope of country to the east. He believed that somewhere in the flat land before him Freeman's company had gone into bivouac ; but there was no speck of light anywhere on earth. He started again, bending his way westward, Squire close behind him. Neither spoke. For a hundred yards thick bushes gave them difficulty ; then they came out into a narrow cowpath.

" Now, Squire, you must lead again," said West, laying his hand firmly on the old man's shoulder.

" W'at I hatto do, Mahs Usheh ? " asked the negro,
excitedly.

" I'll tell you. Right over yonder, not a quarter, you'll
see a shanty. I want you to go to it, and go round it,
and come back. I want to know who's there."

" Yassah ; how I gwine to fine out ef anybody's in
dah ? Want me to knock at de do' ? "

"No ; you just go all around, and find out if everything's quiet, and come back to me. I'll do the balance."

" De' ain't no dawgs dah, Mahs Usheh ? "

West laughed. " No, there's no dog there. It wouldn't
do to keep one a minute. Go on, Squire ; we must try
to get some sleep before day ; I'll not be far behind you."

The old man went slowly on, his reluctant steps almost
noiseless to West even as he started. Squire had not recovered from the fright that his superstitious mind had
taken on the night at Gettysburg. Armstrong, Morgan,
Sency, and Lewis had all endeavoured to laugh and reason his fears away ; but neither laughter nor simple reasoning could have effect against a credulity stronger than
faith. Squire still felt himself doomed, though he must
have been compelled to admit his own wonder that he
had survived so long.

The negro approached a log hut ; in his front he saw
an open window shutter, and a door partly open. Lying
about the place were half a dozen cows ; he walked very
near them, but they did not stir. There was scarcely a
sound. No fence obstructed, and he stole to the back of
the house, keeping his distance, however. He had not
asked West many questions, inferring that the hut was

the residence or temporary quarters of some one that West knew and wished to see; furthermore, he supposed that West wanted to learn whether his approach would be attended with danger, both of which suppositions were thoroughly correct.

Squire completed his circuit, getting momentarily nearer to the lone dwelling, until, when again he stood in front, his sense of insecurity had been greatly lessened; he had been all round — there seemed no danger here. He came nearer the door, and heard heavy breathing within; he returned to West and reported.

" Now, Squire, stick right behind me and keep a good lookout while I talk with that man in there."

Squire took stand; West went to the door and tapped. The breathing stopped.

West tapped again, and then made a peculiar noise by scraping with his nails against the door. Presently the door swung wide open.

" Who is it? " said a low voice within.

" Come out, Swain," said West, recognizing the voice.

" You, Usher? I thought you were in Maryland. The boys have been anxious about you. Glad you've come; I've been expecting some one."

Swain followed West into the woods, going past Squire who was bidden to remain at watch. Fifty yards from the path they halted, and Swain threw himself on the ground. He was barefoot, and in his shirt sleeves — seemingly in the garb in which he had slept.

" Freeman's cavalry are down yonder," said West, as he sat down.

" Freeman ? Possibly ; and many more. Whole brigades of them have gone on toward Snicker's."

" Where are your arms ? " asked Usher.

" Oh, out yonder," waving his hand ; " I'd have slept
out, too, but for thinking some of you would want to find
me."

" Been anywhere, Swain ? "

" Just come from the river, or as near as I could get
to it. God ! How sleepy I am ! " and Swain gave an
immense yawn.

" Well, out with it. Stuart and Lee want to
know."

" What! You come from the army ? " and Swain sat
up straight, with sudden alertness.

" Yes ; Stuart has sent men over here, and I came with
'em. We've got to find out and report what Mr. Meade
is about, and then go on to the major. Tell me what you
saw at the river."

" Saw ? From the top of Loudoun Height I saw more
men at one time than all General Lee's army."

" On this side ? "

" No — about half on this side ; the others coming,"
said Swain.

" That's all I want to know. You've saved me a lot
of hard work, Swain. Saw 'em this morning ? "

" Yes, and they kept coming in two columns, — one
toward Hillsborough, and the other from Berlin. I can't
say for certain, but I believe all of Meade's army will be on
this side by to-morrow night. I saw at least half of it,
I should think, and they were marching south, evidently

to make room for more — camping in Sweet Run Valley," and Swain once more lay back on his elbow.

" You say cavalry has gone to Snicker's ? "

" Gone in that direction ; I haven't been there. Lord ! How sleepy I am ! "

" And where is the major ? " West asked.

" At . . . well," says Swain, yawning drearily, " I name no names. Remember where we found him on the fifteenth of last month ? "

" Yes."

" He's there and will be there till next Saturday, unless something disturbs his plans. You know who looks out for him there, don't you ? "

" Yes ; hadn't you better be a-movin' ? "

Swain was silent, and Usher repeated the question, shaking his companion's knees. " Oh, I heard you ; I wasn't asleep," Swain said. " I thought I'd make a start to-morrow. I certainly must get away before all that infantry shuts me off."

" How long you been here ? "

" Relieved Simpson on the fourteenth."

" And you are to go without being relieved ? "

" Yes — I'll report to the major, and if he wants to send me back, well and good ; but Meade's advance makes this post useless, and another on Bull Run the necessary thing." The last words had been said in tones of increasing sleepiness ; perhaps Usher guessed them from their connection.

" Why not go with *us ?* "

" Well, I take it, Usher, that a man's a good deal safer

at this moment by himself than in a crowd. Now, you
and your friends could hardly be seen without suspicion,
while I am the most innocent clodhopper in the whole
range." Swain's words were now clear, and his tones
were evidence that two seconds of sleep had reënforced
him.

West yawned.

"Whose darky is that you have with you?" Swain
asked.

"Armstrong's," and Usher's voice dropped heavily on
the second syllable.

"What Armstrong? Wake up, Usher! I don't like
darkies. Not one in ten but will give you away."

"Charley. Lives down Middleburg way — you ought
to know him. True as steel."

"But I don't know him, even though I ought. Will
you come in and share my straw pile?"

"Not if I know myself. Much obliged, old man; but
it's a long shot safer in the woods. I've got to make
tracks at daylight so as to get back to my folks; they're
hid over yonder by the knob. Got two signal men with
us — and say, you know George Sency, don't you?"

"Man that was with us last month? struck up with
us over the river, didn't he?"

"Yes, he's along. You won't go with us?"

"No, none of your madding and gadding crowd for
me; I prefer to risk it alone."

The men had risen and were walking toward the hut.

"Well, if you won't go, I hope to see you next week;
you know what Meade's advance means."

" Yes — the Rappahannock," returned Swain.

" And plenty of game in his rear."

" Exactly. I'll be on hand if I keep a whole skin."

" Good-by, Swain."

" Good-by," and the two men clasped hands.

West and Squire plunged again into the woods, but soon halted. It was past midnight, and sleep was necessary. The cautious partisan pointed out a dense clump of cedar bushes and commanded the negro to take his rest ; as for himself, he chose different quarters — even this little force must be divided lest by untoward accident disaster befall them both. He explained to Squire that Meade's army had crossed the river, and commanded that, in case he should be compelled at daylight to run for it, he must make his way back to Morgan with his information. Then he went some ten rods from Squire and slept.

*　　*　　*　　*　　*　　*　　*

Captain Freeman's uneasiness had not been entirely relieved by the departure of the squad under Corporal Cliff, and he decided to send out single scouts northwestward. He commanded Sergeant Walker to summon privates Hawley and Beecher.

" Men," he said, when they stood before him, " I want you two to see that we shan't be surprised from that mountain," pointing. " I know it's not your time for duty, but I have chosen you because I need good men, and I'm going to give you full credit with interest for what you do to-night. Hawley, leave your horse and arms, except your pistols, and go in that direction ; go two miles, or at least a mile and a half, and hold yourself quiet there until sunrise unless you find something. Beecher, you do just as Hawley, only you must go more to the north — understand, both of you?"

"How far apart should we be, Captain, when we take a stand?" asked Hawley.

"Well, say half a mile, and go at once."

They started and held together until they reached the picket-post. Here they agreed on separate directions, determined by two stars, and proceeded apart.

Private Hawley went straight northwest, that is to say, as straight as he could go, considering the obstacles that lay in his course. This man was thought to be the best scout in Freeman's ranks, and he valued his honours. Moreover, he had courage as well as skill, yet on this night he regarded the work outlined for him superfluous; the enemy were known to be west of the Shenandoah, cavalry and all, so his courage was not even to be tested, and he went along utterly void of apprehension. Of course, he would obey orders. He would reach a point on the mountain a mile and a half away, or such a matter, and would take his stand, and remain till sunrise; but he yawned as he went, for he had been waked from sound and insufficient sleep.

At length he decided that he had come far enough; he leaned for a while against a tree. Out here on the wooded mountain there was nothing to interest him; even the stars could not be seen. The night was very calm. Hawley's sense of security and the utter uselessness of this duty yielded in no degree to loneliness and the mystery of a place that would perhaps have made timid men more timid. He had no fears; he sat down, and when he waked the daylight was beginning to show. He rose, stretched himself awhile, and began to walk slowly away. By the time he should get anywhere, at this slow rate, the sun would rise. He had begun really, though he did not admit it, to return to camp.

A dense clump of cedar bushes obstructed his way . . . he moved around . . . he started back, and his hand went to his pistol. Then stooping, he saw under the spreading boughs. "Come out o' that!" he cried, — and old Squire crawled out, shivering with fear.

Hawley had covered the negro with his pistol, but at once had compassion, for the old man's terror was painful even to him who caused it.

"Mahsta, I ain't a-doin' nothin' wrong; I dess be'n a-sleepin' heah, Mahsta."

"Who are you? Where do you belong?"

The lowering of the pistol had restored to Squire some degree of reason. His first thought had been that his impending death was here; had the muzzle still threatened, perhaps his paroxysms of continued terror would have brought complete confession through inability to devise any theory of self-defence; but now, with a possibility manifest that clemency was not repugnant to his captor, his mind went to the fact that Freeman was near, and to the likelihood that this Federal was one of Freeman's men.

"Me? I ain't nobody but ole John, Mahsta! I dess be'n out sheah a-lookin' up de cows in de mounting; ain't shu seed some stray cows, Mahsta?"

"Cows be damned ! You get before me and march."

" Yassah ; w'ich a-way you want me to go, Mahsta ? " and at each word old Squire's voice was higher, and he seemed on the point of breaking hysterically.

" Down the mountain ! That way ! Turn, now, and step out quick ! "

" Suppose *you* turn ! " said a low voice just behind him.

Impossible not to obey ; impossible, as well, not to obey West's further commands. Hawley threw down his pistol, which West kicked toward Squire who at once seized upon it. Then the Federal's other pistol was demanded.

There was now the broad light of day.

West reflected ; then he said, " Squire, you know — but come here."

At the word *Squire* both Hawley and the negro had started, the one with recognition, the other with fear of contingencies in the unknown future. Possibly the old man would not have sorrowed had West slain his prisoner on the spot.

Squire came near, and West, with finger on trigger and eye on his captive, whispered, " Go to the house and tell Mr. Swain to get away ; tell him about this business : hurry ! "

Squire darted through the bushes.

" Well, what do you mean by this caper ? " asked Hawley.

" I mean to prevent you from interfering with my business," was the reply.

" Yes, and you'll ketch hell for it. I'm obeyin' my orders, and you're opposing the authorities of the United States, and you'll ketch hell for it."

West kept his temper; he saw that his own quality was a matter of doubt to the Federal, and he had no wish to relieve the doubt as yet.

" You'll ketch hell! And I'll tell you another thing, young man; your neighbours will ketch hell, too, for what you're doing."

Hawley still thought that his captor, in ordinary farmer's clothing, was some dweller on this mountain, yet he was by no means sure; he knew that the clothes do not make the man; if he must remain a prisoner he preferred to be in the hands of a soldier; it would be hard to confess to his comrades that he had yielded to a single civilian. And if Hawley was in a quandary, the Confederate was in a worse one — always excepting the immediate danger pertinent to the situation. He knew not what to do with the Federal, and he knew not what declaration to make of his own character. To allow the man his liberty, would be to invite distress upon the people. Hawley had spoken but too truly : West knew that the neighbours would ketch hell for this deed. Should the prisoner be held, Freeman would miss his man, would suspect the work of bushwhackers, soon or late would take vengeance on the community that tolerated such ; on the other hand, if the prisoner should be turned loose he would at once report and the same consequences would ensue. But West must decide, and he decided.

" Then I shall not let you go very easily," he said.

"What you goin' to do with me?" demanded the Federal.

"I shall send you to Lee's army as a prisoner."

"Pretty big job for one man," says Hawley, with something like defiance.

"One man? You'll soon see."

West's mind had formed its scheme. He continued: "You think me a citizen? I am a regularly enlisted soldier of the Confederate States."

"Then you are a spy."

"No; I am no spy. I have not been in your lines. But there's no use in this talk; you go with *me*."

Squire came up breathless.

"Everything all right, Squire?"

"Yassah."

West ordered his prisoner to march in front and followed with drawn pistol, and in less than an hour brought him into the presence of Morgan's men.

If the Federal was astonished to find himself in the hands of half a dozen well-equipped rebel cavalrymen, he gave no intimation of such feeling. Truth was that he much preferred his present situation to what he had feared, for his mind had been full of the possibility of bad treatment from bushwhackers, but from the moment of his seeing Sergeant Morgan he felt safe, for he recognized in him the prisoner who had escaped from Freeman on the night of the 6th, and that prisoner, certainly, had been no bushwhacker. So, too, had Morgan recognized Hawley, even at once; for the sergeant, being told that Freeman's company was near, felt greater interest in his individual enemies than the Federal could have previously had. Yet neither of these experienced soldiers thought it wise to betray the fact that he knew the other.

Morgan and West held a council, and it was decided that the imperative duty resting upon the signal men in consequence of the alarming news of Meade's advance prohibited their encumbering themselves with a prisoner ; the signal men must get to their work at once, and the captive could not be taken to Lee's army. Moreover, West was strong in his opinion that Hawley should be paroled.

"Of course, Sergeant, I know he won't observe any such parole ; but it will have an effect. He will be more than ever convinced that we are not bushwhackers. What I want, Morgan, is to give him no cause to harry the people ; he has already said the neighbours are going to ketch hell for my work."

"We cannot keep him," said Morgan.

The signal men were getting ready ; they would return to the spot pointed out on the preceding day, wave their information, which their comrades would repeat, and then would recross the river, for both Morgan and West had complete confidence that Swain's news was valid and conclusive. As for Morgan and his men, the very contingency that had come would cause their remaining in Loudoun, Stuart having commanded that in case of Meade's advance the sergeant's little force should not attempt to overtake Lee's army, which would at once march up the Valley ; but should, on the contrary, attach itself to Mosby, not only for its own protection, but also

s

that strength should be added to the major's against the Federals when they should have passed on to the Rappahannock. No, it was impossible to hold the prisoner.

"Well, Usher, we'll let him loose on parole ; but suppose he won't accept?"

"Then we must let him escape," said West.

But Hawley showed no reluctance to give his parole, which in duplicate was written out in form as accurate as the sergeant could remember, and was willingly signed.

So Hawley started eastward afoot, and at once Morgan's party began to move south, while the signal men went west, — Morgan intent upon heading around Freeman and all other Federals, and getting to Mosby before the enemy's advance should cut him off.

And Squire had little comfort in the knowledge that his own name would once more get to Freeman's ears.

CHAPTER XX

A HOME-COMING

" What think you ? have you beheld,
Or have you read or heard ? or could you think ?
Or do you almost think, although you see
That you do see ? Could thought, without this object,
Form such another ? "

— SHAKESPEARE.

MEADE'S advance was pushed without opposition to Warrenton, where his headquarters were established on the 24th. On the same day General Lee, with Longstreet's corps, reached Culpeper. On the night of the 18th, while Freeman's small force had been in bivouac near Hillsborough, Pleasonton's cavalry held Snickersville, Bloomfield, and Upperville, and a brigade had already passed on to occupy Ashby's Gap.

Before Morgan and his men had ridden three miles on the morning of the 19th they learned from citizens that Snickersville was in the hands of the Federals, with the whole country near the eastern slope of the Ridge under their power. Too great discretion might have determined the little party to remain hidden in the mountains until night, but West was confident that he could get across the roads on which the bodies of Federals were moving. He reasoned that as yet the eastern side of Loudoun Valley was comparatively clear of the Federals, so that the only great danger of the journey would come almost at the start; better make the movement at once ; the delay of a few hours might fill the Valley with enemies. Morgan also believed that once across the roads that connected the gaps of the Blue Ridge the party might feel reasonably safe ; while he shared but little in Usher's desire to speedily join Mosby in order to make use of the great opportunity for reaping glory and spoil when Meade's army should have passed on to the Rappahannock, the condition of his brother, whom it was now possible to see again, had become a subject of deep interest, and he required but little urging to take what proved in the end a successful if not the wisest course.

In the meanwhile Private Hawley, after wandering over the mountain as West had counted upon, succeeded in reaching camp, where he found that the company had marched to Purcellville, Captain Freeman having left O'Donnell with orders to wait a given time for the missing man.

" And it's yerself that's been getting yer purty face torn — and yer hands torn — and yer breeches all torn, and making the captain as mad as a hornet wid je."

"Couldn't help it, O'Donnell. I've seen hell, and I don't know how it's going to end."

" Faith, and hell shall niver see the day whin she shuts up shop."

"Do you know a man named Squire?" Hawley's intonation revealed certainty of the reply.

"That dam black naygur, ye mane?" and O'Donnell's eyes met his questioner's with a demand for more than the words required.

"Yes, that's exactly who I mean. And I want to know if you remember a man that you called your number eighteen."

"And hwat d'ye mane be assking me that, now? Why cahn't ye say hwat ye're going to say and have done with ut?"

"Well, I've seen both of 'em, and I've seen more. I'm a paroled prisoner," said Hawley, with dignity.

"D'ye mane ut?"

"I mean it. I was in the hands of a party of six rebels, and that nigger was with 'em, and they were under Sergeant Morgan, and he's your number eighteen. It's true, by — !" and Hawley held up his hand, and looked very solemn.

"And how did ye get yerself caught, if ye plaise, Misther Hawley?"

"To tell you the straight truth, O'Donnell, it was all along o' that dam nigger," replied Hawley, shaking his head. "I had him; I got him dead, an' was bringing him back, and all of a sudden I found myself looking into the barrels of half a dozen carbines. I tell you the fact, O'Donnell, I was never so skeered in all my life."

"The farchune of warr, Misther Hawley. And ye say, do ye, that me frind Squoire it was that paroled ye?"

"Oh, go to hell! You know better'n that."

"Oi do, sor; Oi know betther; but hwat Oi mane to impress uponn ye, Misther Hawley, is that wanst ye

spurned me wid ridicule whin Oi made me claim to that
same Squoire as me own take, and ye said ye had killed
him.   Remimber that now, Misther Hawley!"   The
charge was delivered with a smile designed as a crusher.

"Yes, I'm compelled to admit that I was wrong in
that," returned Hawley; "but I was telling you that
they paroled me."

"And ye say it was the inimy's cavalry it was that did
ye that koindness, Misther Hawley?"

"Yes; they were a squad of Stuart's men, I suppose.
Didn't you hear that Captain Freeman wormed it out of
Squire that he belonged to a man in Fitz Lee's brigade?"

"Sure, and Oi've been told that same."

"I don't believe they knew what to do with me,
O'Donnell. At first I was afraid I'd got into a gang of
bushwhackers; but they showed up all right, — gray
uniforms, carbines, and everything. Same man you had
over yonder — that same sergeant — wouldn't give his
right name then — Morgan's his name. I've got his
parole in my pocket, and he's got my name in his pocket;
but if I've got any sense, his parole is not worth a dam,
and Freeman's not a-going to recognize it. I wish he
would, but he won't," and Hawley sighed.

"A sergeant, ye say? And sure me number eightain
was a sergeant. But Oi tell ye that Captain Frayman is
not the man to swallow such a parole; no, no, Misther
Hawley, we're not to lose the great pleasure of yer
sosoity for anny sergeant's parole. Make up yer mind to
that at wanst, and save yerself from suspinse. And ye've
had good luck, Oi say, in getting away so loightly. Me

number eightain thraited ye mighty well intirely, Misther
Hawley; did ye say they wor aiger for ye to go?"

"I thought so. They were ready to move, and I thought
they wanted to get rid of me. There was one time when
I was afraid they'd put me out of the way; they treated
me all right, though."

The foregoing version of the adventure was repeated
to Captain Freeman, who demanded Hawley's duplicate
parole and examined it.

"Aha! First Virginia! Then I suppose Fitz Lee's
crowd has crossed over. Sergeant D—or is it a D?
Yes, a D. Sergeant D. Morgan, First Virginia cavalry.
Why, Hawley, this thing is not worth the paper it's written on. You will get back to your duty, man."

"Then I must ask you to protect me in this, Captain."

"Protect? I tell you to get back to your duty. A sergeant has no right to administer such an oath as this. Such
authority is high. It must come with high command.
If it should be the case that a man who violated such a
pretended thing as this were taken again and maltreated
in any way, General Meade himself would see after it."

"Yes, sir, I suppose so; but it wouldn't do me very
much good if they had already shot me."

"Do you want *me* to assure you? My dear fellow,
just hold me responsible. But there's not a particle of
danger. And you're lucky in not being sent to some rebel
prison; and if you feel ticklish about it, and happen to get
caught again, just follow that sergeant's example and give
'em some other name. Morgan—Morgan," continued
Freeman, soliloquizing, "I'm not sure that's a D. It may

be an O, or it may be a D, and more likely D than O. But what does it matter?" Then, quickly, to Hawley, "You say Squire was with these people?"

"Yes, sir."

"How can you be sure? Did you see him when we had him at Rowser's? See him in good light?"

"No, sir, I didn't see him there, except in the dark; but the rebels this morning called his name more than once."

"Ah! By Jupiter, *Morgan!*"

Captain Freeman put the paper into his pocket-book; afterward he showed it to Lieutenant Brock, who also was puzzled concerning the first initial. Brock thought the letter was an L, with a long upward stroke to the tail. The whole thing had been written with pencil, and showed effects of unclean friction.

"Brock, there hasn't been a word from Lacy or about him since we left him down yonder."

The lieutenant recognized in his own mind the association of ideas that had called up Freeman's remark. The name Morgan and the name Squire were coupled on this day with as great distinctness as formerly they had been by Dahlgren, and previously by Squire when he had visited Freeman's bivouac with the purpose of arranging for the delivery of the wounded Morgan. These compound coincidences could not be accidental.

"It's a tangle, Captain."

"Don't you suppose Lacy's got away from West's long ago?"

"It has been very nearly a month, sir, and the road to Washington has been open all the time."

"But Doc wouldn't move an inch if he thought it would hurt his patient."

"No, and he may be there yet. But would you suppose that Lacy has found out that he's been nursing the wrong man?"

"It wouldn't make a dam bit of difference; he'd just keep on with his nursing. And I'll tell you what I'm going to do, Brock. Just as soon as we get in reach of that place I'm going there, and, if I can't go, then I'll send somebody. I'm going to see who that man *is*. It'll take a positive order from Pleasonton to keep me back. And if that nigger knows what's good for him, he'll never let me lay hands on him again."

From Purcellville Captain Freeman marched his command to Philomont, and on the 22d he was ordered to occupy Aldie, his scouts reporting the road clear. By this time the most of Meade's infantry had passed south and reached the line of the Manassas Gap railroad, and Freeman was practically in the rear. And though the captain's duties were not light, extraordinary vigilance having been urged by headquarters lest attacks be made upon the long wagon trains by enterprising partisans supposed to be ready to seize upon such prey, yet he found time to keep his word so emphatically pronounced to Lieutenant Brock.

* * * * * * *

By the virtue of hard riding at short times, long rests at others, and close watching always, Usher West had succeeded in reaching the point in Goose Creek swamp nearest his home, and had hidden his companions far from any

road, Baxter, however, going on to see how the land lay
with his own people and affairs, and to learn, if possible,
the whereabouts and purposes of Major Mosby.

As night fell on the 23d West set out alone for home —
alone, for although both Morgan and Armstrong were
intensely anxious concerning conditions at the farm-house,
yet it was felt that it would be too great a peril to be
seen by Lacy, who by all means must be prevented from
suspecting that Usher was other than he pretended to be.
So, in an hour's time, West had covered the distance and
had hitched his horse, and was approaching the rear of
the dwelling when he heard the sounds of riding and
men's voices in the front yard. He stopped short, but
soon felt confident that the men were leaving. He went
on and was about to go up the back steps when he
thought it possible that the departure of the visitors had
not been final. In this doubt he went round the house
toward the room — his own — which he knew the Federal
Morgan had occupied almost a month ago; approached
the window through which Tom Baxter had spoken to
Dr. Lacy. Usher cursed his fate, and the Yankees yet
more, that he should be compelled to act like a thief at
his own father's door; but secrecy had become a great
part of his profession, so that in itself the measure was
distasteful only because of the time and labour involved,
and he went on slyly past the window, beyond the light,
in order to make a complete circuit of the house, in which
he now heard the voices of strange men. He stood for a
short minute behind the corner of the dwelling, and saw
toward the front two horses hitched at the fence, and heard

the noise of hoofs down at the Aldie pike, and knew by these combined sights and sounds that Federals were visiting the house — probably officers, for the men down at the road had been stationed there as pickets, doubtless, to protect persons of importance. West now went oñ entirely around the house. His sister's window was alight, yet he feared to speak ; there might be guards out in this direction. He went back to the lot and into the farm road, and found all safe; seemingly the front was the only quarter concerning which the visitors felt any fear.

He again came to the window of his room ; he bent down and knelt, with all his body in the shadow; he could not see, but he could hear.

" Never was so astonished in my life."

" That is what every one says when he is surprised." This voice the listener recognized at once as Dr. Lacy's.

" Yes, I know it ; but I maintain it. Never in all my life have I heard a thing so surprising. Why, do you know that I had your brother in my hands hardly two weeks ago? Oh, he's a sharp one! Just slipped through my hands like an eel. What do you think of it, Brock ? "

" Very much as you do, Captain. I've read of such resemblances, but never gave them any credit."

" But, gentlemen," this was a new voice, and not nearly so loud as the others, a voice familiar to Usher, who, if he had not known otherwise, would have believed that Sergeant Morgan was speaking, " gentlemen, if you are so astonished, what do you think of *my* sensation ? "

There was a laugh, and mingled with it the words of the first speaker: "But won't I have one on Dahlgren! You know Dahlgren, Lieutenant?"

"Yes; what has he to do with it?"

"Oh, by the way, I'm afraid we won't see the poor fellow any more. He was knocked down over at Hagerstown two weeks ago, and I'm told he has lost his leg."

"Ah? I'm exceedingly sorry to hear that. Indeed, I am deeply grieved. There are many men of higher rank that the army might better afford to lose. Poor old fellow; I've been with him in more than one close place. And now he's done for?"

"Completely out of the ring hereafter. But I started to tell you about him. He met me over in Maryland the day after we left you here, and swore that he had just talked with you for fully an hour. Ha! ha! Knew all about you! Called you Junior."

"Now, come, Captain. He said a quarter of an hour."

"No difference, Brock. An hour or a quarter—it's all one and the same. And he had a tale to tell about meeting that old nigger Squire, who seems to be your precious rebel brother's shadow—and the old rascal did nothing but confirm what Dahlgren thought he knew. I must find Dahlgren's address."

"That Squire is a remarkable man," drawled Lacy. "I am told by the . . . I am told that he is noted throughout this county for more than one quality."

"He got away from my men at Rowser's, and he deceived Dahlgren, and the other day he turned up again,

still following your brother, Lieutenant. Your brother,
who seems to be a sergeant, caught one of my men, who
had previously caught Squire ; and then the sergeant
paroles my man — by the way, I have that document.
. . . Here it is. Of course I couldn't recognize such
an irregular thing."

There was silence now. . . .

" Let me see that paper," said the doctor. . . . " What
is the irregularity here, Freeman ? "

" In the fact that a sergeant exacts a parole."

" And you have ordered the man not to observe this ? "

" Yes, certainly, Doc ; would you observe such a
thing ? "

" I think that if I were a prisoner, and in order to be
released I gave my pledge to fight no more till exchanged,
I should keep my word," said Lacy, with some heat.

" I'll leave it to Lieutenant Morgan himself. He
knows something about such authority. Has a sergeant,
in command of a squad out on a scout, the authority to
grant and accept paroles ? "

" No," said Morgan, slowly, " unless such authority
has been expressly delegated ; and even then I should
hesitate to declare that a non-commissioned officer would
have such power."

" Stuart himself took four hundred of our men — I
believe it was on the very day Dahlgren met you — your
brother, I mean — in Maryland," exclaimed the captain,
" and he paroled them, and our authorities ordered the
men back to duty."

" I suppose that was decided upon the ground that

Stuart couldn't keep them, and by paroling them was endeavouring to benefit himself and not us," said Brock.

"Then your man is not to observe this agreement, Freeman?"

"Not in the least, Doc. He's already back in the ranks, and is doing full duty. What's the matter with you, now?"

"I was merely thinking of the ox and bull story, Freeman."

"What's that got to do with it?"

"Why, sir, you agreed to a truce with this very Sergeant Morgan; now it seems to me that the power to negotiate a truce should be great enough to make paroles."

"Ah, Doc, you're nothing if not argumentative. But are you sure that the man who required us to come under flag for the lieutenant was the lieutenant's duplicate?"

"Sure."

"But don't you see, Doc, that in the first case he grants us a privilege which we accept, and in the second he makes an unlawful demand upon us? He requires that we neutralize a force which it was impossible for him to withhold from us. He couldn't keep Hawley, and, being the brother of our friend here, why, he couldn't kill Hawley, so he assumes an authority and paroles him, and his parole is not binding."

"Captain Freeman, was the truce binding?"

"No, certainly not. I'll leave it to the lieutenant; he has been at headquarters long enough to know all about such matters. What do you say, Lieutenant?"

"I should question its force. Of course, however, it ad a force outside of its formal aspect. For instance, if ergeant Morgan had laid ambush for you, and under olour of truce had inveigled you into it and taken your ompany, or fought you at disadvantage, why then great omplications would have resulted. No doubt our generals would have retaliated in some way, and our plea ould have been that the truce had been taken by us as ffered in good faith."

"Yes, but that doesn't show that a sergeant has the ight to parole a prisoner," insisted Freeman.

"But if we do not keep our agreement with him, how an we expect him to keep his with us?" asked Lacy.

"Oh, that old matter is ended. Besides, it never did ise to the dignity of a truce. It was simply a matter f an hour, and for one purpose accomplished within that our."

"Then my patient is liable to seizure at any moment?"

"Certainly. Why should you think he is not, Doc?"

"Mr. West and I discussed this matter when I first ame here, gentlemen, and our conclusion was that the ruce would not be at an end until its purpose was accomlished, which was the safe removal of Lieutenant Iorgan. We accepted a truce offered by the Confedertes; but you see other Confederates — Stuart and his roops — intervened between us and safety, and we were orced to stop here. Mr. West's mind was in a conflict, entlemen. He is firm for the South, and debated whether e ought not to inform the nearest Confederates in order hat my patient's parole might be demanded; but he

withheld because of our discussion, which seemed to him
convincing."

" I'll warrant," cried Freeman, laughing.

" But now," said Lacy, very slowly, " now I find it my
duty to notify Mr. West that our conclusion was wrong,
and that he is at liberty to get Morgan captured."

" Ha! ha! ha! Just like you, old man. But you are
all right now. Did you expect your truce to be eternal? "

" I know what you would say, Freeman; you would
say that even from my view I ought to have continued
my journey just as soon as Stuart gave the road; but you
must remember that we had been forced to abandon our
means, and were unable to proceed."

" Well, it doesn't matter now, Doc. West will hardly
make any extra exertions in the present state of affairs.
Lee is thrown back, and you're in no danger. When can
the lieutenant be moved safely? "

" He might be moved at once, if necessary; but he is
comfortable enough here, and it would be well to wait
until his bones knit more firmly, say two or three weeks."

" Well, Doc, you needn't fear to stay. By all means
tell West if your conscience needs relief. And now we
must be going. Lieutenant, it is clear that that brother
of yours is a character. He grants truces, and accepts
paroles, and goes through Maryland alone where he
deceives General Meade's staff, is captured and escapes,
and he bobs up over here in Loudoun — wonder if he
isn't somewhere near us now. Good-by, and don't let
Lacy talk you to death. If we get any more mail for you,
we'll send it over."

There was shuffling of feet; West slipped back and
remained in shadow until he had heard them strike the
main road and turn eastward. Then he went to his
sister's window. She was bending over her work, in the
dim light of a tallow candle, her face toward him. His
father sat with his back to the light, reading, his arms
wide-stretched, holding a newspaper which doubtless one
of the Federal officers had brought to Lacy. Jennie's
stitches were regular and rapid. Usher fancied that she
was in serious thought — her sewing seemed automatic.

A face showed at the door — Lacy's. The doctor came
in and stood before Mr. West.

"Here is the *Herald*, sir, three days old, and the
Chronicle of yesterday."

"Thank you, Doctor; your friends have gone?"

"Yes."

Jennie had not ceased her work, neither had she otherwise changed, except that her eyes for one instant had
turned toward the door. To Usher she looked very pale.

The doctor withdrew; relations with the family seemed
to have become quite familiar.

Usher came nearer and stood at the window, his face in
the full light, unobserved for a moment; then he coughed.

"Oh!" she exclaimed, greatly startled; but at once
she knew, and threw down her work, springing forward.
Mr. West was deep in his paper.

"Oh, Usher, I'm so glad!"

Mr. West turned and saw, but he kept his seat. He
waved his hand peculiarly, put his finger to his lips, and
shook his head.

T

Jennie retreated, and Usher went into the back yard. She seized his hands and kissed him.

"You are not safe here. Two officers have just gone."

"I know, Jennie, and I can't sleep here; but I'm coming to breakfast."

"Where have you been so long?"

"Over the river, Jennie; I've got some of the boys hidden out, and I must get back. Guess who are with me," he said, patting her cheek.

"Oh, I can't guess. Tell me."

"Have you heard that Charley Armstrong was hurt?"

"No, we haven't heard a word of anything, except that General Lee is in the Valley. Was Charley wounded badly?" Her voice had not changed.

"You are a cool girl. No, knocked on the head with a sabre, that's all. He is with me, and is fretting to see you, but we don't dare let him come up. And Dan Morgan is with me, too."

"Oh, what a story! Now, Usher, you're not in earnest."

"Yes, it's no time to be joking. He's here."

"Does he know his brother is here?" she asked.

"Oh, yes, and may try to see him; but he may be satisfied when I tell him he's getting along all right. I've been here an hour, and heard the talk in my room."

"How could you be so rash? Usher, I'm so afraid for you to come to breakfast," and she caught his hand again.

"I'm coming all the same; haven't had a thing to eat in two weeks. There's not a Yankee nearer than Aldie."

"But they are passing all the time. Please don't come to the house. I'll bring a basket for you down to the spring-house."

"No, I'm coming; and I want your basket, too. My gang's got to be fed. Say, Jennie, do you have any help?"

"Nobody but Father," she sighed.

"Well, Armstrong's got old Squire along, and I don't see why he shouldn't come up. We've got to be fed and the old man, too, and I'm going to send him up."

"But I'd hate to take him, Usher; don't do it."

"Why?"

"His master will need him," she said, in a strained voice.

"You little cheat, you know Charley will jump for joy to send old Squire up here to help you; and I'm going to do it."

She gave no reply, and her silence struck West as very singular."

"I'm going to send him up, Jennie."

"Not at my request," she said weakly.

"But the more I think of it the more it seems necessary. You see we don't know how long we are going to be compelled to hang around here, and old Squire can be more help to us all up here than he can anywhere else. We'll make him bring you lots o' things, and he'll be lots o' help to you and to us, so don't you say another word; I'll fix it."

"Who else is with you?"

"You know George Sency and Joe Lewis?"

"No; I've heard the names, though, from Mr. Armstrong."

"*Mister* Armstrong! Well, I won't tell Charley. Jennie, Dan's brother will go away soon. I heard that much from Dr. Lacy. Then I hope you'll get along. I know you are having a hard time, but it won't last long now — two or three weeks, Lacy says. Good-by; look for me at breakfast."

CHAPTER XXI

THE PORTENT DEFLECTED

"Like perspectives, which rightly gazed upon
Show nothing but confusion, eyed awry
Distinguish form."
— SHAKESPEARE.

MOSBY was biding his time.

When Dr. Lacy came in to breakfast, he found himself a little late.

"Why, good morning," he exclaimed. "So you are back home again."

"Yes, Doctor," says Usher, rising and shaking hands, "and I wish I could stay. I reckon I'll be compelled to stay. How I'm going to get back now would puzzle a Philadelphia lawyer. Can't you give me a pass through your lines?" he asked, without the shadow of duplicity in his voice.

"Ah, sir," replied the doctor, shaking his head, "I doubt that my signature would have the effect you wish. Do you remember our agreement?"

"Our agreement, Doctor? Let me see . . . what was it?"

"I was to say nothing about your being here, and you were to protect me from your people."

"I'll stand by that, Doctor, till the cows come home.

277

And I'll do more : you just get me a pass back to my regiment, and blest if I don't see that you get safe to Fairfax," and Usher's tones were as earnest as his words were guileful.

"How is Lieutenant Morgan, Doctor?" asked Mr. West.

"Quite bright this morning. His visitors did him good last night. I suppose I ought to tell you, Mr. West, that I hold you no longer to silence in regard to our stay here."

"And what may be your meaning, sir?"

"I mean that last night I was overruled about the truce which you and I discussed when I came here. I am told that the truce is not binding, having been without competent authority ; so I relieve you entirely of any obligation to protect us."

Mr. West's smile was very grave.

"But I step into my father's old shoes," cried Usher, fully prepared with speech. "I don't care a dried apple for the authority so long as the truce is agreed to. I'd stand by a conscript's truce if it had been accepted and acted upon. I'll tell you, Doctor, what we'll do : you just keep mum and say nothing to Father about it, and you and I'll fix up a scheme that'll land you safe and me too. Do you know where I've been?"

"No, I am utterly ignorant of the cause of your absence ; you have been visiting friends, I supposed," said Lacy, somewhat dubiously.

"Yes, Doctor, and the friends I visited are not entirely helpless, although your folks do hold the high hand.

There are a dozen men on furlough within five miles of this spot, and I can get them to come here if need be and see you safe."

Lacy shook his head. "I prefer quiet," he said; "excitement is what I wish to avoid. Lieutenant Morgan is doing very well — better here perhaps than he would be in Washington. No, I want nothing said — though I admit again that I have no right to make any demand. Not that I reject your help, sir, for which I thank you; but, of course, I understand that your suggestion is mere pleasantry in regard to my helping you to get into your lines."

"Pleasantry? Never was more serious in my life, Doctor."

"Miss Jennie, can you tell me whether he is really serious?"

"No, Doctor; he is simply an incurable tease."

"But, Dr. Lacy," exclaimed Usher, "don't you see that everything is altered since our last agreement? Then you had a wounded man unfit for service. To offer you help then, surely is not like offering it now. Then I was not proposing anything against the Confederacy; but now you have here an important officer, almost ready to rejoin his command and go to fighting us again. Do I ask too much of you when I propose that for the safety of this important officer you provide for the safety of a man in the ranks? Why, bless your life, it's like General Lee's exchanging back the officers we caught for privates you caught — man for man!"

Jennie looked at her brother in wonder; his voice had

risen, and she feared that he was feeling in reality what
he had begun in jest.   And Doctor Lacy, too, seemed
more than usually grave ; outside of all relations, the
underlying truth of Usher's false position was evident,
though the surgeon was not convinced that the soldier's proposal had been serious.   He must answer, however.

"But there is no prisoner to be exchanged upon the
one side or the other ; and as for exchanges, it takes the
authorities at Washington and Richmond to decide such
high matters : even the generals have no authority
therein. Of course, if you were a prisoner and Lieutenant
Morgan a prisoner, I should be greatly delighted to see
you both exchanged. But we have nothing to do with
such matters, and I have no power to see you safe into
your lines."

The doctor's tones discovered annoyance, and Jennie's
countenance showed uneasiness if not displeasure, yet
young West refused to abandon the subject.

"And what would you say is my duty in regard to
Lieutenant Morgan, sir ? "

The question was powerful ; Lacy hesitated. "Regard-
ing you as a man the answer is easy," he said at last,
"and the conduct of this generous family has been that
answer ; but as a soldier in the Confederate army, you
must pardon me for not advising you in connection with
your duties."

Lacy went back to his patient, and Jennie gave Usher a
basket.   Mr. West was compelled to be busy at the farm,
or see all his labours lack.

"Usher, please don't worry Dr. Lacy any more; it doesn't seem right."

"Self-protection, little Sis; you see I've got to keep him convinced that I'm in Lee's army. It won't do at all for him to get the notion that I'm with the major; if he get's that notion, I'll have to keep away."

"But he'd never tell!"

"I don't know what he'd do; he's not the sort of man that's always keeping watch of his words. He's an innocent baby, and we've got to give him words to say."

"Well, they'll be going away soon," she said, and sighed.

"Yes, and then I can bring my friends here — at least sometimes. If it wasn't for these people here, Jennie, we could come up and save Father's crop at once. Armstrong has already urged it."

"Oh, it would be too dangerous!"

"Yes, I know it would. Old Squire will be here soon. And you needn't fear his blabbing. Lacy already knows that Squire has lately been with Dan Morgan; but I don't think he'd ever suspect me on that account. And if he does, he can't do anything as long as I keep my eyes open. You trust Squire; he can lie out of it with ease, no matter what they ask him; I've taught him his catechism."

Squire insisted on seeing to his young master's comfort every night; moreover, such duty fitted with the arrangements in other respects, for the party were dependent upon foraging, and the supplies that Jennie sent daily by the hands of the old man were not unneedful. On

the first day of this new service the negro brought up
face to face with Dr. Lacy, out for a stroll.

"Well, Mahsta, an' how izh you a-gittin' awn by dis
time, sah?" says Squire, softly, holding his hat in both
hands and bowing low.

"Why — why — what is your name?" demanded the
surgeon, greatly wondering where he had seen this cheerful little negro.

"My name John, sah; but den mos' ev'ybody dey don't
call me John; dey don't call me nothin' but Squiah, sah,
an' mos' ingin'ally dey calls me ole Squiah; 'caze dat's
the las' name dey gim me, Mahsta, an' dey mos' alluz calls
it fust, 'caze de good book hit say de las' is a-gwine to be
de fust, an' de fust is a-gwine to be de las'.'"

"Oho! and you are the same man, whether first or last,
that came to us down yonder a month ago," exclaimed
the doctor, making connection with past experience.

"Yassah, I's de same pusson, sah; an' sence I seed ju,
Mahsta, I's seed a mighty heap o' hahd times — dat I is,
Mahsta; but I heah yit on savin' groun' a leetle while
oncet mo'e. How you be'n gittin' along, Mahsta?" and
Squire bowed again, and looked ineffable interest in the
white man's welfare.

"Very well, indeed. We've had nothing here but the
very best of treatment — the greatest kindness." Lacy
said the words earnestly; he meant them, every one.

"Now I is proud to heah dat, feh true; yit I ain't
nuvveh s'picioned nothin' else f'om Mahs Tom an' *his*
folks. De good book hit say you kin know 'em dess es
fuh ezh you kin see 'em, an' I be'n a-knowin' Mahs Tom

a-gwine awn fifty yeah, an' Miss Jinnie she dess es good
es de Lawd eveh mek. You ain't got no chance to
grummle, Mahsta, w'en you gits in wid sech folks es
dem. But I tell you, sah, I's be'n a-havin' a hahd
time," and the negro shifted his feet, toward which
his eyes had fallen as though in great distress from
even the recollection of his trials.

"Where have you been, if it's a fair question?" asked
Lacy, his voice showing sympathy.

"Oh, yassah; me, Mahsta? Well, sah, I don't min'
tellin' you whah I's be'n; but I don't know zackly whah
I *hain't* be'n, Mahsta. My young mahsta, he b'longs to
de ahmy, Mahsta — not de ahmy w'at shu b'longs to, sah,
but Ginnle Lee's ahmy; an' he tuck an' tuck me way
oveh yandeh in Mellan' an' Penns'vania de ve'y day atteh
de day w'en I seed ju de las' time befo'e." Squire's face had
been lifted, and his gaze now squarely met the surgeon's.

"Ah, so you've been over there? You admit it?"

"Yassah, an' den I got los' f'om him, sah, an' den I
cotch up ag'in, an' den he got huht in dat battle w'at
dey fit, an' den he be'n tuck back into ole Fihginny
some'h's in de Valley, an' den I hatto come wid 'im an'
tek keeh of 'im tell he git well ag'in; but now he done
got so he kin go, an' he done gawn out o' de Valley oncet
mo'e, an' all o' Ginnle Lee's men done gawn."

"Where is Sergeant Morgan?" demanded the doctor,
abruptly.

"Mahs Dan?"

"Yes; but never mind, I suppose I ought to ask no
questions."

"Yassah, but Mahsta, I ain't seed him sence one day las' week w'en we be'n in de mounting. He be'n a-gwine to git back to whah he b'long to; 'caze Mahs Chahley he tell me up an' down, he say, 'Squiah, ef anything happen to me, an' ef anything mek so you not keep up wimmy, you dess git back home an' dah you stay tell I done sont fuh you to come away,' an' so I done come back."

"I see; and you expect some one to send for you?"

"I dunno, Mahsta; mebbe dey mought, an' den ag'in mebbe dey moughtn't. Mahs Dan he gwine down de country, an' Mahs Chahley he done broke down wid he haid all bunged up wid a swoad, an' den I come along a piece o' de way wi' Mahs Dan, an' in de mounting he cotch one o' de Feddicks an' let him go, and den he tell me to go, too. You heahed anything o' Mahs Dan o' Mahs Chahley, Mahsta?"

"Well, no; at least I have not heard of your master, though I *have* heard of Morgan, and I've heard of you . . . well, never mind." Lacy had been about to say that he had heard of Squire's adventures with Freeman and Dahlgren, but had thought better.

"An' whah is Mahs Dan now, Mahsta?"

"I can't tell you. Don't you know I have his brother here?"

"Oh, yassah; Miss Jinnie she dess now tole me. How come you didn't git no fuhdeh dan dis place, Mahsta?"

"Why, you old sinner, your people cut us off, so we couldn't get back."

"Yassah," and Squire's voice was exceedingly grave and humble, "you p'nounce de Gawd's troof w'en you call

me ole sinneh. I is feh true, an' de good book hit say I
not a-gwine to live out ha'f my days. Doezh zhu know
de signs, Mahsta ? "

" Signs ? What signs do you mean ? "

" De signs w'at folks sees sometimes w'en dey time is
a-comin'."

" Premonitions, you mean ? No . . . well, yes ; maybe
I do under certain circumstances."

" Yassah, hit mought be dat wi' de w'ite folks, but wi'
de niggehs hit's *signs*, Mahsta, an' I done had one."

Dr. Lacy sat down on a stump, Squire yet standing.
The man of science began to flatter himself that he had
found something of interest. Lacy's religion was of the
kind that regards the law of cause and effect as God
Almighty, and he had no objection to hear part of the
crude belief of one who had descended, and not remotely,
from some savage race head-full of its fetiches.

" Tell me what you mean, old man, and if I can help you,
I'll do it."

" Yassah, an' I done say to myse'f, dess es soon es I
laid my eyes awn you, Mahsta, I done say to myse'f dat
gen'l'm'n he a smaht man, 'caze dey done tole me, Miss
Jinnie done tole me you done keohed up Mahs Dan's
brotheh an' I knows hit tek a mighty smaht man to do dat ;
an' I say to myse'f dat de good book hit say dat ye mus'
come to de fountain an' ye mus' lahn o' de wise man.
Now, Mahsta, I gwine to tell you de troof — I done got
my call."

It would now have been impossible for any one to doubt
the negro's utter seriousness, for he was indeed utterly

serious. The purpose for which he had begun this colloquy had momentarily subsided far from the surface of conscious-ness, weighed down by the ghastly warning received at Gettysburg. The effect of time had but little diminished the agony of the first shock in the old man's mind, yet the blatant incredulity of his white friends had brought reënforcement to time, and together they had given the negro a feeble hope—not hope that brings pleasure, but that denies it. And now, in the presence of Lacy, in whom he dimly conceived enlightenment abounded, and who had said a belief that might be construed faith in the general article of superstitious creed coupled with caution in avoiding particular error, old Squire sought help with intense desire to be told and convinced that in some hitherto unrecognized manner or degree his part in the performance had been erroneous, and that therefore the whole was void of effect.

Lacy was far from being blind to the negro's trembling excitation : a student of physiology inevitably enjoys vast interest in the emotions, and that which excites them, and our doctor was a student and a thinker. He became alert, ready to help the sufferer ; he saw that here was a case of illness that needed the delicate treatment of spiritual surgery — the wholesome restoration of faith by the diver-sion of credulity ; he saw that no mere assurance would answer ; no *ipse dixit* of his own could countermand the voice that had already spoken its decision ; he must be careful, must proceed tentatively, and convince this negro, not that his creed itself was wrong,— a hopeless task,— but that this worshipper had himself failed to read its conditions.

"Let me see your tongue," said Lacy, with due solemnity.

Old Squire shut his eyes and obeyed.

"Ah! ah! — partly right — partly wrong — a little farther — there. Pretty bad tongue, but it'll come all right to-morrow. Now tell me about that sign."

"You wants me to tell you how I come to git dat call Mahsta?" asked the negro, with trembling lips.

"Yes, don't skip anything. You see such things depend on a great many other things. For instance, was it in the night or in the day?"

"Hit wus mos' in de night, Mahsta."

"Well, I want to know which. Was it when you were asleep or awake?"

"I wus wide awake, Mahsta, an' hit wus in de night; mos' in de night."

"Well, tell me all about it. Were you alone?"

"No, Mahsta, de' wus anotheh man wimmy, but he didn't git no call."

"Why not? Why shouldn't he be called too?" Lacy was merely reconnoitring; he must examine the ground carefully that he might organize the most scientific attack.

"'Caze I wus de fust one, Mahsta," exclaimed Squire, his manner very convincing.

"Yes, but didn't you tell me just now that the Bible says the first shall be last, and so forth?"

"Yassah, dat de Gawd's troof. But den ag'in he didn't git no call at all, Mahsta."

"Go on, and tell me everything."

"Yassah, me an' him we wus a-gwine along in de wheat,

Mahsta, right by dat place dat de calvry fit so hahd, an'
me an' him we wus a-gwine along, an' fust thing I knowed
I done slap my han' right awn de daid man's face," and
the negro's voice sank to a whisper void of intentional
emphasis, yet full of tragedy.

"And what did the other man do? Do you object to
telling me his name?"

"Oh, Mahsta, he waun't nobody but a po' niggeh lak
me. I tell you w'at he done, Mahsta; he dess tuck out
de pocket-book an' he dess went awn a piece, an' dess got
some mo'e outen some yotheh men w'at was a-layin' down
dah in de wheat."

Lacy's mind immediately became active to contrive
some scheme for diverting the impending calamity from
Squire upon his companion — the wretch that rifled the
dead; but he must feel his way.

"You are sure the man was dead?" he asked.

"Mahsta, he wus dat cole an' stiff dat I couldn't stan'
de tetch," and Squire's head shook, his eyes on the
ground.

"Tell me where it was that this thing happened."

"Hit wus oveh in Mellan' an' Penns'vania, Mahsta, mos'
whah all de people fit so long," said the negro, solemnly.

"Gettysburg?"

"Yassah, dat's hit."

"You say the other man had no call?"

"No, Mahsta, he tetched 'em on puhpose, an' I tetched
dat man onbeknownst."

"What were you trying to do at the time?"

"I was dess a-gwine to git back to my Mahs Chahley,

w'at I got los' f'om," said Squire, brightening a little.
" Hit wus dess atteh dey got th'ough fight'n' in dat wheat,
Mahsta, an' I knowed Mahs Chahley wus dah, an' I wus
dess a-gittin' back to Mahs Chahley."

"And what was the man with you trying to do ?"

" He waun't a-tryin' to do nothin' but a-follin' along to
keep up wid me, an' git back, Mahsta."

" How old are you, Squire ?"

" Mahsta, I wus in my twenty-fif' yeah w'en de stahs
all fell down, an' dat's in thihty-three, an' now hit's sixty-
three, an' I's a-gwine awn an' hit won't be long." The
first half of this reply had been uttered proudly ; the
latter, with great despondency.

" You are fifty-five. How old was the man who was
with you ?"

" Him ? He not ha'f es ole es me, Mahsta. He got a
long time to stay heah yit."

" A long time ? Perhaps he has, but you have a longer
time."

" How you mek dat out, Mahsta ? Good Lawd, how
you does go awn ! "

" The last shall be first. Isn't that true ? "

" Yassah, dat w'at de good book say."

" If there is a just God in heaven, he *ought* to go first."

" An' I got to follow *him*, Mahsta ? "

" Of course ; you see you didn't look into everything,
Squire." Neither was Lacy looking into everything. In
his great eagerness to relieve Squire, his mind was closed
to the fact that the old negro was beginning to think that
Barney's life was — according to the doctor's theories — all

U

that stood betwixt himself and death. " And when a man doesn't look into everything, he's going to make mistakes. You see that oak tree yonder ? "

" Yassah."

" How did it get there ? "

" Hit dess growed right dah f'om a acohn, I 'spec', Mahsta ; leastways ef hit waun't set out," Squire added, guardedly, as though the great man before him required the utmost accuracy.

" Right.   What kind of oak is it ? "

" Hit's a black oak, Mahsta."

" Now if anybody was to show you an acorn of a black oak, could you swear to it ? "

" I 'spec' I could, Mahsta ; but I ain't nuvveh be'n much of a han' at dat kin' o' wohk."

" You are a black man.   Was the man with you a black man, or was he yellow ? "

" He mos' yalloh, sah," Squire replied, compromising.

" If I had in my hand two acorns, — one of a black oak and the other of a red oak, — would you know which one to plant in order for a black oak to grow ? "

" Yassah," said the old man, with great positiveness.

" And do you think that yellow man could do it ? "

" I dunno, Mahsta," said Squire, doubtfully.

" Well, I couldn't do it, not if my life depended on it. And now you see, Squire, how great a thing it is to know little things. A round ball of an acorn makes a black oak, and another makes a red oak, and you can see the difference but I can't.   But you couldn't make a red oak grow from a black acorn."

"No, sah; hit tek Gawdamighty hese'f to do dat," exclaimed the negro, certain of this little spot of ground.

"And you can't tell what made you black, and what made the other man yellow; but I can tell you that the call you had, and thought was meant for you, was meant for that other man."

"De Je-e-e-susgawd, Mahsta! You mean dat feh true?"

"Yes, and I'll show you. Now, you needn't tell me anything more; I see how this mistake happened, and I'm going to prove it to you. Go and bring me an ear of corn."

Squire made haste. Lacy had now placed his cause almost upon the hazard of a die; if the cavalry fight that Squire had spoken of was the great one of the 3d of July, then the doctor's method ought to succeed; and he believed thoroughly that there had been no other cavalry fight worth mentioning at Gettysburg.

"Now, Squire, what I'm going to tell you is this. If that call came to you on any one of six days in the week, it was meant that the first should be first; but if it came on the other day, it was meant that the last should be first. If I had my way about it, it should surely be his call instead of yours, no matter what day it was; because he was younger than you, and yet allowed you to lead. He ought to have gone first; don't you think so, Squire?"

"Yassah; but, Mahsta, he dess stayed behime an' I couldn't git him up; yassah, he done me dess dat a-way mos' all de time. You reckon, Massah, dat call w'at I tuck feh me, hit wus sont to him?" and the old man's face was distorted with hope and pity.

"I say I'm not sure yet; but you've got a chance; just

one chance out of seven ; if it was on a certain day it was for him ; if it was on any other of the seven days it was for you. Must I tell you what days would strike on you ? "

The negro's face became awful. He shifted uneasily about. The chance in his favour seemed terribly small. Yet, previously, he had thought of no particular chance at all. At last he bowed low, and said : —

" De good Lawd's got me in his han' an' ef he gwine to tek me fust he gwine to tek me, an' ef he gwine to let me stay heah some mo'e an' be de las' he gwine to let me stay. Mahsta, tell me w'at days is mine."

" Monday . . . Tuesday . . . Wednesday . . . Thursday . . . " and here the doctor's slow speech paused ; he would not risk the entire overthrow of his scheme ; perhaps there had been some fighting of cavalry on Wednesday or Thursday. If terrible emotion should betray that all interest had been in either of these days, he must still scotch in some way ; but he saw that his patient was in intolerable suspense, anticipating the sentence of the next word — " Saturday . . . Sunday."

But before Lacy had completed the word Saturday, Squire was on his knees.

The doctor patiently waited. At last Squire said in a broken voice, " Mahsta, izh you sho' ? "

" That is to come now, Squire. Give me that corn. There's nothing like being certain of anything, Squire."

" An' dat's de Gawd's troof, Mahsta. But den dey ain't nobody, 'scusin' Gawdamighty hese'f, dat kin expec' sech a no-count ole sinneh lak me to mek sho'."

"Now, Squire, if it was on Friday, you have a chance."

"Yassah ; hit wus a Friday feh sho'."

"Is it possible ! But it ought to be on a certain Friday. Any common Friday wouldn't do at all. And I'm going to tell you beforehand," and now Lacy's voice was exceedingly solemn, "I must warn you beforehand, Squire, that unless it was on a certain number of a Friday, the sign was meant for you after all."

"W'at dat mean, Mahsta ?"

"Well, I'll tell you, if you'll just give me good attention. You know that thirteen is a very bad number, don't you ?"

"Yassah, I done heahed about dat, and I done seed it, too."

"And you know that Friday is a bad day. Now, there were a great many men who had bad luck on that Friday — but there were a great many men who had good luck. You see when thirteen and Friday come together, the signs fall on other men. Understand ?"

Squire shook his head ; he did not understand ; as to that, neither did Lacy, but he was resolved to make Squire easy and to overwhelm that corpse robber, in case the old man should ever tell him this tale.

Lacy shelled corn : "Clear off a level place, Squire — about a yard — there, that'll do ; now, see here . . . I. make some rows for you to plant corn in ; now plant seven grains in the first row — an inch or so apart . . . no, don't cover them ! Now, we begin on Friday ; one grain for Friday, one for Saturday, and so on. How many days in a week, Squire ?"

"Seb'n, sah ; seb'n days in ev'y week."

"Right ; now plant seven more in the next row ; and keep on till you get seven in each row ; . . . there ! "

Squire had succeeded in obeying orders ; the sweat stood on his face as though he were indeed planting corn in the warm springtime.

"Now, Squire, I lay this stick down at the end of these rows, and we'll say it's a fence ; now what day do we call all these grains next to the fence ? "

"Ev'y one o' dem grains hit stan's feh Friday, sah."

"Are you sure ? "

"Yassah, 'scusin' I ain't done mek a misscount an' ain't got seb'n in ev'y row ; but den, Mahsta, we don't plant cawn dat a-way."

"How so ? What's wrong ? "

"We don't tuhn roun' an' walk back to de eend, Mahsta. We dess keeps awn right aroun' dis a-way," showing with his black finger that when the planter ends a row he begins the next one at the point opposite.

"Oh, yes, I know that, Squire ; but we are supposing that we plant this field in the other way. You understand ? "

"Yassah, I know w'at shu mean ; ev'y cawn at de fence hit stan' feh Friday — leastways ef de ain't no misscount."

"Better count over, and see if they are right ; it won't do to make the least mistake, Squire."

When the negro had proved the work, Lacy continued, "What church do your people belong to, Squire ? "

"My mahsta, sah ? De fambly ? Dey b'longs to de 'Piscopal chuhch, sah."

Better than Lacy had hoped for; it would probably save him some labour of explanation.

"Do you know when Good Friday came this year?"

"No, sah, 'caze I waun't at home den, an' in de ahmy dey don't keep much 'count o' dem days, Mahsta."

"Do you remember where you were on Easter Sunday?"

"Yassah, I 'membeh we wus in camp down dah mos' to de Rapidan."

"Yes, so was I. Well, how many days is Good Friday before Easter?"

"Dey is Good Friday, and den Sadday, an' den Easteh Sunday, Mahsta."

"Now I want you to go and ask Miss Jennie what day of the month Good Friday fell on this year, and don't say anything else; don't let her into our plot at all."

Squire went and returned. "Miss Jinnie she say hit come on de thihd o' Ap'l, sah."

"Yes. I was hoping so, but I wanted to be sure. How many days in April, Squire?"

The old man clenched his fist and began to count. His system was that which begins at the forefinger and calls it the first month; the hollow between the fingers, the second month; the knuckle of the middle finger, the third month; the hollow, the fourth, and so on.

"Jinooa'y, long; Febooa'y, shawt; Mahch, long; Ap'l, shawt. Hit's a shawt mont', sah; Ap'l's a shawt mont'."

"Thirty days, then?"

"Yassah, all dem shawt mont's is thihty days, 'scusin' Febooa'y."

"Well, I see you know a thing or two, Squire. Now begin here at this first grain ; it stands for Good Friday, the third of April ; and you count on till you get to the first of May."

Squire counted, deeply interested in this exercise, wondering whereunto it tended, yet hopeful.

"Dis cawn, hit's on de fust o' May, sah."

"And is May short or long?"

"Hit's long, sah."

"Then count thirty-one, and halt on the first of June. Now be careful, or you'll spoil everything."

"Yassah, I sho' gwine to go slow an' git' em right. Dish heah cawn he gwine to be de fust o' June."

"And is June short or long?"

"Hit's a shawt mont', sah, 'caze May's a long 'un."

"Yes ; now count on up to the first of July."

Squire counted and halted his finger.

"Now we're getting right at the truth ; hold your finger on that first of July, and look at me. What day of the week was the fourth of July?"

"Hit come on a Sadday, sah ; dat wus de ve'y day atteh de day dat I done be'n in dat scrape w'at I be'n tellin' you 'bout."

"Then the day of the fight was the third of July?"

"Yassah, 'caze de nex' day hit wus de fou'th."

"Exactly so ; now what day do we call all these days at the fence?"

"Friday, sah, an' I see dish heah is de secon' ; an' dish heah is de thihd ; an' he Friday, too, 'caze he at de eend o' de row. How come dat, Mahsta?"

"Why, you knew beforehand that the third of July was Friday."

"Yassah, I knowed it, but hit don't seem lak I knowed it befo'e."

"Now put a peg down here — there by the third of July . . . so. Now come back here to Good Friday . . . yes. Now, what number was that we spoke of — that bad luck number that works wrong sometimes?"

"Thihteen, sah."

"Very well; now, count all these Fridays, and tell me how many weeks there were from Good Friday till the third of July."

When Squire, trembling more and more as he proceeded, had made out that his portentous day had fallen just thirteen weeks after Good Friday, his amazement was so great that for a time he had no speech. That Lacy was a man specially favoured of supernatural powers there could be no doubt. A man who could thus, without knowing the day on which Squire had been "called," state the conditions which would prove that "call" intended for another, and then show that these conditions had existed at the time, was something far beyond the reach of his reason, though not beyond his faith. When at last he opened his mouth to speak, Lacy prevented him.

"Come with me, Squire. Lieutenant Morgan has a calendar, and I'm going to prove to you again that I'm right."

At Junior's window the doctor halted, and called out, "Lieutenant, please look at the almanac and tell me what day of the month was Good Friday."

After a moment Morgan's face was seen at the window. "Who is that you have there, Doctor?"

"This is Squire."

"Ah! then I am his very good friend. I have heard of all you did, and you may just count on me to return your goodness—"

Squire was bowing and scraping—

"Hold on, Morgan! Tell us what we want to know. What day was Good Friday?"

The lieutenant fingered his pamphlet. "Third of April," he said.

"And now please count how many weeks there were from Good Friday till the third of July."

Junior counted, and said, "Thirteen to the day."

"Thank you, Lieutenant; please hand me a glass, and that flask on the mantel; and that box of powders with the red cover. Squire, let me see that tongue again."

And the whiskey that Lacy coloured brown with some harmless drug so quickened the old man's blood that he was soon singing at his work, even forgetful, for the time, that he must follow Barney—an enormity of an idea in his own brain, though in Lacy's merely the recognition that death, soon or late, must come to each and all.

CHAPTER XXII

ARMED NEUTRALITY

... "So thrive I in my enterprise
And dangerous success of bloody wars,
As I intend more good to you and yours
Than ever you and yours were by me wronged!"
— SHAKESPEARE.

FOR some days Usher West sat at his father's table for
every meal, but Lacy saw him at no other time. Ancient
convictions were strong, yet the doctor asked no questions;
indeed, he feared to learn certainly that the young man's
absence from his command was voluntary, for the good
surgeon had conceived respect for this modest household.

These days were welcome to Morgan and Sency because
of their desire to see Armstrong recover fully. Mosby
was known to be waiting only for the opportunity which
would try the physical powers of the strongest.

Meade had his headquarters at Warrenton, and Lee was
at Culpeper. Federals rode where they would in Fauquier and Loudoun, and our party remained in hiding,
giving their horses exercise by night, and prudently keeping aloof from Mr. West's. Morgan learned that his
brother was allowed to leave his bed for a few hours each
day, and that any apprehension of an advance by the

Confederates would cause Dr. Lacy to cut short his delay
in removing his patient.   Once again Captain Freeman
had come to the house by night, but nothing transpired
concerning the nature of his visit.   Old Squire diligently
served Miss Jennie, and acted as go-between for the bivouac
and the residence, making Armstrong alternately hopeful
and despairing.   Without reason he expected Jennie to
send him some word, and with reason feared that she
cared little for him.   His agony became intense, and his
wish for Junior Morgan to go became so strong that he
urged upon Usher the scheme of frightening Lacy away
with rumours of a contemplated visit by Mosby for the
purpose of paroling the Federal officer.

Junior had no desire to go ; he was happiest where he
was.   To him and to Jennie the day of his departure
would bring sorrow and not joy.   But for his devotion to
the girl he loved, and with whom he had plighted faith,
Morgan would have gone before Meade had advanced into
Virginia — not healed, certainly, but in early convalescence,
which might as well have been continued in Washington
or at his home in Schenectady.

It was toward the middle of August, almost two months
since Junior had been received into this true asylum.
Still unable to use his sword arm, he was strong enough,
with care, to have ridden horseback ; in an ambulance he
would have feared no evil result in a removal to Fairfax,
or even to Washington if need were.   There was no
excuse for remaining longer a burden upon Mr. West.
Morgan was ashamed of himself.   He knew not how to
propose remuneration for the expense and trouble that

had been incurred and undergone on his account; he hoped that the relationship he was resolved to seek would show him the way. Jennie, oppressed with grief and fears, had at last consented that he appeal to her father.

"Mr. West," said Morgan, "I must ask that you grant me leave to speak very seriously."

"Certainly, Lieutenant, let me make you comfortable," and the old gentleman rose and brought out pillows, which he arranged in an arm-chair on the side porch.

"I am so embarrassed by the great kindness you have shown me, sir, that I find no words that would give expression to my present feeling; yet I want you to know that I consider your conduct very magnanimous."

To this opening Mr. West gave no support. His face reddened. To be overloaded with thanks and with praises was, perhaps, more embarrassing to himself than to the speaker.

Junior found the silence disheartening; yet he was compelled to continue.

"I have fought against you, and must fight again; yet you treat me more as a friend than as an enemy — more as a friend than as a stranger."

"Very simple; you were in distress."

"Yes, sir, simple enough to you, but a thing impossible to many others. Do you know, sir, that I have feared in vain that I should see a look of impatience or annoyance in regard to my poor self? I am oversensitive, no doubt, and my dread that my intrusion would call up resentment on your part has been great, perhaps even disrespectful to

you. I have been here so long that many unguarded
moments must have come when one in your place, who
was merely acting the part of hospitality, must have
shown that he was acting; yet at no time have I felt from
you any displeasure or even difficulty. But my judgment tells me that caring for me has been difficult, and I
beg that I may be allowed to — "

"Stop, Lieutenant," exclaimed Mr. West, though in a
mild tone ; "if I have done any good, I don't want to
lose the comfort of it."

"Sir, you may easily understand the difficulty that I
find in this matter ; yet I obey you, and will consent to
remain forever obliged to you."

"Maybe the tables will be turned some day, Lieutenant. I have a son, and if you should ever be able to help
him out of trouble, I am confident of your doing it."

"Yes, sir, and I am greatly afraid that you will see
suffering yourself, Mr. West. It may be a strange thing
for a Union soldier to say, sir ; but since I have seen something of the life here in this house, nothing but the severe
command of duty can hereafter make me raise my hand
against your people."

"But they are *your* people, as well. Perhaps the
knowledge that you are Southern born has something to
do with it."

"I am not sure that you are wrong. I know that the
war has become to me a great tragedy, and only a tragedy.
Formerly there was some insane pleasure in the excitement ; now, everything becomes mischievous and repugnant."

" Yet you expect to continue."

" Of course I understand that you say that without con-
emnation, for you know it to be my duty to continue to
erve what I believe is the right. Yes, I must continue,
hough it break my heart."

" Lieutenant, the doctor tells me that you will soon
eave us."

" Yes, sir."

" Would it please you to leave any message, or any let-
er for your brother, on the chance of my being able here-
fter to send it to him ? " Mr. West was feeling the
'ederal ; he knew that Sergeant Morgan was near by ; if
he Federal's answer should be propitious, a meeting might
e arranged for.

" If you should see him, Mr. West, kindly tell him that
think of him as a brother ; the differences between us
re but political, and amount to nothing in my sight. I
eg you to thank him for his kindness, and to say that I
ray for the war to end, so that I may meet him and show
im ever after what I feel." Sobs were in Morgan's
oice, and tears in the older man's eyes.

" And now, sir, I am compelled to beg more of you."

Mr. West looked inquiringly.

" Before I ask more, however, I must put you in posses-
ion of some facts. You know something of my birth, and
little of myself. My home, sir, is in Schenectady, New
Tork ; my reputed grandfather — who adopted me — left
o me, as he supposed, in the name of Daniel Morgan, a
onsiderable estate. Perhaps you have heard something
f this also. That property at a low estimate might be

valued at four hundred thousand dollars. I am telling
you this, sir, for a purpose ; if I did not think that you
had heard something of it, I would not mention it now.
That property I do not consider mine ; it was left, sup-
posedly to me ; it was left, really to Daniel Morgan, and
I intend to see that he gets it. If he is alive when the
war ends, it shall be his ; it shall be his, or his heirs'. I
shall have nothing. And now, Mr. West, you see how
poor a man it is who comes to you and begs for your
daughter."

Mr. West sprang to his feet. He had indeed suspected
a slight admiration for Jennie, but had certainly not looked
for this declaration. His mind had been fixed on Charles
Armstrong as his daughter's husband, — an arrangement
positively suitable, — and he had regarded the matter
as nearly fixed as such can be. Yet, in an instant he had
been moved by the proud sufferer before him ; this Federal was the queerest claimant in love matters that he had
ever heard of or read of, — a man who voluntarily declared
a determination to surrender what most men demand in
sons-in-law, — a man to stubbornly assert that he should
continue to fight against the South, and such high principle appealed powerfully to him. If Junior had come to
him showing himself rich, offering allurement, the old
man would have spurned the suitor ; the Federal had become glorious in his eyes, yet it may be pardoned to the
Southerner that his first thought had been the equality of
the Virginian with the best. He exclaimed : —

"By God, sir! Dan Morgan wouldn't touch a cent of
your property."

Then Mr. West sat down and said, "Excuse me, but do
ʿou believe that one of *your* blood would consent to the
acrifice you would make ? "

Morgan was puzzled ; though he had indeed thought
ɪf this phase of the matter, not very seriously, however,
ɪis difficulty came from the seeming avoidance of the main
ubject.

"What would you do in his place ? " asked Mr.
West.

"I hope, sir, that I would act justly and honourably in
ɪny case and every case."

Yet Junior's eyes had kindled with pleasure in hearing
ɪis brother's principle defended. He continued, "It is a
[uestion of right and wrong, in which the right is on his
ide."

"I don't look at it that way," said Mr. West. "Likely
ɪnough, at the first, your grandfather's attachment to you
ame from his belief that you were Daniel Morgan; but
vhen he made you his heir, he had become attached to
ʿou irrespective of names. To all intents and purposes
ʿou were Daniel Morgan; and if he had learned before he
nade his will that you were the wrong brother, no doubt
ɪe still would have made you his heir."

Was the old man arguing his daughter into the position
ɪf a rich man's wife ?

"That may be possible, Mr. West; still it is only theory,
ɪnd I cannot accept it as against the great reality that the
vill names Daniel Morgan as the heir. Yet these ques-
ions, Mr. West, interesting and important as they are,
ɪave not a tithe of importance and interest to my mind

x

compared with my great wish to enter into the relationship with you which I have already sought at your hands."

Again Mr. West rose, not as before, but slowly and with seeming reluctance. He stood by the Federal officer, on whose head he laid his large rough hand, and his voice trembled as he spoke.

"My boy," he said, "I hate to grieve you, I'll swear I do; but I must, sir. I can never consent for my daughter to marry an enemy of her country."

Outside, the world glittered in the August sunlight. South and east the mountains hid the devastated fields of Virginia, under whose sod rested thousands of the sons of the South, and thousands of her invaders. Beyond the end of the range was an armed host seeking devices for causing the most successful destruction, and of this host the lover would soon be a part once more.

"But after the war?" Morgan pleaded.

Mr. West again took his seat. He shook his head.

"No, sir; the best you can do for yourself is to quit thinking of it. My answer has been given. You have spoken to my daughter?"

"Yes, sir, and my weakness is my only excuse. She was a very ministering angel, and I could not withhold."

"Oh, as for that, don't give yourself any trouble. I am not the party of the first part."

Mr. West's voice had changed. He understood now that he was bringing sorrow on the one he most loved. He looked at Morgan and saw his face very white, his hand over his eyes. The silence was grievous; both men were suffering.

Morgan was first to speak. "Your will shall be respected, sir. I have too great obligations to you to cause you any displeasure. Yet before I go," he added, rising, "I would ask permission to tell Miss Jennie your decision."

"So be it," was the answer.

The night came, and Morgan was discussing with Lacy the preparations for their departure. Mr. West was alone out in the porch, thinking with little pleasure about many things. The farm was almost a failure; he had been able to get help at planting time, when the armies were facing each other across the Rappahannock at Fredericksburg, fifty miles away; but the demoralization resulting when Lee and Hooker moved northward in June had thrown the crop far behind for lack of labour; still he hoped for enough to supply his own and Jennie's simple needs. The wheat had been good; some had been lost at the critical moment of harvest, but there was enough. This war, with its fluctuations,—wave after wave rolling forward and back over North Virginia,—showed no abatement. Lee had gone back, but would come again. He had no doubt that Lee would come again; yet the Yankees showed such determination that he feared the war had just begun. It was hard on the women, he knew, and as hard on Jennie as on any one of them, harder than on most. He doubted that he ought to allow her to stay here. His mind went back to his youth and early manhood; to his love for Jennie's mother — his only passion ; to her death, and he sighed grievously.

There was a step behind him, and then soft arms were about his neck and Jennie's head rested against his own.

"Father ! "

The word was a sigh. He drew her around, and she sat on the arm of his chair.

"Jennie, it breaks me all up, my girl."

"Not even after the war, Father ? "

"Oh, Jennie, that is a long time. This war may last ten years. And I thought it was to be Charley."

"No, sir, I never cared for him. He made me tell him so before he left."

"What ? Well, well, how you young people do deceive us. And so you are willing to take this Yankee ? "

"Don't call him a Yankee, Father. You know he was born in Virginia."

"Yes, but he fights against Virginia."

"What would you do in his place ? " she asked, using what she knew was his own familiar weapon.

"I suppose I should fall in love with you, Jennie."

"But I mean which side would you fight for ? Does he owe as much to the South as he does to the North ? "

"I can't say that he does; but it seems to me there are enough men in the North without *his* help. Yet I confess that every man must be his own judge and conscience keeper ; and the young fellow has acted very well, I can't deny that."

"Father ! "

"What is it, my child ? "

"He is getting ready to go."

"And you want to keep him ? Oh, little girl, you want to leave your old father ? "

She broke down for one moment, and laid her head on his shoulder.

"You know I would never leave you. But after the war, Father? Then we can all live together," and she whispered, "he has promised to become a Virginian then."

"How do you know, Jennie, that you can trust him so long? Indeed, it may be ten years."

"If he cannot wait ten years, then I shall be grieved; but I shall say that his love had been very light."

"And you would wait ten years?"

"Father, I shall not marry anybody unless I marry him, and I won't do that if you forbid. Would you prefer that I never marry?"

"I told him, dear, that my consent could never be given to your marrying an enemy; but at the same time I'm not going to give you any command in this matter."

"Father, what would you think of him if he were to turn his back on the North and join our army?"

"Oh, I know such is not to be thought of, either by himself or by any one. It is simply his misfortune to be on the wrong side, and I'm fearing that you feel it your misfortune also. But I'm not going to try to constrain you, and for your part you must not expect me to tell you a lie and say that my consent is freely given. Are you determined to marry him?"

"Father, he thinks so much of you that I know he will never ask me again, unless he should believe you were willing."

"Then it's a hard case, Jennie. I don't know how I can be willing when I'm unwilling."

She bent down and kissed him. "But are you not unwilling also to —" she paused.

"To what, dear?"

"To see me serve him so?"

"Ah! You mean to ask if I am not unwilling to cause you sorrow?"

"I know you are."

"Jennie, if what you wish from me is merely a statement that my objection to him is not so great as my desire for your happiness, I make that statement at once."

"And after the war you will make no objection?"

"Well, my child, I see you are bent on it. Of course I can't tell how I'm going to feel after the war, and I can't know how he is going to behave himself all that long while; but I'll say this, that if you are both of the same mind then, and nothing else will content my daughter, I won't say a word, — and that's what I've been telling you all the time, — I won't do a thing against it. But I can't promise you to feel differently. Won't that answer satisfy you?"

"And you will let me see him again and tell him?"

"Oh, yes, see him and tell him, and let him know that I count on his doing me — no! don't tell him that — I can trust him; that's one thing I can say for that young man."

And so it resulted that Lacy and Morgan would linger, yet only for a few days more. Mr. West showed no evidence of displeasure or anxiety in regard to the matter; and Junior was exceedingly happy over the small degree of favour that had been shown him, and swore to himself that he would win a yet greater degree.

On this night Tom Baxter, barely halting on his round, brought word to Usher that Mosby had ordered an assembling of his men near Wilson's for the night following. Little was needed to make preparation complete, and on the next morning old Squire went as usual to the farmhouse ; he was to return early that he might accompany his master upon the unknown expedition. Armstrong, uncertain as to the time required for the enterprise or the result, which might indeed be death or captivity to any or to all, could restrain himself no longer, and though Usher succeeded in preventing him from going in person, he wrote a note to Jennie, to which Squire brought back a reply. She told Armstrong simply and kindly that his suit could not succeed, and begged him to accept the answer as final ; and Usher, who had seen Squire deliver the answer, and saw Armstrong seize upon it eagerly, saw also the reader change expression from one of intense anxiety to that of deep mortification and despair.

CHAPTER XXIII

THE PARTISANS

" *Lor.* Who comes so fast in silence of the night ?
Steph. A friend.
Lor. A friend ! What friend ? Your name I pray you, friend ? "
— SHAKESPEARE.

THE vague and variable force known as Mosby's
battalion, though strong in its entire enrolment, was
weak in its active strength at any one period. Doubtless,
from first to last, more than two thousand men took part
in some enterprise of the band ; yet very many of these
were mere accidents of the day — enlisted men that had
been cut off for the time being from their own regiments
which they rejoined as soon as they were able or willing ;
others, on furlough from wounds or illness, whose convalescence was sufficient for momentary exertion that carried
stimulus with it, but complacently considered inadequate
for the tedium of the great camp ; others still that came
no one knew whence and departed of their own volition ;
even some, perhaps, that were deserters from the Federal
army.[1] The few that the major trusted were expected
to gather as many men as the contemplated achievement

[1] See General Pleasonton's Report, quoted August 10, 1863, by General
A. A. Humphreys, Chief of Staff.

seemed to demand, or rather, it should be said, as few
men as the leader thought would be indispensable, so
that on some expeditions Mosby led perhaps hundreds,
while on others his followers were but scores, or even
fewer; hence, it resulted that his minor undertakings
were almost uniformly brilliant and successful, while
those of greater magnitude frequently failed, the larger
number involved lacking the coherency of a small body
composed of his best and most experienced men.

As night fell once more, Usher West led his party out
of Goose Creek swamp in a northerly direction. The
way was narrow and winding, overhung at first by great
oaks and elms, through which the filtered starlight barely
showed the leaf-strewn path that muffled the horses' footfall. Every man here knew more or less of this district;
it was the boyhood home of three, and they had not made
half a mile when even to Armstrong's preoccupied mind
it became evident that their course was leading directly
away from the rendezvous that day given.

"Usher, how long you going to keep this road?" he
asked, thinking that their guide was purposely throwing
any possible enemy off the scent.

"Keep it a good while," said West, and rode on.

"Well, it's not the right way."

"We'll get there all the same."

"If we do, we'll have to turn off up yonder at Adams's."

But at Adams's Usher went directly on, and now he
condescended to say: "Boys, I reckon I may as well tell
you that we don't go to Wilson's at all. That was all a
blind, so that if anybody blabbed it would do no harm.

You just follow me, and I'll take you through all right."

And soon Usher's pace almost imperceptibly began to quicken. They had started at a slow walk, as nearly noiseless as possible. They had once or twice diverged from the route, and had returned to it farther on, thus avoiding habitations. In this gathering, secrecy must be the very greatest at the beginning, and celerity must be the greatest at the moment of organizing. On this night a score of small groups, twos and threes, were coming from as many points of a circle to meet in a common centre, and the more nearly that each approached that centre, the less danger to each and the greater to all should they dally. So Usher West and his companions rode with speed ever increasing, until Morgan, who had not yet taken part in any of Mosby's raids, began to fear lest the efficiency of their horses should be impaired before actual work was needed, and he spoke his fear to West, who answered that the meeting and organizing would require time in which the horses could rest, adding that sometimes organization was effected while on the march itself, — by preconcerted arrangement the routes being designated for each of the groups to take, in order to intercept the line of main advance at points convenient, — but that on this night, after a long interval in which the band had not assembled, preference had been given to the former method.

They were now on a main highway, and when their horses trod a sandy stretch of the road, they could hear galloping that seemed to preserve its distance — some

man ahead carrying to the rendezvous, and in a little
while a voice came from the front, and there was silence
— no hoofs beating, the man ahead halting to answer
the challenge of a sentinel.

Two hundred yards farther, and West's party came
to an abrupt halt, a clear voice crying, " Who comes
there ? "

" Friends with the countersign."

" Halt, friends ; advance one, with the countersign."

Usher rode forward ; but there was no need to give the
password — the sentinel knew him.

" Hello, Ush ! How many you got ? "

" Four more. Where's the major ? "

" Down at the mill. Better be lively. He's a hornet
to-night. Crowd from above not heard from yet."

" Hell you say ! How long you reckon he'll wait ? "

Passing the sentinel, Usher again took up the gallop ;
the rendezvous was yet a mile away, for Mosby kept
watch all round him and far. But soon the main road
was forsaken. At a slower pace the squad went down a
steep slope to the right, and on this hillside they were
again halted, and subjected here to longer delay.

" That nigger o' yours, West ; I'm going to keep him
here till you bring me the major's word."

" All right ; Squire, you stay here a few minutes."
The white men rode on down the hill.

The old negro had no fears. " Mahsta, I's be'n th'ough
de bresh mo'n oncet. I's de same ole niggeh dat showed
Ginnle Stuaht de haidquahtehs o' dat big Yankee ginnle

lash yeah, way back yandeh mos' to de railroad, down yandeh by Cedah Run."

"Oh, yes, Uncle; I reckon you're all right; but then you know I got to obey orders."

"Yassah, so I is too; but I gwine to gid down an' res' dis ole mule ef you don't mine; I be'n a runnin' dis mule feh who las' de longes'."

"All right, dismount if you like," said the sentinel.

"I boun' to git me a hoss dis time; 'f I hadn' ha' mos' beat dis mule to def, Mahs Chahley an' all 'ould ha' lef' me way behime. I ain't nuvveh be'n right in my mine sence dat day I hatto leave my hoss oveh in Mellan' an' Penns'vania. You be'n oveh dah, Mahsta?"

"Not lately; but you mustn't talk, Uncle."

"Yassah, ef dat's ag'in de rule, den I ain't a-gwine to talk no mo'e, Mahsta."

West, with Morgan, Sency, Armstrong, and Lewis, was in the presence of John S. Mosby: a thin wiry man, with a sandy beard, his face shaded by a soft black hat around which curved a great ostrich plume. He was in full gray uniform, and was seated at a small table, one candle dimly lighting the whitened walls and pillars; outside was the sound of rushing waters.

"Five of us, Major," says West, saluting.

"Good! Why, Morgan, how are you? Haven't seen you since I left the general. And there's Sency, too. Oh, yes, I remember you very well; you were with us in Maryland once. And who are these?"

"Charley Armstrong and Joe Lewis, of the First, Major," said Morgan, "and we have old Squire with us. Don't you remember his showing us Pope's headquarters last year near Auburn?"

"I should say I do. And I know Lewis like a book. Yes, and I can recall Armstrong now. You are the big man who attacked the bridge at Cedar Run. . . . Well, men, make yourselves easy. We can hardly make a start before midnight. Our people from above are delayed for some reason, and I'll give 'em a chance; but we start not later than midnight, and I want you men of the First to ride at the front. Remember that, now; eight men will ride half a mile in front, and you'll be four of them."

One other officer was in the room, Lieutenant Turner. For a short while Mosby retained West; the others of Morgan's squad went out. The horses were unsaddled, were watered and fed — no telling when there would be time for the next feeding. Old Squire was released, and together the party rested, with groups of men all round them on the hillside, most of them very quiet, but here and there one busy with his weapons.

The numbers were growing; the door of the mill frequently showed forms entering and retiring. Perhaps two hours had gone by, when a confused noise began, and then a scramble for the horses. No loud order had been given; the word was passed from man to man. And now there was no light in the mill.

Morgan knew that midnight had not yet come. West whispered that the delayed party had succeeded in sending a man to tell that they were cut off by the enemy and must disband; the march would begin without them.

Somehow, a straggling column was formed, each irregular group recognizing some familiar leader. ✾ West had urged forward ; the column was moving. Yet in motion, West found Mosby at the front.

"You four men lead," said the commander, "you four in uniform. West, give them leeway and give them complete instructions. You ride behind them in speaking distance."

"But old Squire, Major. What shall I do with him ?" asked West.

"Do just what you proposed. I have thought over it, and it's the thing."

The column was moving at a trot.

"Half a mile !" cried Usher, and his companions followed him at a gallop.

On the summit of a high hill whence they looked eastward West called for slower speed.

"Far enough ahead, boys. Now, Sergeant, the major gives you charge of the advance. If you run into the Yankees before we get down to the pike, you may get away if you can ; but you must make a big noise that can be heard behind you. If you should be taken, your uniforms will make 'em think Stuart is coming. Tell 'em you belong to Lee's brigade. Squire is to go first ; you four boys behind Squire a hundred yards ; I ride behind you a hundred yards. Now, Squire, you mustn't let us run into any trap ; you must go first, you hear ?"

"Yassah, de good book hit say de las' gwine to go fust, but I dunno whah you all is a-gwine to, an' I dunno whah to tuhn off, an' I dunno whah *not* to tuhn off."

"Don't turn off at all unless we let you know. We'll

keep you in sight, and won't let you go wrong.   And
after a while we're going slow, and then I'm going to tell
you more.   And if you do this job up brown you're going
to get more horses than you can take keer of — the major
says you shall have a full share.   Now light out ! "

Old Squire lit out.   It is true that he was nervous
enough, but looking back he saw his master and his master's friends following in speaking distance, and he was
comforted.

West, clad as a civilian, rode some eighty yards behind
Morgan's squad ; close behind West came four other men
in Confederate uniform ; behind these, but almost half a
mile away, rode Mosby, ever active in improving and preserving order.

    *   *   *   *   *   *   *

A train of forty wagons was on its way from Alexandria to Warrenton, with supplies for General Meade's
army, under the protection of a squadron of cavalry.
The first night there had been a halt at Fairfax, where
there was a strong force ; now the train was two days out
from Alexandria ; by noon of the next day it would be
safe in Warrenton.   The ground where the wagons had
been parked was of irregular shape — a stream flowing in
a loop at the east, a stream with steep banks, within the
loop an excellent ground for the protection of the train.
On the far side of the creek pickets had been posted, the
main body of cavalry being held a little to the right of
the Warrenton pike, pickets north and south of the road,
west also, in the woods.   There was but the minimum of
apprehension, for the force was sufficient to overpower

any gang of bushwhackers that might be supposed to infest the mountains, while Stuart's entire division of cavalry was known to be south of the Rappahannock; as for Mosby, he had been heard of beyond the Blue Ridge only the day before.

The fires, kindled for cooking only, had long since died out, but in the open the white covers of the wagons were distinct in the starlight. Right of the road were the picketed horses of the squadron — two long rows — side by side, now and then some raw recruit of a horse expressing the restiveness not yet subdued by the discipline of weary marches and short provender. Between the wagons and the rows of horses lay a group of officers, their horses, only four, picketed close in their rear.

Braying mules had ceased to bray, and there was little noise in the camp, the men having long ago settled down to rest. Earlier, a small body of cavalry, protecting ambulances loaded with sick, had passed through from Warrenton en route to Alexandria. These people had told that they would encamp beyond Gainesville; the weather was hot and the sick men could stand the journey better in the early hours of the day and night.

The sentinel on the Warrenton pike, west of the camp, thought that the time for his relief was long in coming. He had stood here from seven until nine, then had rested until one; the sun would rise but little after five, and he imagined that he could see signs of day — a mere fancy of impatience, for his relief would not come until three; but then, you know, the hours of sentry duty, after a hot march in the long days, drag themselves out beyond all sense or reason, and it was only natural for this man to swear, and wonder if all the guard had gone to sleep and left him here to do more than his duty.

The sound of hoof-beats almost succeeded in interrupting a yawn. "Comin' at last," he thought.

He straightened up on his horse in order to appear vigilant and to receive the sergeant with appropriate ceremony.

The sound had died away. "Just now started, by God!" he muttered, and sank almost double again, his chin on his breast.

But the chin remained thus low for only a moment. From the southwest, toward Meade's army, there had come to the sentinel's ear confused sounds — sounds such as he had heard when, left on post, his own company had ridden by on a hard road far at his front, sounds such as he had heard in this night, when the cavalry escort of the ambulances had approached his post.

Yet these noises also died away, or at least he heard them no longer mentally, his head now full of an approaching object, which soon took the form of a mounted man. . . . "Who comes there?" he cried.

"Yassah, hit's me, sah; 'tain't nobody but *me*, sah. Doezh zhu want me to giddown off o' dis ole mule, Mahsta?"

"No; stand right there till I call the corporal," and then he opened his mouth to cry louder for the corporal of the guard. But he did not cry.

From his rear a low voice had spoken. "Dismount,

Y

and hand over your arms! You are surrounded! Be quiet, or you are gone!"

His head had gone round at the instant . . . three men were between him and his camp . . . footmen, with pieces levelled. He hesitated . . . his eyes turned to the front . . . there the one man had grown into the road-full.

"Dismount!" came the command again, nearer, and he saw the three men around him.

Then, quickly, Morgan with his seven uniforms passed the sentinel. In half a minute Lieutenant Turner's section of Mosby's column halted at the sentinel's post, and remained there stiff in saddle.

The sergeant led his men afoot. He was seeking the headquarters' group: at his right a great semicircle of wagons; at his left, beyond the roadway, the long rows of picketed cavalry horses.

Now came the challenge from another sentinel, the picket on the eastern road. Morgan could hear it but dimly; at the next instant a shot, and then the mad galloping of Mosby's men from east and from west, as in both directions they stormed forward to meet in the camp.

At once, everywhere within the bounds of that bivouac, shouts of anger, of amazement, of entreaty, of terror, of command; men were running to their horses; the teamsters were springing from their wagons, others from their places on the ground; horses were stamping and plunging, breaking their picket ropes and rushing here and there in wildest fright; shots were firing in every quarter; disorder was supreme and yet increasing.

In the very beginning of the turmoil the captain commanding had sprung from sound sleep, pistol in hand;
he saw a group of men confronting him, weapons ready.
" Who are *you?* Surrender ! " he cried.

" First Virginia cavalry !   Lee's brigade !   Stuart's
division ! " shouted Morgan in reply.   " Surrender ! "

The captain hesitated.

" Ready !   Aim ! "

The levelled carbines fixed upon their targets; one by
one all of the sleeping group had risen.

The captain threw down his arms, and the others followed his example.

Without a head, the sleeping cavalrymen had become
mixed in hopeless tangle.   Suddenly the cry rose — started
by one stentorian voice, taken up by others whose heads
were cool, and who saw the meaning, saw that it was the
only hope for saving anything from the disaster, the cry
rose and spread: " Stampede ! stampede ! The woods !
the woods ! "

A few of the teamsters had begun to hitch; at the cry
of the stampede they dropped chain and bridle and rushed
away southward, some of them hiding behind the bank
of the creek until all was over.   The cavalrymen who
lingered in an attempt to mount and ride were taken;
those who rushed afoot into the woods were safe from
pursuit.

Mosby's men were soon busy in ransacking the wagons.
The spot was too near the Federal army to hope that
all the material could be carried away into safety.   Everybody began to collect horses and mules, to be started on

the return journey, each man exchanging his own beast for any he liked better. The prisoners, numbering more than thirty, were held together under guard; they, too, must be mounted. Mosby had found valuable booty, mainly medical stores, which required some sixteen wagons to transport; to these wagons double teams were hitched; all others were burnt.

Wearied by a night's ride, to which had been added three hours of exhausting labour, the band started to return. The men knew that rest could not be hoped for until they had passed the Bull Run Mountains; even then they might have no rest; the proper care of the prisoners and of the horses would demand extraordinary exertion on the part of those whom Mosby should choose, and who must attempt their delivery to Stuart, far away covering Lee's infantry; as to the others, a long rest was looked for, with no duty but that of self-preservation until Mosby should call them again from their hiding-places.

CHAPTER XXIV

THE RETREAT

"Who would true valour see,
Let him come hither!"

— BUNYAN.

IT was long after sunrise when the last raider left the desolated camp, and Mosby could not doubt that tidings of the disaster had reached the ears of more than one Federal commander; for, besides the pickets who had been posted at a distance from the main road, and who would at once have ridden fast with the alarm, scores of frightened men and frantic horses had rushed into the darkness; some of these men would have been able to seize loose horses, and would be ready upon the arrival of fresh help, however small the reënforcements might be, to reorganize and join with any pursuing party. Mosby's troubles had just begun.

Indeed, it is an easy thing to effect a panic of sleeping men; one man afoot is better than a thousand such; a frightened cow has been known to stampede a brigade of infantry. You have fought well in open battle; you have caught the flag as your comrade fell, and have carried it aloft and far to the front and felt no dimming of ardour; but you unbuckle your arms, and you lie down

to sleep, and from dreams of home you wake in blackness
total but for specks of light at the mouths of the enemy's
guns environing ; you hear their war-cry while yours is
silent; you know not whether half your comrades are
still alive, or whether your commander is in the hands of
the foe whose successful advance means complete suprem-
acy ; your first sane thought is how to escape, and you
are a cool-headed and brave-hearted man if you have even
that thought.

The surprise had been easy ; to retire with safety would
be difficult.   It is no wonder that Major Mosby's exploits,
for a great part, began brilliantly and ended in sorrow —
always, nevertheless, with the effect of great disturbance to
his enemies.   His profession was that of destruction with a
greater purpose than to destroy — to demoralize.   And,
although his failures to save what he captured were
many, yet it must be confessed that more than one such
failure was to his credit — he abandoned his booty in
order to save his men.

And on this morning he knew that his own place was
at the rear, and until his column should be beyond the
reach of pursuit, his feeling must be all of suspense and
none of gratulation.   For the moment he had spread a
sense of insecurity in the minds of his enemies, in more or
less degree in the whole of Meade's army; but unless he
should succeed in bringing off his band, this feeling of his
enemies would be changed into satisfaction because of his
future inability to endanger them.   Then, too, not only
his men must surely be saved, but his booty also must be
saved if possible ; though by its early sacrifice he should

be able to disband his men and thus insure their individual safety, such sacrifice must inevitably tend to the
abandonment of the partisan warfare which was of so
great value ; for how could he or others hope to sustain
the spirit necessary for these enterprises if they were not
in a measure successful to the individuals engaged in
them ? Doubtless he would willingly have burnt every
dollar's worth of his booty if at the same time he could
have known that his men would follow him on his next
raid with their accustomed zeal. He knew that it could
not be ; he must endeavour at any cost, except that of his
organization, to carry off into the mountains value sufficient to keep the spirit at a high level.

The wagons retained were lightly loaded — for part
with medical stores which Lee's army greatly needed, for
other parts with implements and clothing. Progress was
rapid ; though the men were weary, they were in a high
state of elation. The prisoners had dwindled to less than
twenty ; in the confusion incident to such an exploit
escapes are easy and numerous. Only the officers were
well guarded, the teamsters being forced to handle their
teams and to drive them in the service of their captors.

Far at the front West rode, the advance following ; far
at the rear Morgan and Sency, yet with old Squire behind them, his invaluable services having been proved at
the pistol's mouth. Even granted that Squire be taken,
confidence was felt that he could make his way with his
captors ; for the only man, the sentinel, who could have
told of Squire's part in the surprise was a prisoner. On

either hand, parallel with the column, moved scouts familiar with the country.

Armstrong had shown more than his customary recklessness; now he seemed utterly indifferent; while other men's faces and speech gave evidence of joy over success or at times manifested eagerness in respect to the march into safety, he rode silent and expressionless.

Mosby pushed the retreat with all his vigour; he knew the telegraph would carry the news to every Federal commander in the district, — Warrenton, Fairfax, perhaps even Gainesville; from Gainesville a force might pursue; from Fairfax a force would endeavour to intercept him. He must strain every nerve . . . could it be possible for a swift rider to carry the news to Aldie in time for the Federal cavalry there to throw themselves across his path? He must strain every nerve.

To guard his prisoners and lead the captured horses had demanded half his force. Mosby now had but forty unencumbered men; yet forty were sufficient — provided he should not be forced to fight. Sometimes the teams went downhill at a gallop; oh, for the clear passage of the Aldie pike!

Old Squire kept Morgan just in sight; the negro was mounted on a stout and swift horse — many were the stout and swift horses that were yet loose in the woods, to be ridden by any man who might secure them.

Usher West, also, was well mounted: all unserviceable or weak animals had been abandoned. West rode far at the front, and at every new stretch of the way he rode fast; four holsters hung at his saddle. Usher West, the extreme front, was more than a mile in advance of Squire.

Mosby rode in no one place; his great horse carried him toward the front, where he would urge the men to steady work; then he would halt, and, as the wagons passed, command the teamsters to drive till their teams dropped dead; when the teams had passed, again he galloped to the front, ever pressing the flight, making for the gap in the mountains, which he knew he could defend at least until darkness should enable him to reward his men; after, dispersion could not be commanded too soon.

West avoided Haymarket. Oh, that he had known! the Federal cavalry force that for two days had been there in bivouac had been withdrawn; he lost a mile. He went on by-roads in a detour and came again into the road for the gap; then, looking back, he halted, for he saw no follower. It was ten o'clock — after. West heard shots far to the rear. The pursuit had not only begun — it had struck the column.

Yet West remained stationary.

In the rear old Squire had seen mounted men cut in between him and Morgan — a squad of but half a dozen; had seen Morgan's men turn in their saddles; had seen and heard the fire of both parties; had seen Morgan's men yet stand as though to invite closer contest; then he had taken to the woods at his right.

The advance guard under Lieutenant Turner, at a distance following West, had been commanded to reënforce the main body. With show of strength Mosby must give his pursuers pause. The train and the led horses went on, but under feeble guard. A front attack would prove ruin.

Mosby was now at the rear — farther to the rear than Turner's men — back with Morgan.

" How many were there, Sergeant ? "

"Very few, sir ; I counted only six," was the reply.

" If the same crowd shows up again, you must charge them," cried Mosby, and rode again to the front, urging as he rode. West had started — had seen the wagons coming.

" West," says Mosby, anxiously, " all I fear now is that man Freeman off there by Aldie."

" Yes, sir ; but it would be a pure accident that threw him across our road."

" I don't know so well about that — and accidents will happen."

" Two hours more, Major, and we'll be all right."

" Yes — but the two hours. Well, we don't howl yet ! And if Freeman hasn't come down this way I don't know the man that can stop us. Morgan drove back their advance — and they will be very cautious."

" How many were there, Major ? "

" Only a small squad."

" Plenty more behind," West exclaimed.

" Yes, but they'll be slow. They think we're the First Virginia," said Mosby.

The column had become more compact ; the speed was a little slower, and soon must become quite slow, for the road would ascend the hills.

" If Freeman should try to stop us, Major ? "

" Then we must throw everything we've got right on him

without giving him time to get help," said the commander, sternly.

Again there were shots at the rear, and again Mosby had gone.

The Federals showed stronger, a full platoon, more than equalling the raider's rear-guard. They were advancing rapidly, and to Morgan it was evident that their confidence came from the knowledge of near support.

Armstrong was no longer indifferent; he was raging.

"Dan, let's have it out with 'em!"

"No, Charley; not unless they force us."

The retreat of the rear-guard had become a walk; behind them the Federals were advancing at a trot — some four hundred yards between.

"Dan, you see that bend yonder?" cried Armstrong.

"Yes; when we get there, we'll run for it and gain ground."

"No, by God! If I had ten men behind me like you've got, I'd try 'em right there!"

Three hundred yards separated the parties. The bend was fifty yards away . . . forty yards . . . thirty yards.

The pursuers commenced firing; Armstrong halted, and faced them. Morgan, failing to see Armstrong's act, passed on with the force, but in ten yards he became aware that his friend was not at his side; he looked around, and saw Armstrong stiff in his saddle.

"Dan, I'm a-thinkin' he's a-goin' to make us stop here," cried Lewis.

"Charley!" shouted the sergeant, "come back here, I command you!"

Armstrong seemed not to hear; Morgan, seeing him
draw sabre, spurred his horse, caught his friend's bridle,
and drew him away. The pursuers fired; their shouts
were heard.

"Dan!" yelled Armstrong, seemingly wild, "for God's
sake, let's stop here and charge 'em!"

Morgan said nothing. The men had seen, and were
wondering what Armstrong would do next. Sency and
Joe Lewis rode in Charley's rear.

But behind the bend Armstrong again halted. Sency
cried to Morgan: "Better have it out here, Dan! It's
got to come soon, anyhow; and Charley's giving us
trouble!"

Morgan ordered his men to scatter in the bushes, and
to charge pistol in hand when he should give the word.

And now the Federals, believing that beyond the bend
the slow retreat would suddenly become swift, came on in
disorderly haste.

As the first blue horseman rode into view, Morgan
signalled by pulling trigger; but even before the shot
startled his men into activity, Armstrong urged on with
a shout, his sabre pointing, leaning forward for action,
neither stiffly erect nor bending aside, eager to strike,
careless to avoid.

At the signal a dozen pistol shots had bewildered the
Federals; then, unready, they were instantly charged and
thrown into confusion, suffering the loss of a third of their
numbers; and as the remnant fled, the Confederates pursued, Armstrong ever in the lead, Morgan long vainly
striving to recall him when the pursuit had become
unwise.

The rear-guard slowly withdrew, passing without concern the dead and wounded of the Federals.

But the check had not accomplished safety. From far away, where a flying battery had been planted, shells began to scream over the wagons. The road curved right and left in its ascent, making plain targets for the rifled cannon on somewhat lower ground. The third wagon from the rear was struck; at once the teamsters cut loose the mules and kept on; three wagons had been abandoned. Then Mosby attempted ruse. He commanded the teamsters to drive on; in rear of the wagons he formed all his men in double file, and at their head rode six times in a slow walk around an open bend, making six circles, half of each circle hidden in the woods where he galloped in order to overtake the slow-moving few who were visible to his enemies. Meantime the cannon continued to pound, but the distance was great, and the elevation was at each instant more impracticable.

Unless the partisan should find a force in front blocking his way, there was now no cause to fear the pursuit; he drew Morgan and more than half his men forward, following West closely. Half a mile more and he must cross the junction of the roads, and once past that cross-road he might snap his fingers at his enemies. From his elevated position he could see with his glass a troop of horse halted two miles at the south; they had given up the chase, or they were delaying for a purpose — for what purpose? To deceive the Confederates, who thus would be tempted to slower march and so give time for other Federals to intercept? He decided to urge forward more rapidly.

The loss of a minute at the junction might prove ruin. He turned and again sought the front; but before his gaze quit the south he saw the Federal horsemen begin to move on.

Mosby rode past Lieutenant Turner's men — and then past Morgan's men; and as he rode he cried to both to keep all well in hand, and to seize upon the junction and hold it till the last man had gone by. He kept on, and now saw West ahead steadily moving; he would ride with West, anxiety so pressing him that every moment's doubt was cumulative torture. It was not more than three hundred yards to the junction — was the crossing clear?

West was yet two hundred yards in Mosby's front, and going steadily.

Mosby turned in his saddle; he saw Morgan leading on, not twenty rods away, Armstrong by his side; and at the instant saw Armstrong raise his hand in the air, and also saw Morgan's hand go up. He turned again, and as he turned he saw the smoke from West's pistol; saw West's horse reined back on his haunches; saw the road full of blue troopers in striking distance of his guide; saw West's horse fall; and, all at the same moment, saw also the fall of the foremost Federal.

A great shout came from Mosby's rear — Morgan was charging.

Mosby knew that West was down, and was a prisoner or dead. He waited but a moment. Morgan's men were coming at the variable speed of thirty horses — better let them close — "Steady, men!" — then, "All together!"

Morgan had not stopped, but his speed had lessened. Armstrong with drawn sabre had swept on.

Twenty paces in Armstrong's rear Mosby was now leading two-thirds of his band against Freeman's company ready in the junction — no, not ready.

The numbers were nearly equal. Mosby had the great advantage of present momentum — the other, that of physical strength unabated.

But Freeman's position was the worst he could have chosen ; indeed, he had not chosen — he had but reached the spot. There was no time to take position, or time to meet charge in column with charge in column. His men had but fronted in line — the centre on the road up which Mosby was charging eight deep, woods and steep hillside on either hand.

Armstrong was in the thick of careering horsemen ; his second blow had not been struck when Mosby, Morgan, Sency, Lewis, were all at his back. The Federals in the open road — room there for but few — had fired their pistols without lessening the impact of the charge. No doubt as to the momentary result — the column pierced the line, cutting Freeman's company in two, part fleeing down the mountain, other part to the west. The crossing was encumbered with fallen men and horses.

But Mosby must turn — the Federals on both wings were seeking to rally and reunite — and as he came back he found the enemy again in his road, and growing stronger at each moment.

Yet the struggle was short. Freeman's men, one-half without leadership, for Brock had fallen by West's first

fire, were unable to hold together.   Freeman himself had
been unhorsed, and though his men had remounted him, he
was hardly able now to sit his saddle.   The return charge
of the raiders easily scattered their enemies, who fled down
the mountain road to the east just as Mosby's reserve
reached the scene of conflict.

Three Confederates had fallen ; more than twice as
many were suffering from wounds.   A Federal lieutenant
was among the dead.   The wounded on both sides, as well
as Mosby's dead, were placed in the wagons.   Six prisoners
had been added to those already captured.   The retreat
continued, but it was no longer a flight.

Before sunset Mosby reached safety.   And the night
grew, and waned, and the sun again shone ; but from
Morgan's squad, Usher and old Squire were still missing.

CHAPTER XXV

A FLASK FOR TWO

" Ber. Who's there?
Fran. Nay, answer me! Stand and unfold yourself!"
— SHAKESPEARE.

SAFE, at least for the time, old Squire heard the Federal cavalry march by on the road. It was clear as the sun that he could not overtake Mosby until that leader should halt, and he saw no indications but those of continued flight and pursuit; so he determined quickly that the best thing for him to do was to return to Mr. West's, whither his master, or at least Usher, would not long delay his coming.

He was in the woods. Just how far he must go he knew not, or the precise direction, but Bull Run Mountain was before him; once on its high western slope he would be able to see villages and roads, and make his way; the mountains, in many places, he already knew. He went northwest, keeping prudently in the woods. His horse was a good one, but would need feeding. As for his own needs he was armed with a Federal haversack which he had not yet explored.

After a time he heard cannon, not near enough to perturb him on his own account, but it gave him fear for

Mahs Chahley; his course had led him too far from the
pursuit to enable him to hear the sound of small arms.
He became extremely cautious; in his uncertainty of the
whereabouts of all Federals, he advanced only after looking in every direction; he must cross the road on which
the Federals were moving, but not yet; he would go slow
until safe in the mountain.

Toward noon he found a small grassy glade in the
midst of the low woods. The spot was very inviting.
He was hungry, and his horse strained at the bridle to
crop the good grass; a small brook ran near by.

He dismounted and picketed his horse to graze; then
he sat down and rummaged his haversack.

"Oohm, hahdtack, — man w'at fixed up dis dam stuff
didn't had no likin' feh ole Squiah, — oohm, salt pohk, —
I not a-gwine to run f'om dat, — oohm, cawfy an' sugah
all mixed up — an' w'at dis in de big bottle? Hit shake
lak some'h'm good feh true."

He unscrewed the cover of the metal flask and smelt.

"Oohmoo! dat dess lak dat med'cin' Doctoh guv me.
Hit mek me fohgit all my troubles."

Squire did not make himself entirely drunk, neither
was he able to preserve complete sobriety. When he got
his consent to leave the spot, the sun was descending
toward the mountain tops; he had slept; his horse had
ceased to eat the tall grass.

He replaced in his haversack the remains of his food,
and the big flask atop.

An hour more and he had begun to go up the mountain
side; and now he concluded, after renewing his courage,

that it was no longer needful to keep the thick woods, for here before him was a good open way seemingly untravelled for long, leading in the right direction; he took it and went on more rapidly, for he wanted to attain the western side of the range while yet there should be good light.

Around him, seemingly unconcerned at the nearness or at the noise of the great four-footer that could not climb, squirrels were chattering; one of them scampered across the way, his tail bent in the most ultra fashionable of convolutions, and hung motionless three feet from earth on the bole of a great oak; Squire watched him.

When the negro's eyes next rested on the path before him, he halted — a man was in the way.

Sunlight had not yet gone in the valley, but here in the woods the mountain shadow was gloomy, and Squire at first glance was unable to know more than that the man was afoot and in blue, and seemed unarmed. The face was hidden by a drooping bough very near it; yet Squire could see that the stranger's front was presented, and it required no great reasoning to determine that the blue man had a mighty coign of vantage in relation to that leafy branch through which undoubtedly he was peering at the more distant horseman.

There was, however, in the stranger's attitude an indescribable something — an indeterminate quality akin to hesitation, yet greater. Yes, Squire had no sooner seen the man than he resolved not to flee; for the man surely, though motionless, radiated, as it were, a subtile evincement of tremulous alarm.

Squire himself was first to speak : —

"Mahsta, kin you tell me ef you is seed any stray hosses?"

The man came forward; his right hand was performing violent and mysterious action in the air; in his left was a bunch of live chickens.

"Well, I swaih to God if it ain't *shu*, Unc Squiah!"

"De Je-e-e-susgawd!" exclaimed the old man, holding out his hand. "Bahney, you fool niggeh, I sho' is proud to see you a-lookin' so hahty! I sot on my hoss right sheah, an' I says, says I, 'Dat man yandeh he done plum got los' an' he dunno whah to go, an' so I nee'n' to be skeehed o' *him*, an' bless Gawd, Bahney, I tuck you feh a w'ite man, dess 'cazhe yo' black skin hit done hide behime de bush. But, bless Gawd, I is glad to see you, an' to see you a-lookin' so peaht! Whah you gwine, Bahney?" and Squire's voice was not devoid of suspicion.

"I ain't a-gwine nowhah now, Unc Squiah; I done be'n. An' all I got to do is to git back. But I swaih to God, heah you is oncet mo'e, when I ain't *neveh* been expectin' to see you no mo'e."

Squire gave an indescribable motion of the head, indicating a complexity of ideas.

"Whaffuh you say dat, niggeh? You be'n a-lookin' to heah dat I done daid? You be'n a-cockin' up yo' yeahs to heah dat? You betteh be a-tekkin' keeh o' yo' own skin. Now, I let shu know dat."

"Now, Unc Squiah, don't shu go to gittin' riled about nothin'," says Barney, evidently desiring to conciliate; "you jest git down an' step out here in de bresh an' I'll tell you some'h'm."

"An' whah izh yo' camp at, Bahney? I be'n a-heahin' dat shu hole on to dat Cap'm Freeman oncet mo'e." Squire's gaze was still full upon Barney's face.

"Yes, Unc Squiah; I had to hole on to him yit, 'caze it so fuh back down whah I got to go to. Git right down an' come along out in de bresh. De's be'n some turrible gwines-on dis day, an' I sho' is mighty glad to fall in with you oncet mo'e."

Although Squire was suspicious, yet not a trace of reluctance was in his mind concerning possible danger of betrayal by this brother in a freemasonry old as the race ; he dismounted and followed Barney.

"I sho' is glad to fall in with you ag'in, Unc Squiah, I sho' is," Barney repeated, looking, too, as though he meant what he said ; "I be'n a-heahin' about shu, an' I be'n skeehed dat some wrongdom was a-hatchin', 'caze I knowed dat my name done git to yo' folks, 'caze I helped one of 'em out oveh yondeh, an' I be'n a-wantin' to see you."

"Whaffuh you want to see me, chile ? " asked the old man, kindly.

"'Caze I knowed my name done got to yo' folks, Unc Squiah. Ain't shu done heahed about me f'om yo' folks ? " asked Barney, anxiously.

"Cou'se I is, chile ; Mahs Dan he done tell me all 'bout seein' you oveh yandeh in Mellan' an' Penns'vania, an' he say he gwine to look out an' pay you back ; dat w'at Mahs Dan say."

"He tell you 'bout how I helped him out, Unc Squiah ? "

"Yas, chile, cou'se he do. Mahs Dan he don't hide nothin' f'om *me!* " the old man exclaimed proudly.

"But, Unc Squiah, I's jest been afeahed dat de cap'm'd heah about dat," and Barney shook his head and seemed restless with his thought.

"How he gwine to heah?" asked Squire, assurance in his tone. "Kin he heah Mahs Dan talk six mile?"

"But den he mought tell somebody what'd tell de cap'm," returned the younger negro, uneasily.

"You feahed o' *me*, Bahney? You feahed o' *me?* You nee'n' to be feahed o' *me*, chile; I de bes' frien' you got anywhah, Bahney," and old Squire had spoken as though he was laying down a proposition incapable of denial.

"Cou'se I ain't afeahed o' you, Unc Squiah, and all I axes you to do is to ax *him* not to talk."

"Mahs Dan ain't no talkin' man, chile; but I gwine to ax him fuh you, Bahney. Ain't we got fuh 'nough, Bahney?"

"Yes, Unc Squiah, you jest tie yo' hoss, an' I gwine to tell you some'h'm. Now le's set down right sheah; an' you needn't be afeahed, feh dey ain't no man in three mile dat shu got any call to be afeahed of. You jest set down. Whose hoss is dat shu got?"

"Mine; de cap'm done say he mine feh good. You heah de cannon to-day, chile?"

"Oh, yes, Unc Squiah, an' I done seed wuss'n dat! An' dat's jest what I gwine to tell you 'bout. You know Lieutenant Brock? He dead. You know Laffney? He dead. You know Jinkins? He done dead. You know O'Donnell? He dead. You know Hawley? Yo' folks is got *him*, an' Freeman he got Usheh West." The deliverance of this speech was oratorical and effective;

at each successive gesture Squire had swayed his body forth or back.

"Gawdamighty, how you does go awn!" exclaimed the old man.

"Hit's de troof; an' if it ain't I hope I may die."

"Dat Hirish is daid?"

"Dead as Adam's gran'daddy. An' I ain't de leas' bit sorry — not feh *him*, noh feh Jinkins, but, Unc Squiah, Misteh Brock he a good man to me, an' my bes' frien' in de comp'ny is done gawn."

"But whah izh yo' comp'ny at now, Bahney?" asked Squire, a possible danger recurring to his mind.

"What dat smell so good, Unc Squiah? You be'n eat'n sugah?"

The old man slowly brought out his flask.

"Tetch it light, boy; hit's mighty pow'ful, an' I don't want to see you mek a fool o' yo'se'f."

... "Sho' dat is good! Uhmoo! Unc Squiah, I be'n heahin' about shu. Dat man Hawley done tole de cap'm dat he see you up dah on de Ridge, an' I be'n sawteh expectin' an' a-hopin' to meet up with you ag'in. Now, you done ax me whah is de comp'ny, an' I gwine to tell you; hit's right oveh yondeh, jest about three mile — but hit ain't in no fix to git skeehed at, feh if eveh you seed a comp'ny dat's done got a belly-full o' fightin' hit's dat same comp'ny. An' I gwine to tell you right now, Unc Squiah, dat if ev'ything goes on lak it do to-day, den Ginnle Lee's a-gwine to come back dis a-way befo'e cawn pullin' time. Whah wuzh you at w'en dey wus a-fightin'?"

"Lawd, chile, I's a-way back yandeh; so fuh dat I couldn't heah noth'n' but de big gun. You know ef Mahs Chahley git huht?" The question had been asked indifferently as to manner, yet Squire now held his breath.

"Dat I don't know; but yo' folks jest up an' went th'ough ouan jest lak a doset o' salts. Twicet. An' dey didn't lef' a man behind 'em excusin' of Usheh West."

"An' dey got Mahs Usheh? How come you know *him*, Bahney?"

"'Caze I be'n to de house with Cap'm Freeman, an' I heah Doctoh Lacy talk; de doctoh knowed 'im jest as soon as he laid eyes on 'im."

"You know dat doctoh, too?" Again Squire's tone indicated a lack of interest.

"Yes, I be'n a-knowin' him mighty nigh on to two yeah."

"You heah him say ef he know *me?*"

"No, Unc Squiah; I ain't neveh heahed him call yo' name."

"'Caze I tell you why, Bahney. You know dat time I put my han' on somebody?"

"I ain't neveh gwine to fohgit it, Unc Squiah, an' dat's jest what make me say I so mighty glad to see yo' face oncet mo'e."

"Yas, chile; cou'she you is," said the old man, slowly, not greatly delighted at the implication, yet feeling no revengeful desire to turn the tables on Barney. "Cou'she you is; ain't dat doctoh a mighty smaht man, Bahney?"

"Yes, he mighty smaht in some places, dat he is; but den ag'in he ain't got de sense of a louse."

"He de smahtes' man right now in ole Fihginny," exclaimed Squire, almost angrily.

"Yes, sah; he smaht a plenty in what he b'longs to; but den ag'in he don't know de fust toot on de big brass hawn."

"He de smahtes' man in dis whole wohl'," insisted the old man, hotly.

"How come you know?" asked Barney.

"W'y, ain't I be'n seed him? Ain't I be'n a-wohkin' up dah at Mahs Tom's fo' mo'e'n three weeks awff an' awn? An' ain't I heahed him talk? You see me heah? You see me heah now, Bahney? You see me?"

"Yes, Unc Squiah; cou'se I see you."

"An' ain't shu s'prise to see me? Now, come, ain't shu mighty s'prise to see me?"

"Dat I *is!*" cried Barney, emphatically. "I jest as soon expec' to meet my daddy what be'n dead eveh sence I was knee high."

"An' you know de reason? You know de reason I heah yit? You don't? Den I gwine to tell you. Hit's dess 'caze I mek a mistake in countin'," Squire exclaimed with all confidence.

"What de doctoh got to do with all dat?"

"'Caze he up an' he showed me how come dat I mek dat mistake. He de smahtes' man, — mine w'at I tell you, Bahney, — dat man he de smahtes' man dis side o' up Yandeh! You don't b'lieve it?"

Barney slowly shook his head. "I ain't a-gwine to 'spute dat he ain't smaht, Unc Squiah; but den, signs is signs."

"Yas, an' dat dess w'at he say, too; an' he ain't a-sayin' nothin' ag'in de signs. But shu see me heah now, don't shu, Bahney?"

Barney's assent seemed rather a protest against existing conditions. "Hit mought be so," he said; "cou'se I knows dat as well as he does, dat ev'ybody can't alluz count right; but den ag'in dey ain't no use in fight'n' ag'in —"

"Ag'in w'at, Bahney? Don't shu see me heah?"

"I got to go, Unc Squiah; I got to git back. I's mighty glad I see you oncet mo'e."

"But shu dess hole on, Bahney. I ain't quite done wid ju yit. Tek anotheh mou'f'l o' dis, chile."

"Jest to please you, Unc Squiah, an' bein' as you got so much."

"Now, Bahney, you done say one wohd dat I lak to heah som'h'm mo'e about. You got Mahs Usheh?"

"Yes, de cap'm done tuck him back to camp."

"An' did he git huht?"

"He jest git stunted, dat's all; an' dey done fotch him to. But I tell you what, Unc Squiah, de cap'm he mighty hot; he say he gwine to make a sample."

"An' w'at he mean by dat?"

"He say dezhe heah Mosby men dat ride about in home-made clothes an' kill de Union men, he say dey ain't fitten to live, an' he say dat he gwine to see dat Misteh West don't kill no mo'e. Dat's what he mean. He done kill de lieutenant, an' de cap'm say dat's de las' man what he gwine to kill."

"An' you still sticks to dat man, Bahney?" asked the old negro in expostulation.

"Unc Squiah, I done tole you I gwine back home jest as soon as I can."

"Den now's de time. You kin dess go right along wi' me."

"No, Unc Squiah, I can't go yit. I 'xpec' I've got to wait tell Ginnle Lee comes back up dis a-way; I've got my things in de camp, an' de men dey owes me feh washin' an' I can't go yit; but you can jest count on my gwine with you when Ginnle Lee's ahmy comes back."

"Den w'en you heah de big guns, chile, an' I sen' you wohd, I gwine to look fuh you to meet me."

"I do it, Unc Squiah, sho', ef you jest sen' me de wohd."

"You meet me up to de fawks o' de road, Bahney?"

"What fawks shu talkin' 'bout, Unc Squiah?"

"Up dah dess dis side o' Hopewell. 'Caze we got to go awn de yotheh side o' dis mounting, chile. Hit won't do to go awn dis side — you know dat, Bahney."

"Yes, cou'se I do, Unc Squiah."

"Den, Bahney, I gwine to look fuh you, dess es soon es we heah Ginnle Lee a-comin' up dis a-way — dess es soon es we heah de big guns. You gwine to meet me, Bahney?"

"Unc Squiah, I gwine to do it if you jest sen' me wohd. If I don't, I hope I may die."

"Don't shu fret 'bout me not sennin' you no wohd, chile. I sen' you de wohd all right. Good-by, Bahney; tek keeh o' yo'se'f, Bahney. I gwine to look fuh you. An' yo' cap'm is a-gwine to shoot Mahs Usheh?"

"Dat's jest de way he talks, Unc Squiah; but don't shu go to givin' me away."

"Lawd, chile, you think old Squiah ain't got no sense? Ef you dess tek keeh o' *yo'se'f* dat's all I ax. I's got to go, Bahney. W'ich a-way is yo' camp?"

Barney pointed. Both men had risen; Squire's foot was in the stirrup; another instant he was in the saddle. Then Barney stood alone, listening to the sounds of a fast galloping horse.

"Look like Unc Squiah he git in a mighty big hurry all at oncet," he thought.

CHAPTER XXVI

FOR LIFE AND LOVE

" How many score of miles may we well ride
'Twixt hour and hour ? "
— SHAKESPEARE.

FROM Freeman's camp a messenger, with a led horse,
had come for Dr. Lacy, whose skill was needed for the
wounded.

Junior Morgan was sitting on the porch with Mr.
West and Jennie ; night had almost come. The talk
was not cheerful ; son and brother had been in the fray,
of which the messenger could not say more than that
Freeman's cavalry had met Mosby's men, and that the
fight had been bloody.

" I hear hard riding," said Morgan.

There was no response ; all were listening. Mr. West
rose and went into the yard.

Morgan's wound was still giving him trouble, on this
day more than usual ; he had struck his shoulder against
the door. Jennie had already begged him not to sit
in the night air.

They saw Mr. West go out of the gate and take stand
there. Sounds of furious hoofs rang out on the pike
toward Aldie. Whoever it was he was riding for life.

Morgan rose, but he did not go out . . . at the mouth of the lane a dark spot showed, growing instantly larger as a single horseman came at all speed.

Jennie rose and stood by Junior, a little in advance. The horseman had halted before Mr. West.

"Dat shu, Mahs Tom?"

"It's Uncle Squire," whispered the girl.

They saw a man dismount; they heard speech in low tones.

Mr. West was coming hurriedly back. Jennie saw that he had not closed the gate, a neglect very unusual, and her fears grew into torture; she went down the steps and met him.

"Oh, Father, what is it?"

Outside the yard Morgan, saw a motionless horse, a dismounted man standing.

Mr. West did not at once reply, and when he spoke Jennie hardly knew the voice.

"Usher has been captured, my dear."

The words gave her a little relief. "Oh, but Father, that is not as bad as it might be."

Again he was silent. He doubted whether to tell all he had heard. But would it not be better for her to know now than to be told suddenly when—? He decided to speak; his daughter was strong.

"My dear, Squire says that before he was taken he killed an officer, and that Captain Freeman has sworn to —to—execute him."

"Mr. Morgan!" she called, and Junior came quickly, for the voice was distressful.

"Uncle Squire!" she called, and the old man threw his bridle over a paling and came forward.

"Now, Uncle Squire, please tell Lieutenant Morgan all you know."

Squire gave the facts of his talk with Barney, concealing only his informant's name.

"Can you let me have a horse, Mr. West?"

"Better two and drive — you ought not to go horseback."

"Much quicker," said the lieutenant.

Mr. West went to his stable and chose his easiest saddler and his best — a favourite of his own.

"Uncle Squire, you must go with Mr. Morgan. Won't you go for *me*?"

"Yas'm, I go anywhah you say, Miss Jinnie."

"There's no need of his going; I can ride to Aldie very well," said Junior.

"Yes, but I want Uncle Squire to go with you," she said tearfully.

"Well, of course, if you wish it. I may be delayed; I can send him back with comfort to you. I have no idea that Freeman would think for a moment of it."

Junior needed help to mount, but once in the saddle he said he was comfortable; the thing felt natural. The pressure of Mr. West's hand enkindled the highest resolve.

They had started — the negro riding close to Junior's side.

After a while Mr. West said: "I wonder whose horse that is that Squire is on. I never once thought to ask him."

Junior Morgan in health was a great rider. He had
been in the First New York cavalry until McClellan's
advance to the Chickahominy, and since that time he had
served as a courier in all of Pleasonton's campaigns until
he had received his wound. Now he let his horse go;
for, although he was still very weak, and his enforced inac-
tion had stiffened him, yet the need was urgent and the
road was good.

Morgan spoke but little to the negro. He had seen
Squire at work about the house and yard, and had heard
Jennie and her father speak in great praise of his shrewd-
ness and his fidelity, but had never been with him alone
until this night. He took their word for it that the old
man had brought no false news, although he could not
think that Freeman would be so mad as to go to the
extremity of his power without first referring the awful
matter to his superiors.

Approaching Freeman's camp, Morgan commanded
Squire to fall behind and remain without. He answered the sentinel's challenge, and was held until a
sergeant, who had been sent for, allowed him to come in.
He asked for Freeman, and learned that the captain had
already retired. Then he asked for Lacy, and was soon
in the doctor's presence.

"What," exclaimed the doctor, "you here, Morgan? I
was just going to send an ambulance to bring you."

They shook hands, Junior still in the saddle, the doctor
standing by.

"Is it true that Captain Freeman intends to shoot a — a
prisoner?" asked Junior in a halting voice.

"Horribly true. That is just what I was going to send after you about. And it's young West!" cried Lacy, in growing excitement.

"Can I see Captain Freeman? Can't you come at him, Doctor?"

"Morgan, I have already exhausted every argument. He is firm — worse, he is unreasonable. His head is turned with his loss — with his loss of Brock particularly. I verily believe his reason is in danger; he acts like a madman. He has fixed the time for to-morrow at sunset."

"You know he has no such authority," cried Morgan. "I could have no effect, you think?"

"Not a particle. West was in civilian's clothes, and killed poor Brock."

"But in open fight?"

"Oh, yes; West charged the whole company, it seems, with no help nearer than pistol range. That young fellow has deceived me badly; but I'm not going to allow him to be murdered. Now, mark my word, Morgan, I'm not going to allow it."

"Have you said as much to Freeman?" asked Junior, mildly.

"Yes—and enraged him. But I have an idea," added Lacy, and he shook his hand violently in the direction of the captain's tent.

"Tell me what it is, Doctor."

"Mosby has taken Hawley, who had already given his parole. Don't you remember?"

"Yes, my brother paroled him."

2 A

" Well, I want to get word to Mosby in some way. I'll do it. I don't care if they cashier me. I'll be *damned* if I let Freeman shoot West," and Lacy stamped his foot as evidence of his earnestness.

" I see ; you want Mosby to threaten retaliation upon Hawley," said Junior, calmly, almost dissuasively. He doubted the wisdom of Lacy's policy.

" Exactly, and I'm going somehow to get word to him. I'm going to tell Mr. West, and I'm sure he can find Mosby."

" Doctor, don't go so far as to suggest action to Mr. West. Let him know, however, that Mosby holds Hawley ; that will be enough, I think."

" Well, won't you tell Mr. West ? "

" No, I'm going to Pleasonton."

" You ? "

" Yes."

"I forbid it, sir. It might be your death. I can't think of allowing it, sir. You've already exerted yourself too much."

" But, Doctor, you ought to know how close to me this matter is, and I'll pledge you my word I'll be careful."

Perhaps Lacy knew that if uncompromising issue should be joined, his own defeat was sure. He responded : —

" Get somebody else, sir. You are in my charge, and I can't allow it."

" Doctor, I promise you I won't go alone ; I'll take help. But you ought to know that I can't trust any one to take my place in this. And then you know that the general will be pleased to see me again, and I'm not ready to believe that he will wish to refuse me."

" What help can you take ? "

" Squire ; he came with me."

" I forbid your going," yet the tones were softer, and Junior felt that his conciliatory speech had been better than persevering in an open declaration of resolve.

" Doctor, what would I think of myself if I should leave anything undone ? Now, if you will manage your plan while I try the general, I shall have great hope that we'll succeed. And if I shouldn't go, and we should fail, you know I could never forgive myself ; and you know there are others who would never forgive."

" Go, Morgan ; I see you are determined to risk your life ; " yet the voice was not harsh, for Lacy knew how it was with Morgan.

" Then I want you to come out with me, Doctor ; we can talk as we ride to Squire, and I shall beg you to exchange horses with him, for his has already done a hard day's work."

" I'll go·out with you ; but my horse is not fresh himself, and I don't know that you'd gain anything by changing."

Yet, compared with Squire's, the horse had done little on this day, and the exchange was made.

" Now, Doctor, all you need to say to Mr. West is that Mosby has taken Hawley."

Junior distrusted Lacy's plan ; he could see that it might work contrary to his hopes. A Union general could hardly be expected to lower his plumes at Mosby's dictation ; indeed, would not the demand of the guerilla be rather resented than complied with ? Yet there was the chance that Freeman might be brought to reason by Mosby's threat : better not . give up this chance, for Junior's own mission might fail. And with this thought there came a swift idea into Morgan's brain : he knew how to make the most of the situation.

" You believe he will see ? I tell you, Morgan, if he doesn't, I'll speak out. I'll tell him straight that he must find Mosby and get him to threaten."

" There will be no need, sir ; Mr. West will do that without urging. And you ought to tell him in such a way that he won't see what you intend. There is no use for you to get into trouble about this thing. I don't know but it would be better for me to write to Mr. West."

" Not at all, not at all. What harm can anybody make out of my telling him that Hawley has been taken ? "

" None, so that your motive is not told." `

" But does he know that Hawley accepted a parole ? "

" You can easily find out by his talk ; if he knows it, you will hear from him."   .

" Yes, but if he doesn't, then I'll tell him, and tell him short. I suppose I'll find him awake ? "

" Oh, yes," and Junior sighed, thinking of the sleepless night before one he loved.

They parted. It was already past midnight when old Squire took the front, making for the Warrenton road. A great and slow detour was necessary in order to avoid the camp ; but once in the road for Haymarket, he struck a trot and kept it.

The night was going — neither moon nor stars to light the road — and twenty-five miles to Warrenton. But would Pleasonton be found at Warrenton? To Warrenton the distance was known; but Pleasonton might be elsewhere. And for fear that the general might be called away early on this day, Morgan decided to do his best riding at the first.

" How long till day, Squire ? "

" But a houh 'n' a ha'f o' leetle betteh, Mahsta."

Squire was unused to Junior; his indefinite " Mahsta " sounded wrong in his own ears — this man was so like his Mahs Dan.

" Three hours till sunrise ? "

" Yassah."

" Six miles an hour, Squire; yes, better make it seven — yes, eight."

Old Squire struck his heels into his horse's sides and darted on.

" Halt ! " cried Junior, " that's not the gait; you'll break down at the start," and for a while he rode at the front to set the pace.

" How you holdin' out, Mahsta ? "

" Moderately well; I can stand it," but the words belied the feeling.

Squire himself was not in good shape. Just forty-eight hours ago he had risen in order to reach Miss Jinnie in time to help her get breakfast. His day's work had not been hard, but the night that had followed, and the day that had followed the night — if he had thought of it he would have felt that a bed of flint would be sweet. And there could be no great rest for either until they had covered twenty-five miles and twenty back.

Dawn came upon them at Catharpin Run ; Squire said they had made ten miles. Morgan's shoulder and back were aching horribly ; but he kept his mouth shut, and followed Squire.

While the east was red they rode through Haymarket —losing time here, for they were halted. But the halt was not long, and the cessation from jolting gave Morgan a little relief. Besides, he learned that Pleasonton was just on the edge of Warrenton.

At sunrise they were nearing Buckland Mills, and here Morgan's suffering was so great that he thoroughly decided that he was unable to go on without resting, and he halted ; but at once there came the belief that if he should rest he would never have the strength to remount, even with help — and he rode on, following Squire.

The negro had turned ; he saw Junior reeling in the saddle, the horse keeping a swift amble.

"Mahsta," and Squire halted, and thrust his hand into his haversack, "Mahsta, tek some o' dis. Hit'll do you good."

Morgan seized upon the flask and emptied it.

"God, Squire ! You are a great man ! " Yet the words were feebly said.

Both horses were showing great weariness ; the sun was climbing up ; but around them were camped artillery, and wagons parked. Morgan urged ahead of Squire ; his new-found strength could not last — he must make the most of it.

. . . General Pleasonton was leaning over a table under a great tent-fly, his adjutant, Cohen, opposite. The
Union cavalry leader looked annoyed ; last night he had
learned of Mosby's escape after defeating Freeman's command, and he was now deliberating over the plan for a
formidable movement upon the slippery partisan — a movement from three directions. Outside, a guard stood at
carry arms. The general was speaking to Captain Cohen.

"Halt!" came from the guard, and at once, again, "Halt!
halt ! Have some sense, man, or I'll be compelled to
fire ! " and at the words both Pleasonton and his adjutant
sprang to their feet, for it was evident from the guard's
tones and speech that some rude, perhaps drunken, man
was endeavouring to force his way to the general.

What Pleasonton saw was an old negro, in the act of
sliding from his horse. What Cohen saw was more : he
saw the negro, and he saw a white man — very white —
his hat falling, his body bent aside and forward, hands
clutching, as though by instinct, at the mane of a foam-
covered horse, and the next instant seeming to lose all
strength and go down. Captain Cohen sprang forward,
and with old Squire received the man and let him gently
to the earth.

" Who is it ? " asked the captain.

General Pleasonton was now at his side, in apprehension of alarming news, for the horses showed unmistakable
signs of having come fast and far.

" Mahs Dan Mawgin, sah," said Squire.

" Great Scott ! " cried the captain, " where did you
come from ? "

But General Pleasonton ordered the guard to come, and together they lifted Morgan and brought him into the general's tent. Cohen got water and brandy; he raised Morgan, propping him with camp-stools and whatever else he could quickly lay hands on, and succeeded in pouring some liquor down him. Meanwhile the general had sent for a surgeon.

"Tell us why you've come, Morgan," said the general.

Junior tried to speak, but failed. He looked beseechingly at Squire, and the old man understood; so did the others.

"He wants you to speak," said the general.

"Yassah; dey wants to shoot Mahs Usheh, Mahs Cap'm, an' Mahsta dah he don't want Mahs Usheh to git shot, an' so he up an' he ride down heah whah he say he gwine to fine de big ginnle, 'caze he say de big ginnle he good man w'at not a-gwine to stan' by an' see Mahs Usheh git shot. But we done guv out, Mahs Cap'm, an' we can't git to de ginnle, an' I dess a-gwine right now to beg you, Mahs Cap'm, oh, feh de Lawd's sake, sen' wohd to de big ginnle so Mahs Usheh he won't git shot!" and then the old man, whose voice had broken more and more, collapsed in a mighty spasm of sobs.

"And who is Usher?" asked General Pleasonton, quickly, "and where is all this?"

"Dat's Mahs Usheh Wes'," cried Squire. "You dunno Mahs Tom Wes' w'at live mos' by ouah house, mos' up to Middlebuhg? He de man w'at be'n tek keeh o' Mahsta dah all dis time. But Mahs Cap'm, please sah, won't shu sen' wohd to de ginnle?"

But the brandy by this time had brought back some strength, and Junior feebly spoke, "I'll try to explain, General."

"Take your own time, Morgan. Cohen, give him some more of that brandy . . . no great disturbance anywhere, Morgan?"

"No, General; it is only a matter of one or two men."

Pleasonton sat down; his greater fears were over — and he could take the matter of one or two men easily.

"The old man is right, General. Captain Freeman threatens to execute a prisoner."

"And his reason, Morgan? Why has he not referred the thing to me? He must be crazy!"

"He was taken in citizen's clothing, sir — a member of Mosby's command . . . and I will not deceive you, he had the misfortune to kill Lieutenant Brock . . . but it was in broad day and open fight."

"Why didn't Freeman shoot him at once? This waiting, waiting! He should have shot the bushwhacker in his tracks."

"It seems, sir, that West was taken by one wing of the company and carried off, and that it was an hour or two later when he was brought to Captain Freeman. Kindly give me a little more brandy, Captain; and if you will show Squire there how to get some breakfast, I'll thank you very much."

Junior had made these requests less for the physical wants of himself and the negro than from the wish to see Pleasonton alone.

"General, I'm going to tell you everything. You've
been very good to me."

"Morgan, don't mention it.　This is a personal matter
with you?"

"Deeply and terribly so, General.　You have learned
that I have a brother in Lee's army; when I was wounded
he sent this old negro to Captain Freeman with an invita-
tion to come and get me.　I was taken by Dr. Lacy in an
ambulance — but I suppose you know all this, General;
I wrote you about it."

"Yes, but go on."

"Lacy found Stuart's cavalry in the way and had to
halt.　A gentleman named West took us into his house
and cared for us; we have been there now nearly two
months.　Mr. West's family is himself, a daughter, and a
son, — and the son is with Mosby, — Usher West.　Usher
agreed at the very first to protect Lacy and me from all
trouble by the Confederates.　To Mr. West and his daughter I owe my life, General.　You see how personal this
whole matter is; I am begging for myself, just as I would
beg for my own life at your hands."

"I see; the daughter, eh, Morgan?" and Pleasonton
smiled sagely.

"Yes, sir; but indeed, outside of that, Mr. West is a
noble man, worthy of all respect you may show him in the
way of leniency in this matter, sir.　He has kept me
safe and Dr. Lacy as well, and when I began to speak
of recompense I believe that I offended him."

"Morgan, it is not to my liking to see prisoners exe-
cuted, but what can I do?　Will not every bushwhacker

at once be encouraged to go on with his deviltry? Of course Freeman must be brought up with a jerk, and he must be taught not to exceed his authority; but in the end, what can I do?"

"General, I think you would have ample justification for holding West a prisoner-of-war. Something else has happened that would not only save appearances, but would give you good room for action."

"Ah! What?"

"A man in Freeman's ranks, Private Hawley, was taken about a month ago by a squad of Confederates and was paroled. It was a mere sergeant that did the thing, and Freeman refused to recognize the parole. Now, Hawley has been taken by Mosby, and it is possible that Mosby will hear of West's danger and will notify Captain Freeman that the execution of West would be followed by that of Hawley for violation of parole."

"What!" and the general rose. "Great heavens, Morgan, that would *never* do! No, *sir!* What! to be menaced that way by Mosby! How could we ever surrender? No; I tell you, sir, that if Mosby makes that threat he'll ruin his own plan, and will ruin all your own hopes!"

"Then there *are* hopes, General?"

"Morgan, we must prevent Mosby from making any such threat."

"Mosby's a quick man, General. He may already have threatened," said Morgan, hypocritically, seeing his scheme work just contrary to Lacy's method, and in exact accordance with his own idea.

"No matter. All that the conditions require is that the execution be forbidden before his threat reaches me."

"Oh, General, you are going to do it?"

"I am going to send one of my couriers with command at once."

"Oh, General Pleasonton, I could kiss your hands! But I want to take that order myself. Am I not your courier?"

"But you cannot ride, Morgan."

*　　*　　*　　*　　*　　*　　*

And when Junior, at noon, tried to mount, he failed, even with help. But a way was provided, and he carried the order.

CHAPTER XXVII

ONE WAY TO SWAP HORSES

"Brother, by myn hals,
Now I have aspied thou art a party fals."
— GAMELYN.

LACY gave Mr. West the news that Lieutenant Morgan had gone to intercede with Pleasonton, and had taken Squire with him. Then, without beating the bush, he advised Mr. West of his plan to abet the Confederates in the matter of setting Hawley against Usher. Mr. West at once rode away ; he knew not where Mosby was holding himself, but he had little doubt that he should find members of the band at their homes, and even before Junior reached Pleasonton, Mr. West was in Mosby's presence and had told his purpose.

Sergeant Morgan had already recognized Hawley, and that prisoner was not happy ; but Mr. West himself was the first to bring tidings of Usher's condition and of Freeman's threats. The matter developed into Morgan's going alone to bear a message from Mosby to the effect that Hawley, for violation of parole, would summarily be shot in case Freeman's threat should be carried out.

For all answer, Morgan, after having been held by the sentinel for a full hour, was informed that Captain

365

Freeman had no communication to make to bushwhackers.

Mr. West had waited until Morgan's return.

"How is my brother now?" the sergeant asked, spite
of the farmer's cruel suspense, indeed with a desire to
deflect his thought.

"Gone to General Pleasonton to intercede for Usher.
Oh, Dan, that's a noble fellow; do you know what he
told me? He says that his grandfather's will was in
favour of *Daniel* Morgan, and that you shall have every
cent of the property."

"Tell him I'll share *mine* with *him!* I'm rich enough
for both if he ever wants anything. I won't touch it!"

"Just what I told him," said West.

"Gone to Pleasonton! He'll succeed, I do pray and
hope. But can he stand it?"

"He took Squire. I hope he can make it, but —" and
Mr. West cut his speech short through fear of losing
self-control.

Dr. Lacy had returned to Freeman's camp, but was
holding himself aloof from the captain. The day was
wearing on, the little camp more and more gloomy; every
sound man was on duty, guarding the roads, the entire
company always under arms. Freeman's excited condition
caused much talk; and as it became current that Hawley
was a prisoner under threat of retaliating upon him the
penalty which Freeman seemed resolved to inflict upon
West, murmurs of deep displeasure began to run; while
it was true that Freeman's orders must be obeyed, yet it
was clear that in this matter he was transcending his own

owers, and more than one man swore loudly not to serve
f ordered on the detail for execution. The sergeants
ndeavoured to quiet such talk, but their efforts were vain,
nd at length one of them informed the captain that it
vould be dangerous to proceed ; but the warning had no
eeming effect, and in the afternoon the orderly-sergeant
10tified each man of the detail for execution.

But now, Mosby, who, had he known of the condition,
antamount to mutiny, of Freeman's camp, might have
:efrained from the act, sent Morgan with a second message,
which seemed to increase the violence of Captain Freeman's
:age ; for Mosby served notice that, if West suffered,
:hen every man of Freeman's company who should thereafter be captured by the partisan would be shot down
without delay. To this message, Sergeant Morgan, after
waiting long, returned without answer.

Freeman, however, had been staggered by Mosby's
:hreats, and it was nothing but pride that still held him
:o his resolution — he wished himself well out of the
:rouble. But his men, hearing of the last threat, turned
about, also through pride, and declared that they would
10t bend an inch for Mosby and his high talk — they
would meet death with death.

Lacy's uneasiness had never been shown so great, and
:oward the middle of the afternoon he rode out of the
:amp, taking the way to Haymarket, up which he expected Lieutenant Morgan to come, his nervousness such
:hat he felt the need of ending it at the earliest possible
moment.

He had ridden at a slow walk more than a mile when,

from a height, he saw far at the south a moving spot in the road ; he halted, for he knew at once that here was something greater than a horseman, or even than two. The object was moving northward and rapidly, but soon a turn of the road hid the thing from view, and when it next appeared the doctor saw some half a dozen cavalry-men coming at a gallop, and close behind·them an ambu-lance drawn by four horses.

Lacy had already sent his wounded to Fairfax, and he wondered why this ambulance from the direction of Warrenton was coming to his help ; but almost at once he conceived the truth — General Pleasonton had sent his exhausted aide back in this degree of comfort, and it meant that Morgan had succeeded ; he put spurs to his horse.

The doctor found Morgan propped with mattresses, and incapable of continuous speech. Old Squire was curled up asleep. The tired horses they had ridden had been left behind to be sent on later. In a minute Lacy had the situation. The squad were to go on without Morgan in case the lieutenant should be forced to halt.

Feeling it better that Freeman should not yet learn of Morgan's appeal to Pleasonton, Lacy now commanded the deflection of the ambulance to Mr. West's, and with half of the squad rode back to camp, where he remained until he knew that the general's instructions had been delivered, and that the orderly-sergeant had notified the detailed men that they were discharged ; then he galloped hard and overtook his patient.

Junior's hopeful condition had been greatly impaired ;

he had brought joy in regard to Usher, but extreme anxiety concerning himself, and not only Jennie was oppressed by fears for his life, but even her father failed to conceal his emotion as he assisted in bearing the Federal to his bed.

In the meanwhile Major Mosby had made his arrangements for sending his prisoners and most valuable captures to the army under General Lee, and had distributed to his men whatever would be too cumbrous for such a journey, which must be made with exceeding caution and rapidity. By means of his scouts, he learned that the threatened execution of West had not been carried into effect, and a messenger sent to Mr. West's returned after nightfall with complete information. Then Mosby put his train in motion; all the night he moved southwest through Loudoun Valley, and when the sun rose he was at Orleans, and almost in safety. Here he disbanded his men except but a few, with whom he brought his prizes to Stuart's cavalry. This journey took Sergeant Morgan and his friends back into the First Virginia — yet not all of his friends. West was now in a Federal prison, and Squire had been left with Junior Morgan; for even Armstrong had a bitter pride in insisting that Jennie's only help should not be taken away.

* * * * * * *

Again for long weeks Andrew Morgan lay at West's, his mind always in the fever of hope, his hurts almost beyond it for a time. Upon the matter of his relations with both, Jennie refrained from speech with her father, wisely discerning that Mr. West's opposition had been so shaken

2 B

that with little more it would be entirely overcome. She
would leave all to time ; needless to revive obstinacy by
pressing upon wounded pride, for it was clear that the old
man felt humbled in the presence of a devotion to love
and merciful duty that he had considered the right, by
preëmption, of the Southerner ; yet was there the comfort
that Junior was a Virginian born.

Naturally, old Squire was a great hero, and enjoyed his
high honours ; yet he was at all times weighed down by a
sense of neglected duty in regard to Armstrong, and
every day he would tell Mahs Dan, as he now persisted in
calling Andrew, that the time must soon come for his
departure. Between Squire and Morgan a great attachment seemed to grow — the soldier silent, listening
eagerly to all that the negro would tell of the sergeant,
and of all his friends. Morgan willingly learned to love
his brother even before he knew him.

As to the household, there was no longer any fear concerning Federal or Confederate, Pleasonton's protection
having been accorded to Mr. West, and Mosby keeping
aloof with greatest good-will. At one time Dr. Lacy had
ridden through a squad of armed men clad in civilian's
garb who all raised their hats and gave him the road ; for
now the doctor had more patients than one, his services
being demanded for serious cases at the camp, and even
by some of Mr. West's neighbours. The place had become a haven, protected by breakwaters against which
alone the tides might dash.

Early in October Junior began again to grow better,
and Lacy had fixed the day of their departure — an appoint-

ment that brought greater joy to Squire perhaps than to any other of the family. On the afternoon of the 12th they were all sitting on the wide porch, the negro's slight form on the lowest step, his gray head bowed.

Abruptly Squire moved, and then rose.

" Didn' shu heahed 'em, Mahs Tom ? "

" Hear what, Squire ? " asked Mr. West.

" Heah de big guns. Dah, heah dat ag'in . . . Dah now ! "

But to the ear of none other had the sounds come.

" Mahs Tom, I 'spec' I hatto go."

" I guess it's nothing but some long range firing that he hears," said Junior.

" No, Mahs Dan, dem guns is a-comin'. I be'n knowed dat dey's a-gwine to come, an' now dey's a-comin'. You know Ginnle Lee, Mahs Dan, an' you know Ginnle Stuaht, an' Mahs Fitz, an' all dem yotheh cunnels ? Dey's a-gwine to come back dis a-way feh sho'. Dey not a-gwine to res' easy in dey beds tell dey gits back heah whah dey b'longs to. De good book hit say dat w'at goes up is a-gwine to come down ag'in, an' dat's dess de way dey be'n a-doin' eveh sence dat night w'at de fust Mahs Dan an' Mahs Joe Lewis dey fust come to ouah house — dey dess be'n a-comin' an' a-gwyin' all de time — you heah dat now, don't shu ? " and this time Junior heard.

" Mahs Tom, I 'spec' you all is got to 'scuse me. I dess got to go to my young mahsta."

" Better wait a day or two, Uncle Squire," said Morgan, who had adopted Jennie's mode of address. "If the armies are moving this way, every day's march will help you —

you might get lost or run into some people you don't
want to see, you know. Suppose you should stumble on
the man who owned your horse?"

"Yassah, dat's de Gawd's troof; an' I done had trouble
enough a-hidin' 'im. But I ain't a-frettin' much 'bout any
of 'em, 'scusin' dat same Cap'm Freeman, an' I ain't got
no call to mix up wid *him* no mo'e."

"If he should ever get you, Squire, he will hardly let
you go to the general again," said the doctor, who knew
that Freeman had learned of Squire's ride with Junior.

"No, Mahs Doctoh, but fust I ain't a-gwine to let 'im
git me no mo'e. I don't git along wi' dem big Yankee
ginnles. I dess can't put up wid 'em, nohow. But
Ginnle Stuaht an' Mahs Fitz, dem's de kin' o' ginnles feh
po' niggeh lak me."

"Squire, you are full of mistakes," said Lacy; "your
signs are all wrong. You had a sign once before and it
came to nothing, and now this notion of yours that Lee is
advancing is worth no more than your old sign."

"Yassah, but Mahs Doctoh, me an' somebody's a-gwine
to be mighty bad awff some o' dese days ef dat ole un is
es good es dis un. Ain't shu gwine oveh to de camp
to-day, sah?"

"Yes."

"Den I ax you, sah, dat ef you sees Bahney—you
knows Bahney, sah?"

"Captain Freeman's man?"

"Yassah, ef you sees Bahney, I be mighty 'bleeged to
you, sah, ef you tell 'im dat ole Squiah's a-gwine to light
out f'om dese diggin's, an' ef he got any wohd to sen' to

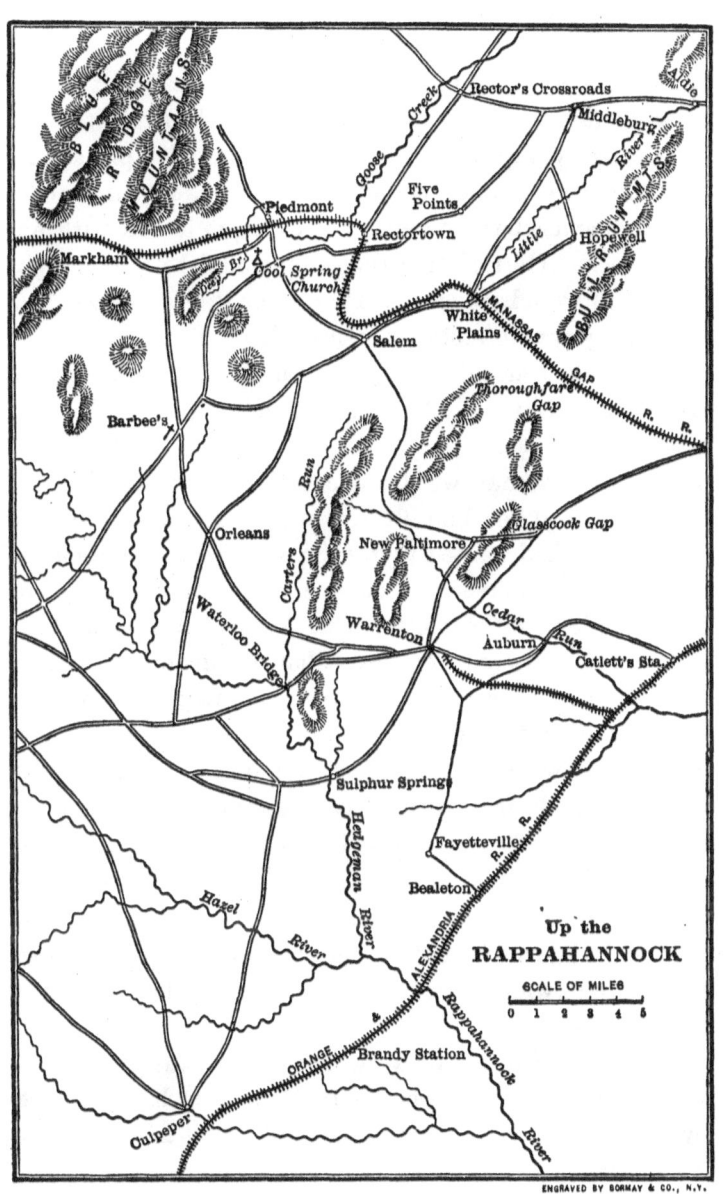

Up the
RAPPAHANNOCK

SCALE OF MILES

0 1 2 3 4 5

ENGRAVED BY SORMAY & CO., N.Y.

he ole mammy he kin git it ready; an' ef he sen' it to me
up at de fawks o' de road mos' to Hopewell, I tek it."

" Certainly, Squire, I'll tell him for you with pleasure."

There were no more sounds of artillery, but Lacy rode
to camp, and when he returned at night it was with an
ambulance. He told that the camp would be broken up;
the troops would move to the front, for it was known that
Lee's army was in motion northward.

On the next morning Lacy took his patient away in the
midst of a scene of silence and grief that must be for-
borne.

Squire rode southward alone. He had provender for
his horse, food for himself, and money given him by Junior. Lacy had wanted to give Squire a written statement
that he had rendered good service to a Union officer, but
consideration of the matter with Morgan had made him
abandon his design for fear that Confederates might
examine the bearer; so, for the contrary reason, lest
Squire should fall into Federal hands, the lieutenant had
decided to write no letter to his brother, and simply
charged the old man with verbal messages of kindness.

In these parts every footpath was familiar to the negro,
every farmer's face and name. North of the Manassas
railroad he had no fear of molestation. As for Federals,
he had confidence that they were having enough to do to
resist Stuart, whose cannon could now be heard with greater
distinctness.

" Wondeh ef dat boy's a-gwine to do w'at he promus'd,"
was the old man's thought. " He done went back awn me
oveh in Mellan' and Penns'vania, an' I ain't had no 'scuse

feh mixin' up wid him no mo'e. De good book hit say
dat ef a man tell you one lie he tell you a thousan', an' I
b'lieve hit's right. I gwine to wait fuh him, but I not
a-gwine to wait tell I git cotch, now I let shu know
dat."

As he rode southward, skirting the western edges of
Bull Run Mountains, the intermittent sound of cannon
grew and grew, and from the varied sounds he knew the
discharges came from no one spot: some were much nearer
than others; they seemed to be pounding along a great
line stretching east and west.

At noon he was near Hopewell. He must halt at the
junction of the two roads where he had given Barney
rendezvous. He would turn into the woods that he might
be secreted from view, and watch toward the north for
Barney's coming. At his left was a natural hiding-place,
a tumble-down fence with great bushes and briers. He
rode to an opening and then turned toward the chosen
spot, but as he turned he saw before him a horse, saddled
and haltered, head to earth, eating; and at the next breath
he saw the dismounted rider spring up — Barney.

"Yes, Unc Squiah, I done got ahead of you feh oncet;
I jest be'n a-watchin' of you, an' I seed ju was a-thinkin'
dat dat good-feh-nothin' Bahney gwine to make you wait.
Yah! yah! Now, Unc Squiah, tell de troof!"

"Bahney, boy, you 'peahs to be mighty high sperrited
'bout some'h'm — you does, feh true. Whah you git dat
hoss, Bahney?"

"I got 'im jest whah you got yo'n, Unc Squiah; dah
now!" and Bahney laughed again.

Squire had also dismounted and was getting ready to feed.

"Dat hawsh you got, Bahney, hit seem to me dat I done seed dat hoss befo'e now."

"Mebbe you did, Unc Squiah."

"Boy, how come you git dis hoss?"

"Don't shu fret shose'f about dat, Unc Squiah; I got 'im. An' it gwine to take a good man's two hund'ed dollahs in gole to git 'im, too, Unc Squiah."

"An' izh you gwine to sell 'im to de Confeddicks?"

"Dat's jest what I 'lows to do. But I make you a good swap, Unc Squiah, if *you* wants him."

Squire coveted the horse, which was a much better one than his own — coveted him for Mahs Chahley; but he shook his head; he had no money to spare.

They made a start. Squire insisted on keeping out of the main roads; for though when alone he had had no fear in this quarter, now, with a companion dressed in blue, he was afraid lest suspicion be aroused; moreover, one negro is an innocent slave on some mission for his master, but two constitute an insurrection.

In the woods the progress was slower. Neither had a definite intention beyond those of avoiding the Federal cavalry, and getting into the Confederate lines. They heard guns, but knew not whether their own approach was toward the backs of Union troops or those of Southerners.

From time to time Barney bantered Squire for a horse trade, but the older man invariably answered that he would swap even, or not at all, while the younger wanted fifty dollars in gold.

Dusk was falling and they were still on the western edge of the mountains, but they had passed the railroad, and were to the south of Thoroughfare. The night would be dark; the autumn wind swept low clouds along the range, obscuring all distant vision before the end of day. A place was chosen, and a halt made for the night; on the morrow they would go up the mountain and see what could be seen.

Barney seemed restless; he persisted in offering to trade horses, slowly reducing his demands. The old negro began to dread some deceit; from the first he had not doubted that Barney had committed theft, and now he believed that the desire for exchanging was based upon fear lest they ride into a Federal camp where the horse would be recognized. As for his own mount, Squire proudly considered him the lawful prize of his bow and spear.

The young negro became sullen. "Unc Squiah, it seems to me dat shu stannin' might'ly in yo' own light. You don't know when you lucky. Dat hoss he wuff mo'e'n two o' yo'n, and dey ain't a man on de top side o' de yeahth dat I let have 'im like I do you."

"Yas, chile, dat's all true, an' I ain't a-sputin' it; but shu see dish heah hoss o' mine? I done got shuse to 'im, Bahney, an' I dess can't mek up my mine to tuhn 'im awff. I ain't a-sayin' dat shyo' hoss ain't wuff de mos', now mine you, but I dess say I don't go back on dis hoss."

"Den 'sposin' I say swap eben, Unc Squiah, what'd ju say to dat? Now, I ain't a-sayin' I gwine to do it, but what'd ju say?"

"Lawd, chile, ain't no use to talk 'bout w'at shu ain't a-gwine to do. You ain't a-gwine to do it, 'cazhe you know you ain't."

On the hard earth, covered by his saddle cloth, old Squire rested for more than half the night in dreamless sleep. Then he woke with a start and listened. Near by he heard sounds of hoofs, growing suddenly louder, and in a moment more receding, galloping away.

"Bahney," he called softly; but the wind in the trees was the only answer. He called louder. Then he moved, and felt where Barney had lain. He rose up and looked all about, groping his way in the darkness.

CHAPTER XXVIII

IN THE NICK OF TIME

" *Mar.* How far off lie these armies ?
Mess. Within this mile and half.
Mar. Then shall we hear their 'larum and they ours."
— SHAKESPEARE.

WHEN it became fully evident that Barney had secretly achieved his wished-for horse trade, and had gone without so much as by your leave, Squire's fears permitted him no longer to rest; anything might be apprehended from the man who had betrayed him, so he gathered his effects and led Barney's horse away.

The clouds were gone; from the stars he learned that day was not far, and he made toward the ridge of the mountain, carefully choosing his way. But present fear was lessened by every step, and before he had made a furlong he halted and sat down, bridle in hand, to await the dawn, his thoughts bitter from loneliness and from dread of a future caused by Barney's desertion; for the younger negro's conduct was now understood — he had forcibly disposed of a booty too dangerous to keep in these parts, where at any moment he might run against Freeman's company; and the act that had helped himself had been done to the peril of him he deserted.

When daylight came, Squire trudged up the mountain side, and as the sun rose looked out east and south and southwest. The region was in a great degree familiar. In his young manhood he had roamed these woods and fields by night, for slaves wandered far at times betwixt sun and sun ; and in the campaigns of Lee and Pope, and of Stuart and Pleasonton, he had learned a little of the more distant country in regard to the main roads and the villages. The smoke at the southwest where Stuart was now crossing the Hedgeman he knew was in Rappahannock County ; and the smoke nearer by, but a little to the left, he thought came from Warrenton, where were many camps. And far eastward the atmosphere was a mingling of dust and smoke, which the negro understood to mean the presence and the movement of a mighty army — which army ? Lee's or Meade's ? It was far away.

Near the mountain the air was pure ; for ten miles there was neither dust nor smoke, except thin spots that indicated dwellings ; here and there in this quarter the roads were visible — but for very short spaces, the region hilly and wooded. Had it not been for hills and woods a watcher with a glass of indefinite power might have seen from this height a panorama which the governments of earth would have trembled to watch, for on this field the Southern army was moving once more in a hope to interpose between its giant antagonist and his Capital.

Squire knew not what to do, and he sat down. He was in a good place ; before he would move he must know more. His fears of Freeman were so great that at one time he had almost decided to abandon the horse which he believed Barney had considered an element of danger; but the thought had followed that by night he might ride even this horse into safety if he could but know whither to ride; he would wait here, if need be, until night. So on this mountain top the slave remained, at each successive moment striving from some new indication thrown vaguely to this far distance by the assembled powers of North and of South to solve its meaning to himself. Down there was Stuart, and he was coming. Squire saw the smoke of his cannon, but the sounds and the smoke mingled with those of the Northern artillery, and he could not divide them. Over at the southeast stood the infantry legions of Sedgwick, and Warren, and French, and Newton, and Slocum — all unseen by the lone spy upon the mountain, while to their north rolled the visible smoke of their camps and the dust of their wagon trains hurrying back to Bull Run; but the dust and the smoke drifted without regard to sectional prejudice, and their political cause was unrevealed.

In the southwest the noise of cannon died away, and Squire still held his post. Yet he thought it prudent to examine the ground near him; he tied his horse, and sought a spot from which he might look more to the west, and now he saw, not half a mile away, a white flag waving from an isolated perch, waving nervously, according to the fitful manner of the signal folk, springing up — jerking down — right — left — left, left — right, right, left, up — zigzag, rapidly and incoherently, lacking utterly the rhythmical succession of the drum-major's conceited baton, jerking and fluttering in spasms of apprehension and warning. And Squire knew that they were signals of warning, but of whom and to whom the warning was projected who could know? Yet, for all his ignorance, was he sure that the flags were waving Federal signals to Federals to tell that Lee was marching. He went back to his former position, and continued to strain his eyes at the landscape under the blazing sun; and as he gazed he still saw the dust rolling northward and now knew that its extreme southern limit had moved. He took an object, and after a little another, and then yet a third, and then he prayed to his God for Mahs Chahley and the Southern cause, for it was plain as day that Meade was hurrying his long trains in retreat; and he knew that between the mountain and those trains, and in rear of the trains, Meade's divisions were seeking some strong position for battle.

Then, in another hour, the atmosphere toward Warrenton became pure of smoke and dust; and in yet another hour the dust was rising there again; and the negro interpreted — the Federals had marched out, and after an interval the Southerners had marched in; and who but Stuart? Yet the negro held his place; he would wait until the rear of the advancing cavalry had passed; then, without fear of the Federals, he could follow and find his master; he would wait, if need be, until night.

*   *   *   *   *   *   *

On this day Stuart marched through Warrenton. The movement had begun on the 9th; at James City on the 10th there had been a combat of cavalry; at Culpeper and Brandy on the 11th more desperate fighting in which Armstrong had ridden ever in advance, seeming to seek

destruction, yet coming out unscathed. On yesterday, at
Jeffersonton, there had been a close but partial engagement, the Federals retiring to the north bank of the
Hedgeman. And behind Stuart, Lee at the west was
endeavouring to repeat the movement that in the preceding year had thrown Pope back to Bull Run.

Fitz Lee held the ground from New Baltimore to Warrenton, and from Warrenton toward Auburn. Stuart
marched with three brigades eastward for Catlett's ; he
left Lomax's brigade at Auburn, and when in sight of Catlett's was forced to halt, for the roads running northward
in his front were full of Federal infantry hastening their
retreat — the two corps commanded by Generals Sedgwick
and Sykes. Though Stuart had been observed by the
enemy, whose flanking parties sent a few shots into his
ranks, he succeeded in withdrawing, and at once de-
spatched an aide to General Lee at Warrenton, advising
that Meade's army was in full retreat, and that now was
the time to strike. At Auburn this messenger found that
Lomax's brigade had been forced to abandon that position
and retire westward ; for on this night the corps of Federal infantry under Warren had halted at Auburn, not
only brushing Lomax aside, but cutting off Stuart's retreat
in the direction of Warrenton. Moreover, the Third
corps, under French, had already passed beyond Auburn,
and was encamping at Greenwich, so that Stuart found
himself enclosed : on the east were Sedgwick and Sykes ;
on the north, French ; on the west and southwest, Warren's infantry and Gregg's cavalry ; while on the south
flowed Cedar Run. But for his ordnance wagons and

artillery, Stuart's predicament would not perhaps have been felt as serious ; but these he could not think of abandoning. Throughout the night extraordinary effort was made to prevent knowledge of his presence from reaching his enemies, and six several attempts by single soldiers to flank the Union lines and tell to Lee the danger of his lieutenant all succeeded.

Stuart's aide had sent back a messenger advising that the road was blocked, and then by a circuitous route had reached General Lee, so that now the situation had become perilous to Warren ; it was a complex case in which accurate knowledge of the positions and designs of the various disjoined forces on either side might throw success to the commander who should acquire that knowledge or conceive it with sufficient clearness to justify action. Stuart was enclosed, and Warren was enclosed ; whoever should strike first and properly, surely ought to gain a great success ; yet the result proved a balance, and added to the fame of both commanders, but perhaps unjustifiably, though surely no criticism can apply against Warren, while adverse comment upon Stuart's course would seem to fall ulteriorly upon Lee — for certainly that great captain failed at Auburn to crush the Second corps.

At daylight Ewell's infantry advanced upon Warren from the west, and Stuart's artillery opened upon him from the east, surprising his men in their bivouacs, creating consternation at finding that the road was blocked to Catlett's.

And Warren succeeded in extricating his command before Ewell could seriously engage it ; and Stuart suc-

:eeded in slipping out with his brigades and his artillery
)efore Warren could overwhelm them ; and in the manœu-
/res incident to these successes, there was close fighting, —
iorsemen riding through hostile infantry, solid regiments
:harging upon cannon, battery replying to battery.

* * * * * * *

Squire reached the First Virginia without difficulty, and
ie soon found friends, one of whom told him that Morgan
ind his group had been detailed to attend General Stuart,
who had marched eastward. No other information could
ie get. His long rest on the mountains had left his good
iorse fresh ; he knew not when his master would return
:o the regiment ; he felt that he must go on and try to
:each General Stuart.

* * * * * * *

At daylight on the 14th Squire was approaching General
Stuart's line. As yet the negro had not seen a Federal,
his acute senses of hearing and sight, coupled with foxlike
:aution, enabling him to avoid their flanks in the darkness.
[ndeed, but for his artillery, which a wood or a gully
might easily have caused to fall into the enemy's hands,
it would have been no difficult matter for General Stuart
and his two brigades to file away into safety by marching
between the corps of Warren at Auburn and that of
French at Greenwich, and it was through this gap that
Squire made his way at an hour later than the march of
any of French's stragglers.

The old man was on a high hill from which a good vision
could be had when the full light of day should come. In
his rear was a wood, covering the crown of the hill ; in his

2 c

front, open ground, but lower, in which depression the Confederate cavalry lay concealed in a heavy fog. Through that fog he saw nothing, yet he heard — he heard the rattle of harness, and the movement of horses ; but soon at the south — though he knew not the south — he saw many fires spring up, and he believed they were made by Federals for boiling their coffee — a luxury that the poor rebels tasted only when they had captured it from their enemies.

At length the fog began to lift, and then Squire heard musketry break out, away at his right ; it seemed a mile, and far beyond the fires. And before it had died away there came other sounds, more fearful and louder — a battery below him was firing with great rapidity. Still he could see no man ; yet under that fogsheet he knew that the combatants could see, could tell what he knew not, could distinguish friend from foe. Again there was thunder — different — a second unknown battery replying, and farther south a crackling of small arms, and then even the mighty tread of horse reached his ears as Stuart threw a regiment forward at the charge. But even yet the negro could only hear. Like a blind man lingering on the edge of battle whose sounds alone come to his smitten brain, the slave stood and hearkened, afraid to go forward because death was there ; yet could he not go back, because of duty.

But the fog continued to rise, and with great suddenness he knew where he was. Over yonder, scarce half a mile, was the spot where his Mahs Chahley had found him one night — that night in '62 when the negro had guided Stuart

to Pope's headquarters ; and in a flash the whole immediate
district sprang into coherence by simple association, — and
for one instant the positions of the hostile forces upon
that night in '62 had well-nigh betrayed him, for here
from the west came Stuart then ; there at the east were
the Federals then ; and he mounted his horse to ride to
the rear of the western battle ; but as he mounted the
scene became clear, and he saw cavalry at the east, with
the Confederate flag ; and infantry at the west, with the
Federal flag ; and he dashed his old heels into his horse's
sides and rode headlong after Stuart's men, now rapidly
retiring southward.

But the rearmost files of the Confederates turned, for
here came thundering athwart the open a company of
Federal horsemen to retard the retreat. Still Squire was
riding ; he saw the Confederates, but not their enemies
behind the swell ; he saw only the gray men halting,
facing west, their flank toward him, he urging on at all
speed in the joyful hope that they were awaiting him.
But all at once the blue men came into view, and not a
hundred yards from their foes ; and as Squire finds refuge
in the rear of the Confederates who advance now to meet
shock with shock, they roll together with one commingled
shout which tells of stern resolve and highest ardour each
for each ; then blades and blades, and shot and shot, and
rider down, and horse overthrown, and all the wild uproar. And then upon the Federals thus struggling comes
back a second gray platoon, and in a time that must be
told in seconds the blue survivors are fleeing over the
field, leaving their dead and wounded. But so their ene-

mies must also flee, for in their rear the bugles call them to save themselves while they may.

Foremost of the Southerners, Armstrong had ridden; foremost of the Federals, Freeman. And Armstrong's horse had been slain, and his comrades were rapidly withdrawing, and Freeman had been stricken to the ground, where he lay in helpless peril; and Freeman saw his own horse — his favourite — dash up to the spot, a negro on his back, and he knew this negro. He saw a white man leap up to the saddle, as old Squire scrambled back to the croup; and then Freeman, lying there incapable, saw his horse, carrying its double burden, gallop after the fleeing rebels.

CHAPTER XXIX

THE FIVE HUNDRED

"Where lies the land to which the ship would go ?
Far, far ahead, is all the seamen know."
— CLOUGH.

THE manœuvres of the cavalry in the Bristoe campaign,
though interesting, were marked by no incident seriously
affecting Squire's history after he returned to his master.
Lee's army settled back beyond the Rapidan, and Meade
resumed his former position in Culpeper County. At
the close of November the Federal army advanced into
Orange County, and was halted by Lee's intrenched
position along Mine Run ; there was much skirmishing,
but no general battle. By the 2d of December Meade
was back in his camps, and everything seemed settled for
the winter, Lee's infantry in huts near Orange Court-
House, his cavalry scattered over three counties, scarcity
of provender demanding small camps widely separated.
Old Squire foraged near and far.

In February Lieutenant Morgan returned to his duty
with Pleasonton. He had interested some influential
people in the story of West and Hawley, and he now had
great hope of seeing the one exchanged for the other,
General Pleasonton himself having recommended it ; as

for the Confederates, they were always willing to exchange. Yet though Junior held desultory correspondence with Jennie, he had not written her concerning his efforts for Usher's release, fearing to excite undue hope.

More than four months had gone by since any of our friends on either side had learned aught of the doings of those upon the opposite side ; neither Sergeant Morgan nor Armstrong, in any skirmish, — and not even Squire with all his foraging, — had met with one small incident relating to Junior, to Lacy, to Freeman, or any of Freeman's company. Yet but few miles divided these parties, and the existing oblivion must cease.

The day on which Lieutenant Morgan returned to duty marked also the return of an old friend. Dahlgren, promoted for gallantry three grades at a stride, had been disabled by wounds since July, and indeed was still disabled, wearing a false leg, and even carrying crutches at his saddle, his chivalrous courage supplying all physical lack.

In whose brain [1] was evolved the wonderful but imperfect scheme which Colonel Dahlgren was first to unfold to Morgan, Junior did not know, but he at once eagerly sought to become an actor in it, responding to Dahlgren's enthusiasm with ardour.

On the morning of February 28, 1864, Morgan was alone in Dahlgren's tent, busy with preparation, the colonel having been called outside by some messenger sent from the provost-marshal. Morgan was hoping that a

[1] General Kilpatrick's, according to War Records, Vol. XXXIII, pp. 172, 173.

guide had been sent to lead Dahlgren's five hundred who were to take the advance.

" Do you know the country below ? " The voice was Dahlgren's, easily heard by Morgan.

" No, Colonel; I was to bring you this negro, and return to Mr. Babcock. That is all I know."

" The negro is sent to me ? " . . . Dahlgren again.

" Yes, sir."

" Dismount, sir, and come in here."

Soon Dahlgren came in, followed by a negro, a young man, brown skinned, slender, seemingly at ease with army people. The negro looked fixedly at Morgan for an instant — then turned his eyes away.

Dahlgren handed a sheet of paper to Morgan, who read as follows : —

" DEAR COLONEL: At the last moment I have found the man you want, well acquainted with the James River from Richmond up. I send him to you mounted on my own private horse. You will have to furnish him a horse. Question him for five minutes, and you will find him the very man you want.

" Respectfully and truly yours,

" JOHN C. BABCOCK.

" He crossed at Rapidan last night, and has late information." [1]

Meanwhile, Dahlgren was questioning the negro.

" Where do you come from ? "

" I be'n down to Goochlan', sah, an' I jest got back," was the reply, the man's eyes shifting uneasily in his head.

[1] War Records, Vol. XXXIII, p. 221.

"You have been with us before?"

"Oh, yes, sah, I be'n with the cavalry, an' I jest went back to see my mammy."

"What is your name?"

... "Bahney, sah." The negro was thinking; he had seen Dahlgren before, and Morgan also; he had no wish to be recognized; he knew, however, that Freeman had been wounded and was now absent from his command, and he tried to take courage. Possibly he had thought of concealing his name, but had thought too late, for he had given it even before seeing Babcock at the provost-marshal's.

"Who can vouch for you?"

"De gentleman dat I waited awn is done got huht, sah, an' he ain't got back, an' I don't know who to say, sah."

"Who is he?"

"Cap'm Bob Freeman, sah."

"And no one else knows you?"

The negro would not say that he had ever seen Morgan; he drew a crumpled note from his pocket, and handed it to Dahlgren, who read that the bearer had successfully guided the writer, after escaping from Libby Prison, through the enemy's country and safely into the Union lines.[1]

The testimony seemed very favourable. Dahlgren dismissed the soldier, who rode away, leading Babcock's horse.

[1] Boudrye's "Fifth New York Cavalry," p. 99; Major Merritt's narrative.

"Now, Barney, I've got a thousand dollars, and I know where there are trees, and ropes are handy. Are you willing to risk it?" Dahlgren's voice was stern, his tones seriously uniform.

"I don't know what shu want me to do, sah," said Barney.

"This paper says you know the James River all the way from Richmond up. Tell me what you know about it."

"I knows de Jim Riveh, sah, in Goochlan'; I be'n a-fishin' all along dah eveh sence I knowed how to bait a hook, sah," replied the negro with assurance.

"Well, what I want you to do is to ride with me and a few more men, and show me the way to get across the James. Can you do that?"

"Jest a few men, Co'nel? In a ferry-boat?"

"No, we'll be too big a crowd to risk a ferry. We must have a ford."

"Yes, sah, we can find a fohd," said Barney, and then added, "if de riveh ain't up."

"Where would you find a ford?"

"Dey's a good un, Co'nel, at Columbia Mills, but dat's up de riveh in Fluvanna. Den dey's anotheh down by Doveh."

"Will you take the risk of guiding me and my men across the James River for a thousand dollars?" demanded the colonel.

"Yes, sah; but I be mighty feahed dat I git cotch."

"We'll be strong enough to protect you. Do you know the roads from Frederick's Hall to the James?"

"Yes, sah."

"Very well; now if you want to make that thousand, I'm going to take you; but I want to tell you plainly, my man, that if you don't expect to guide me right, you'd better let some other man earn that money. Understand me? If you deceive me, you'd better never have been born."

"Don't shu fret about dat, sah. I'll take you right whah you want to go, if it's anywhah in Goochlan'."

*   *   *   *   *   *   *

Old Squire had foraged far. As night overtook him he found shelter in a black brother's cabin near Good Hope Church in Spottsylvania County. He had bought corn, — only a bushel or so, but a little addition to each feed would eke out the forage ration handsomely, — and had bought bread also, and other food, and he would have nothing to do on the morrow except to get back to Mahs Chahley, whom he had left in camp some fifteen miles away. At daylight Squire bade his kind host farewell and started on his return; but he had not got across the road to Frederick's Hall when he heard shouts, "Halt! halt!" and looking northward saw a squad of horsemen, and beyond them the road full of coming cavalry. He had no fears; he halted at once, little dreaming that he had been halted by a force of Federals.

"Hello, old man! Where you belong?" shouted the foremost of the group, and now the negro saw that this man was in blue.

"I b'longs to Mahs Chahley, sah," said Squire, uneasy.

The advance guard had paused; the head of the column was not two hundred yards away.

" Hell you say ! Where ? What's that you got ? Whose mule is that ? " but replies surely were not expected, for the man continued : " Dickson, halt here, and turn over this man to the colonel. Forward ! "

And in less time than Squire would have needed for telling it, he was in the presence of three men whom he knew — three men riding at the head of the column.

Dickson saluted — " Ordered to turn him over, Colonel," — saluted again, and spurred on.

Meanwhile, but one man had paused, Dahlgren himself, who reined his horse to the roadside that the troops might pass.

There had been many exclamations of surprise or gayety, no doubt from amusement at the negro's peculiar appearance, seated on his bag of corn, with three or four fat haversacks dangling on either side of the tough mule which he had cheerfully accepted from Mahs Chahley in exchange for Freeman's good horse. And in these utterances the cry of Junior Morgan and that of Barney had passed unnoticed by the troopers. Yes, both had cried out, and had ridden on without pause, each repressing his emotion alike, but from far different impulses,— the one concerned for Squire's safety ; the other, doubtless, for his own.

" Tell me what you are doing here, and all about yourself, sir. "

The negro's alarm was extreme ; moreover, it was evident. He knew Dahlgren — knew him in spite of the crutches. But he knew not how this great soldier had enjoyed and laughed over Junior's revelations — how he had declared that Squire was a man after his own heart, and the rest of it. Yet, though Squire feared this officer whom he had cheated in a small game of war, his greatest fear was not for himself, but for Mahs Chahley and his friends. This force of Federal cavalry—how strong he could not know—had passed through to Lee's rear; had passed between Hampton and Fitz Lee. What was the purpose of this advance? The idea that Richmond was in danger could not occur to Squire; his thought reached not to such absurdly high emprise. He knew nothing of the fact that at this moment Kilpatrick's division, with artillery, was also approaching the Capital. No, his master was in danger; this cavalry was in Stuart's rear for the purpose of surprise and attack, and he must defend his master, lying, he thought, unguarded in camp. The truth is that Armstrong was at this moment facing the enemy near Charlottesville, where Custer's brigade was making a diversion in favour of Kilpatrick's Richmond movement. Truth is, that Dahlgren cared nothing for Stuart or Fitz Lee, except to learn that they were being enticed away from his own line of march.

" Yassah, I b'longs to Mahs Chahley, w'at's gawn off wid dem yotheh calvry," answered Squire; he was temporizing — and somehow Dahlgren's hopes caught the answer as acceptable. Did not " gone off with the other cavalry " mean that Stuart was engaged by Custer?

"Fitz Lee or Hampton? Speak quick ! "

" Mahs Fitz Lee, sah."

So far, well indeed. " When did they leave camp ? "

" Yistiddy, sah," — a lie and a truth.

" Aha ! Charlottesville or Orange ? "

A stumper, but Squire dodged. " Bofe, sah." He fancied he saw a smile, and was encouraged.

" Throw down that heavy bag," commanded the officer ; but, as Squire started to obey, added, " What's in it ? "

" Cawn, Mahsta."

" Well, never mind, keep it. You come with me ; we'll get rid of it soon enough," and Dahlgren pushed on to overtake the head of his column, Squire following.

Possibly two minutes had been lost in doing what has taken so long to tell. The questions had been fired at the negro like pistol-shots, and the answers had been prompt. Not half of the column had passed ; yet it required ten minutes for the colonel to regain his place, long enough for three men — Junior, Squire, Barney — each to deliberate upon his own proper course.

First : Morgan decided quickly to tell Dahlgren that this negro was Squire. He would do that for the old man's protection. Dahlgren would allow Morgan to defend him. Of course, he could not expect Dahlgren to dismiss this slave — noted for his loyalty to Confederates.

Second : Squire determined to do nothing, and watch his chances. He would see what his acquaintances would do. So long as this body of troops leaned away from Orange, well and good ; if it should change direction and ride toward his friends, he must get away. He doubted Barney, in regard to his own person ; but he had all confidence in his second Mahs Dan. And even though Barney should endeavour to harm him, he felt that with Junior on his side all would be well.

Third : Barney must have felt himself utterly helpless.
What could he hope for? Would Squire betray him in
regard to the theft of Freeman's horse? Would Squire
divulge his desertion at Gettysburg? his assisting Sergeant Morgan's escape near Boonsboro? If Squire should
betray him, he was lost. The morning was cold, but was
not Barney's face glistening with sweat? He was at the
mercy of the man he had deserted — could he hope that
Squire would be merciful? . . . yes, and there was room
for one other hope — the hope that Dahlgren, still toward
the rear, would dismiss the old negro ; but this hope was
gone, for now the colonel reached his place, and Squire
was just behind him.

Dahlgren called a halt and ordered the men to feed.

"Morgan, see to it, please, that this negro's burden of
corn is relieved. I want to keep him awhile ; at least
until we pass the railroad, and I'm afraid his mule won't
keep up. Seems to me I've seen the old chap somewhere."

"Colonel, I want to tell you something. That old man
is none other than Squire."

Dahlgren raised his hand a little way, and let it fall.

"And more," said Morgan, who had now remembered
that Squire had once spoken of a Barney — a follower of
some one in Freeman's camp near Aldie, "I think Squire
knows Barney."

"What! Then keep them apart. Don't let them
speak one word to each other."

"All right, sir. But you can hold me responsible for
Squire ; if he will but give me his word, you may feel
easy on his account. He is an open enemy, so to speak ;

but as for Barney, I am wondering why he doesn't show
that he recognizes Squire."

"Very well, watch them. Find out from Squire what
he knows about the other negro."

When Junior approached him, the old man, having fed
his mule with a small quantity of corn allowed him from
his own bag, was about to get his breakfast out of one
of his many haversacks. "Uncle Squire, you drop from
the clouds?"

"Yassah, Mahs Dan, but I sho' is proud to meet up
wid ju oncet mo'e; an' de yotheh Mahs Dan, he be'n
talk a heap 'bout shu, sah. Whah izh you all a-gwine to,
Mahs Dan?"

The simple question forced a smile. "Ask the colonel,
Uncle Squire. Don't you know him?"

"Yassah, I be'n seed him befo'e now," and the old
man laughed, but somewhat uneasily.

"Yes, but you have no cause to fear. I've told him
about you long before to-day, and he thinks you're all
right. And though he will not let you leave us, he has
given you into my charge."

"Yassah, I sho' is mighty proud to heah dat, Mahs
Dan. Izh you brung de ginnle, sah?"

Again Morgan smiled. "Do you know who that negro
is yonder, Squire?"

"Yassah, cou'se I knows Bahney."

"But he doesn't seem to know *you*."

"Yassah, me an' him dess had a leetle fallin'-out, sah,
an' I see he ain't a-doin' nothin' but a-putt'n' on lak a
fool niggeh do."

"What sort of a man is he?"

"Mahs Dan, I ain't know yit dess w'at kin' o' man Bahney *ain't!* I ain't be'n wid him now so long dat he mought be done got wuss'n he wuz."

More conversation followed, concerning old times at West's.

"Mahs Dan, I ain't got my mine much sot on yo' gwine about dis a-way. You don't look strong yit."

"Well, Uncle Squire, you're right, or almost so; I'm not as strong as I once was; but I get better all the time. The doctor tells me I shall always hold myself a little bent," for Junior supposed that the negro had observed a very peculiar posture which was natural when at rest — a leaning a little forward, as well as a little to the left side. "When did you see my brother last? Was he well?"

"I seed 'im las' week, sah, an' he hol' he'se'f up mighty well, Mahs Dan." As a matter of fact, Squire had seen the sergeant within two days.

"And this Barney — when did you see him last?"

"Mahs Dan, you know dat day w'en we all broke up at Mahs Tom's, an' you went one way an' I went de yotheh way?"

"Yes."

"I ain't laid my eyes on dat niggeh sence dat ve'y day. He come along wi' me a piece o' de way, an' he say he gwine to see he mammy one mo'e time, an' I ain't seed 'im no mo'e tell back yandeh dess aw'ile ago."

"Where was his mother?"

"He tell me, Mahs Dan, dat she live down in Gooch-lan' some'h's."

"Well, Squire, can I depend on you?"

The old man hesitated; he knew not the scope of the demand.

Morgan read his reluctance; he believed that the negro had fears of committing himself against his friends. Squire's evident anxiety in regard to the march had betrayed his thought.

"Uncle Squire, if I will give you my word that we are not going against your people, will you stand by me? You say that I don't look strong; and I'd like to have you in reach if anything happens to me." Morgan really felt no weakness as yet, but he knew how to get the old man.

"You not a-gwine to tuhn off an' go up de country, sah?"

"No, not a foot. If Stuart will let us alone, that's all we ask. And I'll tell you another thing. The colonel wants to keep you, at least for a while; but if you promise to stay by me, he'll take your word — and then I'll see that you are not troubled with a guard."

"Cou'se, Mahs Dan, I gwine to stan' by *you*, sah, an' I do all I kin to he'p *you*, sah; 'caze de good book hit say eve'ybody mus' stan' togeatheh in de time o' trouble, Mahs Dan."

"Well, then, it's a bargain, and I want to ask you now just one thing. Don't speak to Barney unless he speaks to you first."

"Dat don't huht *my* feelin's, Mahs Dan. I dess be'n a-lookin' at dat boy, an' I be'n a-sayin' to myse'f dat ef you too proud to speak to po' Confeddick niggeh, you kin dess up an' go to de debble."

2 D

Again they were marching, and rapidly. Even if
Squire had not had perfect confidence in Junior's assurance that no evil was intended against Stuart's people,
when the North Anna had been put behind them all fears
were gone ; and he now supposed that these troopers were
merely on a raid against some railroad, and when he
heard the whistle of a locomotive, he felt that the
mystery was solved.

A mile or two below Frederick's Hall, Dahlgren's
command tore up track, cut telegraph wires, captured
the court-martial of A. P. Hill's corps, and then
pushed on south.

And to Squire the purpose of the movement was now
made clear, even from the speech of the troopers — the
column was marching on Richmond !

In darkness, under the falling rain and snow, Dahlgren urged on. The roads, bad enough before, became
streams of water ; the column of five hundred stretched
out for miles ; every prisoner who had the desire, escaped
— and it may be questioned whether the romantic leader,
from the moment when black night fell upon him with
storm, had any further hope. His own memoranda contained the item that his command must be in position
south of the city at ten o'clock of the following day ;
yet the column was floundering along quagmires of roads,
in Egyptian darkness — a straggling, broken-down hand-
ful of men, led by an uncertain guide, with a great river
to cross if possible, and yet forty miles ! Surely his
stout heart must have failed even then of hope. Yet he
kept on.

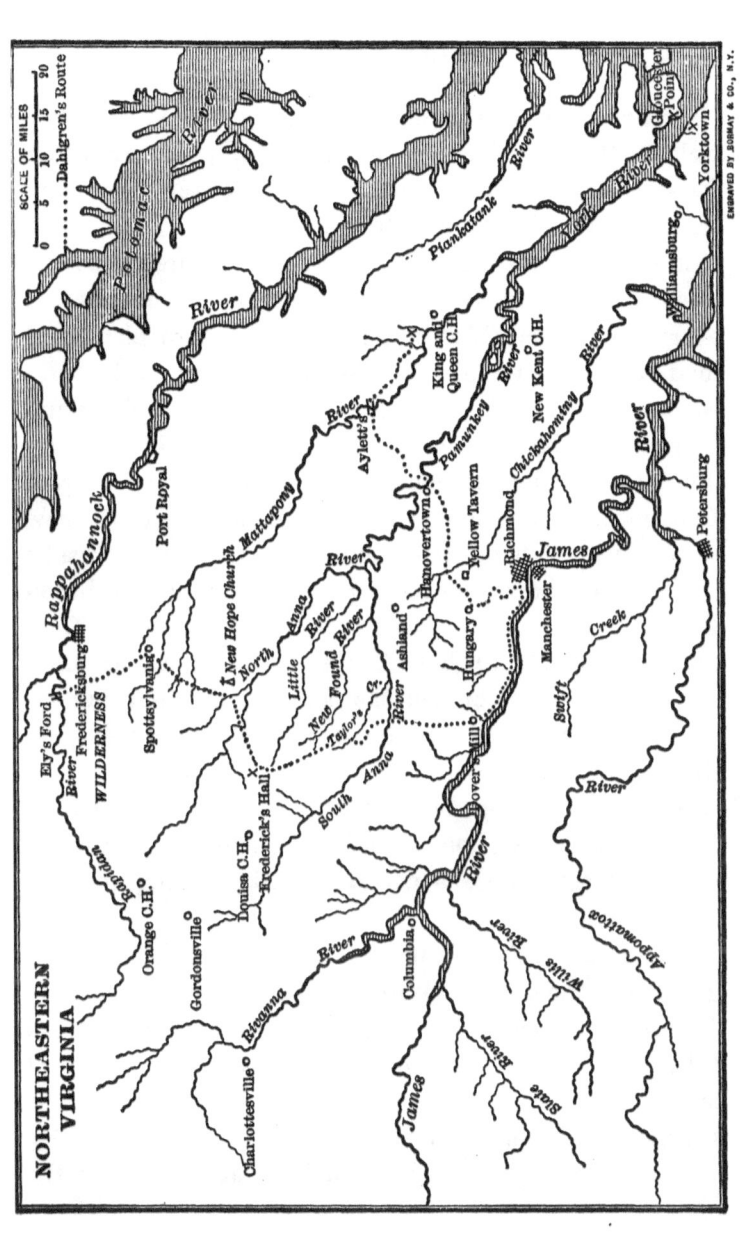

NORTHEASTERN
VIRGINIA

SCALE OF MILES
0   5   10   15   20
······· Dahlgren's Route

ENGRAVED BY SUSMAY & CO., N.Y.

Before midnight the South Anna was crossed. At two o'clock, the rain showing no abatement, Dahlgren felt forced to halt; the column was no longer a column; his men must be allowed to close up.

Ever since crossing the railroad, old Squire's practical mind had regarded the march as folly; he expected every man to be killed or taken. The negro had heard loud boasts from the men : they would take Richmond; some of them said they would destroy it, laughing uproariously; the prisoners in Belle Isle should be freed; Jeff Davis and everybody else should be hanged. Occasionally one would strike up the old tune to the new words, "We'll hang Jeff Davis to a sour apple tree !" and perhaps there were some green recruits who believed they stood a chance of seeing the execution of the Confederate President; ·but all this had been at the first, before the dark night and the rain and the mud and the groping; now there was no cheer, nothing but despondency and weariness.

Yet the morning brought the renewal of hope, at least to the men, for off leftward could be heard the sounds of cannon; was not Kilpatrick clearing the way into Richmond?

But Dahlgren? Whatever he may have felt, he still acted as though he were marching on to success. Whether by accident or design, the road that Barney had taken in the dark night, was not the road to the good ford at Columbia, and Dahlgren ordered him to lead to the nearest place where the river could be crossed.

The column approached Dover Mills at ten o'clock, the

moment when it should have appeared south of the city —
a position not possible now to reach in safety, give what
time you may.

Dahlgren soon learned that at Dover Mills, or anywhere near by, no crossing of the James was practicable
except by boats, and he turned upon his guide and
accused him of treachery.

"You declared to me that you could cross here. What
have you to say for yourself?"

"Co'nel, I swaih to God dat I be'n acrawst sheah befo'e
now, sah; I be'n waded acrawst sheah, and up higheh,
and down loweh, an' I ain't give it up yet, sah. We can
go on down dis side, sah, and I know I can find a place to
git acrawst."

"Then lead on, and I'll swear to *you* that if you do not
speedily guide me to a ford, I'll hang you and leave your
carcass for the birds to pick."

Barney led on, down the James. Captain Mitchell was
commanded to take a hundred men and follow the tow-path
of the canal, convoying the ambulances, the prisoners, and
the crowds of slaves who sought freedom under the protection of the force.

Dahlgren's words to Barney had reached Squire's ears;
they had been heard by many. Morgan beckoned to
Squire to come nearer.

"Colonel," said the lieutenant, "it seems that Barney
refuses to recognize Squire."

"What do you know about this river, old man?" asked
Dahlgren, oblivious for the moment to everything but the
necessity for a ford.

"Mahsta, I don't know noth'n', sah; I ain't nuvveh be'n heah befo'e."

"What do you know about that man?" pointing to the guide, now some yards at the front.

Squire feared that Barney was in peril, yet his fears were not commensurate with the reality of the danger. The old negro had heard too many unexecuted threats to allow him to give complete faith in this terrible menace; yet he feared, for there was in Dahlgren's voice and feature and manner a dreadful compound of resolution. And Squire had no hope of a ford; as he had glanced around his eyes had fallen upon a sail vessel coming down.[1] The broad river at the right, in his opinion, was surely unfordable. The old man answered, his voice trembling, "I dess knows dat he use to cook feh Cap'm Freeman, sah."

"Do you know where he belongs? Where is his home?"

"Yassah — leastways I knows dat he alluz said 'at he come f'om Goochlan'."

The answer was favourable; Dahlgren rode on.

But soon the thing that Squire had seen came into view of all, and it destroyed the smallest lingering hope.

"Halt!" cried Dahlgren.

Every eye was upon the vessel, and the thought of every man was the same thought : that boat was going to Richmond, and it drew too much water to allow the belief that there was a ford anywhere below.

The guide's face was averted. Possibly it will never be

[1] Major Merritt's narrative.

known whether Barney himself had been deceived — possibly it will never be known whether Dahlgren's act was punishment for betrayal, or for incompetency whose result was no less disastrous.

Barney's fear was evident; though his face was unseen by the front files, the fact that he held himself rigid was almost confession.

What Dahlgren's mind, Squire's mind, *Barney's mind*, underwent, who shall say?

Only the deed can be told; the fear, the pity, the horror, all these must forever linger in the hearts of those who saw, those who thereafter shunned the recollection.

Dahlgren pointed to the guide. He said a few words to a sergeant: "Take four men. Hang that negro. Be sure you make an end of it!"

Then he commanded the march; the column moved on . . . no longer following Barney . . . and as they moved the voice of entreaty was heard behind them . . .

*   *   *   *   *   *   *

At a later hour, Captain Mitchell, rejoining the column, reported that he had found the guide's body hanging by the roadside, and had buried it.

CHAPTER XXX

WHERE GLORY LED

"The toil o' the war
A pain that only seems to seek out danger
I' the name of fame and honour, which dies i' the search,
And hath as oft a slanderous epitaph
As record of fair fact."
—SHAKESPEARE.

AT three o'clock Dahlgren halted his column on the Westham plank road within view of the Richmond intrenchments and made preparation to attack the Confederate Capital with his five hundred men. The crowds of negro refugees were sent off toward the north, with a prudence that seems to reveal Dahlgren's hopelessness of success in his present attack; as for his officers, they obeyed his commands.

Squire now had a good rest. He was gloomy, but he knew how to rest. He had already begged Morgan to take measures for his own safety, begged even while he knew that his advice would be scorned; yet the lieutenant was far from believing the negro's opinion unwarranted, and he would go forward without hope.

"You are going to wait for me, Uncle Squire?"

408

"Oh, yassah ; you gwine to fine me right sheah, sah — leastways ef you gits back."

With a line of skirmishers right and left, the column moved forward on the road, and soon disappeared in the dusk. Squire was not alone; there were white men and black men lingering here in the rear to await the result, and he heard their speech, and not one expressed hope; the only spoken opinion was that Dahlgren was but losing time that should be used in retreating. The old negro's head was greatly muddled. In regard to himself had he one intention beyond that of waiting? one purpose that was not merely involuntary? Without the will or even the seeming need for thought, there must have flitted through his brain an incoherent succession of ideas unconsidered because of apathy akin to that which is the effect of a certain drug. From his talks with Sergeant Morgan afterward, we know that the death of Barney had almost unsettled the old man; in a dazed condition he was living moment by moment, with his own future a thing that gave him no interest. True, there were times when his thought of Barney joined fast hold upon thought of Dr. Lacy; but these times were as brief as those moments when he thought of the rain, or of the wet earth, or of aught else too trivial to continue. Instinct alone upheld him, the instinct of loyalty; he had promised; he must keep his promise, for Mahs Dan, this other Mahs Dan, was one of his people — the only one who could now receive his service. Even while he heard shots from the advancing skirmishers, and heard the answering volleys of the Confederates, the old man sank to sleep; and when he awoke he found Dahlgren's command about him, reorganizing for further march, and Morgan standing over him in the rain.

How Junior got through that night he never knew. Gusts of wind tore through the woods. The rain, the snow, the sleet, the darkness, the straggling, disheartened column, the impress of defeat, the almost certainty of capture, were confused into one overwhelming horror against which naught save the influence of discipline might furnish a rallying-point for resistance. Dead and wounded abandoned, the knowledge that Kilpatrick's division had marched away after dismal failure to effect more than a panic of citizens; the sixty — perhaps a hundred — miles to march if safety should ever be reached, the swollen rivers to cross where elated enemies must be met; the stumbling horses, the silent riders, the pain, the torture, the ignominy — all these, who shall tell?

About midnight Dahlgren reached Hungary Station, eight miles north of Richmond. The column closed. The column? There were but a hundred men; where were the four hundred?

The colonel and his few remaining officers held a consultation. It was clear that Captain Mitchell, at the head of the detachment of the Second New York, had been unable to follow in the darkness; four hundred men had turned off upon some other road, to the right, or left, who could say?

It was agreed that to wait would be too hazardous. The next thing to decide was the best route into safety. Dahlgren laid before the little council all that was known, especially the fact that General Butler, near Yorktown, had been ordered to send a force toward Richmond for the support of Kilpatrick, and the opinion that Kilpatrick's division, with the enemy following, had marched eastward to meet the force of Butler's. Only three courses were possible to consider: first, to march back nearly in the way they had come; second, to endeavour to reach Kilpatrick by marching down the peninsula toward Yorktown; third, to make across the Pamunkey and Mattapony rivers and move down to Gloucester Point opposite Yorktown.

Of these propositions Morgan gave his voice for the second; and urged his reasons with force. He contended that the first was in reality outside of consideration. Stuart's cavalry were now alert, and every ford of every river would be guarded; the command would be captured long before the Rapidan could be reached; the third plan involved a journey almost impossible even if no enemy should intervene in their front; the least hope to outstrip their pursuers in a march of eighty miles, their own horses already weakened, was too great; besides, they must make their way across two rivers at either of which they might easily be arrested; the second course offered a possibility, in that, once escaping the enemy who were supposed to hang upon Kilpatrick's rear, an enemy not sufficiently strong to block all the roads, safety would be found within a single day.

The final decision was made: they must attempt to reach Gloucester Point; the column was again in motion.

Now Morgan called the negro to his side, and said,

"Uncle Squire, we have a long march to make, and I'm
going to bid you good-by. You can easily get back to
your people, and I'll keep you no longer. Good-by,
Uncle Squire."

The negro's face was invisible, and Junior could perceive no change in his tones; perhaps he had already
become utterly indifferent to his own fate; he answered,
"No, Mahs Dan, I gwine to stay wid ju; I ain't got
nobody no mo'e to stay wid but shu; an' I gwine to stay
tell I can't stay no mo'e."' And Morgan wrung the
slave's hand and prayed God to bless him, for he knew
that Squire believed all the Federals would soon be in
prison, yet was determined to be faithful until the final
disaster should separate them.

Soon after the column had crossed the Chickahominy a
train of ambulances was met, the Federal wounded of Kilpatrick's division being taken to Richmond, and from
these men Dahlgren learned definitely that Kilpatrick,
attacked by a body of Stuart's cavalry under Hampton,
had retreated eastward, making down the Peninsula.

At dawn the column approached the Pamunkey, and now,
if they had but turned down the river road they would
soon have found Kilpatrick, who waited for them until
one o'clock that day at Old Church. Instead, Dahlgren
led on to the river; here the ferry-boat could be seen on
the opposite side, and adventurous men soon swam the
river and brought it over. Meanwhile the precious rest
of two or three hours was had, it requiring until eleven
o'clock to complete the crossing.

From this time Dahlgren felt no fear of immediate

pursuit by the force that had attacked Kilpatrick; yet
he had come upon ground no less perilous: from the
Pamunkey at Hanovertown Ferry onward to the Mattapony at Aylett's he encountered small irregular bodies of
the enemy, furloughed men who had got together at the
news of the Yankees, and endeavoured to delay their
march; and when, at two o'clock, the Mattapony had been
crossed, the dangers grew until disaster became inevitable.
The road, it is true, turned down the river, but this was
the country of home guards, and the picketing ground
of small outlying detachments of Stuart's cavalry, while
Gloucester Point was yet fifty miles distant. If Dahlgren
had now had his five hundred men, he could have over-
ridden all these foes, but his command had dwindled to
seventy men fit for service, and their cartridges were
almost gone. At six o'clock another halt became horribly
necessary. Rain still, and cold, and greater weariness;
the men and horses must be fed. The barns yielded corn
to force; the men made fires and cooked; the horses
fed; a hundred contrabands in the rear rejoiced in the
prospect of freedom. But meanwhile swift riders were
carrying tidings to Captain Bagby of the home guards, to
Captain Todd of the home guards, to Lieutenant Pollard
of the Ninth Virginia, on detached service, to Captain
Magruder, to Captain Fox, to every furloughed man and
every home guard within reach.

At nine o'clock the column moved on, but moved not far.
From the rear came discharges from carbines, from shot-
guns, from muskets, scattering the negroes, many of whom
at once sought refuge in the woods — nothing seen but

the wet road and the flashes of a hundred guns to which
we could make but feeble reply.   A picket of three men,
sent forward at the last halt, had been seen no more,
and now all knew that the enemy held the ground in
front.   Yet we moved on.

Dahlgren sent forward an advance guard — only six
men — and almost at once rode to their head.

Then the enemy challenged from ambush.

"Surrender, or we fire !" cried Dahlgren.

In reply the forest sparkled with volleys from the
front.

The column fell back in confusion ; and at once a fire
was opened against us on the flanks.

Dahlgren had fallen, pierced with five balls.

In great disorder the men filed out of the road into the
woods at the right.

A guide who had been pressed into service was missing ;
we knew he would tell the enemy that our ammunition
had been exhausted.

The men, helpless, lay on the ground in a small field at
the south of the road.   All hope had long since gone.

Officers counselled the disbanding of the force.   All
around, except on the side next the river, the lights of
fires began to show in the woods — our enemies would
wait till the morning to give the finishing stroke.

Men began to steal away afoot ; they would try to slip
between the fires, thoughtless of the pickets intervening.
Groups went.   The officer now in command, Major Cooke,
ordered all to destroy their arms — except pistols.

Morgan felt a hand laid on his arm.   " Mahs Dan, dey's

all a-gwyin' to go — all 'scusin' dem w'at's done broke down."

" Yes, Uncle Squire, I must try it too."

" Yassah ; w'ich a-way izh you gwine, sah ? "

" Lord, I don't know ; just risk it as the others through the woods ; but I wish to God I could get across the river."

"Yassah, dat's de bes' way ; you come along wi' me, Mahs Dan, an' ef we can't git acrawst, *we kin a'most,* — leastways ef de good Lawd 'll dess be on ouah side dess *one* mo'e time."

Morgan was astounded at the offer ; he knew that this negro must leave his possessions, and must endure hardship after hardship. He pressed the slave's hand.

" Mahs Dan, I got a whole lot o' bread jit, an' I 'spec' we not a-gwine to git no mo'e soon. You kin put awn one o' dezhe heah havehsacks, an' I kin tote two, an' we kin less let all de res' go ; an' you betteh save yo' whiskey."

Morgan gladly assented ; he believed that to recross the river would be to find comparative safety ; true, the Pamunkey also must be crossed, but its banks would not be lined with pickets, and time would be had in which to secure a boat, perhaps ; the Mattapony was the trouble, for only half a mile of its steep banks was accessible because of enemies in front and rear.

" Tek yo' picket rope along, Mahs Dan, an' yo' reins, an' all yo' straps ; I 'spec' we gwine to need 'em. Ef you can't swim, Mahs Dan, we got to mek a mighty big raf', leastways ef we can't fin' no boat, an' I don't 'spec' we kin."

"Swim like a duck, Uncle Squire."

It was past midnight; the dense darkness was in their favour in one respect, against them in others. Squire led to the right, Morgan close behind; and now Junior was surprised at his own strength. Riding, he had felt exhausted; walking seemed a relief; perhaps the excitement due to this individual enterprise had given him stimulus.

At last they stood near the river — a black, indefinite chasm. They dared speak only in whispers.

"You seddown, Mahs Dan, an' stay right sheah tell I git back ag'in," and now Junior was alone.

The sound of a shot broke the silence in his rear, perhaps fired at some Federal stealing between the enemy's pickets.

Morgan's hope of success was small; the river could be crossed, yet he saw not how to prevent freezing in his wet clothes when he should reach the southern bank. Squire was resourceful, but how could he make a raft sufficient to uphold their effects? How, even, could they descend this steep bluff?

But Squire returned and bade him follow; Morgan felt himself going down a gentle slope, and soon was in the midst of bushes.

"Got to be mighty sly now, Mahs Dan," said the slave; "dey's mighty clost by. We's a-gwine down to de mouf o' dis creek, an' den we kin land in de ribeh."

It was a short but toilsome stage; through brush and brier they crept on slowly, at every yard or two stumbling over some log or rail which the back-waters of the

last freshet had stranded; and at every such obstacle the
negro gave a grunt of satisfaction, which Morgan was not
long in construing.

At the mouth of the creek the negro again bade the
lieutenant remain, and soon he could be heard dragging
some heavy thing about. Morgan insisted on helping;
but Squire, with obvious hypocrisy, asserted that one
must hold the point gained, in order to signal the worker
back to the spot. Yet the old man seemed to work in the
darkness by instinct, and in half an hour had dragged to
the place a collection of old timbers that he pronounced
sufficient.

The raft must be made in the water; Squire stripped,
and Morgan helped the negro, now in the creek. With
the picket ropes they succeeded in lashing together two
stout timbers of unequal length, and upon them crosswise
three pieces of rails; on the top of these they tied half a
dozen longer rails parallel with the base. But before this
top layer had been fixed, Morgan was naked and in the
cold water.

At length they tied their clothing, blankets, and haversacks, and fastened them to the floor of the raft; then
they dropped into the creek and pushed their ramshackle
craft out into the main stream, side by side, each swimming with one hand on a stringer.

They landed on the south bank, a quarter of a mile
below, without accident, and, but for the cold, without
great suffering. Lest it be detected at daylight, and pursuit begun, Squire demolished his raft and pushed the
several parts down the stream; and when each had taken

2 E

a great draught of whiskey, and had got his clothes on, the adventure seemed little perilous.

A rapid walk through woods and fields quickly warmed them; then, ignorant of the course they were taking, they slept until dawn, when Morgan consulted his map, and they marched cautiously south for the Pamunkey. He would strike it below White House; it ought to be not more than ten miles away; they would reach it in the early afternoon, in ample time to secure a boat before the day was gone; then, in the darkness, they would cross, and he had little doubt that he should find Kilpatrick or Butler's forces near by. And the result proved that he was correct in all these opinions.

    *   *   *   *   *   *   *

Colonel Spear, in command of a Federal cavalry brigade, had been ordered by General Butler to march up the Peninsula to the support of Kilpatrick. On the morning of the 4th the brigade left camp at New Kent Court-House — Kilpatrick having marched on down, upon the 3d, with Captain Mitchell and Dahlgren's four hundred, who had overtaken him — and began its return toward Williamsburg, which place it reached at four o'clock.

Colonel Spear brought with him a man whom he had found below New Kent — a man seemingly exhausted, and whom the surgeon at once put to bed when he was brought on to Yorktown. This man said that Dahlgren's command had been ambushed near King and Queen Court-House, and the colonel killed; he had been with Dahlgren, and with the help of a negro had crossed two rivers and made his way into safety. The man gave his name

ıs Morgan, and his rank as lieutenant. Questioned by
Colonel Spear as to what had become of the negro, Mor-
ʒan's answers were seemingly reluctant. The negro, he
ıaid, had seen the Federal cavalry coming on the road,
ınd had refused to come farther. He did not tell that
ıe had emptied his purse into the negro's pockets.

CHAPTER XXXI

FATE'S DISCHARGES

"Speak, or thy silence on the instant is
Thy condemnation and thy death."
— SHAKESPEARE.

WHETHER right or wrong, wise or unwise, no sooner
had Squire seen blue cavalry coming than he announced
his decision to go no farther with the Federal lieutenant.

"Mahs Dan, you's done got back to yo' folks, an' now
I's got to git back to mine. Fah you well, Mahs Dan.
An' ef you nuvveh see me no mo'e in dis wohl', 'membeh
ole Squiah."

Lieutenant Morgan was taken to Yorktown, and thence
to Washington, where he long lay ill of a nervous fever,
brought on — according to Dr. Lacy afterward — by ex-
posure and mental distress ; his late companion, meanwhile, made his way back to his master ; and so great
was Squire's success on his return journey that he
appeared in camp without having been missed, Stuart's
men having themselves been out for a full week engaged
in provident blocking of the fords lest Kilpatrick's column return through Spottsylvania ; and Squire's horse,
which he had purchased from a farmer with part of the

money Junior had given him, was almost the only palpable evidence of what the negro had undergone.

*   *   *   *   *   *   *

On the 4th of May General Grant's army crossed the Rapidan and marched into The Wilderness.

At this time Andrew Morgan was still in Washington, and Jennie West was expecting him to come for her, her father's opposition to their marriage having been completely conquered a month before by the return of Usher, exchanged through Junior's efforts. Lacy had found time to devote to his old patient, and had demanded that Morgan should never reënter service. The marriage would take place on Wednesday, the 11th.

On the 4th of May, while the Army of the Potomac was crossing the Rapidan, Sergeant Morgan and his friends at the head of their brigade, with old Squire and other camp servants in its rear, were riding from Orange Court-House toward The Wilderness ; and Captain Freeman, now recovered from his wound, was riding at the head of his company on Grant's flank.

While Grant's and Lee's infantry were wrestling in the dark thickets, the cavalry on the south were frequently in close contact ; where an opening was found, road or field, there the horsemen would meet — on either flank a line of dismounted men in the bushes. In this road or field, for a while, the Confederates would gain ground ; in that, for a while, the Union troops would win advantage; and each side would eagerly strive to make prisoners that through close questioning definite knowledge might be gained of forces opposite. Many of these combats had no seeming connection with each other, and all of them but little result except to increase the number of the dead. Yet, with it all, Stuart's main purpose — to work around Grant's flank and block the roads to the south — was successful, his lines working on and on until his force at the critical moment held Spottsylvania Court-House and prevented the capture of this strong position where Lee withstood Grant from the-9th until the 20th of May.

In one of these many unnamed skirmishes, Freeman's command had driven its opponents back upon a narrow road for more than a mile. The forces contending were about equally small, but Freeman's men had been armed recently with the terrible Spencer repeating carbine, and no enemy twice their number could stand their eight volleys to one. And Freeman, on this day, was trying to do his best.

At length, in one headlong run, the Federal advance, outstripping its main body far, had galloped to the edge of a little bivouac from which the camp followers of the rebels had just retreated. Firing continued ; dead and wounded began to fall on both sides, for here the enemy had made their strong rally ; but as his company came up in force, Freeman again ordered the charge, and his men, with a great shout and a last loud emptying of guns, drove like a storm into the little encampment.

*　　*　　*　　*　　*　　*　　*

A riderless horse had rushed away ; a soldier lay upon the ground in a dense thicket, a negro kneeling over him.

" Izh you huht bad, Mahs Dan ? "

The voice was a whisper, for the conquering Federals were close at hand; their shouts were easily heard, and even the stamping of their horses.

To Squire's speech Morgan made no answer. The negro bent lower; he drew a knife from his pocket and cut the soldier's canteen straps; then he sprinkled water on the face of the wounded man, who soon opened his eyes.

"Izh you huht bad, Mahs Dan?"

Morgan raised his left hand, and muttered, "Turn me over."

The old man succeeded in obeying, and now saw the right arm bent at a horrible angle above the elbow. Squire rose to his feet; he must seek help.

Shots were yet coming from both sides. Freeman held the bivouac, but the negro knew it not.

"Squire," said Morgan, the voice feeble, yet reaching the negro's ear. Again Squire bent.

"You must get help . . . but be very careful; don't show yourself until you *know* that you're right . . . you may run into the Yankees anywhere in these woods."

"Yassah, I sho' gwine to be sho' befo'e I go up to 'em. Izh you huht bad, Mahs Dan?"

"The arm — I suppose I must lose it. But, Squire, you must not let the Yankees see you. I'd rather lie here for days than go to prison. Be very slow and careful."

"Yassah," and the negro went, going, as he supposed, toward the rear of his bivouac. Instead, he ran into the ranks of men, who, too late, he saw were clothed in blue.

Too late, indeed, for as he rushed forward he had cried,

"Oh, Mahsta! please, sah, come an' sen' somebody to git Mahs Dan Mawgin."

"Oh, yes, I know you, dam you! at your same old tricks. Captain Freeman! Captain Freeman!"

The words had been shouted by Private Hawley, who had instantly recognized the old man, and had urged out of ranks and grasped him by the collar.

"What is it, Hawley?"

"That dam'd old Squire, sir, begging your pardon. He comes right out o' the woods, right there, and wants us to help Dan Morgan again."

"So, I've got you at last, have I?" exclaimed Freeman. His tone was very angry, and doubtless the slave's heart sank even yet lower within him.

"Mahsta, I ain't a-doin' noth'n', an' I ain't be'n a-doin' noth'n' but a-tendin' to my mahsta."

"And where is your master?"

Squire was silent; yet in a moment he seems to have conceived that speech was best.

"He done dess now gawn back, Mahsta."

"Yes, yes; you're attending to your master, and I promise you that I'm going to attend to *you*. Where is my horse, you scoundrel?"

Men were pressing around Hawley, who, leaning forward in his saddle, still held the negro. It was getting dark.

"Back to your places!" shouted Freeman, sternly.

"Just look at his hands, Captain; they are all over blood."

Freeman's orders to learn what force was on this road

had been imperative; his personal vengeance must give way, at least for a time.

"Now, old man, I know you. You will answer my questions, and truthfully, or I'll have you shot. I'll not take time to hang you. I'll shoot you here in this spot unless you answer me. So help me God, I will. And you need not think to cheat me. I know you and your ways. You will tell me at once whose troops are in our front, and you will show me the wounded man you're trying to hide. Quick, now!"

"Yassah, Mahsta . . . I tell you, sah; hit's Ginnle Stuaht, an' hit's Ginnle Lee, Mahsta."

The answer enraged Freeman. Certainly he knew already that whatever force he met was Lee's; certainly he knew already that every cavalryman was Stuart's; yet against combined ignorance and obstinacy who can prevail?

"Whose blood is that? Answer me at once."

Squire lifted his red palms. "Oh, Mahsta, dat's w'at I got awff'n a chicken. I was dess a-killin' a chicken right oveh dah, Mahsta, w'en you all come up an' skeehed me away in de woods."

At this instant a terrible blast of cannon, and the thicket rattled with canister shot.

"Dismount and form!" shouted Freeman. He had turned his head and was now giving orders to construct a barricade across the road, and to the men to withhold their fire. Hawley yet held the negro; he was leaning over, still in the saddle, his hand clutching Squire's collar.

And then there came to the poor trembling slave a

wonderful deliverance . . . Hawley's hold relaxed, and at the same second of time the repeated detonation of artillery shook the woods ; at the next instant the cavalryman was falling, and Freeman's horse, frantic with pain, was rushing away heedless of his rider.

Squire's wonder at Hawley's releasing him lasted but a moment ; before the man had begun to fall, he knew by the bursting shell what had happened, and he had lightly stepped aside, and then had thrown himself down by the now prostrate soldier ; a moment more and he was crawling through the thicket in the darkness.

Two hours later, the Federals having retired, he guided men to the spot where he had left Sergeant Morgan ; and before sunrise of the next day that brave soldier had been compelled to submit to the loss of his sword-arm.

CHAPTER XXXII

NO GREATER LOVE

"Bring me an axe and spade,
Bring me a winding-sheet. . . . "
—BLAKE.

SHERIDAN, with ten thousand men, rode around Lee's right flank and marched upon Richmond. Stuart followed, and with three small brigades met the Federal cavalry at Yellow Tavern some seven miles out from the Capital.

It was the 11th of May, Wednesday. Jennie West was married on this day, and on this day Sheridan marched from Ashland upon Stuart, who faced northwest, his line across the road to Richmond. From eleven o'clock until four little impression was made upon the Confederate lines, — the brigade of Wickham on the right, that of Lomax on the left, with a reserve of but part of one regiment — the First Virginia.

Stuart's extreme left was west of the road, two guns in the road, another upon a hill farther toward the flank.

At four o'clock Sheridan engaged the whole of Stuart's line, and at the same time threw forward Custer's brigade to charge the guns on the Confederate left.

427

At this time General Stuart was with his right wing, half a mile away or more, but the speedy report coming that mounted cavalry were threatening his guns, he rode southward in all haste.

Custer's charge was led by the First Michigan, Major Howrigan at the head of the leading squadron.

The Confederates, closely engaged along the entire line, held to their work at every point, until Howrigan rode over the two cannon on the pike, capturing guns and gunners, cutting off Stuart's left, and threatening the destruction of the whole Confederate line.

Now Stuart stormed up, crying aloud to his men to rally.

Yet the guns had been lost beyond recovery. A great gap was in the line, and into the gap, and on, following the scattered Confederates, the Fifth Michigan advanced.

Meanwhile, all the right was holding, and at the left of the captured guns still stood some small companies firing into the flank and rear of the Federals that had moved through the gap — and with these few men Stuart held, in the last effort of his life.

The Michigan regiments, pouring through the gap, were met by the First Virginia.

Now the battle raged along the right where the rebel lines were yet unbroken, and all about the isolated left where Stuart was, and behind this hill, where the First was charging.

Stuart's old regiment, on that day, fought not only its last fight under the eye of its first commander, but it fought for his safety from capture, and its efforts were equal to the crisis, — the enemy were thrown back, and Stuart's person was saved : yet even as the Michigan men were retiring, their fire, directed at Stuart's group, wounded the general to the death.

The First Virginia was already in disorder from its charge ; its success had been but partial, but momentary ; already the ground was spotted with its best.

On that little hill the bloody wave again flowed back, and the Federals held all the line from which Stuart's left had been driven, and the Confederates were forced to form a new line of the left wing, resting at an angle upon the yet unbroken right.

Now the balls from both sides swept the hill between the lines, where lay blue men and gray men, and horses of both.

*　*　*　*　*　*　*

The sun was setting. Gloom and anger, defeat and grief, upon the faces of the Virginians. Their sun was setting. Stuart, had been placed in an ambulance, and had been driven toward Richmond ; men said in whispers that he had fought his last battle.

Joe Lewis had not been injured ; back at the rear he found old Squire, busy over his cooking, near the line of horse-holders.

"Mahs Joe," said Squire, nervously, "how come you don't stay wi' Mahs Chahley ? "

The negro had risen ; his hands were clasped together ; perhaps he read Joe Lewis's face.

"Squire, I'm afeared that George and Charley are both of 'em down. Fact is, I know they're down, and I'm a-thinkin' we can't keep the Yanks from gittin' 'em ; but I'm a-hopin' neither one ain't got it hard."

" Oh, Mahs Joe, tell me whah Mahs Chahley is. Tell me whah dey is."

" Out in front between the lines — out at the left front. I got to go on, Squire; jest got to go on and git cartridges for the company."

* * * * * * *

They had fallen almost together, there on the little hill over which from both directions the bullets were flying.

Sency recovered some strength ; yet when he tried to walk he found he could not ; any motion was with great anguish. He sat up, and saw riderless horses rushing through smoke and dust, and off at the left heard a great mutter of hoof-beats, which sound swelled out louder, and he lay flat again as a regiment of horsemen charged over the hill.

* * * * * * *

Sency again tried to reach Armstrong, and at length succeeded. What he has told of that night's horror has been little ; he seemed always to shun its remembrance.

But we know that still there was fighting — even until dark had set in, the Federals making partial attacks and being repulsed, until in one combined assault they drove the Confederates from all their new position ; and that at eleven o'clock Sheridan marched away from that field of victory and death.

While the bullets were flying both ways, about night-fall, Sency heard a cry, and answered as best he might

—a cry and an answer not for him who answered, but for him who could not.

And then Sency became aware that a negro had come.

The bullets were flying both ways.

Perhaps George Sency became unconscious for a while ; he tells us nothing of detail . . . the bullets were flying both ways.

*   *   *   *   *   *   *

At dawn four men came. They lifted Sency to a stretcher and bore him away.

*   *   *   *   *   *   *

At sunrise came other men, but these bore no one away. They buried the soldier, and another body at the soldier's feet. And then Joe Lewis stood alone, weeping bitterly.

www.ingramcontent.com/pod-product-compliance
Lightning Source LLC
Chambersburg PA
CBHW020503020726
47493CB00001B/163